Praise for *Aegis Incursion by Amazon* bestselling author S.S.Segran

"An electrifying thrill-ride over *Hunger Games, Maze Runner & Percy Jackson* territory."

— *Amazon Reviews*

"If Daniel Silva and Rick Riordan had a love child, it would be the young S.S.Segran. With the intensity of an adult spy thriller and the relatable characters that teenagers enjoy, Aegis Incursion takes YA Action, Adventure, and Fantasy to a new level."

— *The OnlineBookClub.org*

"Five Stars! A great book to dive into and a fantastic follow up to the first. One of the best things author S.S. Segran has done here is to produce a sequel that can be read as a standalone."

— *Readers' Favorite Reviews*

"If I could give this series more than five stars I would! Excitement, drama, heartfelt characters and an excellent plot make these books hard to put down!"

— *Teri Colglazier, Amazon Reviews*

"A good sequel stands alone as a strong work without the accomplishments of its predecessors, but a great sequel inspires readers to go back and relive a book they've already read, and that is precisely what this book accomplishes."

— *The US Review of Books*

"S.S. Segran did it again. Aegis Incursion was an awesome read. It made me laugh, cry and worry. That was in one chapter alone."

— *Candy Canfora, Amazon Reviews*

Publication Information

This book is a work of fiction. Names, characters, places and incidents are either the product of the author's imagination or used fictitiously. Any resemblance to actual events or locales or persons, living or dead is entirely coincidental.

First Published by INKmagination March 2015. Second Edition September 2019

Printed in the Unites States of America

Cover Design and Illustrations © 2015, 2019 by S.K.S.

'REAPR' designed by Jace Kim & S.K.S.

Book Teaser & Trailer by: INKmagination.

Image of CAT797 Mining Truck used with permission from Caterpillar Inc.

Caterpillar recommends operation of heavy machinery by trained operators using safe, industry standard methods.

S.S.Segran asserts the moral right to be identified as the author of this book.

ISBN: 978-0-9910813-3-2 (Paperback)

ISBN: 978-0-9910813-4-9 (Hardcover)

eISBN: 978-0-9910813-5-6

Receive free short stories, exclusive giveaways, advance reader opportunities and updates directly from the author. Visit www.sssegran.com to subscribe as an Aegis Insider.

AEGIS INCURSION

AEGIS LEAGUE - BOOK TWO

S.S.SEGRAN

Dedicated to you,

the dauntless reader who explores uncharted literary-scapes of unknown authors.

"Whatever lies within our power to do lies also within our power not to do."

— Aristotle 384-322 BC

"There is a difference between knowledge and wisdom. Wisdom gives us lucidity so that we may use our best judgment, completely detached from impulse, and distinguish the right path to tread."

— Elder Nageau

PROLOGUE

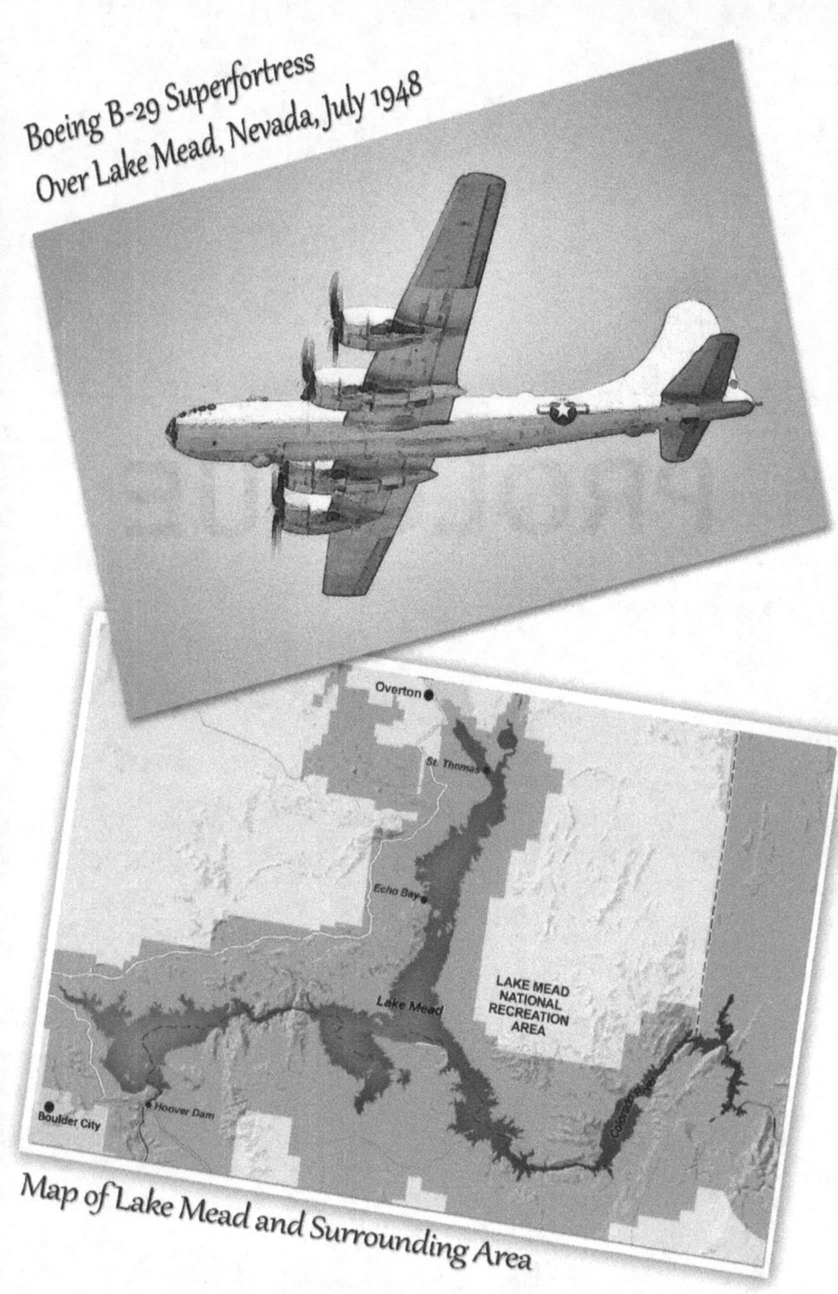

Boeing B-29 Superfortress
Over Lake Mead, Nevada, July 1948

Map of Lake Mead and Surrounding Area

Lake Mead, Nevada
July 1948

"*Gotcha!*"

The wiry teenager, dressed in faded blue jeans and a red flannel shirt, vigorously reeled in his fishing line the moment he felt a hard tug. Careful not to tip the canoe, he pulled his prize closer and closer, a triumphant grin plastered on his face. Judging by the drag on the line, he could tell that it was a big one.

There was a splash as the largemouth bass leapt out of the water, struggling to get free of the hook. Startled, the sixteen-year-old yanked on the suddenly slack line as the fish fell back into the lake. The bass, with a flap of its fin as if waving goodbye, disappeared underwater.

The boy stared after it in dismay, then yelled, "Elwood, you knucklehead!"

He'd spent the last two hours trying to land a catch. Tempted as he was to hurl his fishing rod into the manmade lake, he forced himself to set the pole down and ran his hands over his face.

He sat quietly for a while, taking in the striking contrast between the beautiful teal-blue waters of the lake and the red sandstone hills. Once he was ready to give it another go, he picked up the rod. He opened his tackle box to grab a new hook and sinker, then rigged them to his line.

He took a few calming breaths and gazed around. There wasn't a hint of a breeze and the cloudless sky was sunny and bright. The surface of the lake looked smooth and glassy, like a mirror.

Elwood had brought out the small canoe in the wee hours of the morning. He knew he'd be in trouble for missing his chores at the farm, but all he wanted was to catch his first fish of the season. If he was lucky, he would get a nice big one—maybe he'd clean it and give it to that pretty girl next door that he fancied so much, Rosemary. He smiled goofily at the thought, playing with the fraying brim of his father's old Army Air Force cap as it shaded his eyes from the sun.

He knew Rose found aviation exciting. That, on top of his own passion for planes, drove his interest in wanting to follow his old man's footsteps. What better way to impress a girl *and* do what he loved? Not only that, but she liked motorcycles! How he wished his next catch would be a chest full of treasure so he could buy his dream bike, an Indian Chief Roadmaster. Maybe they could ride across the country together, wind in their hair. He would make her laugh and she'd smile that angelic smile that never failed to brighten his day.

A sound in the distance snapped him out of his daydream. It was a low rumbling, like thunder. But that was impossible; the sky was still cloudless. As the sound gradually became louder, Elwood was able to pinpoint the direction and slowly looked toward the east. He squinted against the sun, then gasped when a shimmering silhouette emerged from the glare.

It was a large airplane.

Flipping through the deck of spotter cards in his mind, trying to find which plane would best fit what he saw, it hit him: A B-29 Superfortress, big brother to the B-17s his father had flown during the war. He stared in both amazement and fright as the aircraft began to descend and continue its path—in his direction.

He covered his ears as the roar of its four engines nearly rendered him deaf and watched with wide eyes as the plane flew straight toward him. In his fear, he sat paralyzed in his boat though every fiber in his being screamed at him to jump into the safety of the lake. He realized that he could see the pilot of the aircraft in his cockpit, could almost imagine the horror on the man's face.

The plane thundered right over Elwood's head, the vortex of air it created churning the water violently and capsizing the canoe, pitching him into the lake. He struggled in the depths, forcing himself not to cry out in reflex. Heart thudding, he floundered back up to the surface and sputtered and spat as he tried to regain his bearings.

Catching sight of the plane as it boomed overhead, he traced the aircraft, agape, as it hit the surface of the lake on its belly. The massive propellers struck the water, ripping three of the four engines from the wings. The aircraft skipped along, much like a flat stone would, before plunging into the lake for the last time a few hundred yards from Elwood.

Debris from the impact rained down around him as the waves resulting from the crash rolled to and fro. He paid no heed to the falling fragments and, with some effort, righted his canoe, thankful that it hadn't sunk. His tackle box and rod were gone, and he feared for what his father would say after finding out that not only had he taken the canoe without permission, he'd lost their fishing gear as well.

Elwood pulled himself into the craft and sat down, only to find his feet submerged in ten inches of water. Groaning, he tried to scoop it out with his hands before giving up and looking back at the B-29.

The plane's nose rose, pointing toward the sky as water flooded into its aft section. Slowly, the aircraft began to sink into the lake. He watched as five men scrambled out of the escape hatch and clambered into life rafts. Four of them wore green Air Force flight suits and the fifth appeared to be a civilian.

The civilian, safely on the raft, started to argue loudly with the men in uniform. Elwood could hear him from where he sat in his canoe: "It must be retrieved! We cannot lose it!"

Elwood hesitated, then cupped his hands around his mouth and yelled out. "Hey! Are you fellas alright?"

The argument stopped momentarily as the men searched for the source of the voice. When they saw the boy, they waved their arms over their heads and the civilian called back, "Yes, I think we are!"

Elwood slipped his paddle into the water as he made ready to reach the men, then paused. He was closer to the small beach than they were. He gestured to them as they began rowing over to him. "Can you make it to shore?" he shouted.

"Yes!" they answered.

"Good! I'll go on ahead and get help!" Elwood gave them a confident thumbs-up before picking up his paddle and hurrying toward dry land. He hopped out of the canoe and pulled it as far up the beach as he could, then started running toward the town; his shoes squished with water at every step.

It wasn't long before fire trucks and sheriff's cars came onto the scene, sending dust flying everywhere as they pulled up on the beach. The men from the plane, who'd made it to shore just minutes before the emergency responders arrived, were quickly tended to.

Elwood quietly returned for his canoe and left without a word, knowing that the survivors were in good hands. Neither he nor the men from the B-29 could have ever fathomed that the plane that had sunk to the bottom of the lake would remain hidden in its watery grave for over half a century.

The mystery of its missing cargo would be a secret for a long time to come.

Northern California
The Present

The white delivery van cruised along a mostly empty highway. Sage bushes flanked both sides of the road but were barely visible through the pouring rain in the dark of the night.

Behind the wheel of the vehicle was a man in his early thirties. His dirty-blond hair was cut in a matte side-part and he sported a carefully trimmed beard. He was built tough, with a strong chest and biceps that stretched the sleeves of his collared t-shirt. *Semper Fi* was inked around his right wrist; it was his only tattoo and he bore it proudly. With his height and impressive build, he could have passed for a younger Hugh Jackman.

Bored with remixes of Top 40 tunes, he switched the radio to another station. A loud voice resonated through the speakers, familiar to his ears. With a small chuckle, the driver thought, *Shock jock hour.* As he listened, though, he was rather surprised to hear a slightly mellower version of the usually obnoxious radio host he was used to. Currently, the jockey was conversing with a female caller from North Dakota.

"I just don't understand," the woman was saying, sounding breathless. "*All* my crops. Can you imagine that? This is how I make my living, you know, and they're gone! I wake up this morning and all I see are my crops—dead in one night."

"Yeah, I've been getting a few other calls like yours over the past couple weeks," the radio host answered. "Some crazy things are going down! Let's get the tinfoil hats out, yeah? Next caller, whatchu got, man?"

"Hey, I'm a long-time listener, first-time caller . . ."

The new caller went into an earnest ramble and listed off what he thought might be the causes behind the dead-crop phenomena that had been sweeping across parts of the mid-west. The driver of the van grimaced; most of it was conspiracy theories. He understood why some minds would drift toward that kind of thinking. If it had only affected a farm or two, it wouldn't have been such a big deal. This, unfortunately, had spread across a couple of states, thereby feeding more than a few wild theories.

The driver quickly checked his GPS to see how much time he had before his freeway exit. The wipers were working hard to clear the heavy rain. He shook his head in disbelief at the weather blanketing California. The state was experiencing its heaviest rainfall in ages.

He drove for a while longer, listening as the shock jock moved on to other topics and returned to his usual gaudy and boisterous self. As the driver exited the freeway near the town of Redding, the rain started to ease until it stopped completely. He turned off the wipers and passed several small homes and businesses, breathing a sigh of relief.

Industrial buildings began to appear along the sides of the road. The driver instinctively turned the volume down on the radio, then caught himself and made a face. *Why do people do that? It's not like reducing the volume helps us see better.*

He sped past a few large parking lots and more buildings until he found his destination. It was a gated single-story structure, built long and rectangular—generally looking like any other ordinary manufacturing facility.

He pulled up to a guard post and stopped before the boom gate. There were four guards inside. *Why so many?* he wondered.

The guard closest to the window peered out at him from under thick brows. "State your business, please."

"Delivery."

The guard checked his clipboard, then looked up at the clock in his post. Noting it was nearly midnight, he said, "You're late."

"Oh, lighten up. I'm not more than ten minutes behind. With the rain pouring the way it did for the past three hours, I had to stay well below the limit."

The guard grunted. "Alright. Head toward the loading dock. Remember, in and out, that's it. You don't go anywhere else."

"Yessir."

The guard pressed a button and the boom gate rose. The driver gave the other man a nod of thanks and drove toward the back of the building where the loading dock was located.

When the truck was positioned properly, he turned off the engine and hopped out. Striding around to the rear of the van, he threw the doors open and began offloading the heavy boxes. A couple of workers from inside the building came out to help him. Once everything was unloaded and documents were signed, the workers disappeared without so much as a word.

As he fished his van keys out of his uniform pants, the driver paused as an uncomfortable feeling grew in his stomach. He knew right away that it had been a horrible idea to grab a late dinner at the Chinese takeout. He should have known; the Kung Pao chicken had smelled and tasted funny. Just thinking about it now made him queasier. He needed to find a restroom, and quickly.

He glanced around. *In and out, don't go anywhere else* had been the guard's orders. The driver couldn't wait; not with the way his insides were churning. He quickly made up his mind. Ignoring the 'Authorized Personnel Only' sign, he tried the door that the workers who'd helped him had gone through. It hadn't closed completely, thank goodness. The driver entered the building and hurried down a narrow corridor, hoping that no one would see him.

A sense of urgency took over the further he went. *Come on, come on*, he silently pleaded. Then he spotted it: A stick figure nailed to a dark blue door. He practically bulldozed his way through the entrance and found a stall for himself. Once he was done, he reached out to open the stall door but froze when he heard the creak of the bathroom door swinging open. Two men in mid-conversation entered.

"But yeah, we really appreciate you coming all the way in from Reno," one said. He spoke as though he had a cold. "Your approval of the components will help us firm up the production schedule."

The second man cleared his throat and responded. "Well, we *are* on a tight timeline. Anything I can do to speed things up. We need to get the parts to Quest Defense as soon as possible."

The first man lowered his voice. "I know it's none of my business—we're just producing components here—but, ah, there have been rumors spreading across the floor among the engineers."

"Rumors? What kind of rumors?"

"I'm not sure if I should say this, but a couple of engineers are thinking there's a link between what we're doing here and . . ." The man trailed off.

"And what?" the second voice demanded.

"And the farm phenomenon that's been making news."

"Garbage!"

"I didn't mean to upset you. I just wanted to let you in on some of the chatter that's been percolating along the production line."

In the stall, the driver was breathing lightly through his nose, doing his best not to make a sound as he listened.

"You know what? There are rumors in every corporate corridor. It's your job to keep it in check."

"I get that, but there are a number of things that have happened lately that are feeding into this."

"Yeah? Like what?"

"For one, the company invested heavily in upgrading our cleanroom to a Class One facility."

"Go on . . ."

"And the fact that we're producing a component for which we're not given information about its intended purpose—that's never happened before. There's also been talk about supplies of a rare mineral that were brought in, possibly illicitly, from Northern Canada and Siberia several months ago. Add to that the bolstering of the site's security with guards from Quest Defense. You know we only hire the best people to work for us, and these are pretty smart engineers I have in here. They're quite capable of putting two and two together and with the news of the outbreak in Kansas and North Dakota, the question is: Is this more than mere coincidence?"

The driver of the van made the mistake of shifting his weight. A loose tile under his foot cracked as he moved, and the sound was as loud as a gunshot in the enclosed space. He froze as the voices went silent. Then footsteps approached.

Expecting a knock, he was caught by surprise when the door burst inward and smashed into his face, sending him stumbling backward. Dazed, he lifted his head and found two men staring at him. The younger of the pair wore a white lab coat and the other, slightly older, was clad in an expensive-looking suit.

"What are you doing here?" the man in the suit asked sharply.

The driver straightened himself and raised his hands in a non-threatening manner. "I just really needed to use the restroom."

"You would have been told that you weren't allowed in here," growled the second man.

"Yes, I was. I'm sorry. It was an emergency. Look, I'm leaving. I'm gone." He started to push his way past the pair but was held back.

"He's heard too much," the one in the suit muttered. "Call security."

"Whoa, whoa, relax," the driver coaxed. "There's no need for that. I'm just a delivery guy. I'm on my way out now."

The men said nothing as the one in the lab coat moved to block the bathroom door and spoke quickly into a small radio. The driver sighed inwardly. He didn't like where this was going.

The guards arrived within a minute. As they entered, the driver assessed them. Both were wearing black coveralls with handguns at their hips. Mean-looking batons were in their hands, and the guards didn't appear to be the types who'd shy away from using them. The driver could only conclude that the newcomers were not there to merely apprehend him.

In a motion honed by years of practice, he grabbed the man in the suit and flicked out his box-cutter knife from its belt sheath. He held the blade to his captive's throat. "Now," he said quietly, "I'm going to leave. You try anything and he'll be a bleeding mess on the floor."

The guards hesitated. The fact that they did meant that the driver was using someone of importance as a shield—and that was the only advantage he had.

"Move away from the door." When the guards glared at him, he snarled and pressed the blade harder against his captive's neck. "I said, move away from the door!"

Seeing that he meant business, the guards and the man in the lab coat reluctantly stepped away toward the sinks. The driver's eyes followed their every move. When he was satisfied with their distance from the exit, he walked backward toward the exit, dragging the suited man with him. He kicked back and the door flung open. In a blink of an eye, he sheathed the knife and pushed the man toward the guards before turning and barreling out of the restroom.

He sprinted down the corridor in the direction he'd come from and threw himself at the door, pushing it open, and ran to his van.

As he jumped into the vehicle and started the engine, he caught sight in the side mirror of the guards racing toward him. Without another thought, he stomped on the gas and sped headlong for the exit. He smashed through the boom gate, ignoring the shouts from the men inside the guard post. As he swerved onto the road, he heard the report of gunfire. The rear of the van took the bullets and he fishtailed away from the site.

He turned northbound onto Interstate 5, pushing the bulky vehicle up to its limit. When he glanced at his side mirror again, he saw two pairs of near-blinding headlights following close behind. As they accelerated toward him, the driver recognized the vehicles as Dodge Chargers, commonly used as police interceptors.

The odds were not in his favor, not when all he had was a box van that could barely reach eighty miles per hour. He wasn't going to lose his pursuers with speed. An idea formed in his mind but, before he could act, shots rang out and he heard the back of the van taking more bullets before one zinged past his window and shattered the left-side mirror. Not so easily fazed, he pushed on as the leading Charger hastened to catch up.

He counted silently to three then slammed on the brakes. His vehicle skidded to a stop but the guard behind the wheel of the Charger didn't react fast enough. The Charger slammed into the rear of the van and the car's momentum forced it up on its front wheels. The driver of the van quickly switched pedals and floored it. As he resumed speeding north, the Charger, in its precarious balancing act, flipped over on its roof.

The van mounted the crest of a hill bound by steep drop-offs on either side and passed a sign that read 'Lake Shasta'. Ahead, the driver saw the long bridge that spanned the lake. He took a quick look at his right-side mirror. If he'd expected a break, he wasn't getting one. The second Charger was hot on his tail. The lone guard inside was evidently none too happy about his colleagues being bested by a delivery man. Wary of falling for any more of the driver's tricks, he switched into the next lane, out of sight of the only mirror the driver had to work with.

The driver wound down his side window halfway and risked a look back. Craning his neck, he saw the guard use his baton to smash out the Charger's windshield. Most of the glass broke away from the pursuing vehicle though some jagged shards remained.

What is that nut do—

The driver halted mid-thought when the guard lifted his gun and pointed it toward him through the broken windshield. He recoiled as a bullet obliterated his windshield, shattering it into countless pieces. He bit back a cry of pain as dozens of glass pellets struck his face. Momentarily distracted, he swerved in the wrong direction. He was still trying to regain control when he heard a loud bang, and the van suddenly veered right toward the guard rail. Knowing one of his tires had been shot, he stomped on the brake but the vehicle continued to skid before crashing through the railing and plunging over the side.

The van tumbled down the two-hundred-foot cliff at terrifying speed. Doors and parts broke away. The vehicle went airborne one last time before crashing to the ground right next to the lake and rolling onto its roof.

The guard brought his car to a screeching halt and leapt out. He ran to the edge of the road and peered over, drew his gun, took careful aim at the van's exposed fuel tank, and fired. On the third shot, the tank exploded, engulfing the van in flames.

The guard watched for a few moments, then unclipped a radio from his belt. "It's done," he reported. He stared at the blazing wreckage for a moment longer before heading back to his vehicle. With a powerful roar of the engine, he drove away from the scene.

A dozen feet below the edge of the road, the battered and bruised driver of the van hung onto an exposed root that stuck out from the side of the ravine. He listened as the sound of the Charger's engine grew distant. Then, mind racing, he looked down at his destroyed vehicle. Grateful as he was to be alive, his intuition told him that he'd stumbled upon something big in that facility; something clandestine and dark.

As he dug his fingers into the slope and clawed his way back up toward the road, dirt-stained and bleeding, he allowed himself a small, furtive smile. It seemed like a good time to do something he hadn't done in ages: Reach out to the Council.

PART ONE

The Five's Road Trip Route

It was a scene of complete mayhem. Remains of destroyed buildings and vehicles were strewn across a mountaintop landscape. Shots rang out and bullets flew in the early hours of the misty morning. The heat of the battle drew cold sweat from the teenager who stood amidst it all. He watched, horrified, as a large black beast leapt and dug its massive fangs into a woman who was firing arrows from her bow. Unable to tear his gaze away from the ghastly sight, he looked on as the woman's life was taken right before his eyes.

He heard someone call out. At an agonizingly slow pace, he turned to see a man running toward him. The stranger, perhaps in his mid-fifties, had flaming red hair with a matching beard, but what captured the teenager's attention was the look of pure terror in the man's gray eyes. Behind him, gouts of earth erupted as bullets struck the ground. The projectiles burst forth from the ramp of a strange, imposing aircraft that hovered above the site.

The teenager found himself running toward the man. He willed himself to move as fast as he could, yet time seemed to have slowed. Everything became crystal-clear. He; could see every little detail, from a minuscule piece of broken glass to broken arrowheads on the dirt, though his focus remained on the flame-haired stranger. He shouted to him but his voice was drowned by the sounds of the aircraft's thundering engines.

As the gap closed between them, the man let out a pained cry that rose above the noise. He lurched forward before falling to the ground and lay motionless as his blood began to stain the dirt.

The teenager screamed in terror and stumbled toward the man. Before he could reach him, everything went dark. Painful silence ensued. Then a voice spoke, rich and firm, with a touch of a peculiar accent:

The storm is gathering, Jag. You must wake up.

Wake up!

JAG!

Jag Sanchez bolted upright in his bed, gasping for air. As he caught his breath, he stared at the wall ahead, not realizing he was sweating but very aware that every part of him was trembling. He ran a hand over his face and shut his eyes tightly.

That voice had been haunting his dreams for the last nine months, since . . .

He looked at his phone and yelped when he saw the time. Late, *again*. He leapt out of bed, staggering around his room as he got ready, then grabbed his bag and flew down the stairs toward the front door, not bothering to stop for breakfast. How was it that he lived only five minutes from the high school but was constantly late, even when he put his alarm on?

"Jag, you gotta quit waking up this," his brother called from the living room where Jag could hear him playing on the Xbox.

"Easy for you to say, you're done with school," Jag growled. "When you decide to apply for college, Tristan, then you can talk."

"Touché," Tristan chuckled. "Have a good day, bro."

"Have fun rotting your brains out playing Halo."

"I will. And don't act like you wouldn't enjoy it, either!"

"Pfft!"

Jag was still jamming his feet into his shoes as he headed out the door. He was half-tempted to take his brother's newly acquired motorcycle from the garage but knew he'd get a good beatdown if he dared. So, relying on just his legs, he hurried along the sidewalk that turned up into the school's front parking lot.

As he rounded the turn, he stopped short. A group of four guys his age were laughing at someone on the ground. To one side, a wheelchair had been overturned and the contents of a backpack were strewn over the grass.

When Jag took a closer look at the boy on the ground, his heart sank for a moment before fury overtook him. He made his way over. "What do you think you're doing?" he snapped.

The ringleader, a stocky sophomore with a gray ball cap, looked up in surprise. When he saw who the newcomer was, he smirked. "Hey, look who it is. One of the amnesiacs."

Jag said nothing. He straightened the wheelchair as the black teenager who'd fallen off it sat up on the ground, glaring defiantly up at his intimidators. He got a pat on the head from one of them.

Jag saw it and fought the powerful urge to throttle the boy. "Roderick isn't a dog. Show some respect."

The one who'd patted Roderick on the head laughed. "Roddy's a tough guy, he can take a little shoving. You, on the other hand . . . heh . . ."

"Don't test me."

"Jag, don't bother," Roderick said quietly.

"What's up with you anyway, Jag? You don't get into fights as much anymore." The boy with the ball cap lowered his voice and whispered mockingly, "Was it the aliens? Did they take away your urge to fight? The same way they took away your memories of last summer?"

"Shut up."

"It's been a year, guys," Roderick sighed. "Find some new material."

The boy ignored him and pressed on. "Did they probe you, too, Jag?"

His friends guffawed. Jag's amber eyes were twin flames of anger as he stepped forward. "You're garbage. You and the other rats around here have done nothing but harass my friends and me since we came back. If I hear another word come out of your mouth, I'll gladly make you eat your teeth."

The boy in the ball cap stared at Jag for a few moments, then broke into an unkind grin. "I guess the aliens didn't take the fight out of you after all."

Jag struck without warning, his fist catching the other teenager squarely in the jaw. The boy fell back, stunned and in pain.

Jag snarled. "You want another? Keep talking and I'll be more than happy to supply!"

"Oh-ho, tough guy!" The boy held his jaw, wincing. "Your hit's harder than I remember . . . Did the aliens inject you with super strength? Were you and your friends a part of their experiments?"

Fists raised, Jag was about to throw himself at the ringleader when Roderick's voice rang out. "Jag! Stop!"

Jag caught himself in time and slowly lowered his hands, but the flames in his eyes didn't die. "Watch your mouth," he muttered icily before turning his back on the boys and reaching down to help Roderick into his wheelchair.

The teenager in the ball cap looked ready to utter a snarky comment but thought better and resorted to kicking Roderick's backpack into the middle of the street. Then he and his friends left.

Their departure allowed both Jag and Roderick to breathe easier. Jag quickly went to retrieve the bag and gathered the books that had tumbled out. As he zipped it up and passed it to Roderick, he asked, "What was that all about?"

Roderick waved his hand impassively. "It's nothing."

"Roddy . . ."

"Don't worry about it, man. It's all good. Come on, we're late."

"It's the second-to-last day of school. We can't really get in trouble for not being on time anymore. We can talk for a bit."

Roderick looked amused. "Says the guy who came running all the way from his house . That may be your thinking, Jag, but I don't like rolling into class after everyone else." With that, he guided his wheelchair toward the school.

Jag kept pace with him. "Tell me what happened."

Roderick sighed. "I don't want it to bother you, Jag. Look, the school year is almost over—"

"Just tell me."

Roderick was quiet for a moment, then said, "They were walking behind me on the way here and I heard them making fun of your . . . amnesia. All I did was tell them to back off."

Jag flinched slightly. *Amnesia.* "I'm sorry."

Roderick looked up at him with a frown. "Why?"

"Because . . ." *Because I put you in a wheelchair and now you get pushed around for being friends with the amnesiac that got you paralyzed.*

Roderick seemed to understand what he was thinking and offered a small laugh. "I hope you're not still blaming yourself for the accident two years ago. The cam was defective. You didn't know, it wasn't your fault. Whoever said rock climbing was a safe sport?"

"I promised you and the other guys that you'd be safe. That I'd look after you."

"Jag, look at me. I'm alive! As long as I'm right here, you don't have to be all down about me not being able to use my legs. God is good, man! Yeah, I can't do some stuff anymore, but there's a whole bunch of things I can still experience. I can rock out at concerts, throw a football, get a date with a girl—and I have!"

Roderick sat confidently in his wheelchair, a bright smile on his face as they made their way to the school's main doors. Jag glanced at him and felt a surge of admiration. He didn't know where his friend found the strength to look on the positive side of his life, but Roddy never wavered from his optimism.

They reached the main entrance and Jag held the door open for Roderick. As they parted ways to head to their classes, Jag said, "Roddy, can we talk at lunch?"

"Sure thing, man. See you in the cafeteria." With another bright smile and a fist bump, Roderick entered his classroom.

* * *

Jag was sitting by himself at a table in the school's cafeteria, fiddling with his phone, when Roderick rolled up. "Hey."

Jag looked up from his phone. "Oh, hey."

"You're not having lunch?"

"Not really hungry."

Roderick helped himself into a chair; Jag would have offered, but he knew Roderick wasn't always fond of being assisted, especially with things he considered easy.

Once he was settled, he pulled out a sandwich from his bag and began eating meticulously. After a few mouthfuls, he looked Jag in the eye. "You look horrible," he said. "You sleeping okay?"

"Yeah . . . I mean, no. That's kind of why I wanted to talk—I need to get something off my chest." Jag paused, hesitating. He'd sought to share his dream but was unsure now whether to mention it. The more he thought, the sillier he felt for even wanting to speak about it.

Again, Roderick seemed to read his mind. "I'm all ears. You know that. I don't laugh at your problems—you've never laughed at mine."

Jag slid his phone into his jeans' pocket and leaned back with a sigh. "It's just . . . I've been having these dreams. And they're *always* the same."

Roderick frowned as he munched on his sandwich. "Is this a nightly thing?"

"No. Happens often enough to bug me, though."

"How long has this been going on?"

"A few months after . . . after returning home last summer."

Roderick stopped mid-munch. "Oh." He put his sandwich down and cleared his throat. "I know I've asked before, and I know other people have, too, but you really can't remember a thing, not even in the slightest?"

Jag shook his head and ran a hand through his dark brown hair. "The only thing I remember is the crash in Kody's dad's plane over Yukon, and then finding myself in a hospital. But there's like a three-month gap in between and no matter how hard I try, nothing comes back to me."

"And you really weren't injured? Head trauma or something?"

"I mean, according to the docs, we'd walked into that town in perfect health so I'm guessing we're fine. Except that I—we—remember none of it."

"That's just strange." Roderick picked up his sandwich again. "You, Tegan, Aari and the others don't really hang out anymore, do you?"

"We're a bigger target when we're together in this place," Jag said wistfully. "We do meet up after school sometimes, but it feels different, you know? Like a huge part of us is missing. Which is true, I guess. And we're all frustrated because of people like that idiot and his friends this morning."

"They're just a handful of dimwits who are all bark. Yeah, they're loud and rude, but most people are sympathetic toward you guys."

"I suppose. But sometimes it's a handful of people that do the most damage."

Roderick smiled sadly. "I get that." He pushed the last piece of his sandwich into his mouth. "So, about that dream."

"Right. Basically, I'm in the middle of some kind of—I dunno, it feels like a battleground. There are these people, two groups of them, and they're fighting each other. One side has guns and the other is using bows and arrows. And there are these animals that I'm pretty sure were spawned from the depths of hell. Ruthless killing machines. And then . . . and then there's this man I keep seeing—an older guy. He moves really fast, but each time in my dreams, he gets shot down by a machine gun in a plane flying overhead. And each time, I can never save him."

Roderick's frown seemed to be plastered onto his face. "That's a bit spooky, if you're dreaming about it often."

Jag nodded. "When I wake up, I usually have the urge to throw up. Seeing that man get shot, seeing the blood, and having it be that vivid . . . every emotion, just . . ." As he spoke, he felt bile rising in his throat.

Roderick reached into his bag and pulled out a water bottle which he passed to Jag. Jag gratefully took a few sips.

Rubbing his face, Roderick said, "Well, that's definitely not a pleasant dream to have, even once."

"No kidding. And then this morning, I had it again, but this time there's this voice at the end. I can't place the accent, but it's a man speaking and he's telling me about a gathering storm and that I need to wake up."

"Hmm . . . This may be a bit silly, but have you talked to anyone else about this? Parents?"

Jag let out a sharp laugh. "Hah! No, definitely not. It's bad enough that one of their sons is a clinical amnesiac who disappeared without a trace for months. I don't need them thinking I'm a nut, too."

"They're your parents! They know you're a nut anyway." Roderick smiled good-humoredly.

Jag, despite himself, smiled back. "Ha-ha."

"But in all seriousness, maybe it's just a psychological reaction to everything you've gone through."

"If you're implying that I should see a psychiatrist, the answer is *no*."

"Just trying to look out for you. You tried taking some sleeping medications?"

"I did, but I stopped. They didn't help much and I didn't want to get hooked on them." Jag poked at the water bottle that was sitting on the table. "Thanks for listening, Roddy."

"Anytime, man, anytime. There may be jerks roaming this place, but you've got friends who have your back."

The moment the bell rang, Jag was out of his classroom; he didn't want to spend a minute longer in the building. He exited through the main doors of the school, making his way through the throng of students who were also leaving the premises, and found Aari Barnes waiting for him outside.

Aari was several inches shorter than Jag, who stood six feet tall. He had short, dark red hair and ice-blue eyes that made him appear both intense and friendly. His intelligence was well-known throughout their grade, but he was not a teacher's pet and disliked being labeled so.

Like Jag, Aari was one of the so-called amnesiacs, along with Tegan Ryder, Mariah Ashton, and Kody Tyler. The five of them had known each other all their lives and were like second family to one another. Ever since their mysterious reappearance after vanishing in Yukon, though, they'd subconsciously avoided being seen together during school to escape the stares and taunts.

Jag went up to Aari and grabbed him in a headlock, grinning. "Hey, Barnes."

Aari, who'd long since learned that attempting to get away from Jag's tight grip was futile, stood still and smiled, arms dangling in front of him. "Yo."

"How you doing?"

"Okay, I guess." Aari looked at his watch. "Should we get going?"

"Yep." Jag let his friend go and stepped back. Aari straightened his black button-up shirt, and together the two started toward Jag's house.

They didn't speak much as they walked. It was a particularly warm day and they were glad for the modest cooling breeze. Jag glanced up at the large trees that bordered the sidewalk as the leaves rustled in the wind. Great Falls, Montana, was a beautiful place and he was thankful to be living in such a wonderful town. However, all he'd wanted to do as of late was just get out and find himself.

They reached the house and Jag led the way to the front door. Inside, the smell of melted butter stopped them in their tracks. Aari blinked, then marched into the living room where the aroma was coming from.

"Oy, who's got the popcorn?" he called out.

Jag quietly repeated 'Oy' out of Aari's earshot and smiled to himself. It was an exclamation that Aari had fallen into the habit of using, taking after his grandfather, a Jewish Holocaust survivor. Jag always enjoyed hearing the story of how Aari's grandparents met—his grandmother's family had risked their lives to provide refuge for numerous Jews in Germany, her future husband included.

Tristan looked up from the television and hoisted a big bowl over his head. "That would be me, the popcorn goblin."

Jag's two older siblings were relaxing on the couches. Tristan was lounging sideways with one leg dangling off cushions. He was still in his pajamas, indicating that he'd been a couch potato the entire day. His hair, which was usually done up James Dean style, was tousled. He was taller than Jag but both shared the same athletic build and a passion for parkour. The brothers were often found practicing the sport in the town's many parks, unwittingly attracting curious onlookers.

Sitting on the other couch was Jag's twenty-two-year-old sister, Camilla, in sweatpants and a baggy t-shirt. Her hair was up in a messy bun but she still had makeup on, which meant that she'd only returned from work shortly before Jag and Aari arrived.

Evidently, it was a lazy day at the Sanchez household.

Jag vaulted over the back of the couch and landed beside his brother. "Have you been vegging here since I left?"

"Yeah. Oh, Mom called, by the way. She and Dad will be back after dinner, so we're on our own in terms of food." Tristan threw a piece of popcorn in the air and caught it in his mouth. When he saw Aari flop down on the carpet in front of the couch, he grinned and raised his hand. "Hey, man. What's up?"

Aari high-fived him, then grabbed a handful of popcorn for himself. "Nothing much. Counting down the hours till the school year's done. Just under twenty-four hours left."

"So how come you're here?"

"I just wanted to look over the route that we're gonna take for the trip."

Tristan shook his head in disbelief. "You need to explain that to me. How is it that after last year's mishap, you five are allowed to drive all the way to California *by yourselves?*"

Jag and Aari glanced at each other but neither answered. Camilla looked over at the pair sympathetically, then said, "They need it, Tristan. They need to hang out and do stuff like they used to. This trip will help them."

Tristan shook his head again but let it go. He picked up the remote and switched the channel to a national news station. When he saw the headline on the screen, he frowned and turned up the volume.

". . . Additional reports are coming in of more crop failures in parts of North Dakota, Kansas and Montana," the news anchor was saying. "For further details, we now turn to our correspondent in Baldwin City, Kansas."

As the camera cut away to show a man with a microphone standing among burnt crops in a farmer's field, Jag turned to the others, puzzled. "More crop failures? What's going on?"

Camilla shrugged. "Don't know. I heard talk at work. Rumor has it that it's a new viral bug, but no one has come out to officially say anything. It's not just wheat, either. Apparently corn and rice crops have been destroyed too."

"I hope Gran and Gramps are alright," Tristan murmured. "They make their living off their farm . . ."

They continued to watch the news for a little while longer until Jag got to his feet. Taking the cue, Aari got up as well and the two excused themselves. Jag led the way to his room and threw the door open. The first thing that greeted them was a large map of the United States pinned against a wall decorated with posters of cars and musicians.

Aari went up to the map. He used a finger to trace the route that the friends had begun planning several weeks back. "I'm looking forward to this," he muttered.

Jag stood beside him, arms folded. "Me too."

He saw Aari glance at his desk where a small stack of newspaper clippings was pushed up against a corner. Aari went over and spread them out on the tabletop. When he took a proper look the content of the articles, his expression grew stony.

The clippings were of media frenzy when the friends had gone missing the previous summer. Everyone had been stunned when Samuel Tyler appeared in a small town many miles distant from the crash site, battered and distraught. They were even more baffled when his teenage passengers were nowhere to be found.

When the five showed up weeks later in a hospital at the same small town, the media tripled its craze. The friends had obviously been taken care of as they were healthy, save for some bruises and scars. What happened during those missing weeks remained a mystery that, over time, the media had slowly lost interest in.

Jag silently restacked the clippings and pushed them back into the corner.

"Why do you keep them?" Aari asked, rubbing his temples as if he'd gotten a headache.

Jag sat on the edge of his bed and sighed. "I'm not sure. I just know that when I look at them, I—"

"Want to burn them?"

"Yes, burn them. But they also make me want to do this trip even more. Clear our minds and all that. Prove that we can be together without this cloud hanging over us."

Aari looked back at the map and pointed at it. "If this doesn't help . . ."

"I'd rather not think like that."

"You're right. Positivity. Be positive." Aari rapped his knuckles against the side of his head. After a moment, he smiled slightly. "Can't wait for the barbecue on Sunday."

Jag's face lit up. "The food's gonna be great."

"Food's always great when Kody's family is involved."

"True." Jag pushed himself off the bed. "Let's grab a bite. Pretty sure there's leftover cheesecake in the fridge."

"Thanks, but I think I'll be heading home. Gotta babysit the kid for a few hours while Mom and Dad run some errands."

"Your little sister has a name, you know," Jag teased, walking Aari to the door.

Aari slipped his shoes on and picked up his bag. As he stepped out of the house, he raised his fist over his head and hollered, "One more day and school's out!"

Jag chuckled as he shut the door. *This trip really is what we need,* he thought. *No misadventures and no idiots to mock us. Just fun times with the group. It'll be good.*

The smell of grilled burgers rode the cool evening breeze as laughter and shouts filled the air. Samuel Tyler glanced over his shoulder from where he stood on the deck by his barbecue and watched his eldest son toss around a football with his friends and their siblings. He smiled to himself. It was great to see the kids being together and having fun.

Someone tugged at his pant leg. He looked down to see his five-year-old looking up at him with big, dark eyes and a large, life-loving smile on his face.

Samuel scooped up his youngest child. "Roshon, my little man! What do you need?"

The boy squirmed in his father's arms. "When are we gonna eat? I'm huuungry," he complained, grabbing Samuel's face in his small hands.

Samuel grinned. "Ah, you and your appetite. Just like your brothers."

"Fooood, Daddy!" Roshon wiggled his father's face. "Pretty please?"

"Not for another few minutes, baby."

"Aww!" Roshon pouted and squirmed again, so Samuel put him down. He watched his son run toward his mother, who was seated at a large table at the other side of the deck, and clamber onto her lap to snuggle against her chest. With a soft smile, Samuel turned back to the barbecue and closed the lid, then went to join the other parents as they lounged and chatted around the table, drinks in hand.

As he sat down, Roberto Sanchez looked over at him. "Smells good, Sam!"

Samuel laughed. "It's nothing fancy, Rob, just an old family recipe."

"All the same." Jag's father took a sip from his glass. He was tall and athletically built, much like his two sons. With his charming smile and easygoing ways, he didn't look fifty and certainly didn't give off the impression that he was a scientist working at a biomedical firm.

He nodded in the teenagers' direction as they threw the football around and called out to each other. "It's nice to see them hanging out like that."

"Remember how we used to goof around?" Samuel mused. "Our kids may be tame by comparison, but they're definitely an adventurous lot."

"Yeah, they're a good bunch. Proud of them all."

"How's Jag been?"

"No calls from the school about getting into fights for the last seven months, so it's been getting better. Guess he's finally learned to keep his temper in check."

"Good to hear."

Samuel helped himself to a drink then leaned back and observed the property quietly. Life with the Air Force was good. The base near Great Falls, now reopened after a decades-long closure, was a good place to raise a family.

As he sipped his drink, his thoughts rewound to the previous summer. He was still baffled by everything, from their surviving the crash to the teenagers' disappearance and sudden reappearance. It had been an unwelcome burden when the media and various investigators kept questioning and probing the kids for months after their return. None of the five had ever wanted to be in the spotlight like that, and the persistence of the press made them dislike it even more.

Kody's memory loss had been difficult for the Tylers, and Samuel knew it was the same for the other families. It was not an illness and they didn't treat it as one, but it was hard to believe that the five couldn't remember a single detail about all those weeks they'd been missing. Upon their arrival back home, Kody had spent more time than ever focusing on schoolwork and aviation—he'd been learning to fly since he was twelve and was working on obtaining his Private Pilot's License—and Samuel figured that was his son's way of regaining some normalcy in his life.

"Penny for your thoughts?" Roberto asked.

"Ah . . . just the kids and everything they've been through. The scorn they had to put up with at school and the harassment by the media."

Roberto snorted. "Downright irritating, that's what they were. Wouldn't leave a group of *kids* alone. It's sickening."

"It's newsworthy, I guess."

"All they want is ratings and they'll go after it like bloodhounds. Respect for privacy means nothing to most of them."

"No argument there," Samuel sighed. He passed his hand over his short afro, a haircut his three sons wore as well. Roshon and George both had his dark brown eyes, whereas Kody's were green like the boys' mother.

As he downed the rest of his drink, he said, "So, about this upcoming trip. to be frank with you, I'm still worried about letting them go off on their own."

Roberto smiled. "I know. We all are." He motioned toward the other parents who were caught up in their own conversation at the other end of the table. "This was definitely not an easy decision for any of us, but we all know that the kids haven't been quite the same since their return. We've raised great sons and daughters, and it pains me to see them this way. They need the space to find themselves again. I'm praying that this trip will provide them the healing and strength to be as they were before."

"That's my hope too. It's just . . . I'm still concerned. They'll be on their own for two weeks, and Jag's only had his full driver's license for a few months."

"I understand your concern, but they're responsible kids. If it helps, I can vouch for Jag's road skills. And the bulk of the trip follows along one highway, Sam. That shouldn't be too difficult for him to handle."

"I suppose. I heard you're letting them take your Jeep?"

Roberto nodded. "It's a gas-guzzler, but it'll keep them safe and I'm happy with that."

Roshon suddenly piped up. "Daddy, dinner!"

Samuel jumped up. "Whoops!" He hurried to the barbecue and opened the lid to let the smoke escape. He checked the beef patties to make sure they were thoroughly cooked and began sliding them onto hamburger buns as Roberto called the friends and their siblings over.

As they ate, jokes were cracked and laughter was plentiful, as were the smiles. The families were close to one another, mainly because the parents had been good friends since they themselves were teenagers.

Ice cream was served for dessert as the sun began to set. Kody caught his father's eye. Samuel smiled and nodded. Excusing himself, Kody ducked into the house, then returned a minute later with a big tote bag.

"And what do you have there, Kode-man?" Jag asked, one eyebrow cocked.

Kody wore a sly look. "When you guys are done eating, come join me." He headed out to the center of the backyard and sat on the grass, waiting.

The friends and their siblings looked at each other, then gobbled down the remainder of their ice cream—with Roshon saying "Owie, brain freeze!"—and hurried down the steps to Kody. The adults finished a little more slowly, then made their way over.

From inside the bag, Kody carefully produced five rocket fireworks. The group gasped in delight and Roshon clapped his hands. "Yay!"

"I got these for a couple of reasons," Kody said as he rose to his feet and began setting up the rockets on the ground. "The first is for fun, of course—just all of us being here and having a great time. The second reason I got these is to kick off our road trip."

A whoop came from Jag, Tegan, Mariah and Aari. They raised their fists in the air and wore huge smiles. "Love you, man!" Jag laughed.

Kody raised his fist as well, a large grin on his face. "So the idea is, we'll each fire a rocket and see how high it goes."

Roshon ran up to Kody and wrapped himself around his brother's leg. "Kody, I wanna fire a rocket."

Kody picked Roshon up. "Tell you what, why don't you help me with mine?"

Roshon draped his arms around Kody's neck happily. "Okay!"

It warmed Samuel's heart to see them like that. Looking at his boys, he felt reassured that he and his wife had done right by their children. It had always been a question in the back of their minds—in the back of any good parent's mind—whether everything they were doing as they raised their kids was shaping them to be the best they could be.

Jag lit the first rocket, and there were cheers as the missile flew up before exploding into bright colors. Tegan launched hers next, then Mariah, then Aari. When it was Kody's turn, he kept to his word and let Roshon help him light the rocket's fuse before scooping him into his arms and bounding off to a safe distance. Roshon watched along with the others, his mouth open and his hands covering his ears, as the final rocket burst and lit the darkened sky with vibrant hues.

Another round of cheers swept over the families. Samuel regarded it all with a small smile. While the chat with Roberto had allayed his fears, he couldn't help but feel some trepidation as he watched the friends enjoy each other's company, their arms around one another.

He could clearly recall the heart-stopping moment when he'd regained consciousness after having been flung far from the plane, only to realize the teenagers were nowhere to be found. He'd searched for them, limping and falling and yelling out until he eventually ended up at the edge of the forest and passed out from hunger and exhaustion. When he awoke next, he'd been taken to a hospital in a nearby town but there was still no sign of his son or his other passengers.

Samuel slowly looked up at the sky as the stars began to appear. He offered a silent plea: *Keep them safe.*

Kody packed the last of the friends' baggage into the back of the black Grand Cherokee. When he was sure everything was stowed properly, he readjusted his sunglasses, closed the rear hatch and gave the others a thumbs-up. "We're good to go!"

The families were crowded in the Sanchez's driveway to see the group off. Jag, Tegan, Aari and Mariah went to their parents and siblings to give them one last hug. Kody turned to his own family and embraced his mother and father tightly before gathering his brothers in a huddle. He nodded at the youngest Tyler and removed his shades. "Alright, Roshon, you gotta be good, okay? Don't be a brat all day long."

Roshon looked thoughtful. "Is half a day okay?"

"As long as that half a day is when you're sleeping." Kody winked and faced his ten-year-old brother. "George, you know the drill."

"Of course I do. Don't worry about me." George lifted his chin and grinned.

Kody hugged them both, then put his shades back on. Someone placed a heavy hand on his shoulder and he looked to see his father gazing down at him with hopeful confidence and a hint of concern. "Take care, okay? Be safe. Don't do anything senseless . . . please."

Resting his hand on his father's, Kody gave him a reassuring smile. "We'll be fine, Dad, don't worry. No dumb stunts, I promise."

He heard a whistle and saw his friends already piling into the Jeep. He waved goodbye to his family then jogged back to the vehicle and slid into the backseat with Mariah and Aari while Jag and Tegan sat up front.

"Get the AC on," Aari said, grimacing.

"If Aari of all people is complaining about how hot it is, when we're in trouble." Jag started the engine and quickly turned on the air conditioning. The five breathed a sigh of relief. It was only eight in the morning, but the heat was building up rapidly. Kody turned around so he could see their families standing at the back of the vehicle. He waved as Jag drove the car onto the road. Aari and Mariah joined him.

"Okay, keep waving, keep waving." Kody watched carefully until their families were out of sight, then faced the front, whooping. "And we're clear! Woo!"

His friends laughed. There was an air of release as they left behind their school and homes. For the first time in nearly a year, they were starting to feel truly at ease and their sense of adventure was returning, coursing through their veins like fire.

They drove by a small park, barely noticing the parents on benches and their little ones monkeying on the playground. As the Jeep rolled past, an African-American woman with jet-black hair sitting astride a motorcycle picked up her phone. She tapped the device a couple of times before placing it to her ear, staring at the retreating SUV as she waited for the person on the other end to pick up.

There was a click and a voice came on. "Hello?"

The woman only said two words before hanging up: "They've left."

* * *

Kody watched as Aari pulled a slim laptop out from his black sling bag. As he opened it and booted up a coding program, Kody let out a mew of incredulity. "Are you serious, dude?"

"Huh?" Aari didn't look up from the screen.

"We've only *just* left for a trip and you've already pulled out your inner geek."

"Inner geek?" Tegan echoed. "He's never had to bring it out. He pretty much wears it all day, every day. Like a cape."

"Captain Geek," Mariah said with a grin. "No, wait. Super Geek."

Aari raised an eyebrow calmly without taking his eyes off the screen. "Laugh it up all you want, powder puffs. Who's the guy who fixes your tech, takes care of malware and all the bad stuff you let onto your computers?"

"I'm sticking up for Aari, here," Jag chimed in. "I've saved a lot of cash with him helping me out."

"What else do you do on that little computer of yours aside from surfing and gaming?" Mariah asked.

Aari's fingers moved quickly over the keyboard. "I don't use a laptop like this to game. That's what an actual computer's for."

"But what do you *do*?"

"Stuff."

"What stuff?"

"Programming and whatnot. Nothing any of you would really be interested in."

"Try us," Jag said.

Kody rested with his head back against the headrest, eyes half-closed as he listened. Aari spoke about some of the knowledge he'd been picking up on his own for the past few years. Kody managed to follow along for a bit but was completely lost—and somewhat bored—after Aari explained different methods to achieve denial-of-service. His thoughts wandered off and he slipped into his own world, his friends' voices melting into the background.

He wasn't sure how long he'd been absent, but Jag must have noticed his quietness because he asked, "Hey, Kody, you alright?"

"Huh?" Kody blinked. "Oh, yeah. I'm fine. Just thinking."

"Uh oh," Aari said jokingly. "'Thinking', he says. Something's definitely wrong."

"Let's hear him out before jumping to any conclusions," Jag replied, somewhat amused. "What's on your mind?"

Kody rubbed the top of his head. "It's nice to be away from . . . from home. It's weird to say that, because you'd think of home as a place of safety and warmth. Home is where you'd want to be. But we're pretty much running away from it."

The others were silent for a few moments until Aari spoke up. "We're not really running away. We just need a break from it."

"Because home's not home anymore."

The words sank in and silence took hold of them again. Jag glanced at Kody through the rearview mirror. "Home . . . home is where *we* are. As long as we're together, nothing will change that. Not the idiots in Great Falls, not the media, not the doctors."

They sure played a huge part in making home feel unfriendly, Kody thought, but kept it to himself. Out loud, he said, "Sorry for bringing it up. It just bears down on you after a while, you know?"

Mariah smiled comfortingly at him. "Let it out. This trip is for healing."

He gave her a half-smile in return.

"How about some music?" Tegan asked.

"Anything but the radio," Aari said, lacing his fingers behind his head. "Everything is so repetitive nowadays."

"Agreed. That's why we've got these"—Tegan connected her phone to the car's system—"and voila! No need to worry about recycled tunes."

They drove for a few hours, taking in each other's company and jamming to the long playlist of songs. The scenery of shrubs and faraway mountains rolled by and they stopped noticing it after a while. They were nearing the Montana-Idaho border when there was a brief pause as one of the songs ended. In that period of silence, a collective rumble sounded from their stomachs. Laughter ensued. "Guess it's time for lunch," Jag said.

Kody nodded. "I think you're right."

Tegan stretched back to poke his knee. "*You* don't get a say in this, Mr. I-Eat-A-Lot-But-Never-Gain-Weight."

He adopted a snobbish, miffed tone. "How dare you, peasant? I must eat, otherwise my metabolism will end me." He reached over to mess up her ash-brown hair. She retreated instantly and grumbled something incomprehensible as she combed her fingers through her layers.

"Let's check this place out," Jag said as he turned off of the highway into a town. A sign greeted them.

"Welcome to Llama?" Kody read, frowning.

Jag chuckled. "It's Lima, not llama."

"Oh, good. I'd hate to have lunch where a bunch of fluffy long-necked animals spit at me."

"Right . . ."

As they drove up and down the streets, they realized quickly that Lima was a very, very small town. Kody pressed his face against the window. "Where's the food?" he moaned. "The restaurants? The takeout?"

Mariah pushed Aari's head back so she could look out of his window. "Hey, what about this little thing?" She pointed to a small building with her free hand as Aari flailed. "Mountain High Subs."

"Let's give it a shot." Jag carefully parked the Jeep and the five got out, hastily making their way into the air-conditioned shop. Once inside, they looked around, pleasantly surprised by how charming the deli was. They ordered their sandwiches and happily munched away before thanking the storekeeper and scurrying back into the Jeep. Jag drove toward the highway, leaving Lima behind.

They crossed the border into Idaho and traveled for a while until they reached a town, whereupon Kody cleared his throat. "Um, I gotta take a leak."

Jag made a sound of exasperation. "Dude, you should've gone when we stopped for lunch!"

"I didn't have to go at that time, though."

"Okay, okay—here's a donut shop. Be quick."

As Kody hopped out, he heard Tegan murmur, "Is I it smart to let him go into a shop that sells food?"

"We just had lunch," Jag said. "He's not gonna get anything."

A couple of minutes later, Kody walked out of the store balancing a large cardboard box in one hand and a half-eaten donut in the other. As he got into the Jeep, Jag groaned and slid down in his seat. Tegan smiled, her gray eyes alight with laughter. "Never underestimate that guy's appetite. After seventeen years with him, you should know that."

"Glazed delights, anyone?" Kody asked, mouth full.

"Why not." Aari reached past Mariah and took a fudge-covered donut for himself, then said thoughtfully, "Hey, if we were to head thataway to Highway 20, we'd be heading toward Yellowstone National Park."

"As much as I'd love to visit, I don't think we have time for a detour," Jag said wistfully as he put the Jeep into drive.

"Yeah, but what I was getting at is . . ." Aari took a bite. "You guys know that there's a huge active volcano in Yellowstone, right?" When the others nodded, he continued. "Did you know it's actually considered a super-volcano?"

"A super-volcano?" Tegan repeated.

"Yeah, the Yellowstone Caldera. Some folks are saying that it's long overdue for an eruption."

"That's a real jolly thought."

"It gets better. Because of its sheer size, when it erupts, the effects would be devastating. Everything within a hundred-mile radius would be destroyed. Ash would hang in the air for ages. With so much of all that stuff in the atmosphere, it's not just North America, but the entire planet that would be affected. Sunlight would be blocked, making the temperature fall. It'd be nature's equivalent of a nuclear winter."

Kody, who had been silently listening with a perturbed look on his face, emitted a funny sound. "Can we *please* not talk of depressing doomsday scenarios? Donuts are present here, and all you guys care to chat about is the end of the world as we know it. Come on, people. Priorities."

"Alright, alright,", Mariah groused. "Teegs, where are we spending the night?"

"I think we were gonna stay at a motel in . . . hold on, let me check the GPS . . . aha, right. Salt Lake City, Utah."

"Three states in one day. Neat."

Tegan grinned. "I have a funny feeling Jag's gonna be so done with this car once we return from this trip, what with all the driving we have to do."

Jag scoffed. "How could I ever get tired of a car? Especially a beast like this." He patted the dashboard affectionately.

Kody rested his head against the window, yawning, then muttered, "Food coma."

Mariah glanced at him. "All the food's catching up with you now, huh? How many donuts did you eat?"

"Like four," he groaned. "And they were pretty darn big."

She sighed. "Well, I hope you don't get carsick. I wouldn't want to be next to you when you throw up."

"Gee, thanks for the concern."

"Anytime, buddy boy."

As they drove on, the chatter slowly died. Kody fought to stay awake as Tegan, Aari and Mariah nodded off. He wanted to keep Jag company, but Jag must have been able to tell that he was struggling to remain awake. "Take a nap, Kode-man," he advised. "I'll be fine."

Kody stifled another yawn. "You sure?"

"Yeah. You look barely alive right now."

"Mmh . . ." The sound had hardly left his mouth when his head lolled back against the headrest and he fell into a deep sleep.

One of the most family-friendly places in the United States, Provo, Utah was teeming with activity this particular day. With summer in and school out, people were biking, hiking, and enjoying the many outdoor activities that the town offered. Families swarmed the parks, trails, and recreation centers. Drivers had to be careful around neighborhoods and look out for kids and pets.

In a neighborhood made up of different-colored homes with single-car garages, a small blue house sat nondescriptly near the end of the street, overlooking Utah Lake. The view was splendid. The front yard was well-kept, with trimmed hedges and a perfectly manicured lawn.

Inside, the house was equally neat and organized except for a few papers strewn on a large teakwood desk next to a window. Upon the mantle of the living room were several framed photos. In between them, a carefully placed box held a United States military decoration of valor, the Silver Star Medal.

A man dressed in a dark polo shirt and fitted jeans sat on a sofa facing a television that had been muted. He tinkered with a tennis ball-sized device in his hands; a light-shelled glass container that looked like an oval perfume bottle with a notched surface. Attached at the top was a safety lever and a pin. The container was filled with luminescent blue liquid.

The man glanced at the watch on his wrist and continued to fiddle with the device for a minute more before placing the object into a pouch. He then very gingerly tucked the pouch into a pocket in his backpack and headed to the bathroom where he splashed himself with cold water. It was late afternoon, and the heat clung to the day as it always did this time of year.

He grabbed a towel off a rack and patted himself dry, then studied his reflection in the mirror. Eyeing the scars on the left side of his face, he scowled at the memory of his mishap two months prior. Looking down at his arms where longer scars were somewhat visible, he shrugged to himself. At least he was alive and in terrific physical shape.

Running his hands from his blonde hair to his short beard with a sigh, he strode out of the bathroom to the coffee table and picked up a small, beautiful chip-carved wooden box. He opened it and peered in. Then, with a glint in his eyes, he latched the lid and carefully slid the box into his backpack. Grabbing his car keys, he quickly made his way to the garage and flicked on the light. His prized Shelby GT500 greeted him. The classic red Mustang was continuously maintained to preserve its pristine condition.

Once inside the car, he opened the garage door and started the engine, then backed out onto the street and activated the home security system via an app on his phone. With that, he drove toward the highway and hoped that the events scheduled for the evening would go as planned.

Someone was shaking Mariah's knee. She slowly opened her eyes and saw Jag and Tegan looking at her. "Oh, hi," she said, letting out a large yawn. She noticed Tegan seemed a bit groggy, then realized that Kody and Aari were asleep on either side of her. "Gosh, how long have we been out?"

"A few hours," Jag answered.

Mariah was apologetic. "And no one kept you company?"

He smiled. "Nah, but I'm fine. Mind waking the two clowns up?"

Mariah picked up a donut from the box and held it in front of Kody's face until the scent reached him and his nose began to twitch. His eyes eased open after a few moments. When he saw the donut, he sat up and plucked it from her. "Now that's the proper way to wake a man up," he said approvingly as he took a bite.

Mariah rolled her eyes and shook Aari's shoulder. As he sluggishly awoke, she gazed out the window. The sun was only just beginning to set, so it was still rather bright out. Curious as to why they were parked on the side of a busy street, she leaned forward so she was between Jag and Tegan. "Where are we?"

"Salt Lake City," Tegan answered.

"We're already in Utah?"

"Yep. It's almost eight, so we're trying to find somewhere to eat before getting a place to rest."

"See if there's a Denny's around here," Kody suggested.

"Sure . . . okay, yeah. There are a few." Tegan tapped the GPS screen a couple of times and the robotic voice of a woman came on, giving directions. Jag guided the car back into the traffic and drove along.

It was nearly ten minutes later when the yellow sign of the diner cropped up with a motel nearby. The parking lot was half-filled. Jag, not fond of parking near so many vehicles, headed to a back lot where there were no cars or motorcycles.

The friends hopped out of the Jeep and made their way toward the diner, stopping only to let a red Mustang pass as the driver searched for a spot to park. Mariah thought she saw the man behind the wheel scrutinize them for a fleeting moment.

Inside, they sat in a booth and ordered to their heart's content; Kody naturally ordering the most. They chatted for a while as they waited for their meals to arrive. Mariah's eyes flicked up, locating a man sitting alone at another booth, sipping his drink and fiddling with his phone. She stared at him for a moment, wondering why he looked so familiar, then realized that it was the driver of the Mustang.

The man glanced up and caught her watching. She quickly shifted her attention elsewhere—it was strange how some people seemed to have a sixth sense about being observed.

"I can't wait to hit those Carpinteria beaches," Tegan said dreamily. "Just lying in the sun, taking a nap . . . you may have to drag me away from there when it's time to leave."

"Carpinteria?" A young man sitting at a table beside them and having pancakes for dinner looked up. He had short, honey-colored hair and a bright smile that was as sweet as it was rascally. "You guys heading that way? It's quite a drive."

Tegan nodded. "It is. And we'll be checking out other places in California as well."

"Have you been to Cali before?"

"When we were younger, yeah. Our families went together. Don't remember much about it, though."

The young man's eyes lit up. "Oh, you're going to love it there. I'm driving that way, too. Took a week off work so I can visit my girlfriend in Morro Bay."

Mariah smiled. "That's really sweet. What do you do?"

"I work for a security contractor."

The friends all tilted their heads. The guy was slim-bodied and didn't even touch the six-foot mark in height. He most certainly didn't seem threatening in his flannel shirt, skinny jeans, and striped socks with penny loafers.

He noted their looks and laughed. "I know what you're thinking. I actually have black belts in taekwondo, karate and judo." When he saw that they didn't believe him, he pulled out his phone and tapped it a few times, then passed it to them. "Proof. Go through the album."

Tegan took the phone and held it, the others craning their necks to get a closer look at the screen. Jag let out a low whistle as she swiped through the photos of the honey-haired fellow sparring in the black belt division of various martial arts competitions. "Dude, that's insane."

"Looks are deceiving, aren't they?" Kody muttered in awe.

Tegan passed the phone back to its owner. "We didn't mean to doubt you, it's just . . ."

The young man laughed again. "Don't worry about it. But that's the beauty, right? I don't look like I can defend myself, but if someone ever tries to best me, they'd be in for a nasty surprise!"

Jag grinned. "Good stuff." He reached past the others and held out his hand. "I'm Jag. This is Aari, Tegan, Mariah and Kody."

"Pleasure making your acquaintances. Name's Anthony, but you can call me Tony." He shook Jag's hand.

The five chatted with him until their meals arrived a few minutes later, at which point Tony smiled at them and returned to eating his pancakes.

The friends gladly dug into their food. "Who's paying, by the way?" Kody asked as he munched through his dinner.

The others just stared at him and grinned in response. He stared back at them, then groaned. "I had to ask . . ."

While the five ate and laughed over stories, Mariah couldn't help but notice that the Mustang driver in the other booth constantly glanced in their direction. For some reason, it made her skin prickled.

They spent nearly an hour in the diner before Jag finally said, "Alright, we should find a place to stay the night. We've got another early morning tomorrow."

"What about that motel right across the street?" Mariah asked. "It looks decent enough."

"Let's go check it out, then. Kode-man, you're up."

Kody grumbled as he grabbed his root beer and trotted to the counter to pay for their dinner. The group then said goodbye to Tony before leaving.

As they headed toward the exit, Mariah saw the bearded man get up. He ignored them completely as he went to the cashier, but she was still uneasy and hurried the others out of the door.

They passed the rows of cars until they reached the Jeep in the back. Mariah pinpointed the red Mustang parked a few slots away from them and frowned slightly as the five of them got into their vehicle and buckled in.

Jag was starting up the engine when a knock on his window startled them all. They looked out to see who it was. Mariah's eyes widened when she saw that it was the bearded man who had been surveilling them.

As Jag was about to press down on the button to lower his window, Mariah stopped him. "What are you doing?"

"Seeing what this man wants."

"I don't think we should."

"Why is that?"

"I . . . I don't know. We should just get going."

"That would be kind of rude. Look, he's holding up a map. I think he needs directions." Before Mariah could protest further, Jag lowered his window and smiled at the man. "Hello, sir."

"Hiya." The man's voice was low and pleasant, his smile cheery and disarming. Mariah noticed some scars on the left side of his face as he brought up his large map to show to Jag. "Could you tell me where exactly we are on this thing? My phone died and I have no GPS, so I'm stuck using this dinosaur."

Jag chuckled. "Sure. We're just passing through here ourselves, actually, but we are right—" As he raised his finger to the map, the man suddenly shoved the chart toward Jag. Mariah heard a quick metallic clinking before seeing the man toss a spherical object through the window. Jag let out an oath. Before anyone could react, a pall of light blue smoke filled up the car completely.

Mariah's chest tightened, her breaths suddenly short. She tried to yell out but it was as if invisible hands were wrapped around her neck, choking her. Terrified, she reached out to the others for help but saw them all struggling to breathe through the strangling smoke.

Jag was the first to open his door and throw himself out. Tegan followed suit, as did Aari and Kody. Mariah was the last one out of the vehicle. She fell onto the gravel as she desperately tried to gasp for air. Her mouth and nose, filled with smoke, rendered her attempts futile. After several panicked moments, minute streams of fresh air seeped into her lungs. With a glimmer of hope, she gulped in as much as she could.

She lay on the ground for a while, feeling weak, before slowly rolling onto her back and covering her face with her hands. The others' sputtering and gasping reached her ears from where they were splayed out on the asphalt, exhausted.

It took a couple of minutes before Jag was able to pull himself up. "You guys alright?" he wheezed.

"Think so," Mariah answered feebly.

Aari coughed for a bit before replying. "Well, I can breathe now . . ."

'Yeah' was all Kody could say before he resumed sucking in air.

"Teegs?" Jag called.

"I'm okay," Tegan responded from the other side of the Jeep. "Just trying to get my breath back."

The friends eventually got to their feet and staggered to the front of the vehicle. "What just happened?" Kody rasped. "Who was that man?"

"And where is he?" Mariah looked around; their assailant was nowhere to be found, and neither was the red Mustang.

"He drove off," Jag said angrily before erupting into a series of coughs. "We should report this."

A silver SUV pulled up beside them. To Mariah's surprise, Tony jumped out and ran toward them. "Hey!" he cried. "Are you okay?"

"Yeah, I think so." Jag dusted himself off. "Thanks."

"What happened?"

"Some guy acted like he wanted directions. Next thing we know, he popped a smoke bomb into the car and drove off."

"You guys know him?"

The five shook their heads.

"Going after a bunch of kids . . . that's just sick." Tony stared at the exit of the parking lot, eyes narrowed. "You know what, you guys stay here. What car was he driving?"

"It was a red Mustang." Mariah was weary. "But what are you—"

"Stay put!" Tony was already running to his SUV. "I'll be back as soon as I can!"

The friends watched the silver vehicle tear out of the parking lot. "What is he doing?" Aari asked, bewildered, between sporadic coughs. "Is he really going after that jerk?"

"He's like a guardian with black belts in multiple forms of self-defense." Kody paused dreamily. "Gotta say, I kinda like that."

Mariah sighed and rubbed her eyes as Jag took it upon himself to check on everyone and ensure that they were, in fact, alright.

It was nearly fifteen minutes later when the SUV returned to the diner's parking lot and pulled up beside the friends. Tony got out, wearing a look of satisfaction. "That guy's not going to be bothering anyone anytime soon."

Jag looked over at him. "What did you do?"

Tony shrugged and smiled a little. "Taught him a lesson he's bound not to forget. Don't worry. You guys are safe."

Kody pumped Tony's hand eagerly. "Thanks, man. Really. We owe you one."

Tony gave him an almost reprimanding look. "No, you don't. I'm just glad I could help in some way." He nodded at the others. "You guys found a place to rest tonight?"

"We were gonna check out that motel there," Aari said, pointing to the building across from the diner.

Tony grimaced when he saw it. "I wouldn't suggest staying there. Weird stuff goes down inside—not particularly family-friendly. There's a hotel a few blocks away where I'm staying. I'd recommend that one. Not too expensive either."

Jag nodded. "Thanks for the heads-up."

"Anytime. I could lead you guys there. Just follow my car." The young man turned and started toward his vehicle.

"Sure," Jag called out after him, then shepherded the others into the Jeep.

Inside, Mariah picked up the small glass container that had been tossed in and was about to chuck it out of the window when Aari intercepted her.

"I'd like to have a look at it later," he explained when she looked at him questioningly.

Jag pulled out of the parking lot and followed the SUV down the road. They turned into a small but clean hotel a few minutes later and got out. As they stood in front of the building, sizing it up, Tony joined them. "Not too shabby, right?" he asked.

Jag gave a half-smile. "Nope. Just hope there are a couple of rooms available. And thank you again, by the way. We really appreciate your help."

"Hey, don't even mention it. Come on, let's get you checked in."

"Hold on, someone's gotta make the call," Mariah reminded her friends.

They stared at her blankly. She folded her arms. "We call one of our parents every night we check into a hotel, remember?"

"Oh! Right, right. I'll do it." Aari took out his cell phone. "You guys go ahead, I'll join you in a bit."

Later, the teenagers gathered their bags and headed up the elevator to the fifth floor where they found their rooms, which were right across from Tony's.

"Alright, I'll be on my way now," Tony said, stretching. "I'm exhausted. Have a good night, guys." He waved at the friends before entering his room.

Tegan turned to Aari. "So what exactly did you tell your parents when you called?"

Aari wore a sheepish look. "That we'd arrived safely in Utah and just checked into a hotel. I opted out of telling them about the, ah, incident. I mean, just imagine how they'd react. On the first day of our road trip, we get attacked by some lunatic with a smoke grenade. We'll never be allowed to leave our rooms until we're forty. And even then they'll probably have us on a short leash."

The others exchanged uncertain looks, then Jag grunted. "Aari's got a point. I'd hate to have our trip cut short within the first fourteen hours because of some nutcase. And you guys know that we *need* this."

"And Tony did deal with him," Kody added. "No need to worry anyone."

"Yeah . . . alright." Tegan heaved a sigh and opened the door to the room she and Mariah were sharing. "I'm really tired. Bedtime for me."

Mariah yawned. "And me. Good night, knuckleheads."

Jag smiled as the guys headed into their room as well. "Sleep tight, ladies."

* * *

It was half past three in the morning when Jag woke with an outcry. He threw his blanket off and stumbled into the bathroom, slapping the wall, trying to find the switch. The light came on, nearly blinding him. He quickly turned on the tap to splash ice-cold water on his face. His undershirt became soaked but he didn't notice as he stared himself in the mirror, eyes stretched wide.

Aari and Kody poked their heads in. "Hey, what's the matter?" Aari slurred, looking confused and sleepy.

"I—nothing. Nothing at all."

Kody snorted. "I'm not even going to tell you how weak that sounds. Come on, Jag. Nightmare?"

Jag continued to stare at himself for a while longer, then picked up a towel and dried his face and neck. He remained silent, which annoyed the other two.

"Jag, we've been best friends all our lives," Aari said. "If you can't talk to us, then something is really wrong."

Jag glanced at them. "It was a nightmare."

"There you go," Kody said triumphantly and turned to walk back to his bed.

"No, hold on." Aari grabbed Kody by the collar of his shirt and yanked him back. "Jag, this isn't like you. I know there's more to this. What's going on?"

Jag took a deep breath. As he readied himself to tell them the story of his recurring nightmare, there was a scream, followed moments later by frantic pounding on the door. The boys hurried over and threw it open. Tegan staggered in, Mariah following closely with a worried look on her face. Tony was behind them in shorts and a sleeveless shirt, his hair tousled.

"What's wrong?" Jag asked, alarmed, as he reached out to hold Tegan.

"I heard a scream and ran out of my room to find these two in the hallway," Tony said, sounding as if he'd just woken up. He cocked his head at the girls. "What happened?"

"She had a nightmare," Mariah started, "and she woke—"

"Nightmare?" Aari interrupted. Frowning, he pointed at Jag. "She's not the only one."

"Hey, Teegs, come here." Jag gently guided Tegan to a chair and sat her down. Slowly, he asked, "What was the nightmare about?"

She covered her face with her hands. "There was . . . I was in a battle or something. I saw a woman collapse in front of my eyes. There was blood on her. A . . . a bullet wound to her chest." She absently rested a hand under her left collarbone, presumably where the bullet had struck the woman in her dream. "And what makes me feel sick is that it felt real. All my senses were engaged throughout. I could smell things and hear screams and . . . and it was as if I was actually there."

The blood drained from Jag's face. "Did the dream end there?"

"No. It went dark at one point and I thought it was over, but then a voice spoke. Directly to me."

Jag paled further. "What did it say?"

Tegan just shook her head and slumped down in the chair, looking spent. Aari got her a glass of water, of which she only took a sip.

There was a pregnant silence, broken a minute later by Tony. "At least it was just a dream. I thought someone was attacking them." He gave Tegan a comforting pat on the shoulder. "You should get back to sleep."

She licked her lips and nodded. Jag and the others watched as she and Mariah silently headed back to their room. Tony left after them.

Kody shut the door and suppressed a yawn. "I'm taking Tony's advice." He returned to his bed and was out within moments. Aari gave Jag a reassuring look before he retired as well.

Jag, however tired he was, couldn't bring himself to fall asleep until an hour later. He and Tegan would have to talk. It was too much of a coincidence that they'd had similar nightmares on the same night and woke up around the same time.

Can it get any weirder than this? he wondered as he finally drifted off to sleep.

Tegan and Mariah stepped out of their room with their bags at ten the next morning. The boys were already packed and waiting in the hallway. Aari playfully tugged at Tegan's earlobe, mindful of her numerous piercings. "Morning. Did you sleep okay the rest of the night?"

"Considering what happened, yes." Tegan glanced at the time on her phone. "We really should get going."

The friends descended to the main floor. As Jag checked them out of the hotel, a voice behind Tegan sang, "Good morning!"

Startled, she turned around but relaxed when she saw Tony with his bags, fresh-faced despite having had his sleep interrupted. She smiled. "Hey!"

"You're looking much better than the last time I saw you," he noted.

"Thanks. And you . . ." She scanned him from head to toe. ". . . are still wearing striped socks."

"Life's too short to wear boring socks," he responded poetically with a dramatic wave of his hand. "Oh, whoa, who's got that flowery perfume?"

Mariah snickered. "That's probably Tegan's shampoo. Her mom made it. We've all gone nose-blind to it, though."

"Your mom makes shampoos?" Tony inhaled deeply, puckering his face in thought. "Lavender and . . . lilac?"

"It's her hobby," Tegan said. "She crafts handmade soaps and bath bombs, too. And sheesh, what kinda honker do you *have?*"

Tony smiled and bobbed his head as if he was about to break into a dance at any moment. "My girlfriend is a florist, so my nose has gained new knowledge over the years. Oh, man, I can't wait to see her again."

By this time the others had noticed Tony and greeted him warmly.

"So you're driving all the way to Cali today?" Tony asked as they exited the lobby.

"That was the plan," Aari said, "but we're off to a late start. We'll be staying in Vegas for the night instead."

Tony's eyebrows rose. "We may as well be traveling together. I was planning on stopping at Vegas for dinner, but I'll be continuing through the night. Maybe I'll see you guys there."

"In a city like that, the chances are slim. But who knows? Sure would be cool if we did."

They arrived at their cars. Tony shook hands with each of them as they stood under the blazing sun. "It was a pleasure meeting you guys," he said with a slight bow. "Take care, you hear?"

Jag grinned. "You too, Tony. Thanks again for helping out yesterday."

"Anytime. Hopefully this won't be the last time we talk. You guys seem like a really great bunch." Tony gave them one final smile before getting into his car and driving off the premises.

The friends watched until the SUV was out of sight. Kody sighed. "Such a shame to meet someone like that, only to never see him again."

Jag slid into the driver's seat of the Jeep. "Come on, we really need to get going. We were supposed to be in Vegas by noon, but that's not happening now."

"We needed the sleep," Kody said as they clambered into the vehicle, retaking the same seats as the day before. "Matter of fact, I *still* feel like I need to grab a catnap."

Aari rested his head against the window. "Judging by the bags under everyone's eyes, I'm guessing the feeling's mutual."

Jag pulled out of the parking lot. "Sleep, then."

"We'll be leaving you alone again," Kody said.

"I don't think I want to nap," Tegan muttered. "I'll keep Jag company, don't worry." She could hear the three in the back wiggling around until they were comfortable. Soon the only sounds in the vehicle came from the air conditioner blowing cold air into the cabin and from Kody's and Aari's quiet snores.

Jag was silent for a while before saying, "Hey, Teegs?"

"Hm?"

"About last night, the dream you had . . ."

Tegan winced. "What?"

"You mentioned that you heard a voice, but you didn't tell us what it said."

"What does it matter? It's just a nightmare."

"Teegs . . ."

She curled her fingers into the hem of her t-shirt, nearly tearing the light fabric. "No, Jag. Let it go. It meant nothing. It's just a dr—a nightmare."

"You said that it felt real, as if you were actually there."

"Jag, I don't want—"

"I had a nightmare too, and it was basically the same as yours."

Tegan snorted and stared ahead at the lines on the freeway. "Yeah, right."

"I'm not joking. Some kind of battle, right? Destroyed buildings and vehicles all around you? Feels like some isolated place on a mountain . . . a construction site or something?"

She looked at him sharply. He continued. "My dream took place during the early morning."

"Mine . . ." She pulled her gaze away. "Mine, too."

Jag slowly let out a long breath, then filled her in on every detail of his nightmare. "And I keep having it over and over and over." He ran a hand over his face. "Since school started, that's the only dream I can ever remember."

Tegan was shaking slightly as she listened to him. "This is just some weird coincidence. It's got to be. There's no other explanation. There isn't."

"Some coincidence," he murmured as he sped up to pass a slow driver before merging back into the travel lane. "I heard a voice at the end of my dream as well. A man, calling me by name, and—"

"Telling you to wake up?" Tegan's words was soft, nearly inaudible.

"Yes." He glanced at her. "I guess the man you heard told you the same thing, huh?"

Tegan folded her arms and chewed on her bottom lip. Neither she nor Jag spoke for the next while. She was glad that he wasn't pressing her any further on the matter, although there wasn't much else to speak about; all the facts were laid out but none of them made sense. She tried to find every plausible reason to explain this coincidence but nothing worked. *If you can't figure it out, it's best to forget it,* she thought. *It's nothing.*

She inhaled and exhaled a few times as she clenched and unclenched the fingers of one hand. Just as she started to calm down a little, there was a terrified bellow from the backseat. Jag slammed on the brakes. Tegan lurched forward with a gasp, gripping her seatbelt.

The driver behind them held down the horn angrily. Jag returned to his senses and eased his foot off the brake to press down on the gas pedal.

Tegan snapped around. The three in the back were clearly awake. Kody looked frightened out of his wits. Tegan reached out to grab his hand. "Kody?"

He had fear in his green eyes, fear she'd never seen in him before, and right then she knew. She tightened her grip. "Was it a battle?" she whispered.

He nodded slowly. "They were torn apart," he said in a low voice. "Just . . . murdered."

"Black creatures?" Jag asked; he and the others were listening in carefully.

"Beasts. They were beasts. I—" Kody looked at Jag through the rearview mirror. "Wait, how did you know?"

"I saw them in my nightmares," Jag answered softly.

Tegan swallowed. "I saw them, too."

"That's impossible." Kody pulled his hand away from her. "That's impossible."

"Did you hear a voice telling you to wake up?" Jag asked.

Kody shrank back. "You're freaking me out, man."

"You did, didn't you?"

"I . . ."

Tegan tilted her head. "Kody?"

Kody rapped his forehead with his knuckles. "Yes. I did."

"I'm sorry, are you guys saying you all had the same dream?" Aari asked incredulously.

"Not exactly," Jag said. "More like . . . different perspectives of one elaborate dream."

Mariah's brow crinkled. "What do you mean?"

Jag lifted a hand from the wheel and curled his fingers slightly, as if he were holding an imaginary sphere. "I've been thinking about this. Imagine the dream as this reality where there is one timeline. Many things are happening, all at the same time. I see one part—my part—in my dream. Tegan sees her part in hers. Kody too. The dreams aren't totally independent of each other. What we see are different perspectives of the same dream, one event. In this case, that event is apparently some kind of a battle."

"But how is that possible?" Kody demanded.

"Beats me."

Tegan gave Kody a gentle pat on the knee to soothe him even though she was in a daze herself. She could hear Aari muttering "This isn't possible" repeatedly in the backseat. Despite agreeing with him, she had a funny feeling that either he or Mariah would be the next one drawn into the nightmare.

On the outskirts of Concordia, Kansas, a farmer backed his truck and a trailer filled with bales of hay toward a large barn. His skin was tanned and weathered, the palms of his blemished hands callused and seasoned like a sailor's. A scar ran from the side of his nose to his cheek from a mishap during his teenage years. Though he looked to be in his seventies, his amber eyes, half hidden by a cap, shone with youthful curiosity and the resilience of a man who'd overcome numerous hardships in life.

He aligned the trailer by a bale elevator that extended to the hayloft where two young farmhands were waiting to stack the hay, then turned off the engine and hopped out to load the bales onto the elevator. The men conversed as they worked, laughing and bantering as they often did to make the routine job go by a little faster.

"Hugo!"

The farmer turned to see a woman with her graying hair in a side bun standing behind him. A yellow Labrador retriever sat next to her. The man smiled and reached down to stroke the dog's head, then looked at the woman. Removing his cap, he bowed playfully.

She rolled her eyes good-naturedly. "Oh, don't you do that now. How many times do I have to call you in for supper?" Her voice contained a hint of the Portuguese accent that he too carried.

Hugo leaned in and kissed her forehead. "I'm sorry, *meu amor*. I wanted to get as many of these stacked before calling it a day." He nodded up at the hayloft. The young men grinned and waved down at the couple.

The woman placed her hands on her hips. "Has he been holding you hostage?" she called out to the farmhands.

They laughed and one of them called back, "No, ma'am! We're just happy to help a great fella like your husband. You've both been very good to us since we began working for you."

Hugo beamed and his wife gently cuffed him before addressing the farmhands again. "Go home, dears! You can help him finish this up tomorrow."

"Yes, ma'am!"

As the woman took Hugo's hand, he waved at the young men as they exited the barn and locked its doors. "Have a good night, boys!"

"You too, Mr. Sanchez!" They smiled and headed to their cars, then drove off the property.

Hugo laced his fingers with his wife's as they walked toward their two-story home. The Labrador trotted ahead and entered the house, then waited patiently for the couple to come inside.

Hugo closed the door and took a deep whiff. "It smells so good in here." He removed his checkered shirt and went to throw it into the laundry basket.

"It's just corn and roast beef," his wife said, though she sounded pleased.

As he walked through the living room toward the kitchen, something on the television caught his eye. "Julia, have you seen this?"

His wife came to stand beside him while wiping her hands on a dishcloth. She frowned and tucked some loose strands of hair behind her ear. "It's the crop failure we keep hearing about, isn't it?"

Hugo reached for the remote and turned the volume up. "*. . . the phenomenon appears to be spreading rapidly. Reports from the last few hours indicate that major crop failures have* *been observed across Kansas, the Dakotas, and now Oklahoma and Texas."*

Julia gasped. "It's spreading so quickly?"

Hugo regarded the television, eyes narrowed. Having worked the fields for decades, he had never heard of simultaneous crop failures like this. He listened as the reporter discussed the occurrence with a panel of experts. The crop failures that had begun in the farms of the Midwest did indeed seem to be spreading across the country at a frighteningly quick pace.

Julia looked up at her husband, searching his face. "Hugo . . . our crops."

He gathered her into his arms. "Shh, we'll be fine."

"A couple of fields around here have already been destroyed . . . You heard how badly the Jacksons were hit in Baldwin City. And the Moores! They're not too far from here and they lost all their crops."

"Julia, please, don't worry."

"It's just a matter of time, isn't it? We're going to lose our crops soon, aren't we?"

"Don't think like that, Julia." He shut his eyes tightly. "We can't afford to think like that."

"Hugo . . ."

Keeping an arm around her, he pointed the remote and turned the television off. "Come, supper is getting cold."

As he led his wife away from the living room, Hugo swallowed the lump that was rising in his throat. He kept telling himself that they had gotten lucky; that whatever virus or bug was killing the crops had missed their farm. To think any other way would not bode well for him, and especially not for Julia, whose health was easily affected by stress.

They ate silently. His attempts at making her smile were met with barely a lift of her lips.

"We'll be fine, *meu amor*," he murmured. "You'll see."

Rows of serrated teeth gnashed menacingly below a flattened, cone-shaped snout. The head merged with a grayish-brown body with two dorsal fins. Cold, dark eyes followed the curious beings that, in turn, seemed to be watching it without a trace of fear. It stared them down for a few moments more. Then, with a swish of its tail, the sand tiger shark swam away.

The friends stood in a circular swimming pool at the Golden Nugget Hotel in Las Vegas, peering into a two-hundred-thousand-gallon shark tank located right at the center. The Tank, as it was known, hosted three hundred different types of fish, including sixteen sharks. A water slide went right through it, allowing vacationers to zip past the marine life that resided outside of the tube.

"I'm glad we're staying here for the night rather than rushing to Santa Barbara," Aari said, smiling as the fish he was having a staring competition with swam away. "Feels nice to unwind, especially after what happened yesterday."

The four of them turned around and motioned for Kody to join them, but he hung back.

"Come on, Kode-man," Jag called. "You'll get a better view from here."

Kody folded his arms.

"What's up with you?" Aari asked.

Kody pointed at the tank. "Look, I like food. I just don't want to *be* food, okay?"

Jag pursed his lips and went over to splash Kody in exasperation. "There's acrylic between us and the sharks, dude!"

Kody waddled away as fast as he could. "Only six inches of it! How can anyone feel safe?"

"You're missing out, Kody." Mariah looked back at the marine life. The smaller fish moved around with ease, not seeming to be bothered by the eight-foot-long predators circling in the tank.

As she observed them, something caught her eye in the glass. She squinted slightly, then froze. There was a reflection of a man staring in their direction. Her heartbeat quickened. It was the bearded man from Salt Lake City—the one who'd attacked them.

She spun around, sending water spraying everywhere, and scoured the crowd, once, twice, three times. The man was nowhere to be seen. She raked over the visitors again but he seemed to have disappeared into thin air.

"Mariah?"

Tegan was staring at her. Mariah reached out and grabbed her friend's wrist tightly. "He's here," she told her in a low voice, teeth clenched.

"Who is?"

"The guy with the smoke grenade."

Alarmed, Tegan scanned around. "Are you sure?"

"Yes!"

"I don't see him. Where is he?"

Aari overheard them and looked over. "He who?"

"Mariah's saying she saw the guy who attacked us yesterday," Tegan replied.

"Where did you see him?" Aari asked.

Mariah waved her hand vaguely. "I was looking into the tank and I'm sure I saw him in the reflection, but when I turned, around he wasn't there."

Aari took a careful look at the crowd, then gave Mariah a reassuring smile. "He's not here, 'Riah. Maybe it was just someone who looked like him."

Mariah's cheeks flushed; her friends were thinking she'd lost it. "I know I saw him. He was right there, watching us and—"

She halted midsentence when she saw Jag grab Kody in a headlock and drag him over to the shark tank. Kody was trying to resist the entire time but gave up when Jag pressed his face against the glass.

"Jag, you're—" Kody's complaint ended in a startled yelp as a shark swam by. "I'm done! I'm so done!"

Jag let him go. Kody, in his attempt to distance himself from the Tank, tripped over his own feet and fell backward, splashing everyone around him. The others stepped back, protesting, but Mariah remained where she was, too preoccupied to be bothered.

Jag noticed. "Hey, space cadet, where you at?"

"She's convinced she saw that guy from yesterday," Aari explained, completely doused and shaking water from his hair.

"What? Here?"

"Yeah. She said she saw his reflection in the tank but we can't find him."

Jag inspected the mass of holidaymakers for himself for a minute, then went over to put an arm around Mariah. "Are you absolutely sure, 'Riah?"

Mariah nodded furtively, though now she was beginning to doubt herself.

Jag gave a gentle squeeze. "I know you're still spooked about what happened, but it looks like he's not here."

She looked away, feeling only somewhat reassured. Jag gave her another squeeze before letting her go.

The friends made their way out of the pool and grabbed their towels before heading up to their rooms to change, then strolled down the street to a Mexican restaurant for dinner. As they were guided to a table outside, Tegan burst out laughing. "I don't *believe* this!"

Mariah gazed around to see what she was talking about. Her eyes landed upon a familiar face. Despite being distracted with what happened at the shark tank, she broke into a delighted grin. "Tony!"

Tony, who was sipping on a cold beverage, looked up from a few tables away. When he saw the five, he nearly choked on his drink. Coughing and laughing, he stood up and waved them over, pumping the boys' hands and quickly hugging the girls.

"This is crazy!" he exclaimed as they sat down at his table. "When I said maybe I'll see you guys here, I didn't think I actually would!"

"Maybe we should travel together," Kody joked as they picked up their menus and looked through the dishes that the restaurant offered.

Tony waved a waiter over. "I just got here a couple of minutes before you. You guys know what you want?"

They nodded and placed their orders. Once the waiter left, Tony leaned back and stretched. "This place is so alive," he noted. "Kinda wish I could spend a night or two here."

Aari removed his sunglasses and tucked it into the collar of his t-shirt. "Why don't you?"

"I haven't seen my girlfriend in four months and I really don't want to spend more time than necessary away from her."

"That's really sweet," Tegan said as she and Mariah beamed at him.

Tony turned a little red but smiled and changed topics as he looked at their hair. "Been swimming?"

"Yeah. The shark tank at the Golden Nugget."

Mariah stared down at the table, rubbing her shoulder absentmindedly. Tony tilted his head at her. "You okay?"

She glanced at him, debating if she should tell him about what she'd seen at the Tank, but Jag beat her to it. Tony listened, wary, a slight frown on his face.

"You saw his reflection?" he asked carefully.

Mariah nodded. He turned to question the others and when they said they never saw the bearded man, he looked back at her. "It's probably the lack of sleep getting to you. It can do things to your mind." He smiled, though Mariah thought it seemed morose. "Trust me, I know."

Aari tapped the lens of his shades. "That's what I was saying."

Tony gave Mariah's hand a soothing pat "Don't worry about it, okay? I mean, how does it sound to you that someone would follow a group of teenagers from one state to another? It's not like you kids are celebrities and he's some nutcase or paparazzi."

"Aren't the paparazzi nuts anyway?" Kody piped.

Tony grinned. "True, but not all nuts are paps."

Their meals arrived a short while later and they dug in hungrily. Once the check was paid, they lounged at the table, the friends wanting to stay with Tony as long as possible. He was easy to talk to and knowledgeable about a range of subjects. He seemed to enjoy their company as well, and was nearly in tears from laughing so hard at the group's constant repartees and wisecracks.

The sun had almost completely set when Tony reluctantly pushed his chair back. "That was a great meal, guys. I'm glad you could join me."

"Likewise," Jag said as they all got to their feet. "We should keep in touch."

"Definitely. Here." Tony passed his phone to Jag, and Jag handed his to Tony. They exchanged numbers before returning the devices. Tony got his keys out of his pocket and gave the girls another hug before bumping fists with Jag, Aari and Kody. "You guys have a great trip!" he called as he started toward his car.

"You too!" the five chorused as they watched him leave. Once the SUV rolled onto the street, they headed back to their hotel. Mariah, who'd nearly forgotten about the incident at the shark tank, returned to a state of high alert as they entered the air-conditioned elevator that took them up to their floor.

Tegan lightly nudged her as the elevator dinged and its doors opened, allowing the group to step out. "Hey. Stop that. We are *not* being followed, okay?"

Mariah tittered guiltily as she trailed Tegan to their room. The guys headed to their own suite, which was several doors away.

Once inside, they showered and wound down for the night. Mariah curled up on her bed as fatigue overtook her. It probably was her over-anxious mind that fooled her into seeing the strange man. She sighed and closed her eyes. "Night, Teegs," she murmured.

"Night, Mariah. Sleep tight—"

"—don't let the bedbugs bite."

Aari and the boys were wakened several hours later by heavy knocking on their door. Groaning, Aari rolled off his bed and went to open it, revealing Tegan and Mariah in their pajamas. By the looks on their faces, he instantly deduced what had happened. Quietly, he stepped aside to let them in.

"Dreams?" Kody asked blearily, turning on the lights in the room.

Mariah flopped down on one of the beds and covered her face with her hands, nodding.

Jag was trying to blink sleep out of his eyes. "A battle, kind of like on a mountain? Someone with a strange accent telling you to wake up?"

Mariah nodded again as Kody sat down beside her and gently rubbed her back. "Why is this happening?" she whispered.

There was a stretch of silence. In the stillness, Aari could hear his pulse in his ears. He cleared his throat. The others looked up at where he stood leaning against a wall. Slowly, he said, "Nature abhors a vacuum."

Jag's eyebrow lifted. "Come again?"

"It's a quote by Aristotle. Way back when, he would observe the world around him and concluded that nature requires space to be filled with something. Anything. Doesn't matter what." Aari tapped the side of his head. "We have an emptiness—a vacuum, if you will—in our lives. I know we don't really want to talk about it, but it's there. A void. I think that, maybe, these dreams . . ."

"What?" Jag prodded.

Aari let out a breath and directed his gaze toward the smooth, white ceiling. "I don't know. This might sound crazy."

"Aari, four out of five of us have basically had the same dream. Any explanation is probably going to sound normal in comparison."

Aari pinched the bridge of his nose as he gathered his thoughts. "Okay, here's my wild theory. Our collective loss of memory is like a vacuum in our minds. We don't remember anything that happened to us last summer. These dreams that you guys had—I think that's nature's way of filling in that vacuum, and by doing so, giving us our memories back."

"You can't really be telling me that by some weird stroke of . . . of randomness, we're beginning to remember, at the same time, what happened to us?" Mariah finally lowered her hands from her face. "Because if that's the case, then we seem to have been surrounded by mayhem and death. I'm *pretty* sure I'd remember something like that!"

"But that does fit, doesn't it?" Jag asked quietly. "For whatever reason, our . . . memories . . . are returning. How else do you explain the dreams?"

"Nightmares," Kody corrected. "I believe the scientific term for such horrible dreams is nightmares. But I'm with Mariah on this. This is way too far-fetched."

Tegan, who'd sat down on Mariah's other side, spoke up. "Whether or not this is true, let's get the facts straight. We survived a plane crash in Northern Canada. We're found weeks later. We remember nothing in between those two events. Jag apparently has been having his dream often, before any of us had ours. In the dreams, it's always some kind of fight between two groups of people. One with modern weapons, the other using primitive methods. We see destroyed buildings and debris everywhere. There are living, breathing killing machines around us. And then, at the very end, there's a voice telling us that we need to wake up." She glanced at Aari. "What he's saying, no matter how absurd it is, actually makes sense."

Kody fell backward onto the blanket. "This is insane!"

"There are many mysteries in the world," Aari said simply. "Some can be explained, and others can't."

Kody grunted. "You sound really calm about all of this."

"Because it makes *sense.*" Aari pushed himself away from the wall and went over to flop down on his bed. "Not gonna lie, I'm actually expecting to have that dream now. All of you have had yours, so it looks like I'm the last one."

"If you do have it," Tegan said, "then there's absolutely no way any one of us can deny that the dreams are significant."

"Nightmares," Kody muttered.

Jag stretched. "Nothing more we can do for tonight. Let's get some more shut-eye. We're not going to oversleep like we did in Utah."

The others agreed. Once the girls were gone, Aari went to bed, bracing himself for the nightmare to seep into his unconscious and trap him in its dark realm.

Come on, just do it, he pleaded, covering his head with his arms. *Get this over with.*

The city of San Francisco boasted many high-rise buildings, granting one particular structure the ability to assimilate with the rest of its surroundings. The nondescript gray-colored edifice hosted a large boardroom on its fortieth floor that offered a stunning view of the city's azure bay, which—on sunny days—would have speedboats and sailboats alike exploring its waters as if it were a playground.

Today, however, storm clouds shrouded the sky. The gloom was broken only by near-blinding streaks of lightning, illuminating the city with electrified veins. The sound of rolling thunder could be heard over the rain pounding against the windows.

Within the boardroom was a broad, oval mahogany table; its presence both commanding and elegant. The impressive deep-red centerpiece was surrounded by twelve opulent black leather chairs. At one end of the table, standing in the place of a thirteenth chair, an eight-foot high silver screen was mounted on a curved wall.

A tall, Caucasian man sat facing the screen, his fingers laced together and his thumbs supporting his chin. His dark hair had recently been cut short and his long face was clean-shaven.

Adrian Black was the chief executive of Phoenix Corporation, a wealthy establishment with a global reach that, among other things, owned many properties including this one. It also had its hands in a number of industries, ranging from biotech and armaments to mining and construction.

Though ordinary in appearance, the building housed secrets accessible to only a select few who worked within its walls; hence the name "Tower 51", a joke spun from America's top-secret military base in Nevada. The boardroom, as remarkable as it was, withheld from view a smorgasbord of concealed high-tech devices that connected all of the corporation's activities worldwide—operations that Black was ultimately responsible for.

Despite the restless, intense weather outside, Black felt more at peace than he had in months. Two major operations had produced some challenges for a while but now everything was on track and finally running without a hitch.

There was only one other person in the boardroom this afternoon. Jerry Li, the corporation's chief financial officer, was a short and tubby fellow of Asian descent, sporting thick-rimmed glasses and an infinite collection of bowties; or at least it seemed so to Black as, in all the years they'd worked together, Li had never worn the same bowtie twice.

Currently, the two were in the midst of a video conference with Vladimir Ajajdif, the head of one of the company's major operations. Black leaned back in his chair as he scanned through a report on his tablet. "You are working on private land that the company owns, Vlad. The authorities aren't breathing down your neck. I thought your progress would have been far more substantial."

The auburn-haired man on screen sighed, then took a drink from a Styrofoam coffee cup and replied in a deep, Russian-tinted accent. "My group's progress has been great, Adrian. I dare say we're one of the better teams on this project."

Black raised an eyebrow and smirked. "As good as you think you're doing, Vlad, you're still behind the other five Sanctuary operations."

Ajajdif scowled for a second before plastering on a smile that never met his eyes. Through his teeth, he muttered, "*Mudák*."

"What was that?" Black asked.

"Nothing." Ajajdif took another sip from his cup. "I'll let my team know that we're falling behind. They're a motivated bunch. The moment they hear those words, their productivity will double. Triple, even."

Black nodded slowly. "Good. This has to run much smoother than your operation in Canada last year, hm?"

Ajajdif bristled. "That was uncalled for, Adrian." He absently ran his middle finger over his nose. It had been surgically reconstructed after being severely broken nearly ten months prior while he was working on a clandestine mining operation in Yukon.

Li coughed, interrupting the tension that seemed to always emerge whenever Black and Ajajdif addressed one another. "How is the weather treating you there?"

Black noticed that Ajajdif looked relieved to be speaking with someone else. "It's fine. Hot. We're on the New Mexico-Arizona border, so what do you expect?"

"I trust the men with you are well-occupied?"

Ajajdif snorted. "You bet they are. They work like mules. When they get time off I let them visit Silver City. It's a fun little town. They don't complain much." He looked around him as if to ensure no one was within earshot, then asked, "How's the REAPR project going?"

"You don't need to be concerned with that," Black said sharply. "I want you to stay focused on your assignment over there. I have to make a report to the Boss in twenty-four hours and I've vowed that there will be no more fiascoes. I appreciate that things are running smoothly now. We don't want a repeat of last year."

The other men in the meeting went completely silent. Even though Black and Ajajdif were rarely on good terms, the one thing they shared was a fair dose of fear of the Boss and a hunger for the realization of their leader's plans for the future—not just for Phoenix Corporation, but the whole world.

After nearly an hour of further discussion on operational matters, Black took in a small breath. "Anything else to report, Vlad?"

"No."

"Good. We'll keep in touch."

The feed from the screen and sound from the hidden speakers went dead. Black pushed his chair back and stood up. "And so another day comes to an end. Would you like a drink, Jerry?" he called as he made his way to the fully serviced bar behind the curved wall. "Never mind, I'll get you one anyway. I think we deserve it." He returned a minute later with two glasses and passed one to the other man.

Li smiled as he took it. "Thanks." He held up his drink. "To the Boss—a brilliant visionary, a benevolent liberator, and a ruthless trailblazer."

Black smiled in return and clinked his glass with Li's. Reverently, he echoed, "To the Boss."

12

Soft, warm sand cushioned Tegan's feet as she and the others took in Carpinteria's golden coastline and picture-perfect cobalt waters lapping at the shore. A gracious ocean breeze cooled the heat of the day. It was just after noon and the friends were looking forward to relaxing on the beach they had last visited as children.

Kody trotted ahead, weaving his way between kids building sandcastles and people sunbathing as he led the group toward a spot he'd pinpointed the moment they'd stepped onto the beach. Jag and Mariah followed while Tegan trailed behind them with Aari.

Tegan glanced to the side. Aari's eyes were narrowed against the sun's glare and, though she knew his thoughts were roiling, he was careful to not show any emotion.

After Mariah's nightmare, the five had anxiously waited for Aari's dream to occur. It was only two nights later, once they'd arrived in California, when it happened, and he told them about it before leaving for the beach. His words had been met with silent pats on his shoulder. There truly was nothing that could be said to comfort him, and the group agreed not to discuss their dreams for the time being—they wanted to take it easy and forget it all for a while.

"And here we are," Kody said, looking pleased as he shook out his beach towel and spread it on the sand. He plonked himself down and turned his baseball cap around so the brim could shade his eyes from the sun.

The others settled down on their own towels as well, deciding to put off plunging into the water for a bit. Tegan looked out at the ocean where a handful of surfers were attempting to ride the waves. Most of them seemed to be novices, but one dark-haired teenager about fifty yards out exuded confidence as he stood atop his surfboard. She observed him quietly, watching how he carved a wave with ease. Obviously native to the area, he was bronzed from many hours outdoors and navigated the waters well.

She continued watching him for a while as the other four either read books, ate, or dozed. A group of children ran past, giggling ecstatically as a couple of older kids chased after them with foam noodles. Tegan smiled, then returned her attention to the surfer.

Seeing a perfect swell approaching, he paddled out to meet it and climbed upright. He'd barely started to ride the wave when he unleashed a spine-chilling scream and fell off his board, disappearing under the water. Tegan shot to her feet, blood running cold. The board rolled among the waves, jaggedly torn at one end.

Jag, who'd been dozing, bolted upright, as did the others. "What—"

Before the rest of his question slipped past his lips, the boy's head broke surface and his cry rang out. "*Help me!*"

Several people on the beach heard it and caught sight of the fallen surfer struggling amidst the waves. A dark shape slowly rose from the water about thirty feet behind him, moving in his direction. Gasps and shrieks came from the beachgoers. Some started sprinting toward a lifeguard post some distance away, kicking up sand and yelling for help.

Tegan stared in helpless horror as the fin sliced through the subsiding waves toward the boy. There was a brush of wind against her cheek and the next thing she saw was Jag sprinting toward the water as he removed and tossed his t-shirt aside.

"What are you doing?" Mariah screamed.

As he reached the shoreline at blurred speed, Jag leapt with the full force of the momentum he'd built up and traversed nearly a hundred feet over the waves before plunging near the surfer. Tegan's mouth fell open.

Startled by Jag's sudden appearance, the approaching shark quickly maneuvered away and turned back toward the open ocean, its dorsal fin slowly vanishing under water.

There was stunned silence as those on the beach watched Jag hook one arm around the surfer and use the other to swim to safety. As they got closer, there were a few murmurs that broke into a cheer from the onlookers. Tegan, Mariah, Aari and Kody ran into the water until they were nearly waist-deep, urging Jag and the surfer on.

Kody, standing beside Tegan, suddenly stiffened. "No!"

"What?" she asked.

"The shark . . . it's coming back."

"What are you talking about? It swam away."

Kody's eyes narrowed. "No, Tegan. It's coming back." His voice dropped, and the color drained from her face at his next words. "I can smell blood in the water."

The cheering from the onlookers faded into the background as Tegan slowly looked back at Jag and the surfer. The surfer, eyes shut and face contorted in pain, rolled his head to the side while Jag dragged him along. Tegan saw the injured boy's eyelids lift slightly before both she and he caught sight of a fin—so dark in color that it looked black—resurfacing.

"Jag!" Aari boomed. "*Shark!*"

Jag didn't have to look back to believe him. He redoubled his efforts but struggled to drag the injured surfer along. Aari and Kody, despite knowing the danger, waded further out to try to help.

Tegan stood frozen as water lapped around her waist, soaking her shorts and t-shirt. Fine ocean mist lightly sprayed her face and she could taste the salt in the air as she stared at the rushing shark. Her mind reeled in frustration. She wanted to do something, anything, but she felt so powerless.

Time seemed to slow before there was a sudden flash in her mind. It blinded her momentarily before quickly disappearing. She stumbled back a step, then the flash exploded again. There was an image this time. She could barely make out a flurry of feet underwater before the vision disappeared. "What the—" she began before the vision returned.

She could see it clearly now: Two humans in the water, moving away from her as frantically-kicking feet churned the water behind them. The strong scent of something metallic hit her nose and she could see a dark trail under the salty waves. A part of her wanted to gag at the smell but another part was hungered by it. The realization of what she was witnessing hit her like a hammer to the chest.

She was seeing Jag as he swam surfer to shore . . . through the eyes of the shark.

Unable to grasp what was happening, and just as panic started to reach its brink, an inexplicable calm welled inside her, easing her terror. It was as though someone had placed a reassuring hand on her shoulder as if to say, *You know what to do.*

The sensation brought a reprieve, but it was short-lived. As she felt the shark open its jaws to snap at the injured surfer, she let her consciousness join completely with the beast and wrenched its head away from the boys just as the jaws filled with rows of razor-sharp teeth came crashing together. Then, with some effort, she took control over the rest of its body and forced the shark as far away from the scene as she could until the connection faded.

She blinked once, and when her eyes opened, she saw Kody and Aari helping Jag and the other boy onto the beach.

The crowd converged upon them. Tegan ran over, pushing her way through the throng with Mariah close behind. Aari had already helped Jag to his feet. Kody crouched beside the surfer, gently talking to him.

Tegan's eyes traveled down to the wound on the boy's left leg but she had to quickly avert her gaze from the sight. The surfer, shivering and in near shock, raised a shaky hand to Jag. Jag looked down at it for a second, then knelt and held it firmly. He gave an encouraging nod and the surfer just barely nodded back.

A lifeguard broke up the crowd from behind, advising them to give the injured boy some space. They obliged, but eyes started to turn to Jag with a mixture of confused awe and intense questioning. Jag hurriedly picked up his t-shirt and joined Tegan and the others as they moved away from the beachgoers.

An ambulance and police cruiser arrived shortly and paramedics loaded the surfer onto a stretcher. Tegan watched it all in silence. Once the vehicles were gone, the friends turned to one another, saying nothing, until Aari pointed at Jag. "Dude, I swear I saw you fly."

Jag looked uncomfortable and busied himself with dusting the sand of his t-shirt. "I didn't fly, knucklehead," he muttered. "I just . . . jumped."

"A great distance," Mariah said matter-of-factly.

"I smelled the guy's blood in the water," Kody cut in, voice cracking. He looked ill as he spoke.

Jag eyed him. "Come again?"

"You heard me." Kody lowered himself to the sand and sat down heavily.

Tegan wanted to tell them about her own experience but feared that they would find it absurd. Still, she could not keep it to herself. "I don't know how, but I controlled the shark," she blurted, then turned red when the others faced her. "I . . . I mean, I made it turn away from you. Somehow I was able to . . . jump into it and . . . take control."

To her surprise, the others regarded her without much disbelief. Jag quietly slipped his t-shirt back on. "We should—"

He was cut short when Tegan let out an earsplitting cry and fell to her knees, digging her fingernails into her head as a torrent of images exploded behind her eyes. The visualizations—hundreds of them—flashed by with dizzying speed. Fragments of different voices filled her mind, growing riotously louder in her ears. Letting loose another cry, she curled up on the sand and pushed the heels of her palms against her temples as the images sped by faster and faster.

She didn't know how long it took for the surge of visions to pass but when it did, she continued to lay on the beach, numb. It wasn't until she saw Jag standing over that she made the painful effort to sit up. He pulled her to her feet and she leaned against him for support.

The first thing she saw when she regained her senses was Kody coiled into a ball nearby. Not too far from him, Aari was unsteadily helping Mariah up from where she was kneeling on the ground, holding her head and whimpering, "Why is this happening?"

Together, Jag and Tegan pulled Kody to his feet, each draping one of his arms over their shoulders. "What happened?" Tegan croaked.

Jag pursed his lips, jaw tight. He urgently patted Kody's cheeks to get him to open his eyes but the other boy seemed to be unconscious. "Come on, brother, come on . . ."

As Mariah and Aari joined them, Kody's eyes slowly cracked open. Relieved, Tegan looked at Jag for direction. He was glancing over the beachgoers. People were coming toward them, looking worried and even a little frightened.

He started moving in the direction of the parking lot, away from the crowd, aiding Kody along. "We need to get out of here. The media will probably arrive to cover the shark attack soon and that's the last thing we need."

"People might have already taken videos on their phones," Aari said softly.

"All the more reason to leave."

The others hastily grabbed their beach towels and bags and followed him. At the Jeep, Tegan helped Jag maneuver Kody into a seat. "Jag, I saw—I saw things. I—"

"I know," he said, ignoring the stares that the group was getting in the parking lot. "I did too. We all did. I think . . ." He exhaled slowly. ". . . I think the pieces are finally falling into place."

After a quiet drive, the friends returned to their hotel and converged in the girls' room. Aari scrubbed his face with the hands, then flopped back on one of the beds and stared at the ceiling, legs dangling over the side. Mariah, next to him, gently patted his knee, then the two of them glanced backward to where Jag stood staring out the window.

"So what exactly is falling into place?" Tegan asked, curled up like a cat on the opposite bed.

Jag remained statue-like.

Aari grunted. "It's like he completely zones out when he goes into his head to puzzle things over. Jag, come on."

Still no response. Aari turned over so he was on his stomach and stared at his friend, unease now replacing gentle mockery. "Hey, you're starting to worry us."

Jag abruptly wheeled around. "Tegan, do you have that bouncy ball you bought from the souvenir store yesterday?"

"It's in my knapsack," she said, waving her hand to signal permission to rummage through her belongings. He did, then lobbed the small ball with California's flag printed on it to Mariah, who caught it just as it sailed over Aari's face.

From where he lay on the floor between the beds, Kody—now completely back to himself—stretched his arms noisily. "I fail to see what this has to do with anything."

Jag took a seat beside Tegan and nodded at Mariah. "Try to move it. With your mind."

She stared at him like he was crazy. "Excuse me?"

"Just try. Please."

Aari pushed himself up on his elbows, swapping bewildered looks with Mariah. Even Kody sat upright, forehead crinkling. Then he laughed. "Right, okay. Seriously though, what's going on?"

"I don't think you'd believe me if I told you," Jag said. "So I want Mariah to prove it."

"Prove what?" Mariah squeaked before catching herself and clearing her throat. "That I have powers? That I have *telekinesis*? Please."

Jag responded by jerking his chin at her hand. She rolled her eyes but stared at the ball anyway. The others watched, skeptical, but a pinprick of anticipation started to grow somewhere deep in Aari's chest. His pulse quickened.

No way, he thought. *There's just no way.*

Then his mind spooled back to the beach and he saw again what Jag had done, the way his friend had traversed an impossible distance. He froze, feeling like he was on the cusp of an awakening, the kind that would jar him to his bones.

It took him a minute to realize he'd been caught up in his thoughts for too long. When he returned to the moment, something was hovering inches from his face. His eyes stretched wide.

The red ball hung in the air over Mariah's open palm. Her face was slack with shock, her mouth parted slightly. The only thing she managed to utter was a whispered "I remember".

No one else spoke a word.

Then Tegan slowly leaned forward, careful not to step on a frozen Kody, and swiped her hand above and below the ball as though checking to see if invisible strings were tethered to it.

"What in the world?" she breathed.

Aari wasn't sure why, but something compelled him to pluck the ball out of the air. As he stared at it, his mind calmed and focused as if of its own accord. For a few moments, nothing happened. Then one side of the ball began to shimmer slightly and vanished before reappearing. He tried again. This time, the other side of the ball faded from view. He tried a third time, and both sides of the small sphere shimmered toward the middle before the ball vanished completely

"Gah!" Kody pressed himself back against the nightstand. "What is this?!"

Aari couldn't answer. Something had sucked him back into his mind and all he saw was images zipping by like they had on the beach. Except this time, no matter how fast the memories flew, he was able to grasp it all.

And then he remembered everything: the village nestled in a hidden valley they'd stayed in after their plane crash the previous summer; the Elders who trained them and helped develop their individual abilities, and who spoke of a prophecy depicting darker times on the horizon; and the mountaintop where a battle had taken place between the villagers and a mining operation that had poisoned the inhabitants of the valley.

"*Saplings of Aegis*," he wheezed, coming back to himself again. He clenched the ball tightly and pressed the back of his wrist against his lips in disbelief. "That's what we are. We're . . . holy smokes, we're supposed to save the world."

Light seeped into Jag's eyes. "Yes."

Tegan, who'd been silent the longest, had a clouded, faraway gaze. Jag rubbed the back of her head. "Teegs?"

"Yeah." She shook herself and released a long breath. "Yeah. It feels like someone just pulled a cloth off the missing parts of my memories. Like everything just clicked into place."

"It feels *weird* is what it feels," Mariah mumbled. "Everything's off its axis because now I see things and they fit, but the emptiness from before—its memory is still there and . . . and I don't know how to explain it."

Aari looked down at Kody, who had his eyes screwed shut. He lightly tapped the other boy's shoe with his foot. "If it's all coming back to you, don't fight it," he advised.

To his surprise, a grin formed on Kody's face as he opened his eyes. "Dema-Ki. That was where we were last summer." He looked down at his hands as if seeing them for the first time. "And . . . we . . . have . . . *powers!*"

"Guess that explains how you could smell blood in the water," Aari said. "Hypersensory abilities. And Tegan with the shark—linking minds with animals."

Jag raised his hand. "Extreme speed, agility and strength over here."

"Okay, okay," Tegan said, spreading her arms to quiet everyone. "Timeline. Quick rundown. Plane crash, taken to Dema-Ki, trained by the Elders—"

"Don't forget nearly getting killed by an egotistical lunatic," Mariah snorted.

"Right. Then the Battle of Ayen'et—"

"Where Jag took down a plane on his own and nearly got himself killed in the process," Kody supplied. Jag shot him a look.

"Yup. Then back to training. What I'm still missing is how and why our memories were taken away."

"Same here," Aari said, rubbing his chin. "Maybe they'll return later? The bigger question is, what now? What are we supposed to do? We have almost everything back in place but we're on our own. How do we even contact the Elders?"

Jag cleared his throat. "Actually, I don't think we're completely on our own."

Aari and the others frowned at him. He continued. "The Elders told us that we wouldn't be alone when we returned to the outside world. You remember that?"

Tegan suddenly sat up straighter. "They said that there would be people . . . Sentries . . . looking out for us."

"So that we're protected while trying to fulfill the prophecy," Aari added slowly as the memory surfaced.

"And who's been with us almost every step of the way since we started this trip?" Jag prompted.

Aari and the others came to the same conclusion simultaneously and looked at each other in amazement. Mariah hugged her knees to her chest. "I mean, that would explain a lot."

"Are we sure it's not just coincidence?" Tegan countered.

"No, but the signs don't really point to anything else," Jag said. "We should be sure, though. I'll make the call."

Once the meeting was scheduled, the friends just stared at each other, still trying to come to terms with everything. The hum of the air conditioning unit kept the room from being plunged into complete silence.

"We have the world on our shoulders," Aari said at last, and the notion finally sunk in. His insides churned, shorting his breaths. "How did this happen?"

Kody, upon hearing that, seemed markedly less enthusiastic about his abilities, even a little sick. "You know this means bad things can happen to us? We could get seriously hurt, or even—"

"We are not talking about this," Jag interrupted. He swept over them with a firm look. "One thing at a time. That's how we dealt with Dema-Ki last year, that's how we'll keep doing it."

"We just need some time to adjust," Tegan said, nodding. "Or readjust, I guess. But Jag's right. We have to accept that this is our reality, and we'll just . . . continue as we always do."

Kody raised his hand, palm down. Jag and Tegan placed their hands over his, Aari doing the same. Mariah bit her lip, then followed suit.

"We'll work through this," Jag said. "Together. Always."

The next morning, the friends sat at the end of Stearns Wharf, feet dangling over the edge of the pier as they enjoyed the spectacular views of Santa Barbara and the surrounding coast. Dark blue water frothed twenty feet below them. A few anglers along the sides of the wharf had their fishing lines cast, and every few minutes someone would call out gleefully, signaling a catch.

The five had talked long into the previous night, each emerging memory triggering another along with visions of familiar faces and conversations. Now they yawned almost every other minute, although anxiety about the meeting prickled the air.

Mariah kept herself occupied by surreptitiously levitating the small bouncy ball in her hand. The others spoke quietly amongst themselves, still discussing everything that had been brought to light.

"Seriously," Tegan murmured. "How could we ever forget all this? The village, its people, the Elders, our powers . . . the flat-out war at Ayen'et."

Mariah dropped the ball back into her hand. "I can't believe we were part of that."

"All that death and destruction." Kody shuddered and stared down at the water. "And those things—those beasts of murder."

Tegan nestled her head on his shoulder. "You saw everything from your vantage point with Elder Nageau . . . Can't imagine how horrifying that must have been."

Mariah made sure no one on the wharf was looking, then hurled the ball as far over the waves as she could. Just when it was about to hit the water, it came flying back toward them. Kody put up his hand and caught it right before it hit him. He tossed it back to her. "Careful. You could've nailed me in the face with that."

She looked at him apologetically, then sighed. "What I want to know is, why is it that none of us except Jag had those dreams until this trip?"

Aari rested his hands behind him and leaned back a little. "I may have an explanation—not for why we started having our dreams—but why Jag's been having his for a while."

Jag's eyebrows rose. "I'd love to hear this."

"You're somehow the only connection that the Elders have had with us since we left the valley."

"You mean my dreams were some sort of a link with them?"

"Maybe."

"But why?"

"My guess is that the Elders wanted to maintain some point of contact with us. They trained us for a reason and maybe they were keeping us close through you."

Tegan rubbed her forehead. "But, again, why did we lose our memories of Dema-Ki and everything we learned there?"

Aari shrugged. "Dunno. It could be that our abilities needed to be concealed for some reason."

"Then why is it all coming back now?"

"I wish I knew."

"Well, point is, it's back and that makes us a force to be reckoned with," Kody said; Mariah could see him making an effort to shake off his gloom. "Because we've got powers!"

"Not that we should flaunt it," Jag cut in firmly.

"Yeah, yeah, whatever you say, Captain." Kody gently butted heads with Tegan. She shoved him playfully.

Mariah swung her legs back and forth over the pier. "Do you think it was the Elders who wiped our memories clean?"

"Why would they do that?" Aari asked. "Especially when it's connected to something as important as the prophecy—"

"Prophecy? What prophecy?" asked a cheery voice.

The friends started at the sudden interruption. They craned their heads to their right and breathed sighs of relief as Tony sat down beside them. Jag shook the newcomer's hand. "Tony! It's good to see you, man."

The young man smiled brightly. "Likewise. When I got your call last night, I knew I had to come see you guys again."

"Hey, Tony," Tegan called. She pulled up her jeans slightly, revealing striped socks.

"No way!" Tony looked as if he'd just seen the greatest thing in his life and reached out to high-five her. She laughed and slapped his hand. He then looked back at Jag. "Okay, so, over the phone, you mentioned something about memories that you'd lost starting to come back?"

"Yeah. Sorry for not telling you much, but we thought it would be best if we could speak with you face-to-face."

Tony nodded slightly. Mariah watched him closely as the five quickly filled him in on the events of the previous summer, leaving out crucial details regarding the prophecy and their innate abilities. They wanted to play it safe first, opting not to divulge anything else. By the end of it, Tony looked blown away, which Mariah wasn't sure was a good sign. Still, she was hopeful.

"We're not making this up, I swear," Jag said.

"No, no," Tony assured him hastily. "I believe you. Just . . . wow. Now I know why I thought you guys looked familiar when we first met. You were in the news." After a brief period of silence, he said, "So . . . how do you think I can be of help?"

"The Elders told us that, when we returned to our lives, we wouldn't be alone," Aari answered. "There would be people here who would help us."

Mariah swallowed nervously, the moment of truth hanging over their heads like an axe on a fraying rope.

"They said that they'd placed special people around the world and . . ." Jag wavered. ". . . and we wondered if you were one of them."

The group's hopes sank the instant they saw that his words had left Tony completely nonplussed. The young man shook his head, pained. "I-I'm sorry. I have no idea what you're talking about."

Doing all they could to hide their disappointment, the friends looked away. "It's alright," Jag said through a tight smile.

Tony seemed distraught. "I wish I knew what you meant, but—"

"It's alright, Tony."

There was another pause in the conversation. The group looked on as two dragon boats practice-raced; the crafts carrying ten rowers on each side who energetically worked their paddles.

Tony shifted uncomfortably, then asked, "What will you do now?"

Mariah and the others didn't take their eyes off the dragon boats. "I guess we're just gonna continue our trip," Jag responded. "We checked out of our hotel a day early. All our stuff's already in the car."

"Where to next?"

"We're driving down to San Diego in a bit."

Tegan stretched out her feet. "I can't wait to check out the zoo and Sea World."

"And the *USS Midway*," added Aari and Kody in unison.

"Sounds like you'll be having a blast," Tony said. He rubbed the back of his neck. "I'm just sorry I'm not who you thought I was."

"Don't worry about it," Jag said. "If anything, we should be apologizing to you. We called you away from your girlfriend and had you drive out all the way from Morro Bay."

Tony gave Jag a friendly smack on the back. "I like being with you guys! Trust me, there really was no harm done here. I learned a lot about the five of you. It was enlightening. But there was something you said, right when I joined you guys—about a prophecy?"

The friends froze. Thankfully, Jag recovered with quick enough. "It was an inside joke," he said dismissively.

Mariah couldn't tell if Tony bought that, but the young man didn't push further. He looked at his watch. "Mind if I catch lunch with you guys before we part ways?"

The five lit up. "Of course not!" Kody exclaimed.

The group pulled their feet back from the edge of the wharf and helped each other up. Together, the six of them made their way to a fish-and-chips place not far down the pier.

From behind the window of a crowded restaurant, a man watched the group stroll past. He inspected them with a careful eye as the teenagers chatted animatedly with a light-haired man.

When they turned out of sight, he leaned back and rubbed his short beard, then glanced down at a black bag that lay by his feet. He picked it up. Unzipping it, he reached in and cautiously removed a pouch. When he was sure no one was looking his way, he opened the pouch and pulled out a glass container that was filled nearly to the top with a glowing liquid. It was exactly like the one he'd tossed into the teenagers' Jeep a few days before.

He stared at it for a while, debating with himself, until finally reaching a decision. Pressing his lips together, he glared and placed the container back in its pouch. He would wait and see if he needed to use the device again.

The friends arrived at San Diego smack in the middle of rush-hour. They'd been happily following their GPS to their hotel along the freeway but were stunned to see the lines of cars ahead of them as they neared the city.

They sat with the air conditioning on full blast, not aware how hot it was outside their vehicle. They'd tried to pass the five-hour drive from Santa Barbara with some games, but after playing scavenger hunt on an app and a run of thumb wrestling, they'd gotten bored and couldn't wait to get out of the traffic. They hadn't spoken for a while now, each retreating into their own personal space.

Jag rested his chin on the steering wheel and glanced at Aari, who was fiddling with his phone as he rode shotgun. His sling bag sat across his knees. Every time Jag made an attempt to engage him in a conversation, he only received distracted, one-word responses.

Letting out a sigh, he leaned back and tried to stretch the kinks out of his legs. He knew the silence that had converged upon the friends was largely due to Tony not being a Sentry. They'd had such high hopes. That wasn't the only thing that was unsettling the group, though—all five of them were at a loss. They'd wanted someone to tell them why their memories and powers were just returning and what they were supposed to do.

We need guidance, Jag thought sullenly, but with no one around them providing direction, the friends were nothing more than wanderers who harbored abilities and didn't know where to start using them. *What do we do now?*

He sighed again and looked up at the rearview mirror. Kody was reading a brochure with such intensity that he didn't notice Tegan balancing an empty plastic bottle on his head.

"What's that you got, Kode-man?" Jag asked.

"I'm trying to find a good restaurant around here," Kody answered. "By the time we get out of traffic it'll be dinnertime."

Mariah snorted. "You and food."

"We have a beautiful relationship. If food wore a white dress, I'd marry it in a heartbeat. I'd put a ring on it."

Tegan threw her head back, laughing. "It's scary that I don't doubt it."

The traffic moved in starts and stops. Jag grumbled as he scratched his temple. "When we get to the hotel, take twenty minutes to freshen up. We'll meet in the lobby and head out for dinner."

"Yes, sir," Tegan barked, looking dead serious.

Jag smirked, glad that the group was perking up. "Ha-ha, Ms. Funnypants."

"Hey, hasn't that van been following us since that gas station several miles ago?" Mariah asked suddenly.

Jag frowned and checked his mirrors. "What van?"

"That black one a few cars behind us, in the other lane."

He spotted it a second later. "I don't think so. There's a ton of vehicles going the same way. Are you still worried about us being followed after Vegas?"

Mariah pouted. "Maybe."

Aari yawned and put his phone down. "This traffic is ridiculous. Hope it's not this busy when we visit the Midway museum tomorrow." A smile worked across his face. "I can't wait to see that ship. We're actually going to be on an aircraft carrier that saw action during the Vietnam War *and* Desert Storm."

"That's all good, Brainiac, but I just found a Malaysian restaurant," Kody said, looking up from his pamphlet, "and I'm ready to get my satay fix."

Aari gasped in mock astonishment. "Food trumps an aircraft carrier?"

"Only until my hunger's gone," Kody promised.

"Even when you've already eaten, something tells me it'd still be a hard choice." Aari turned on the radio and shuffled through a few channels before landing on a talk show that caught the friends' attention.

". . . But does this mean we'll see rising gas prices soon as well?" a gravelly-voiced man asked. *"I mean, that's how it tends to work, right? I don't want to be driving to the studio one afternoon and get a heart attack 'cause gas shot up to ten bucks a gallon!"*

"I dunno," joined another voice, a woman this time. *"I think the main worry right now is food. The prices of bread and other grain products in some places have nearly doubled in the past two weeks alone. Had to do a double take at the baked goods section while doing groceries yesterday."*

"Just a matter of time before we're going to have to pay more for red meat too, then," the man moaned.

"Give up on meat!" the woman said. *"Being vegan is a much healthier lifestyle."*

"Hey, if I want to eat meat, I'll eat meat. Besides, I heard that even San Joaquin Valley's been hit hard. Hundreds of acres of fruits and vegetables, gone. And—hold on."

There was a moment of silence followed by the sound of shuffling papers on the radio as the group waited intently.

When the male radio host spoke into the mic again, he sounded solemn. *"We've just received some news and it ain't good. Looks like whatever's hitting our crops at home has spread to other parts of the world. Scattered reports are beginning to trickle in from farmers in Asia and Europe claiming substantial loss of crops."*

"That's not something we want to hear . . . I hope someone gets to the bottom of this real soon," the woman muttered,

"because if it doesn't stop, things are gonna go south faster than you can say 'What on God's green Earth!'"

The hosts soon moved on to other local happenings. Jag turned down the volume. "That's not good," he said darkly.

"This crop disease or whatever it is that's going around, has anything like this happened before?" Mariah asked.

"Well, yeah," Aari said. "But I don't think it's ever spread this wide or, for that matter, this quickly."

The traffic began to ease up at last. Jag stepped on the gas, relieved to be moving. They drove through the city, taking in the sights that zoomed by. It wasn't long until they found their hotel and checked in. While Jag went to park in the basement, the others carried their bags to their rooms.

Once the friends had freshened up, they regrouped in the lobby and made their way back to the Jeep. They piled in, Aari beside Jag again and Kody in between the girls in the back. "I guess we're going to that restaurant you found, huh?" Jag asked as he passed Kody the GPS to key in the restaurant's address.

"No question," Kody said.

As Jag put the car in reverse to back out of the slot, the sound of screeching tires filled the underground parking. Alarmed, the friends turned to look through the rear window. A black cargo van was stopped right behind them, blocking their exit.

Jag heard Mariah breathe in sharply. "Oh my God! It's the same van I—" Her sentence ended in a scream when her door was thrown open and a figure clad all in black yanked her out of the car. She struggled violently against her assailant but a rag was slapped onto her mouth and nose; she passed out almost instantly.

At the same time, Tegan's door was flung open, as was Aari's. They were both pulled out of the vehicle by two more dark figures. Their cries for help were muffled by rags held up to their faces. They barely had any time to fight back and Jag watched in terror as they lost consciousness.

"Jag, what—*no!*" Kody yelped as he in turn was pulled from the car.

Jag moved to get out of the Jeep but stopped short when he saw an attacker headed to his side of the car. He thought of locking the door, but another idea came to mind. He braced himself, waiting until the assailant was close enough. From the build of the body, he could tell that the man was a regular gym rat.

Jag hesitated, now unsure of himself and his plan. As the man reached for the door handle, the only thought he had was: *Here goes nothing. Come on, you jerk.*

He lifted his feet and the moment his door was wrenched open, he struck out at full force, catching the aggressor square in the stomach and throwing him back a good ten feet. Jag was out of the vehicle in an instant. He saw his friends' limp forms being tossed through the rear door of the van like rag dolls. The girls were the last to be dumped in.

With a roar of outrage, he leapt toward the van. Before he could get close enough, he heard what sounded like the muted report of a gun. Something hit his back. He lurched forward with his arms outstretched to break his fall but his strength was failing rapidly. He fell onto the concrete floor as his vision began to blur. His muscles wouldn't respond to his will and he found himself a helpless, limp mass on the ground.

A dark shape stepped in front of him. Heavy, rough hands grabbed him by the arms and dragged him up. Jag tried to fight, but all he managed was a weak twitch of his fingers.

He was shoved unceremoniously into the large vehicle, on top of his friends. The last thing he saw before blacking out was the back doors being slammed shut, blocking out any light from the outside.

16

W*ake up, Jag.*
You must wake up.
JAG!

Jag groaned quietly as his eyes opened. He could see nothing but darkness. For a moment, he thought he'd somehow lost his sight until his senses slowly started to function again. He could feel something wrapped around his head, covering his eyes. His arms were behind him and his wrists were secured together with some kind of binding.

Whatever he was lying on suddenly rattled, bouncing him. He let out another quiet complaint before realizing that he was swaying ever so slightly, as one would in a moving vehicle. Two male voices speaking softly to his right reached his ears. He could hardly make out what they were saying, but judged that the voices were coming from the driver and his passenger.

Slowly, he began to recall the final moments before he'd lost consciousness. *Oh, awesome,* he thought bitterly. *Kidnapped.*

He should have been scared, and rightly so, but he was irate—mainly at himself. Why had he dismissed Mariah's concern when she pointed out the van earlier? Why hadn't he reacted quicker to save the others from their attackers?

As his head cleared, he caught part of the conversation between the men. ". . . and besides, you know how the client is. Once they've got what they want from these kids, they'll be discarded quickly."

"That's not our problem," rasped a deeper voice. "We just get paid for delivery."

Jag's lethargy vanished at once. He tried to move his legs but could barely even lift his feet. While his mind was nearly functioning at full capacity, his physical self was still trying to catch up. He felt something to his right; presumably a person. He hoped it was one of the others.

A voice near him made him jump. "Hey, we got a wriggler here. What dosage did we use on them?"

One of the men whom Jag had heard earlier spoke up. "Enough to knock 'em out for a few hours. Even if they wake up, their hands are tied and they can't see a thing. They're a buncha kids. They'll be too terrified to try anything."

Wrong, Jag wanted to hiss, but instead told himself to calm down and think. He was sure now that there were two men at the front of the vehicle, with another somewhere in the back, closer to him. The van made a sharp turn and then straightened out onto a rough road, rattling the passengers and making a rumble in the cabin.

The three men got caught up in a conversation about a cohort who'd disappeared with money he'd borrowed from them. Over the noise inside the cabin they argued loudly on how to track him down and what they would do when they found him.

Seizing his chance, Jag whispered to the body on his right. "Tegan? Mariah?"

No sound.

"Kody?"

Still nothing.

"Aari?"

A groggy voice whispered back, "Jag?"

Relief flooded him. "Aari. You okay?"

He strained to hear his friend's voice in the din. "Maybe. Feeling weak."

"I know."

"Shoot—we were nabbed."

"Yeah. Need to figure out how to get out of here."

"Are we . . . are we in the van?"

"Yeah."

Jag strained to hear Aari murmur. "There's something against my back. It hurts."

"Your hands. They're tied back."

"No, it's something hard. Feels like metal and—*argh*, it's digging into my spine!"

The wheels in Jag's head spun as his body began to respond. He had a suspicion that if the two men at the wheel were to his right, that would mean that the back of the van was to his other side. He stretched his left leg little by little until his shoe hit something flat and solid with a hollow kind of thud.

Doors. He grinned to himself as a plan took shape. If they could force the abductors to stop the van, it just might give them a chance to escape. "Try grabbing that metal thing under you," he told Aari.

"Why?"

Very quietly, Jag laid out his idea. In response, Aari told him that he was out of his mind but he would go along with it anyway.

Aari's shoulder kept butting into his as he tried to grasp the object beneath him. "Got it."

"Wait for my word."

The vehicle stopped rattling as it made a turn onto a smoother road and accelerated, indicating that they were on a stretch of highway. Several minutes later, Jag felt the van slow down again. His weight shifted to one side and he realized they were turning onto an exit ramp.

Here we go, he thought, preparing himself, then shouted, "Now!"

He quickly twisted around to position his feet toward the back doors. As he curled his legs toward his chest, he heard shouts as Aari lurched forward to stand up.

Jag uncoiled his legs and smashed the doors open. The sound of cars on the road and horns blaring filled the van. More shouts ensued, followed by a heavy clanking as Aari swung around and launched his prize—a wrench—toward the front of the vehicle. At least, Jag hoped it was the front of the vehicle. His answer came soon enough when he heard a crunch of breaking glass; the van swerved sharply as the driver wrestled for control.

"Damn!" someone bellowed just before the vehicle leaned too far over and crashed onto its side.

Jag was thrown brutally out of the open back doors. He hit the ground hard and tumbled a good distance. Two cries of pain, sounding as if they came several yards away from him, followed shortly after he rolled to a stop. He groaned as he turned over onto his stomach and pushed himself up to his knees. "Aari?"

"Oy!" Aari yelled. "That was hands-down *the dumbest* idea ever, you lunatic! I wouldn't be surprised if I've cracked a rib!"

Following the voice, Jag unsteadily made his way over to his friend. "Where are you?"

"Jag? Aari?" Kody, near Jag's left, sounded as though he had just regained consciousness. "What happened?"

"I don't—"

A vehicle skidded up behind them, tires screaming. Jag froze. A man shouted, "Hit the deck!" before the boys were tackled to the ground. At that instant a volley of gunshots rang out.

The three of them stayed down. Jag felt someone pull his blindfold off. When his eyes adjusted to the twilight, his gaze focused on the newcomer who was removing Aari's and Kody's blindfolds as well. His blood turned to ice and he scooted away, wrists still bound behind him. "*You.*"

The man glanced at him. When Aari and Kody at last got a chance to see who the stranger was, they stumbled on their knees toward Jag.

"You *did* follow us!" Aari snarled. "Mariah was right!"

Two more shots flew over them. They ducked but kept their distance from the man. The stranger held his hands up where he lay on the grass. "Look, I'm not here to hurt you! You have to believe me!"

"You attacked us!"

Bullets hit the man's red Mustang, which was positioned between them and the crashed van. "They're shooting wide," he said. "They want the three of you alive."

Jag ducked again, then a stinging realization hit him: the girls were not with them. He looked around frantically, then peeked past the side of the Mustang in time to see one kidnapper flagging down a car, then pulling a woman out of the dark blue vehicle. The other black-clad men were throwing two smaller bodies into the trunk.

Jag leapt up and ran toward them. "Tegan! Mariah!"

He couldn't get close enough. Two strong arms wrapped around him and carried him back behind the red muscle car. "What are you doing?" he bellowed.

The man held him down and shouted at Kody and Aari to remain on the ground.

Jag pulled away and pushed himself up in time to see the blue vehicle speeding off. The woman whose car had been hijacked lay still on the road. Jag hoped she hadn't been shot.

Aari and Kody slowly went to stand beside him. They watched in subdued shock as the car grew smaller and smaller in the distance, taking the girls with it. Though the abductors' bullets had completely missed them, two voids grew in the boys' hearts, bleeding agony.

Jag, his hands still tied behind him, rested against the Mustang. His voice, usually calm and even, was quiet and broken even to his ears. "We need to call the cops."

"No."

The boys slowly turned to glare at the tall stranger. "What do you mean?" Aari seethed. "Our friends have been taken. And you—you've been tailing us for *days*."

"I have a good reason," the man said quietly.

Kody bristled. "Who are you? What do you want?"

The man rolled his shoulders back. He raised his right fist over his heart and bowed his head. Then, he lifted his chin and his baby blue eyes bore through them. The boys stared back.

That gesture—it was as though a memory was inching its way out of the shadows.

"The reason you can't go to the authorities," the man said, "is because it's beyond their power. They are not equipped for the darkness that's been cast. What was foretold in the prophecy can only be ended by those appointed by the prophecy. The five of you know that."

Jag, Aari and Kody nearly collapsed. "You're a Sentry," Kody gasped.

The man said nothing. He pulled out a switchblade from his back pocket and moved to cut the boys from their bindings. They rubbed their wrists, grateful to be free, but Jag was still antagonistic. "If you're a Sentry, why didn't you try to save Tegan and Mariah?" he demanded.

"There's no time to explain right now. People must have already alerted the cops after witnessing your crazy stunt with the van." The man inspected his car, pursing his lips as he took in the bullet holes and flat tire. "We need to get out of here. I'll fill you in as we go, you have my word."

When he saw the boys hesitating, he sighed impatiently. "I have someone following the girls, someone skilled and capable who will do everything possible to get your friends back. Just, please, we have to leave. Right now."

The boys glanced at one another. Jag, face taut, walked toward the car. He pointed at the busted tire. "You can't drive on this!"

"We don't have a choice. We're going to go after your friends, but we need to get to a safe spot nearby first to replace the tire."

Jag reluctantly got into the passenger seat as Aari and Kody piled into the back from the driver's side. The man hopped behind the wheel and, as he started the engine, Jag looked over to where he'd last seen his friends being thrown into the trunk of the car.

We'll find you, he promised silently.

PART TWO

CAT 797 Mining Truck

Reprinted Courtesy of Caterpillar Inc.

Map of New Mexico Showing the QMI Mine

Snowapped peaks glowed with golden light as the sun began its slow ascent from behind the mountains. Sunrise occurred early during this time of the year in northern Canada, usually around four in the morning.

The mountains were adorned with a shawl of pine trees that thickened on the slopes toward a valley that lay snugly in between the rocky behemoths. Weaving through the length of the basin, a slim river divided the valley. To a casual observer in an aircraft flying over the valley, the landscape below would appear remote and uninhabited.

The valley, however, was home to a village that straddled both sides of the river. The secret sanctuary housed over seven hundred inhabitants, descendants of a hybrid community that had remained hidden from the rest of the world for centuries.

All man-made structures were camouflaged to blend in with the surrounding foliage, and all access routes to the valley were well-protected by five mysterious and powerful creatures known as the Guardians.

The picturesque village was usually serene. But not today.

A group of villagers anxiously moved from one cluster of buildings to another, scouting the barn, stable, storehouse, and the temple while another group searched the greenhouse, community hall, school, and youth center.

On one of three wooden bridges that linked the north and south sides of the valley, a man in a long black-and-silver cloak—one of the five Elders of the village—directed the search. He was calm but his tone conveyed urgency. Most days, it would be impossible to tell that he was well into his late seventies. His blue eyes, an intriguing contrast to his brown skin, would shine brighter than a thousand suns. He was regal yet approachable, a shared trait that ran through the genes of the people of the valley. Lately, though, he'd started to notice deep lines carved around his eyes.

He quickly finished instructing the villagers he was speaking with and watched wearily as they sprinted away before turning to rest his elbows on the railing of the bridge. He stared at his reflection in the river's beautiful emerald waters.

His ears, far sharper than any untrained listener's, picked up the sound of hurried but delicate footsteps approaching well before the person arrived. He knew who it was without turning around—after all, he'd lived with and loved that woman for over forty years.

"Tikina," he murmured.

"Is it true?" she spoke, hushed. "Hutar is . . . is gone?"

His shoulders slumped slightly. The woman, an Elder herself, let out a small breath. "Oh, Nageau." She leaned against him, resting her head against his.

"There is no sign of him," Nageau said grimly. "He would have fled before dawn."

He heard another set of footsteps hurrying in their direction. He looked up and saw a youth of nineteen summers running toward them. He and Tikina both straightened as the youth slowed to a halt in front of them.

"What is it, Akol?" Nageau asked.

The youth wiped his brow and smoothed down his moose-hide shirt before answering, breathlessly, "Aesròn is gone as well, Grandfather."

Though disappointed, Nageau had suspected as much. "I suppose it would make sense for Hutar to take his only trusted comrade with him."

Akol pursed his lips, hand curling into a tight fist around the staff he held. "They must have been planning this for some time." He turned away so his grandparents could only see the side of his face. "By no means do I intend to be disrespectful, but . . . why did you not consider my words, Grandfather?" He was clearly doing all he could to keep his emotions in check. "They were trouble if put together and yet they were still allowed to interact. Hutar was not going to change, that was clear to see after only a few sessions."

Nageau looked up at the sky for a while, then slid his hand under Akol's chin and gently turned the youth's face toward himself. "You were right, Akol. Your intuition about Hutar is something I should have noted. I am sorry." The Elder slowly lowered his hand. "I had only hoped that the boy would change, that he would be rehabilitated and become as responsible and, above all, as nurturing as his father was."

"He is no longer a boy," Akol said quietly, dark eyes boring into the Nageau's.

Nageau tilted his head. "Neither, it seems, are you."

Akol flushed. "Would you have me lead a patrol outside the valley to search for the escapees?"

"I would. Thank you, Akol."

Dipping his head at the Elders, Akol left them at a brisk pace to gather a few villagers. Nageau returned his attention to his reflection in the river. "I would appreciate it if you could search the forest yourself," he told Tikina softly. "Create a mindlink with one of the animals. Perhaps the lynx, Tyse."

"Of course. She cannot travel as far and as swiftly as Akira, though."

"Akira? That old eagle is still around?"

"Yes. She has simply decided to make herself scarce since the siege at Ayen'et." Tikina rested against the wooden railing and took a proper look at Nageau. "Are you alright, my love? Has news changed regarding the boys and the Sentry?"

Nageau smiled only slightly. There was never a time when his mate could not see through him. "Nothing has changed. He is telling Jag, Kody and Aari as much as he is permitted even as we speak. The other Sentry is still following the girls, but . . . how did I not see this coming?"

Tikina looked puzzled. "No one could have, Nageau. But the one consolation we have lies in the Sentries. We know they will not let us down."

Nageau remained gloomy. Tikina prodded, "There is something else that is bothering you."

He turned around, cloak sweeping, and strode off the bridge toward the south side of the village. Tikina kept pace with him.

"I do not expect the five to take kindly to the knowledge that we suppressed their memories," he said, "especially considering that the memories concerned are very delicate and an important part of their lives."

"They will understand the necessity of our actions, Nageau, I am sure of it. It may take some time, but they will recognize that we did what was needed to protect them. They are too important to be exposed when the time was not yet right." Tikina lightly squeezed his forearm.

Nageau glanced at her, meeting her tender green-eyed gaze. "And still they were abducted."

"But you know that the Sentries will do all they can to get Tegan and Mariah back," Tikina reminded him.

Nageau massaged one of his hands with the other before murmuring, "I do wonder if . . ."

"If?"

"If this has something to do with . . . the expulsion."

Tikina stopped in her tracks and folded her arms. "You are still dwelling on it, Nageau. I have been trying to tell you, the past must remain in the past."

"And yet it seems that it may have clawed its way into the present. Not a day has gone by that I don't question my actions all those years ago; question if the decision that was made was the right one. It is difficult, knowing . . ." Nageau trailed off with a sigh and pulled out a silver coin from inside the folds of his cloak.

Engraved into the center was a symbol that vaguely resembled the letter Z with a short horizontal line crossing midway.

He stared at it for a few moments, throat constricting. "It is difficult," he repeated, "knowing that the prophecy may be unfolding through a decision that was made in this very place."

Tikina took the coin from him and slipped it into one of her moccasin boots. "We cannot know that for certain. A coin like this could mean anything. That . . . that individual's presence, have you felt it at any time?"

"No. I have been trying for the better part of the last two decades but I am unable to sense it. I did in the beginning, right after the event, but there has been nothing since."

"It seems likely, then, that this person is . . ." Tikina slowed down, choosing her words carefully. ". . . no longer in existence. From what we know, the five were subjected to all kinds of scrutiny when they returned to their homes. Their abduction could be the work of some devious minds from the world outside."

Nageau was unconvinced. "Possible, I suppose." He turned and gently pushed back his mate's chestnut hair. Tikina smiled comfortingly at him. He said nothing more, but he needn't have. Their relationship was one where words were seldom necessary to express their true and deepest thoughts.

As they made their way through the trees toward the western end of the valley where the temple was located, Nageau hoped the five would forgive the Elders for their actions and understand why they had to do what they did.

They're too young!

The Mustang hurtled down the highway with Marshall Sawyer at the wheel. Jag, sitting beside Marshall, kept fidgeting and drumming his fingers on his knee. Aari and Kody shared the backseat. The bullet-holed tire had been replaced, costing precious time that they were frantically trying to make up for. They'd now been in pursuit of the girls for a few hours, and the sun had yet to rise over California.

Having just finished filling the teenagers in on what he was permitted to divulge—with them barely uttering a word but looking more dazed by the minute—Marshall and his passengers sat quietly, no one sharing even a whisper.

The Sentry rubbed his short beard. A group of teenagers were the fulfillment of the ancient prophecy . . . He had difficulty wrapping his mind around that. They were too young and inexperienced to have such a heavy burden placed on their shoulders. *How can this be right? They're just a bunch of kids—lambs among lions. The world will not be kind to them.*

Aari spoke up, interrupting his thoughts. "So our memories were wiped clean and we were deprived of the knowledge we had a *right* to keep?" There was no mistaking the resentment in his tone.

Marshall looked at him in the rearview mirror. "For one, your memories were not wiped clean. If they were, they would be irretrievable. They were just . . . suppressed."

Aari responded angrily, "Six of one, half a dozen of the other. Whatever."

Marshall pinched his earlobe but kept a neutral expression. He knew the boys were hurting, what with Mariah and Tegan missing, and trying to take in all that he'd disclosed to them.

"It was a necessary evil," he said. "If the Elders had any alternative, I know they wouldn't have resorted to suppressing your memories. You know that too. They only wanted to keep you protected by ensuring that your knowledge and powers remained undisclosed to the world."

Aari looked away but Marshall could tell that he was still crushed. *Must be so hard, having the people you trust take away part of your life, even if it was well-intentioned,* he thought.

"What do we do now?" Jag asked. It was the first time he'd spoken since Marshall picked them up several hours ago. "So we got our memories back and found our powers. Why now? What's happened?"

Marshall's eyes flicked to the speedometer before returning to the road. "That was my doing. That little device I tossed into your car—the vapor that was released helped stimulate your suppressed memories. Other than that . . . things are at play here, Jag. I'm piecing it all together as I go along. I don't have all the answers. Right now, I'm hoping that your abductors will take your friends straight to their client, whoever that is. I know it's not ideal at all, but maybe this happened for a reason. Maybe the Sentry following the girls will find out who it is that wants them. Once we know their identity, or at the very least where they're located, we'll have a better idea about who we're dealing with and how to move forward."

Jag looked out of his window. "So tell us again why we can't contact the authorities. Because it feels like that would make a lot of sense right now."

"I know. And you'd be right, if it weren't for the prophecy. Your memories have all returned now, so you know more than anyone else how accurate the prophecy is. It foretold your arrival in Dema-Ki and the abilities that you possess. So there can be no doubt about its validity, right?"

"I guess, yeah. But by that logic, doesn't that mean that the prophecy is the cause of everything that's happening?"

"Is the prophecy the cause of mankind's slide into the abyss?"

"Well . . . I suppose not."

"Mankind chose a path of greed, corruption and destruction all on their own. The prophecy merely foretold this. So when the same ancient verses tell us that the gathering storm can only be stopped by the chosen ones of the prophecy, we can't waver. Think, Jag. Do you really believe the authorities will be able to handle what could come their way? The darkness that's brewing is outside of their understanding. I'm sorry, I know this is difficult to hear, but the authorities can't come into the picture. Not yet, at least."

Jag closed his eyes tightly.

Marshall hated being the bearer of bad news. He would have rather been shot clear through the foot than see the distress in the teens' faces, but it was part of his duty and he needed to keep that in mind. He couldn't afford to falter. There was too much at stake.

He tried to inject some hope. "We're making good speed. At this rate we should be able to catch up with the abductors soon."

All he got was a pensive nod from Jag.

"Who are you, anyway?" Kody asked.

Marshall paused abruptly, taken aback by the sudden, strange question. "Um, well, as I introduced myself earlier—"

"I mean you, aside from your role as a Sentry. Who are you?"

Marshall ran his hand around the steering wheel lightly as he considered the query. "I'm a descendent of the people of Dema-Ki. My great-grandparents were from the valley and they passed their knowledge and duties to their descendants."

"Is that what you've been doing your whole life, just Sentry stuff?" Kody asked.

"No. I enlisted with the armed forces when I turned nineteen and was with the Marine Corps for over a decade."

Kody whistled, and Marshall caught Aari giving a begrudging look of surprise.

After a moment of hesitation, Kody reached over to poke Marshall's bicep enviously. "No wonder you're so ripped. You gotta be real fit to be a Marine."

Jag and Aari rolled their eyes. Kody noticed and glared at them. "What?"

Marshall, who'd taken an instant liking to Kody, appreciated the teenager's presence even more. The boy came across as the type who wouldn't hold a grudge for too long; hopefully that would rub off on the others.

Kody wasn't done yet. He noticed the tattoo on Marshall's right wrist and pointed at it. "*Semper Fi*," he murmured, reading the ink. "Always faithful."

Marshall softened slightly. "I got it to represent my faith to my brothers and sisters in arms and this nation, as well as to my dedication to the duties of a Sentry, which transcends artificial boundaries on a map."

Aari, who'd had his arms crossed, now unfolded them. Through the rearview mirror, Marshall could see a raging sea of curiosity behind the teenager's hard gaze. "How many Sentries are there? Are they everywhere in the world?"

"We're all over, yes. We're part of the League, as the first-gens coined it. But we're not that many considering the scope. I don't know the exact number, but I've been told it's from several hundred to a thousand."

"Are you forced into this responsibility?" Aari asked. "I mean, what if someone doesn't believe in the cause?"

Marshall scratched the back of his head, subconsciously taking care not to disturb his neat blonde hair. "I wasn't forced. It just . . . I don't know. I guess the best way to explain it is that it's an instinctive sense of duty. To wax poetic, the ancient blood coursing through us seems to dictate our purpose in this world. Our duty, and I believe the Elders may have shared this with you, lies not only with standing by the five of you, but also in protecting the good in humanity, the flame in people's souls. We are driven by the knowledge that darkness is but the absence of light."

The teens looked quizzical as they absorbed Marshall's explanation.

"What exactly do you guys do, though?" Kody asked.

"It varies from Sentry to Sentry. Most of us have regular jobs and we serve the communities we live in by carrying out and encouraging deeds that bring out the best in people. Others serve and protect the people as firefighters, doctors, educators, law enforcement officers and such. Some try to influence society through different forms of art. A handful are tasked to uncover and, where necessary, bring to light that which poses a serious and imminent threat to society."

"Meaning . . .?" Kody probed.

"Meaning that they have to go underground, get their hands a little dirty and drag out those who bring darkness into the world. It isn't a pretty job, but someone's got to do it."

"Isn't that the job for the police and other agencies, like the FBI?" Aari asked skeptically.

"Yes, but not even they can uncover everything. So some Sentries have actively taken it upon themselves to, as I said, uncover the filth. There's a pair I'm good friends with. Welsh twins. Rascally guys, but definitely not ones to mess with . . . Anyway, no matter who we are—community-based Sentry or field Sentry—when called upon, we all commit without hesitation. One thing we will *not* touch with a ten-foot pole is politics." Marshall wrinkled his nose distastefully. "It's a messy field, that one. And extremely divisive."

That earned him small grins from the trio, which made him feel more at ease. He understood why they were taking a long time to warm up to him, especially Jag and Aari. The conditions in which he'd met them were nowhere near ideal. Not even close.

"Oh, Aari, I nearly forgot—thought you might want this." Marshall reached between his seat and the car door and gently pulled out something black, which he passed to Aari.

Aari took it, eyebrows swept upward. "My bag!" He unzipped it hastily to ensure that his laptop and cell phone were intact. When he saw that they were, he looked at Marshall through the rearview mirror. "I, uh . . . thanks."

"Anytime."

Suddenly, Jag groaned. "Problem. Our folks are gonna freak out when they find out we're not exactly on our planned trip anymore."

Marshall saw Kody and Aari swap alarmed looks.

"What do we do?" Aari asked. "They'll go *ballistic* when they find out what's happened to Teegs and 'Riah."

Kody looked almost fearful. "Oh, man, this isn't good."

Aari was panicking. "What are our options?"

"Do we even have one?" Kody demanded.

"Well, we can't hide this from them," Jag said quietly.

"If I may," Marshall cut in. "I wouldn't want you lying to your parents, but you're aware of what's at stake here. This is much bigger than any of us. Maybe you might want to consider holding off on telling them, at least until the girls are safely back with us?"

"We take turns calling home every day and our parents fill each other in. We might get away with it for a while but not for very long."

"We'll figure it out," Marshall replied kindly. "Don't worry." He took his eyes off the road to steal a quick look at his watch. "We've still got some ways to go. Try to catch some shut-eye, if you can."

The boys slowly leaned back but remained tense. Marshall understood then that there was no way the trio would even attempt to sleep. In a soft voice, he said, "Know that the Sentry following them is a tiger. She'll stick with them until they're rescued. Don't worry, we'll get them back."

The red-and-black Ducati roared over the asphalt, its passage rattling a farmer's handmade sign that hung from a post thrust into the shoulder of the freeway. The rider of the motorcycle was a fit and striking woman in her early forties. Her long black hair, mostly hidden under her sleek touring helmet, was tied in a ponytail. She wore leather gloves and a comfortable jacket over a white top.

She kept her distance from the blue car she was tailing, using the sporadic traffic of mostly semis and smaller trucks to maintain her cover. The car carrying the three abductors with the girls in the trunk was some five hundred feet ahead of her. She glanced at her watch. It showed a few minutes past four in the morning. There was still no hint of the rising sun, but it wasn't pitch-dark either.

A sign overhead indicated that the New Mexico border was not far off. The Sentry had been following the car for nearly six hours, across California and into Arizona. She ought to have been tired, but it was the exact opposite. Being on the open road woke a part of her that was repressed when confined in a city. She thrived on the freedom of riding a powerful motorcycle on a freeway.

Up ahead, the abductors took an off-ramp toward a gas station. Eyes narrowed, she weaved her way between three large trucks and accelerated to catch the ramp. She spotted the blue car parked at one of the pumps where a few other vehicles were filling their tanks.

A man with long red sideburns and dark clothes stepped out of the driver's side. He'd taken off his mask, and a peek into the vehicle showed that the other two abductors had done the same. Making his way to the convenience store to pay for the gas, the driver didn't seem to notice her as she pulled up to the pump ahead of him.

She topped her motorcycle's tank and paid with a card, but when the man still hadn't returned, she went into the store. Inside, she found him ambling down the aisles, grabbing junk food as he went. Taking a risk, she hurried to the bathroom to relieve herself. When she came back out, she was thankful to see that the man was waiting in line at the counter.

The Sentry paused, pretending to adjust her helmet strap, and darted a quick glance at the man. To her surprise, he was watching her over his shoulder. He took in her face and heavy biker boots before meeting her eyes and leering. The Sentry ignored the degrading look and gave him a nod and a tight smile.

Only when the man had paid for his snacks and fuel did she slink out, again keeping her distance. He tossed the food to his cohorts in the car and pumped the gas. The Sentry headed back to her bike and pretended to check its tires, muttering to herself and showing no interest as the captors pulled back onto the freeway. She allowed them a few seconds' head start before swinging her leg over the seat and following, staying behind several cars until they were in her sights again. Her eyes went to the vehicle's trunk where the girls were crammed, and her heart wrenched.

The kidnappers and their unseen pursuer rocketed down the wide lanes of the freeway for a couple of hours more before they approached a small town. The blue car exited the highway and began to pull further ahead. It maintained its increased speed briefly before disappearing around a curve behind a small hill.

The Sentry leaned forward, urging her bike on. She pulled away from the other vehicles, leaving them far behind her, and rounded the bend.

The blue car was nowhere to be seen. There was no sign of its retreating taillights down the road. The Sentry slowed to a halt, baffled. This wasn't possible.

Is there a hidden turnoff somewhere? she wondered, looking around. There was no traffic on any of the lanes and big sagebrush carpeted the sides of the roads. The area was darker than the surroundings as the small hill blocked what little light there was in the sky. She used her headlight to try to see into the shadows.

The Sentry turned her head to the left when she thought she saw something odd in her peripherals. She pointed the headlight and froze. An outline of a car just barely visible against the sagebrush. It was parked, engine off, on the side of the road.

It seemed as if the car's occupants had abandoned it. The Sentry quelled the panic creeping up her throat. She hadn't lost them. They couldn't be too far away. She'd find them, and the girls.

As she moved to get off her bike to investigate, a sound of metal on metal caught her attention. She quickly turned and saw a stocky, broad-shouldered form in the shadows. Its arms were raised, a gun pointed at her.

The Sentry threw herself off her bike but was a fraction of a second too late. She heard a bang and felt a blow to her abdomen as she hit the ground, scraping the side of her helmet against the pavement. She let out a gasp and pressed her hands where she'd been hit. Steeling herself, she slowly sat up only to be forced back down by another bullet. It struck her a few inches above the first wound. She bit into her lip to stop herself from letting out any sound of pain.

The roar of an engine coming to life made her raise her head. The blue car's headlights glared into her face and she closed her eyes just before her head hit the ground again. Helpless, she listened as the vehicle rumbled back onto the road and sped away.

The Sentry pulled her helmet off and unzipped her jacket. She could feel no exit wounds; the bullets were still inside her.

Her entire body trembled from shock but she forced herself to plunge her fingers into the holes to stem the bleeding as much as she could. With one hand keeping pressure on the wounds, she weakly grabbed her customized phone out of her pocket and called one of the few contacts she had listed.

A man's voice answered after the first ring. "Is everything alright?" were the first words he said.

The Sentry's breathing was heavy and uneven. "Marshall . . . they're gone."

"What? What are you talking about?"

"I lost them," she whispered.

"You . . . what happened?"

"They got me. Ambushed—shot twice."

There was a curse on the other end. Then, "How badly are you hit?"

The Sentry didn't reply. She could feel her energy steadily leaving her body and knew her time would be up before she could get to a hospital. Marshall said, "Look, hang tight. I'm not far behind. I'll be there—"

"Marshall, you need to worry about the girls. I lost them."

"Where were they headed?"

"We just crossed the state line into New Mexico and . . ." She grimaced as the pain intensified. ". . . and took the exit at Deming, heading north. I don't . . . know . . . the final destination."

There was silence before he said softly, "I'm so sorry about this."

She managed a bleak smile. "It's what happens in the line of duty. You know that better than most."

"But I should have—"

"We're here for a reason." She let out a shuddering breath and shut her eyes tightly. "I just wish I'd made my time count."

"You did . . . you did make your time count. Thank you, Gwen."

The Sentry ended the call. Her vision was darkening around the edges. She went to the settings on her phone and tapped the

'Wipeout' option. With a sigh, she dropped the device as all its data was erased permanently.

She could hear a vehicle approaching but never got to see the wide-eyed truck driver who stopped his semi and ran to her, never got to hear the frantic emergency call he made, never got to take more than two excruciating breaths before her heart stopped.

When Marshall's fists came crashing down onto the Mustang's steering wheel, Jag knew something was horribly wrong. He saw that the Sentry's eyes were red as the man tore away his Bluetooth earpiece and threw it down.

"What's happened?" Jag asked, gripping his seat belt as they raced down the freeway.

Marshall's jaw worked for a few moments before forced out, "Gwen's been shot."

"Gwen?"

Marshall didn't respond. From behind, Aari said, "Wait. Is that . . . is that the Sentry who was following Tegan and Mariah?"

Marshall pressed the fingers of one hand against his eyes. Jag stared at him, aghast, his heart plummeting to the pit of his gut. "I thought you said she wouldn't fail!"

Dropping his hand back onto the wheel, Marshall muttered, "They caught onto her somehow and they . . . ambushed her."

Jag looked back. Aari had his face covered with his hands and Kody was staring up at the roof of the convertible. He turned back to look at Marshall, wanting to break something, but stopped himself when he saw the Sentry staring at the road ahead with tightened lips and his shoulders slumped. The man looked . . . broken. Guilt prickled Jag's skin; the first thing that had left his mouth when he found out the other Sentry had been shot was accusation.

A few seconds of silence passed before Marshall spoke. He looked dejected but his voice was strong and determined—or so it seemed to Jag. "We're going to have to find your friends on our own. Gwen said that the abductors turned off the freeway at

Deming, New Mexico." The speedometer needle moved farther to the right. "We'll get them back."

They drove onward without talking as Marshall kept a heavy foot on the gas pedal. Jag glanced at him every so often as the thoughts swirling in his mind grew into a crescendo. *Where have they taken Tegan and Mariah? How do we get them back? Why are we with this stranger, this Sentry? Do we know for sure if we can trust him? Why is this even happening? We didn't ask for any of this! I don't want anything to do with this prophecy anymore . . . I just . . . I just want my friends back. I want our lives back.*

In the midst of the tempest in his mind, a man's voice, rich, dignified and slightly accented, quietly parted the raging sea of thoughts. *Jag.*

Jag froze, eyes darting to Marshall and his friends in the rearview mirror, but none of them seemed to be paying attention to him.

The voice called to him again. *Jag.*

It was the voice from his dreams. Now though, he knew who the speaker was. *Elder Nageau?*

Yes, youngling. The Elder's comforting tone seemed to dispel a great deal of tension in Jag's shoulders.

Jag slowly pressed himself back against his seat. *What . . . how . . . ?*

Understand, Jag, that my physical self in this, the biosphere, remains a long way from you, but we are connected through our consciousness in the novasphere . . . The Elder's voice broke off, as if a call had dropped, then returned a few moments later. *Do you remember this from your training?*

I . . . I think I remember. The novasphere is the higher plane where consciousness is, uh . . . projected. Where we're able to seek out those that are ready to connect with us.

Very good, youngling. I am pleased that you still recall that.

But I thought the five of us weren't ready to communicate this way?

Jag could hear Nageau's chuckle as he responded, *You, Jag, were more than ready. You always have been, though I sense Tegan will soon find this ability as well. The mighty hand of the universe has tilled the earth and now tends to the saplings of Aegis. You should know by now*—the conversation halted again before Nageau's voice came back to Jag—*you and your friends are indeed the ones promised in the prophecy. However, a repeat of an old lesson was not why I connected with you. I know you are uncertain and have your reservations about the Sentry. Let me assure you, Marshall is a man of honor and integrity. He is fully devoted to his duties. It did not sit well with him when he found out we had suppressed your memories.*

Jag glanced again at Marshall. *Yeah, I guess I can see that. It's just . . . was there really a need to remove our memories, even temporarily?*

Yes, and as I am certain Marshall has told you, it was for your safety.

So then why were we allowed to regain them?

When he received no response, he asked, *Elder Nageau? Are you there?*

The man's voice returned. *Yes, I am. This form of communication will not be perfect in the beginning, but you are doing remarkably well. Now, do you recall the warnings of the prophecy, Jag?*

I do now, yes. The dark clouds that are gathering on humanity's horizon. A catalyst at the center of this storm that the five of us will need to face to save the world. That's still something I'm trying to wrap my head around, to be honest.

Understandably so, Nageau said softly. *I do not believe anyone expected the ones from the prophecy to be so young. But life works in strange ways, with reasons unfathomable by our limited comprehension. To answer your question, the motive for reinstating your memories is simple. We believe that the time has come. There is a plan we think is unfolding even as we speak. We have read the signs and are almost cer-*

tain that it is being initiated by the catalyst we were warned about. However, we have not been able to completely verify this assumption. I have been trying for a long time to seek out this catalyst in the novasphere but alas, my efforts have been in vain. As such, I have yet to determine the intent or the capability of this entity. I believe that the five of you—his voice disappeared again—*and hold the key to revealing this catalyst and neutralizing its malevolent intentions.*

I still don't get it. Where do I—we—begin?

Start by trusting and having faith in the Sentry, Jag. He will do everything he can for the Chosen Ones. He understands how precious and important you are and stands ready to give his life to protect you if he must. Trust him, as you trust us.

Jag pressed his thumbs to his eyelids, then turned slightly to study Marshall again. The Sentry gripped the wheel with steely hands as determination returned to his countenance. *I . . . I will.*

Thank you, Jag.

Elder Nageau?

Yes?

Jag took in a shaky breath. *Despite everything happening right now, I—we miss you all.*

We miss you dearly as well, youngling.

Could you please pass Akol and Huyani a greeting from the group?

Most certainly. We will speak soon, Jag. I promise.

It felt as if a comforting hold was ebbing away as the Elder withdrew from Jag's mind, like someone pulling back from a hug. Jag wondered if all cognitive presences felt the same.

The Mustang flew over the road for nearly another hour before Marshall said, "We're here . . . exit to Deming."

They made a couple of turns before driving straight up North Golden Avenue as the first light of dawn crept in. The land was flat save for a small hill and the mountains in the distance. Creosote bushes, desert grasses and some deciduous trees made sporadic appearances by large empty lots and buildings. All in all, though, the place seemed barren.

As they drove further up the road, bright flashing lights came into view. When they rounded the bend, Jag, Aari and Kody leaned forward to get a closer look. They saw an ambulance, a couple of police cruisers, a semi-truck, and yellow barricade tape. A black-and-red motorcycle stood upright on the side of the road. A woman in civilian clothes was taking photographs while uniformed officers were talking to an older man next to the semi-truck. The man looked distraught.

Marshall slowed his vehicle down to almost a crawl and stared out of the window. The Sentry and the boys watched, mute, as two paramedics gently slid a stretcher carrying a sheet-covered form into the back of the ambulance. Marshall's throat throbbed and his knuckles whitened on the steering wheel but he continued on, gradually picking up speed once they were away from the scene.

They drove north for the next five minutes when suddenly Jag let out a yell of dismay. Aari and Kody jumped. "What?" Kody asked.

Leaving the key in the ignition, Marshall put the car in park and got out, as did Jag, slamming the door shut. Aari and Kody followed them out into the arid environment and, when they were standing in front of the car, realized what was wrong.

The headlights behind them cast their shadows onto a fork in the road. Jag shoved his hands deep into the pockets of his jeans. "Gwen wouldn't have mentioned which road they may have taken, by any chance?" he asked, sounding miserable.

Marshall laced his fingers behind his neck and glared ahead, eyes red, though whether from unshed tears or anger, Jag didn't know. "Unfortunately, no."

"How are we going to find them?" Kody asked quietly.

He received no answer, and even their shadows seemed to have taken on an air of despondency as they stared at the divide that cruelly taunted them.

Tegan slowly lifted her head, eyes barely open. She felt lethargic, dizzy, and had a bad taste in her mouth. Lying on her side on the hard ground, she could feel a throbbing pain from her shoulders down to her hands, which were bound behind her back. She forced herself to open her eyes further but couldn't see anything through the darkness. Was she blindfolded? No; there was no pressure around her head to indicate so, and she could blink easily.

Struggling, she used her arms and torso to pull herself into a sitting position. The soreness spread to her back and she groaned in protest. As she looked around, her eyes slowly adjusted to the darkness. The small, musty-smelling chamber she was in was devoid of any light save for a crack under a door. There were things that looked like cardboard boxes in one corner of the room and a few buckets lay around.

As she assessed her surroundings, a loud growl came from her stomach. All at once, she remembered what had happened to the friends. *Abducted before dinner,* she grumbled to herself. She knew she should have been afraid, but her hunger made her irritable. *Why did they take us?* Where *did they take us? Oh God, where's everyone else?*

A grunt beside her nearly made her yell out. Turning quickly, she squinted in the dimness and saw Mariah lying beside her, nearly facedown. Tegan hung her head in relief before her ears picked up a male voice from the other side of the door.

". . . yes, I know. I'm sorry."

Tegan raised her head again. Maybe her ears weren't fully awake yet, but she thought the voice sounded familiar. The man spoke as if he were on a phone call, and there was a jittery inflection to his tone. She strained to listen in.

"I know, those guys were my responsibility . . . yes . . . I didn't mean to—no, there was no way of knowing. They didn't expect the two to regain consciousness so quickly . . . yes . . . They know what they're doing, and the tranquilizer dosage should have knocked them out for at least five hours . . . I understand . . ."

Tegan fought feverishly against her bindings but ended up whacking her elbows hard against the wall. Thankfully, the man on the phone outside didn't hear her muffled curse and continued his conversation.

"I'll take care of it, I promise . . . I know what I'm doing. I'll take care of it personally if I have to . . . What? No, there was no mention of that . . . just something about a prophecy but they brushed it aside . . ."

Tegan, now certain she knew the voice but barely able to bring herself to believe it, got her feet under her and stood up. She shakily made her way over to the door and lay down by it, pressing her cheek against the ground as much as she could to peek through the inch-high gap under the door.

She saw a pair of low-cut leather shoes pacing back and forth; the man was extremely close to the door. His voice was clearer now that she was closer to him.

"Believe me, I've worked with them for a while, they're good . . . something strange happened, that's all I know . . . Yeah, I'll get them back . . . you can count on it . . . I'll keep you updated. We'll get them back for you." The voice paused, before asking tentatively, "Do you plan to see them here? . . . Yeah, alright. Of course. Have a good day, or night, wherever you are." The man gave a forced laugh.

Tegan watched the feet as they stopped pacing and heard a grumble from the man. Then the feet turned away from the door and retreated, displaying the man's socks that rose past the rolled-up cuffs of his pants. Tegan couldn't hold back her gasp.

The socks were striped.

Tony. A surge of revulsion welled up inside her. She quickly scrambled to her feet and ran back to Mariah. In her haste, she kicked a box into a wall and the resulting thud echoed around the chamber.

Rapid footsteps came toward the door. In a panic, Tegan flung herself down beside Mariah and lay in her original position, tilting her head to her chest so she could have a view of the entrance as it unlocked. She closed her eyes most of the way but kept one open a slit, watching through her eyelashes as the door buzzed quietly and opened outward. Light from outside illuminated the room.

A silhouette was outlined against the brightness. Despite not seeing any part of the man's features, she recognized Tony's deceptively non-intimidating frame. She held herself back from storming up to him and hurling questions. Where were they? Why did he have them abducted? Who had he been talking to on the phone?

The silhouette must have been peering at the girls for a full minute. Tegan could feel the suspicion emanating in waves from him. She kept absolutely still and made sure her breathing was even.

Finally, the door was shut and relocked. Tegan blew her cheeks and sat back up to face Mariah. She extended her leg, nudging her friend urgently. "Mariah!" she hissed. "Wake. *Up*!"

The other girl didn't stir. Tegan nudged her harder. "Come on! Mariah!"

Still nothing. Exasperated, Tegan jabbed Mariah's ribs several times with the toe of her shoe, hard. "Mariah!"

When her friend refused to budge, Tegan gave up and leaned back against the wall as best she could, jaw ticking. *Tony, you have a lot of explaining to do when we get out of here. Mark my words.*

The boys and Marshall scouted the fork in the road, praying with every fiber in their being to find a hint that would tell them which way the girls' abductors had gone. They searched for trash recently thrown out of a window, a piece of fabric, anything at all. They had no luck. Marshall had parked the Mustang on the side of the road so it wouldn't be in the way of other drivers. That seemed unlikely though, as no other vehicles came by.

"Where do both of these lead?" Kody asked, stepping onto the right side of the fork and stomping on it as if the road would suddenly open up and a huge flashing arrow would point them in the right direction.

Aari scratched his forehead, then reached into his pocket and drew out his phone. "Gimme a sec while I—"

He stopped himself when he saw Marshall pull a physical map out from his cargo pants and unfold it with a serious expression. It looked exactly like the one he'd held out to them the evening he'd tossed the smoke bomb into their car. The Sentry studied it for a few moments. When he noticed that the boys had gone completely silent, he looked over at them. "What? You can't have too many of these, right?"

The trio stared at him as if he'd just sprouted four extra arms and a tail. Aari slowly slipped his phone back into his pocket. "Not sure how quick and effective that will be, but okay . . ."

"Deming, Deming . . ." Marshall scanned the map. "Here we go. If we keep heading north, the next major town is Silver City. If we were to take the road to the right and head east, we'll hit a town called Hatch."

"Which way would they have gone, though?" Jag asked, fiddling with the crucifix around his neck.

"Well . . ." Marshall pulled the map closer to his face, but Kody caught sight of Aari impatiently whipping his phone back out and furiously tapping away at the screen.

"Okay," the redheaded boy said, "to the left is . . . almost nothing. To the right we have a long, mostly empty stretch with houses that are really spread out."

"Wouldn't that make sense?" Kody asked, staring down the fork. "If they wanted to keep the girls out of sight, they would have taken them to somewhere secluded and out of the way, right?"

"Possibly," Jag said. "But that's not for sure."

Kody snorted. "Do we have anything better to go on?" He turned to Marshall. "What do you think?"

Marshall lowered his map, then nodded slowly as he folded the chart. "We need to cast the net as far and wide as we can, so why not? They've only got an hour's lead on us."

"Hold on," Aari interjected. "What are we gonna do? Go knocking door to door and ask if there are a couple of kidnapped girls inside?"

"You're forgetting something, smart guy," Kody said. "My hypersenses. I'm sure I'll be able to hear them or pick up a scent if they're within range. And remember, Tegan uses that lavender-lilac shampoo her mom makes—don't look at me like that, I'm not being creepy, it's just a unique fragrance—so I should be able to pick it up."

"Oh, good, I forgot we had our own bloodhound."

The four of them hurried back to the car and took the right-hand road.

"Hey, Marshall," Kody said, leaning to the front, "what are *your* powers?"

The Sentry smirked slightly. "My *abilities*, Kody, will be revealed in time. Maybe. They're definitely useless right now, anyway."

Kody, though wanting to question the Sentry further, chose not to. They drove for a bit, then stopped near the first cluster of houses that came into view. "Man, this place could do with a facelift," Kody observed. "Let me out here."

Marshall stopped the car and Kody hopped out of the back. Quickly but light-footed, he ran to the first house, listening and trying to pick up scents. All he got was the smell of stale food somewhere inside the building and diesel fuel from the trucks parked in the yard. As for his ears, they picked up three distinctive snores from within the household. At one point he caught the howling of coyotes but quickly came to the realization that the animals were some distance away. He even heard the flutter of a bird's wings but that wasn't nearby, either.

He moved swiftly, raking through each residential building with his senses, but gave any sign of Tegan and Mariah. He loped back to the Mustang and jumped in back beside Aari. He shook his head at the others and sighed. "I wish my enhanced vision would let me see through walls. It would make this a lot easier."

"Wouldn't that be something," Aari muttered.

At the next group of houses, Kody was out of the car before the vehicle had come to a full stop. He went around sniffing and listening once more, and had to scale a couple of pitiful fences. The thought of being caught intruding on private land didn't even occur to him—he wanted to find his friends and that was all that mattered.

At the last house, he quietly crept around the side but paused mid-step. A large pit-bull was chained to a tree, fast asleep. Though Kody's experiences with the breed had been positive, he only did a three-second scan of the house before tiptoeing all the way back to the car.

"They're not here, but there's a pooch in the back that could wake up at any moment," he said to the others.

"Must be nearly deaf if it didn't hear the car come up in the first place." Marshall put the Mustang in drive. "All the same, let's move out before it does decide to get up and wake the entire neighborhood."

They continued for over an hour, Kody repeating his methods with the other houses along the road. There were a few long stretches with no buildings at all. In some areas, Marshall had to go onto dirt roads to check out the homes that were more remote. They kept the search going until they approached the town of Hatch, where traffic slowly began to build.

When they arrived, Kody was done in. The anxiety and the exhausting search, coupled with the lack of sleep had all but completely drained him.

Not wanting to drive further into town, Marshall dolefully pulled the car over to the side and turned on his hazard lights.

Jag banged his head with his fist. "They're. Not. Here."

"Maybe they took the road that led north to Silver City," Kody said wearily.

"If they did, then they've got at least two hours on us." Jag turned around to face Kody. "Are you a thousand percent sure you didn't miss anything?"

Kody was defensive. "My senses work just fine. If the girls were there, I would have picked up something. I want to find them as much as you guys, so why wouldn't I have searched properly?"

The hardness in Jag's expression dissipated. "You're right. I'm sorry."

Aari ran a hand through his hair. "Let's think this through. Why would they drive all the way out to Deming, New Mexico—a place that's pretty much in the middle of nowhere—just to pass through it if their destination wasn't nearby? I think they were closing in on their final stop not far from here. Their destination must be either on this road or the other. When was the last time they stopped for gas?"

"Gila Bend, where Gwen refueled as well," Marshall answered.

Aari looked down at his phone. "Okay, that's nearly five hours from their last fuel stop, but if they were making good speed, it would have taken them three and a half hours, maybe four to get to Deming. A midsize car like that would run for about six hours on a full tank at the speed they were doing. That would put them within a hundred to a hundred-fifty-mile radius of Deming."

Kody was lost. "So?"

"*So,* that means it's very likely that they're not far from here. They would have around two hours' worth of gas left. Our search grid should be, as I said, within a hundred or a hundred-fifty-mile radius."

"They wouldn't have used this road to go past Hatch, then," Marshall said slowly.

"Don't think so. The road to Hatch leads to CanAm Highway, and CanAm actually merges with the highway all of us traveled on. It would be really dumb to use this route when they could have just stayed on the original highway. Their destination can't be too far from here."

"Back toward Deming we go, then." As Marshall turned the car around, he added, "Great deduction, Aari."

Kody took notice of Aari looking a bit surprised and even pleased by the praise, though he didn't respond to the Sentry.

Marshall floored it all the way back to the fork and continued on North Gold Avenue this time. Kody, although worried sick about the girls, couldn't hold back a large and noisy yawn. Aari and Jag yawned shortly after him.

"If you guys need to grab a nap, feel free to do so," Marshall said. "You're gonna need your energy."

"You can probably expect Kody to pass out, but not Aari or me," Jag said thickly.

"I'm not going to," Kody grumbled. "I may be tired, but if you think I can sleep with Tegan and Mariah missing, you're mistaken." He slouched down in his seat. "I just hope we find them sooner rather than later. If something horrible happens to them, so help me God I'll make someone pay. We're family and you never, ever mess with family."

A shrill cry severed the peace and quiet of the house. "*Hugo!*" Hugo Sanchez scrambled upright in his bed as his wife charged into their room. He yanked off the blanket, nearly falling in his haste to get up, and rushed to hold her. "Julia! What—"

His wife curled his nightshirt into her fists and wept against his chest. She was still in her sleepwear and her hair fell messily around her shoulders. "The crops, Hugo . . . they're . . . they're all *dead*."

Hugo guided her to the edge of the bed and sat her down. His first instinct was to hurry outside and take a look for himself, but he needed to keep Julia calm for the sake of her heart. "They're not really gone?" he asked as he passed her a tissue.

She took it from him, hand shaking. "They are. I—I woke up a few minutes ago, before the alarm was set to go off. Something didn't feel right. I don't know what it was. I went outside with the dog and . . . and I saw the crops, completely destroyed. I couldn't believe it, Hugo, I just couldn't." She had wiped her tears away but more still spilled down her cheeks. "The outbreak got us after all."

Hugo rested his hands on either side of her face and leaned over to kiss her forehead, resting his lips against her for a few moments. Julia shut her eyes and wrapped her arms around herself.

"Let me take a look," he said softly. "Rest, *meu amour*, catch your breath. I won't be long."

She opened her eyes slightly and nodded. Hugo rubbed her shoulders before heading out of their room. He grabbed a light jacket as he slipped his sandals on.

The couple's Labrador was curled by the front door and stared up at him with big brown eyes as he approached. Gently shooing her away from the entrance, he pulled the door open and stepped outside.

It was six in the morning and the air was only a little crisp. He could see from afar that the wheat stalks were plainly visible and standing. *Julia's mistaken*, he thought as he walked toward the crops. As he neared the field, though, it became clear that his wife was right after all. He quickened his steps along the tramlines in the field. The stalks may have been untouched, but the wheat heads—ripe and ready for harvest—were all gone.

Distraught, Hugo crouched to see if the heads had fallen but only found fine, yellow-green dust covering the soil by the bottoms of the stems. He picked up a handful and let it fall from between his fingers before standing up. What kind of an ungodly infection could cause such destruction? He slowly turned around, taking in all of their lost crops, before continuing down the tramline in a daze.

His feet carried him mechanically through the field. He extended his arms, letting them brush every stalk he passed. He didn't look left or right and watched, uncomprehendingly, as the rising sun cast its golden tint onto the land below, illuminating the ruined wheat field with a surreal glow. It was both strangely beautiful and appallingly devastating.

The sun doesn't care that whatever its rays touch have been ruined, he thought, fighting against the mounting lump in his throat. *This can't be really happening. Our crops can't all be gone.*

He carried on with his arms reaching out, bending the stems and letting them bounce back upright once he'd passed. His hopes of seeing even one stalk of wheat that still carried its head were cut down soon enough. There was nothing salvageable.

He came to a stop. What were he and Julia supposed to do now? More importantly, how was he going to comfort his wife? She was especially sensitive to stress and did not respond well to anxiety. He needed to be strong for her above everything else. He needed to show her that they would be able to pull through this.

When he returned to the house, he headed straight for the kitchen where Julia was making breakfast for the two of them. He could tell that she was doing everything in her power to distract herself, but there was a tautness in her face, and a severe crease on her brow.

She heard him enter and turned around to look at him. Hugo did what he could to put on a smile for her, but she saw right through him and found the shattered man behind the futile mask. Tears spilled anew from her eyes and she leaned back against the counter, hiding her face from him. Her body lurched violently with what Hugo thought were sobs, but he realized in terror that she was gasping deeply for breath. Her hands slid down to her chest and she pierced his gaze with a frightened stare before collapsing to the floor. Her wheezes and her weeping were a haunting call to Hugo's ears.

He ran to her and with some effort lifted her into his arms. Her body kept heaving painfully against him as he laid her down on the couch and picked up a phone to dial 911. Once he'd completed the call, he sat on the coffee table in front of the couch and took one of Julia's hands. She didn't notice him, lost as she was in her world of torment.

"Help will be here soon, Julia, just hold on," he whispered. The moistness in his eyes formed wet streaks down his face as he watched his wife wheeze in agony. "Hold on . . . please just hold on."

24

A groan made Tegan look up from her efforts to free her wrists from remove their bindings. Her eyes, which had long since adjusted to the darkness, caught sight of Mariah turning over. Tegan scooted over and gently prodded her friend with her knee. "Hey," she said.

"Teegs?" Mariah sounded drowsy.

"Yeah, it's me."

"What's going on?"

"I don't know. Some guys jumped us, and the next thing I know, I woke up in here. It's like some kind of storage room."

"How can you see anything?"

"Your eyes will get used to it. But listen, you're not going to believe who's involved in all of this."

Mariah was wriggling into a sitting position, not seeming to have heard Tegan's words. "Ugh, my arms are sore . . . Oh, great, I'm tied up. That's why."

"'Riah. There's someone here who's behind our abduction."

"Who?"

Tegan had to force the name out. "Tony."

"Right. Sure."

"I'm not kidding. I heard him. He was on the phone talking to someone and I heard his voice. And I saw his shoes and striped socks. That's pretty much signature Tony."

"Anyone can wear striped socks, Teegs."

"You think I don't know that? And I already said I heard his voice too."

Mariah shook her head. "I don't know who you saw, but it can't be him. Tony dropped everything and drove out all the way to meet us when we needed him. He went after the guy who threw the smoke bomb into our car. Whoever you saw, it wasn't Tony."

At that moment, the door buzzed quietly and opened. A brilliant glare flooded the room as an overhead light came on. Tegan and Mariah looked away, shielding their faces.

"Oh, good, you're both awake."

Mariah met Tegan's eyes and a look of horror darkened her features. Slowly, they turned to the source of the voice.

Tony stood at the entrance, sliding a keycard into the back pocket of his pants. As usual, he was smartly dressed, his hair was immaculate, and his face carried a certain rascally charm.

"Tony . . ." Mariah said weakly.

"Hello again." He smiled a little. "How are you doing?"

"What's going on?" Tegan asked.

"Ah, yeah . . . apparently, you guys have piqued the interest of my employer. They seem to think that the five of you are—how do you say—*significant*, in a way that I definitely don't understand. Got a few questions for you, you see."

"What questions?"

Tony shrugged. "Beats me. But"—he shut the door behind him and, to the girls' surprise, sat on a chair he'd dragged in, legs crossed—"if my employer wishes something, then I will make it so. And here you are. Pity my men couldn't get the others, though."

Tegan's back straightened. "You mean the guys escaped?"

Tony studied her with unnerving intensity. "We're going to get them, not to worry."

"I still don't understand what's going on," Mariah cut in. "Why are we wanted? Were you just playing us the entire time, with that story of taking time off work to see your girlfriend? Were you actually following us?"

Tony turned to her with an almost pitying look. "It was my assignment to meet you and get to know you. I take orders and follow through with them. What my employer wants, I deliver.

There's always a good reason for it. But I do like you guys—you're bright and funny."

"Then what are you doing?" Tegan asked. It didn't matter what he said, she felt betrayed. He'd seemed genuine. He'd given her hope that not every stranger was someone to be wary of.

"As I said, it's just my job." Tony ran his thumb under his chin. "Strange, though, that the Boss would take such interest in you five. Stranger even that the Boss may decide to question you personally."

Mariah glowered at him. "We're not talking to anyone. We were kidnapped. That's a serious crime. If anything, we ought to be questioning your boss."

Again, Tony smiled. "You're spunky, aren't you?"

Mariah's anger remained plastered on her face.

"You cannot begin to fathom what's at play," he said. "It's huge. It's going to fundamentally transform the entire world. It may take a few more years before the last piece is put into place, but it'll be worth it. It'll be nothing short of astounding."

Tegan leaned away from him. "I don't know what *it* is, but you sound calmly fanatical about it."

"If my employer permits, maybe you'll discover what the final outcome of this vision will be. Then perhaps you'll understand why so many are heavily invested into this organization." As he picked some lint off his shirt, Tony continued, almost as if to himself, "But this is very unorthodox. Even the people high up in this organization have never seen the Boss in person, and yet you soon may."

The girls watched, stone-faced, as he got up. "I don't know when exactly we'll pull you out for the interrogation. When the men come to retrieve you, don't fight them. You'll only give them reason to hurt you, trust me."

He exited the room, then closed and locked the door behind him. The girls didn't move after he left, and remained still even as the lights went off in the chamber, submerging them in darkness once again.

***

Tony drove slowly through the cavern where the storage room was located and into a concealed underground tunnel, being careful to avoid the dirt-stained vehicles driving into the cave as he exited. The tunnel was lit by bright LED lights to allow the drivers to see their way over the packed dirt roadways.

The SUV rolled out into broad daylight onto a makeshift road that was part of a restricted area of the mine site. He circled a huge waste rock dump to leave the zone and was nearly flattened by the thirteen-foot tall tire of a four-hundred-ton mining truck.

"Moron!" Tony yelled, then got an unsavory amount of dust whooshing through his open windows, which he hastily wound up. He glared at the monstrous vehicle as it lumbered past and bitterly thought, *I've been here for a few hours and I've already developed a hate for mining sites.*

Why the Boss had wanted the five teenagers brought to the company's copper mining facility in New Mexico was not his concern, but it irritated him how loud and raucous the place was, not to mention dirty. The workers were hardly any better, with their shouting and general unkemptness.

He refused to look anywhere but forward as he made his way to the main office complex. Once in the parking lot, he braced himself and opened the car door. A blast of hot air and diesel fumes assaulted him. The rumbling of rock crushers sounded in the distance of the open-pit mine.

Tony quickly dodged into the slightly cooler office building and went straight to the receptionist behind the counter. "I'd like to speak with Mr. Ajajdif, please."

"He's at the main security post checking up on things," the woman said nasally, not looking up from her work.

Tony pulled a face. "Of course he is. Thanks."

The woman didn't respond as he headed back into the heat. Getting into his vehicle, he wound down his windows again and pulled out of the lot. Just when he thought nothing could annoy him further, he found himself stuck behind a large truck that was spraying water to keep the dust down on the dirt road. Tony made an obscene gesture toward the driver of the tanker even though the man would not be able to see him.

Oh, yes, thank you. Muddying up this place makes things a whole lot better, doesn't it? I need to get out of here.

He made a left turn to the main security post and saw two men outside; one was medium-built with auburn hair, and the other was a bald giant who had his back to Tony. The giant was holding a cigarette between his fingers.

When Tony parked beside them and got out, the men looked over. "Well, well," said the Lebanese-born hulk, sneering, "if it isn't Tony Cross, the tiger who couldn't capture five measly children. I'd say you're more of a mewling kitten, truth be told."

Tony's mouth curled back as he looked up at the towering man. "How's the weather up there, Elias? Getting enough oxygen for that tiny brain of yours?"

Elias Hajjar's lips twisted downward.

Tony masked his satisfaction. "If the Boss is right, those *children* were in league with the group that gave you that disgusting injury. Truth be told," he mimicked the big man's voice, "it improves your looks."

Hajjar, standing nearly seven feet tall, looked as if he wanted to squash Tony under his boot. Instead, he blew a thick cloud of smoke into the young man's face. He was a heavily tattooed ex-mercenary with black holes for eyes and tree trunks for limbs. Tony appeared tiny and malnourished by comparison.

Hajjar's face had been severely disfigured in a horrible accident the year before when a large shard of glass had fallen onto his face. There was an untidy, jagged scar that extended from his forehead down to his chin. He'd lost most of his sight in one eye but was doing remarkably well—well enough to be reassigned as the head of security for Quest Mining, a division of Phoenix Corporation. He'd had to go through intensive surgeries just to regain the semblance of a human face. That the man was even alive was a miracle. Or a shame, as Tony saw it.

Tony held his breath until the smoke abated. "Classy," he muttered.

"What is it you're here for, Tony?" Vladimir Ajajdif asked. For some reason, the hint of a heavy Russian accent struck Tony as funny but he didn't dare show it. He knew, as many did, that Ajajdif was one of the very few people who had actually seen the Boss—indeed, Ajajdif claimed that the Boss had personally saved him from a life on the streets of San Francisco nearly two decades ago.

Sliding his fists into his pockets, Tony said, "I have an assignment to complete because the men I hired were unable to do so." He heard Hajjar snicker but continued. "I've got the girls safely locked away in the storehouse underground."

Ajajdif looked toward the tunnel, which was hidden by a huge pit at the center of the site with tall mounds around it. While the mining activity was legitimate, it was merely a cover for the massive project that was being worked on beneath their feet.

"I might be tempted to check on these girls myself," Ajajdif said. "See if they're actually the ones who took part in wrecking my operations last year."

"No," Tony said sharply. "No one's to go near them except those under my direction. I came here to tell you that. You need to keep everyone else away from them. Besides, it's none of your business. The Boss happens to be very interested in them and may interrogate them soon."

At that, Ajajdif's head snapped up. "The Boss is coming *here?* You're sure?"

"I was only told that the kids are meant to be questioned."

Ajajdif turned away, uttering what Tony could only guess to be Russian curses. "Why wasn't I told about this?"

"I only found out myself a couple hours ago." Tony glanced at his watch. "I need to get going."

Ajajdif waved his hand dismissively. Hajjar placed his cigarette between his lips and regarded Tony through half-lidded eyes. "Make sure you get them this time, runt."

"Make sure the devil doesn't find your filthy soul and drag you back to where you belong," Tony said coolly as he shut the car door.

Hajjar spat in his direction. "You're no angel either, Cross!"

Tony could see Hajjar's contorted face getting smaller and smaller in his rearview mirror as he drove away. With a smile, he left the mining site.

It was early morning when the red Mustang pulled into Silver City. Aari was barely able to keep his eyes open. Marshall had miraculously not fallen asleep at the wheel and Jag seemed to be holding up as well. The one person Aari was worried about at the moment was Kody. The poor guy looked like a walking corpse, and super-hearing wasn't needed to catch the earthquake in his stomach.

They'd scoured every small town between Deming and Silver City. Kody had run through all the streets, checking each residence thoroughly while avoiding detection before returning to the car with drooping shoulders each time. The mad running, lack of sleep and hunger combined with the heat was weighing him down. Aari would often have to reach over and shake Kody to keep his friend from passing out.

"You guys need to eat," Marshall said. His words were less distinct than before but he seemed to be faring better than the boys. "I'm guessing the last you ate was lunch yesterday."

"We need to find the girls," Jag responded dully. "We can't stop the search just to sit in a diner."

Marshall sighed. "You need the energy. How about a compromise—we get takeout."

"I think we should, Jag," Aari said. He glanced at Kody who was curled up beside him.

Jag looked back at them, then nodded in resignation at Marshall. The Sentry continued down the road before turning into diner with a drive-thru. As they pulled in, Aari caught sight of a dirt-caked SUV exiting with the driver typing one-handed on a phone. For a second, he thought the man could be Tony, but the vehicle was gone quickly and he dismissed the thought. Tony was in California with his girlfriend, and that was hundreds of miles away from where the boys were right now.

"One thing, Marshall," Aari said as a thought came to him. "There was a guy we met at the diner in Salt Lake City—he was very helpful. He went after you to teach you a lesson for . . . attacking us with your smoke bomb. I guess I kind of want to apologize for that. We didn't know you were a Sentry at that time."

"Huh?" Marshall sounded baffled.

"You were attacked. A dude came after you when you drove away from the Denny's we were at."

"Erm . . . nope. I didn't run into anyone after the incident, much less get taught a 'lesson'."

Jag turned back again to share bewildered looks with Aari and Kody, but they said nothing.

They ordered their food and scarfed it down once Marshall parked the car. For a few minutes, there was only the sound of food wrappers unfolding and chewing.

Silver City's population was only a little over ten thousand but the roads were busy with morning traffic. Aari sluggishly dragged his gaze away from the cars to the interior of the Mustang. Their little group wasn't looking too well. No one smiled. Faces were taut and mouths drawn down. Black circles had appeared under everyone's eyes. But Aari noticed a little bit of energy would return with every bite they took.

As he munched at his meal, his thoughts drifted away without him realizing. "Why here?" he asked.

"Mmh?" Jag mumbled through his burger.

"Why New Mexico? Why around Silver City? Why is this place so important? Why did they, whoever *they* are, choose this area as the destination? Nothing much happens here. The only notable thing I can think of are the mines, like the Chino mine east of here. I think it's east, anyway."

"So then . . . what now?" Kody asked.

"We're gonna check out every inch of Silver City, of course," Jag said.

"What if they're not here?"

Aari winced inwardly. He wished Kody hadn't voiced what had been in the very back of his mind.

"If not," Marshall said bluntly, "we'll check out all the other places around here. I know there are a few towns close to some mining sites. Hanover, Pinos Altos and Tyrone to name a few."

Jag swallowed a couple of French fries before giving the Sentry a look. "Marshall?"

"Yes?"

"I know you haven't told us everything. I really do trust you now, because Elder Nageau advised me to—"

"Waaait," Kody said. "What do you mean, he advised you? When did you talk to him?"

Jag tapped his temple. "He reached out not long after Marshall picked us up."

Aari's mouth fell open. "I thought that sort of thing was only possible with more training! And even then, it's not guaranteed!"

"Yeah, well, the point is," Jag said impatiently, "you haven't told us much, Marshall. I know you're holding back. Considering we've been dragged into this mess, I think we have a right to know what you know."

Marshall slowly set his food down and reached for his drink. After a few sips, he said, "I was being honest when I told you that I don't have all the pieces. I probably don't have most. But you're right. I can offer you the little more that I do know."

He took a few moments to collect his thoughts, then continued, "First of all, the Sentries have knowledge of the warnings in the prophecy and we take it seriously. Unfortunately, we haven't been able to pinpoint what or who is at the center of the dark storm that is gathering.

"To varying degrees, the Sentries and our brethren in Dema-Ki are able to feel significant changes in the fabric of existence. So when there's a serious disturbance in the field, as there is now, we can sense it. It's as though someone has cast a rock into a calm pond and the ripples created from it eventually reach us.

"Most of the time, we're able to locate the source and do what's required, but in this case we've been unable to identify it. What makes it worse is that the ripples from this disturbance are exceptionally strong and the frequency, instead of abating, is increasing. No Sentry alive has ever witnessed anything like this before. And here's the real kicker: Neither have the Elders. There is a real fear that this disturbance may reach a critical mass soon, making it imperative for us to identify the catalyst and put an end to it.

"You would have been told sometime during your training with the Elders that the Sentries would watch over you upon your return. The Sentries are privileged and honored to protect you and to be at your service. The five of you mark the beginning of the triumph of light over darkness.

"It may not seem that way to you at the moment, but you're destined for greatness beyond your imagination. You will be the ones to save humanity from certain destruction. But it will not come without sacrifices. The Sentries will walk through the gates of hell to protect you if we must. The Sentry whom we lost today . . . her name was Gwen, and she was the one who had been watching over you in Great Falls." Marshall's mouth flattened into a line.

The boys looked at one another, feeling a pang in their chests. *Gwen?* Aari thought, overwhelmed by unexpected sorrow. *We didn't even know her. And . . . now she's gone.*

Marshall nibbled half-heartedly on his meal as he spoke. "She gave her life believing it was her duty. She never wavered from the cause, not for a second."

The trio leaned closer to him, silently urging him to continue. Marshall glanced at them as he took the last bite of his food, then said, "A few months ago, I was doing a late-night run for some kind of lab in California—I worked as a delivery guy for a while after I retired from the Marines—and after dropping off some boxes, I went into the building to use the washroom. Mind you, I wasn't supposed to be inside. It was by chance that while I was in a stall two men came in, talking about some project they were working on. One of them asked if what they were doing was somehow related to the crop failure that's spreading across the country."

"*This* crop failure?" Aari demanded. "The one that's all over the news *right now?*"

"Yes. But they discovered me before the conversation could get much further. They called in some guards but it wasn't normal security; these guys looked mercenary. I took off in my van and they came after me with guns firing. They rammed my truck off a cliff and thought they had killed me. I was lucky they didn't come down to check. Guess they figured my body would have been charred after the van exploded."

The boys stared at him with wide eyes but Marshall paid no heed. "Remember I said something about Sentries and our senses? Mine were going off the chart. Something big was brewing in that facility and I think I stumbled into it. It was at that point when I decided it was time to contact the Elders after over a decade of silence between us. That was when Elder Nageau told me that the time to reactivate your memories was close, and he would instruct me when to do so."

"Whoa, okay, wait. Wait." Kody slid his hands down his face. "Are you saying this whole crop thing is connected to the prophecy?"

Marshall looked from one teenager to another, searching for words, before saying quietly, "Yes."

Aari tapped his knees, thinking hard. This was too big and coming in too quickly. "I guess . . . I guess I can see the dots beginning to connect for this to be more than just a coincidence . . . but this is insane."

"It certainly seems that the dark clouds foretold in the prophecy are descending," Marshall said, staring out at the sky. "We will have to be ready. The assault on humanity has begun."

Tegan waved her paper plate around aimlessly. Dully, she knew there was no possible way she and Mariah were going to be able to use that as a weapon against Tony and his men. She flung the plate aside, but it fluttered pathetically to the ground a foot away from her.

The last thing they'd wanted to do was consume anything Tony had given them, but the girls were parched and starving and the sandwich looked absolutely delicious. At least this time he'd left the light on. Tegan had gulped down her sandwich and now sat staring at the door of the storage room. Mariah was nearly done with hers, but she'd left the crusts behind.

"I just don't understand," Tegan murmured. "He played us so well. No one saw it coming."

Mariah shoved her plate aside, glaring. "Mind not talking about that dung beetle for a while?"

Tegan absentmindedly reached down and grabbed a piece of the crust. She rolled it between her fingers, staring at it for a long while. Then, slowly, an idea started to take shape in her mind. She grinned. "We're gonna get out of here."

Mariah rested her chin in her palm. "Well, I sure hope so, but—"

"No, no. I mean, we're gonna get out of here. On our own."

Mariah cast a tired look at Tegan without responding. Tegan grabbed the rest of the crust from her friend's plate and went to the opposite side of the room. Quickly, she began breaking off pieces of the bread and dropping small crumbs that led back to where Mariah was sitting.

Wary, Mariah asked, "Teegs, what are you doing?"

Tegan sat down beside her and leaned back against the wall, legs crossed. "Shh, you'll see. Talk quietly from now on, though."

"Okay, but what's the bread got to do with—"

"I told you, you'll see. Now hush!"

Though bewildered, Mariah complied and slumped down against the wall beside her friend. They spoke in whispers for a stretch, their conversation returning to Tony, all the while berating themselves for being blind to what he really was—although deep down they had to admit that Tony was a phenomenal actor.

Mariah curled her hair around her hand and observed the ends. "Then who was the guy from Salt Lake City, the one with the smoke bomb?"

Tegan frowned. "Tony said he took care of him . . ."

Mariah snorted. "Yeah. Tony said a lot of things, didn't he?"

Sighing, Tegan leaned her head back and closed her eyes. No more words were exchanged between them until they picked up the quiet sound of tiny scampering feet. Tegan's eyes snapped open and she looked at her trail of breadcrumbs expectantly.

Mariah followed her friend's gaze and her eyes widened. A tiny, dusty-brown creature had crept from behind a box and was sniffing at the trail of bread crumbs. Its nose twitched incessantly.

"A mouse?" Mariah hissed, horrified.

"Quiet," Tegan breathed, watching the small animal, a pocket mouse, eat through the trail. It squeaked once, probably in excitement at finding so much food. Tegan was delighted that, even though it saw the girls, the mouse didn't exhibit fear, merely caution.

Having an uncle with a small family-run zoo, Tegan and her cousins had grown up around animals. She was extremely comfortable with nearly every creature, no matter the size. Animals seemed to love her in return; it was as if they could sense her earnest affection for them and were naturally attracted.

The girls kept absolutely still as the small creature picked up crumb after crumb, drawing ever closer to them. Tegan slowly rested her hand on the ground, exposing some bread on her upturned palm. The mouse slowed its approach as it neared the friends but still advanced.

"Tegan . . ." Mariah warned quietly.

Tegan ignored her and waited patiently as the mouse drew closer until it was sniffing her hand with utmost prudence. It nudged her pinkie finger with a cold nose before quickly pulling back. Tegan didn't move a muscle and eventually the creature returned. It put off making a move for the crumbs she held, instead opting to explore the hand on which the tempting morsels rested.

Tegan glanced at Mariah. Her friend didn't seem at all comfortable as she regarded the mouse.

Very slowly, the small furry animal clambered onto Tegan's hand, its little feet tickling her palm. As it nibbled on the crumbs, she stroked its head with her other hand. It stiffened for a moment but relaxed in the end, and even seemed to enjoy the gentle attention. It was a little over four inches long, with half its length comprised of the tail.

"It's so soft," Tegan said, delighted.

Mariah wasn't impressed. "It's a rodent."

"Look how tiny and cute it is! You can't deny that it's adorable."

"It's a rodent."

"But look at it!"

"I'm looking. It's still a rodent."

Tegan rolled her eyes as she continued to fawn over the mouse. Mariah, keeping her distance, said, "So tell me exactly why you lured it out?"

Tegan's only response was a flash of an impish smile.

* * *

The view was a lot different than any Tegan had experienced—mainly due to her close proximity to the ground—and getting used to the accelerated heartbeat had been a task. She could see every little speck of grime on the dirty concrete floor.

When she turned around, she found herself peering up at Mariah who towered over her like a gargantuan statue. She could also see herself, resting against the wall in deep meditation with her eyes closed, looking disheveled.

Tegan loved seeing through the eyes of the animal. The experience felt both right and surreal to her. As she got used to the mouse's movements, she was able to take over and guide the little creature to the door of the storage room. As she got nearer to the crack under the door, air circulating through the opening ruffled the mouse's fur. She pushed her snout through the crack and wriggled the rest of her body through. It stunned her how the creature was able to flatten itself enough to fit under the door.

When she popped out the other side of the chamber, she found the mouse's feet pattering on a hardwood floor that was even dirtier than the storage room. There were stale crumbs everywhere and she could smell many things, mainly diesel fuel and musty air. She leaned back onto her hind legs and looked around, nose twitching.

She was inside a cluttered office with a small pantry set against the far wall. It looked cavernous to her as a mouse, but she reckoned that at a human scale it would be a fairly small room. A coat-hook some distance away had a dirty work shirt hanging from it. Metal half-lockers were mounted against one wall of the office. Her nose told her that there was food somewhere in the vicinity.

Tegan could feel tremors beneath her feet and heard the sound of what she recognized as heavy drilling. She turned the mouse around so it faced forward and froze. A man in black attire sat at a long wooden table, reading a monster truck magazine. Long sideburns and a pompadour of flaming orange hair gave him the appearance of an intimidating Elvis Presley.

The drilling sound was coming from a door to her right. Tegan carefully guided the mouse forward, hoping that Elvis, engrossed in his magazine with one hand digging into a bowl of potato chips, wouldn't notice her. She could hear the loud crunching from his mouth as he shoved in a handful at a time.

Tegan made her way past the table and saw another door looming ahead. She skittered toward it but halted when she heard the crunching of chips stop. She turned and saw Elvis staring at her with eyes as wide as full moons. Then, with a Tarzan-like yell, he hurled his magazine at her.

The mouse squeaked in alarm and everything seemed to slow down. As the magazine neared, Tegan saw a fearsome machine on the front cover with the name *Devastator* emblazoned on its hood. Then the magazine hit her, sending the mouse skidding. Not needing further prompting, Tegan wiggled through the narrow crack under the door and fled to the other side.

She froze. A cacophony of sounds and smells hit her ears and nose all at once. The thundering decibel level initially frightened her, but she eventually got used to it. The mouse looked around, sniffing. Dust hanging in the air, and the sounds of construction equipment at work filled the mouse's ears, as did distant yelling. There were large mounds of dirt and rock, as well as tall piles of building materials. *Good hiding spots*, Tegan thought.

She scurried around, taking in as much as she could. As far as she could gather, she was inside some kind of a massive cavern. Buildings were being erected in several locations within the enormous space with bright lights illuminating each work site. Dozens of workers in orange coveralls and white hardhats were drilling, laying down pipes and digging trenches. The closer she looked at the men and women working, though, the clearer it became to her that most of them were merely teenagers around her age. She found it strange but had a more pressing objective to attend to.

She quickly darted under some wooden pallets when a worker carrying a wrench shuffled by. She stared after him. *What are they working on down here?*

Once the worker was out of sight, she whizzed around a mound of dirt and came face-to-face with a steel building. A sign on the door read 'DANGER! DO NOT ENTER!' She would have walked right past it if not for the intimidating scent traces around the structure, and the rippling snarl that emanated from within.

An ice-cold finger ran down her spine. There was something disturbingly familiar about the snarl. A chilling image began to surface in her mind but she shoved it down before it could come fully to light. She scampered away, mapping the area and committing the layout of the site to memory.

She traversed gravel roads used by huge trucks loaded with dirt or construction material. To her left she noticed a large tunnel that seemed to be the main conduit to the outside. It was busy with traffic flowing in and out of the cave.

Too much activity here, she decided. *We wouldn't even take one step in and we'd be caught.*

She had gone nearly half a mile eastward when she came upon two buildings. One was in mid-construction while the other was nearly complete. A sign mounted on the wall of the finished structure indicated that it was an aquaponic farm. She continued east until she stood across from a large blue building. The sign on it read 'Water Treatment & Storage'. Sitting still for a moment, she wondered, *Where's the water coming from?*

She hurried around the water treatment plant and noticed a smaller concrete edifice, about twenty feet wide and just as long, with the words 'Hydro-Power Generator' painted in green on a steel door. A large steel pipe led into it from a small, dimly lit tunnel thirty feet away. Curious, she followed the pipe into the tunnel and scurried up a gradual slope for several minutes before reaching a dead end as the pipe disappeared into a rock wall at the end of the tunnel.

Oh, come on! Don't tell me I've hit a dead end!

As she anxiously searched for an exit, her eyes fell upon a narrow opening in the tunnel's roof. She peered up into the vertical shaft and saw a metal ladder bolted to the wall. It was partially extended and a few rungs reached halfway down into the main tunnel. Her gaze followed the ladder into the opening, which ended in a flat circle some ways up.

It took Tegan a few moments to realize that she was looking up at some kind of a service access to the water supply tunnel. The mouse's body started to shake in excitement. *A way out! Yes!*

She turned around and hurried back down the tunnel. As she ran back toward the storage room, she wondered how she and Mariah would slip past all the workers and the traffic while crossing nearly a quarter mile of the cavern.

As long as there's a way, she told herself firmly, *we'll find the means to make it out.*

Mariah had been pacing back and forth, looking over at Tegan every once in a while only to see her friend still in a meditative state. It was agonizingly quiet inside the storage room, and lonely. Tegan may have been there in body, but not in mind. Heaving a sigh, Mariah continued her little restless march.

She heard a squeak a few minutes later and looked down. The pocket mouse was wriggling under the door. When it got its rear end through, it stopped moving for a couple of seconds. A deep intake of breath signaled that Tegan had ended her mindlink with the creature. The mouse scampered to hide behind one of the boxes in the room.

Mariah hurried over to Tegan and knelt beside her. "What was it? What did you see? Did you find a way out?"

Tegan looked up at her, blinking several times, then grinned. "Sure did. We're gonna have to plan this carefully."

"Why? Where are we?"

"I think we're underground in a cave. It's huge and there's a lot of construction going on . . . It's strange, though. Most of the workers seem to be teenagers."

"Huh?"

"It's weird, I know. I'm not sure what's going on."

Mariah rubbed her arms. "Forget that, then. How do we escape?"

Tegan pushed herself up and pressed her ear against the door for a few moments, a finger to her lips. Then, looking reassured, she went back to Mariah. "There's a guy out there," she said softly. "He's got an Elvis hairdo going. Guess he's supposed to be guarding us."

"So what do we do?" Mariah asked.

"Let me explain the layout first. On the other side of the door there's an office with a small pantry. There's a long table that Elvis is sitting at. Past that, there's another door that leads out to the construction area. There's a network of gravel roads and huge mounds of dirt, rocks, stacks of pipes and building material. We'll have to hide behind those while we make our way through."

"There's a main tunnel not far from here that I think leads to the surface, but we can't use it because there's heavy traffic. Unfortunately, we're gonna have to cross a road connected to that tunnel to escape."

Mariah was hopeful. "Escape?"

"Yeah. There's a smaller tunnel with a pipe that supplies water from the surface to this site. I found a manhole at the end of the tunnel—I'm hoping it'll lead us out."

Courage and anticipation surged through Mariah. "Perfect. This is good . . . really good. But how do we get past the guard?"

Tegan winked. "That's where you come in."

"Me?"

"I'm gonna yell out that I need to use the bathroom. Hopefully he buys that and responds. When he does, you need to be quick. There's a toaster on the pantry counter. Use it to knock him out."

"You know I'll need line of sight to the object to do that, right?"

"I know."

Mariah stretched out her arms in preparation. "Okay, let's do this."

"Gimme a second." Tegan went behind one of the boxes and bent down to pick something up.

When she returned, Mariah groaned. "Are you serious? You're gonna bring the mouse with us?"

"Of course I am. He was such a great help, and may still be later." Tegan held up the mouse proudly so it was just inches from Mariah's face. "And I think I'll name him Devastator."

The mouse looked from Mariah to Tegan, seeming for all the world as if it were smiling at them. Mariah, though far from fond of rodents, couldn't deny that the tiny, furry creature was indeed adorable.

As Tegan helped Mariah to her feet, Mariah asked, "Why Devastator?"

"Elvis tried to hit him earlier with his monster truck magazine. One of the trucks on the cover of that magazine was called *Devastator* and that was the last image I saw before scooting outta there."

Mariah lifted an eyebrow and smiled slightly, then nodded at Tegan. Tegan slid the mouse into her shirt pocket, then went up to the door and banged her fist against it. "Hey! I need to use the bathroom!"

When nothing happened, she tried again. "Come on, for heaven's sake! I really gotta use the bathroom! Can anyone hear me? *Hey!*"

The door buzzed and opened so suddenly that she jumped back in surprise. Mariah took stock of the man in the doorway. Tegan was right; he really did look like an orange-haired Elvis. *Those sideburns are a sin, though,* she thought with distaste.

Elvis glared at the girls. "What do you want?" He sounded Australian, much to the pair's surprise.

Tegan glared back at him. "Bathroom."

"You can hold it in."

"I really need to go."

"Too bad."

"But I really need to go!"

"Not my problem."

"Tony didn't say anything about denying us the bathroom," Tegan snapped.

While they argued, Mariah was trying to look past Elvis to locate the toaster. *This oaf needs to move his fat head,* she seethed.

"Fine," Elvis growled. He pointed at Mariah. "You. Stand back. Back of the room. Further. No, further. Back against the wall. There you go."

Mariah snorted but complied, and was glad she did. She could now see half of a microwave oven on a counter some ways behind Elvis. It wasn't going to be as easy as a toaster, but she'd have to make it work. Focusing, she saw the appliance begin to shake for a few seconds before its cord was yanked from an outlet as it careened through the air.

There was a dull but painful-sounding thud when the microwave hit the back of Elvis's head before falling to the floor with a loud clang. Elvis swayed as if drunk and then tipped forward into the storage room. Tegan quickly sidestepped as the man came crashing onto the concrete floor and lay there, out cold.

"I said toaster, but a microwave'll do too—ten points to Gryffindor! Let's go!" Tegan ran over Elvis, Mariah at her heels. The girls cautiously opened the same door the mouse had earlier slipped under and peeked out. Seeing that the coast was clear, they sprinted to the first rock mound. Mariah hoped Tegan remembered which way to go.

The clamor of drilling was the most noticeable sound. This end of the cavern was dimly lit, but Mariah could see a glow from work lights in isolated sections of the construction area. The girls had to take care not to trip over equipment as they cautiously avoided workers, dump trucks and Bobcats moving around the site.

They ran past a fair-sized steel building to their left. Something about it seemed vaguely familiar to Mariah. The 'Danger! Do Not Enter!' notice on the door gave her a chill and she was glad when they were past it.

They went from mound to mound swiftly, crouching so as not to be seen. "What are we gonna do if Tony's around here somewhere?" Mariah asked.

"I'm gonna take one of those pipes over there and hit him with it," Tegan replied flatly.

"Sound plan. I like it."

They snuck past a pile of two-by-four lumber but quickly had to dance back around it to avoid being seen by a young man in orange coveralls hauling a wheelbarrow filled with bricks along a path next to a dirt road. Once he had passed, they darted over the path to the next stack of lumber.

"This place is so huge," Mariah whispered. "Why? What are they doing down here?"

"Don't know, and right now, really don't care." Tegan peeked around the stack. "Okay, main road is up ahead. Looks clear, except for a couple of guys walking away from us. Remember, quick and stealthy."

The girls ran across the gravel road, eyes shifting rapidly between the main tunnel and a pair of workers ahead of them. They had just crossed the road when someone thundered in an Australian accent, "Stop those two!"

The workers ahead of the girls turned around. At first they appeared confused, but when the shout was repeated, they sprinted toward the escaping pair.

The girls spun around to make a break for it in the other direction but found their way blocked by Elvis. The man looked as angry as a bull. He had fresh scrapes on his nose and cheek, and a fresh bruise forming between his eyebrows.

Before either Mariah or Tegan could move again, they were grabbed from behind. They struggled indignantly but were shoved roughly to their knees.

"You two've got some guts," Elvis said, his fingers extending as if they were claws that he wanted to dig into the girls' faces. "You're a right pain in the arse, you are. Tony would have slain me if you'd escaped."

The pair kept their mouths firmly shut but gave the man loathing, spiteful looks.

"You're lucky I saw you runnin' off, else I would've been forced to use a more *drastic* method to find you." Elvis observed them disdainfully. "Who helped you? Who hit me? I know it was someone around here. Tell me who it was." When the girls didn't answer, he drew himself to his full height. "Fine, don't speak. We'll find the tosser, and we'll make sure to take very good care of them."

Mariah angled her gaze at the dirt.

"Did you really think you could get away so easily?" Elvis asked, sneering. "Where were you plannin' to go?"

Instinctively, both girls glanced at the main tunnel. Elvis saw them and guffawed. "You were hoping to go through there? I should've just left you to it—wouldn't have been able to go more than two steps before getting caught, you wouldn't."

Oaf, Mariah thought again.

Elvis gingerly touched the back of his head and flinched. "We left your hands untied, too—tried to be nice. Bloody ingrates. That privilege is gone now, that's for sure." He pointed at Tegan. "Bring that one here."

Mariah watched as Tegan was pulled to her feet and pushed toward Elvis, who had plastic zip ties ready. As he bound Tegan's hands behind her back, Tegan muttered something that Mariah didn't catch. Whatever she'd said, it riled Elvis. He lifted his arm and backhanded her across the face. Tegan gasped out a breath but said nothing more.

Mariah glimpsed around, frantically trying to find something they could use to escape.

"There you go," Elvis said, handing Tegan back to the worker that had been holding her. "There'll be no more trouble from you. Bring the other one."

Mariah was shoved from behind. She stumbled forward, then turned around and spat at the worker. The young man, caught off guard, punched her and sent her tumbling back onto a pile of tools. She fell hard onto her back and let out a groan before being hauled to her feet again.

Elvis moved quickly to tie her hands, then the girls were led to the storage room. He gave them a scowl. "I'll be posting another bloke out here to help guard you two, so no more dirty tricks." He slammed the door shut.

Tegan swung her foot at the door angrily before slumping against it. "That nearly worked," she fumed. "Now we're back in this stinkhole."

"We're not out of the game yet, Teegs," Mariah said quietly.

"What are you talking about?"

Mariah backed up against a wall and started to wriggle uncomfortably against it. Tegan gave an equally uncomfortable look and said, "Um, do you have an itch somewhere there, or . . .?"

"Oh, shut up." Mariah wriggled a little more before something green dropped onto the floor behind her. She grinned as she kicked it over to Tegan.

Tegan crouched down to take a look, then gawked. "How . . ."

"Box cutter," Mariah said victoriously. "We can use it to get free—somehow."

Tegan looked at her friend, awed. "Was that why you spat at the guy? So you'd get shoved onto that tool box?"

Mariah grinned again. "This black-and-blue's worth it, if we can make good use of the box cutter."

Nodding, Tegan used her foot to move the green tool behind the boxes. "We'll keep it hidden until we can work out another plan."

Then she stared at Mariah for the longest time without saying anything. Mariah stared back, beginning to feel self-conscious. "What?"

"Nothing. It's just . . . don't take this the wrong way, but you seem more ready to kick butt. Like, you're not letting these guys get to you. The Mariah I grew up with, she was spunky, sure, but—"

"Didn't like dealing with any kind of bad situations?"

Tegan nodded, looking apologetic. Mariah looked down, shuffling her feet as happiness bloomed inside her. "It's okay. I've started to realize it too. Kinda feels good to not let fear control me as much anymore." She pointed at Tegan with her chin. "How's Devastator doing, by the way?"

"Warming up to the little guy, aren't you?" Tegan looked down as the mouse poked its head out of her shirt pocket and stared up at her. "Looks like he stuck through the scuffle. Hey, buddy. Hope you're okay, we may need you again later."

"Second time has to be the charm," Mariah said. The small happiness gave way to a growing tightness in the pit of her stomach. "Or else I don't think we're gonna be able to pull off another attempt. They'll have tighter security and we'll never be able to get out of here. Unless the guys miraculously find us, we're gonna be here for who knows how long." She took in a breath. "Next one has to count, or we'll be out of silver bullets."

Jag had his face pressed up against the window of the air-conditioned Mustang as he and the others watched Kody walk around an abandoned warehouse. The afternoon heat was nearly unbearable, but Kody braved the temperature and was sniffing and listening intently as he scouted out the building.

They were running on no sleep, but their breakfast had restored some energy and they'd continued the search for the girls. It was a cumbersome task. Silver City was the largest municipality they'd had to scour so far and they weren't halfway through the area yet. Jag and Aari offered to search with Kody, but the boy insisted that he do it on his own so he could have complete focus. Currently, they were probing industrial buildings on the outskirts of the city.

Jag watched Kody for a minute more before turning to adjust the air conditioning vents. The phone in his pocket vibrated and he hurriedly pulled it out. When he saw the caller ID, he shushed Marshall and Aari, then answered the call. "Hey, Tristan."

Jag's brother let out a long groan. "Jag! I've been trying to call you but you never picked up the stupid phone!"

"You were worried?" Jag teased.

"Of course I was, you idiot! You're my kid brother! Besides, if something happened, Mom and Dad would be pretty ticked."

"Very touching. I didn't get any miscalls from you, though. But the signal's been spotty for a while, so that's probably it. What's up?"

"I, uh . . . it's about Gran and Gramps."

Jag slowly sat up straight. "What's happened?"

"You know the crop virus has been spreading, right? Did you watch the news last night?"

"No . . ."

"Concordia has been hit. I don't know if Gran and Gramps' crops made it through. I've been trying to call them, but no one's answering." When Jag didn't respond, he said, "Jag?"

"I—I'm here."

"Listen, I'm still trying to reach them. When I get ahold of them, I'll call you back and get you up to speed."

"Yeah . . . okay. Mom and Dad know about this, right?"

"No. They're on a plane to Switzerland right now."

"*Switzerland?* Why?"

"They were called in for an emergency meeting at the UN. They're flying in microbiology experts from all over."

"Oh." Jag stared down at his fingers.

"Try not to worry about Gran and Gramps just yet. Maybe it missed them."

Though Jag highly doubted that, he said, "Yeah, maybe. Hopefully."

"Alright. Talk to you soon. Say hi to the others for me, okay?"

"Sure. Take care, Tris."

"You too, kiddo."

Jag hung up and rubbed his hands over his face.

"What's up?" Aari asked.

"Tristan says hi."

"That's not it. You look like you've just lost a leg."

Jag turned around and quickly filled his friend in on his conversation with Tristan while Marshall listened attentively. Both Aari and the Sentry were grim. When Kody returned, head shaking, Jag brought him up to speed as well. Kody instantly adopted the same look Aari and Marshall wore.

Not eager to linger on the subject, Jag asked, "So no luck with the girls here, huh?"

Kody held his head in his hands. "No. I've lost count of how many houses and buildings I've checked, but it's in the hundreds for sure. There's still no sign of them."

"They've got to be around here somewhere," Jag said. "Aari's calculation *has* to be right."

Kody leaned back beside Aari. "Alright, big guy. Alright."

Jag faced the Sentry. "Marshall?"

The man nodded. "Let's keep going." He put the car into drive and headed back into town.

They searched a few more houses. At one property, Kody had been spotted and was consequently chased away by a plump, angry woman brandishing a spatula like a sword.

An hour later Marshall made a comment about needing to refuel and pulled into a gas station. While the Sentry was paying for the gas at the checkout counter, the boys zoomed through the aisles, picking up food and drinks. As they went to join Marshall at the counter, the muted television overhead caught Jag's interest, though his curiosity soon turned to dismay.

On screen was a live newscast of a riot outside a grocery store in Florida. Men and women were pushing each other to the ground and kicking one another while appearing to be shouting.

"What's going on over there?" Jag asked, appalled.

The clerk behind the counter glanced behind him as he passed Marshall his change. "Haven't you been following the news?"

"We haven't turned on the news since last evening," Jag said.

The clerk pulled a face. "Boy, oh boy. Well, that's the sixth riot they've shown today. They're saying that folks are getting real worried about a shortage of bread."

Kody opened a pack of Doritos. "Bread can do that to people?"

"It's a staple food, Kody," Aari said. "Wheat's the second or third major crop grown in the USA, *and* the global trade for it is bigger than every other crop combined."

"But people are rioting over bread?"

"It's not just bread, it's all wheat-based products. What would you do if you ran out of them and found empty shelves in your local grocery store?"

"I'd probably go look at another place."

"And what if that store had run out as well?"

Kody shrugged. "I'm sure I'd find them at the next store or two."

"Let's say you get lucky and you eventually find a store that has, maybe a few loaves of bread left. Then you notice that the price of a loaf is now ten bucks."

"That's nuts! Nobody would buy bread at that price."

Aari clicked his fingers. "Wrong. When supply runs out, demand goes through the roof and prices skyrocket. Only those with extra cash can get what they need, but there'll be countless others who won't be able to afford it. What are their options to feed their families then?"

Kody stopped munching on his Doritos. "No . . . no. This can't be happening here. This is America, man. It can't happen here."

"Dude, take a look." Aari nodded up at the television. "It already is. Seems like it's sporadic right now, but if they don't find a solution quick it's most likely gonna spread across the country."

As the Sentry and the boys got back into the car, Jag couldn't help but fear that the riots would only worsen. He had a feeling that they were staring at the tip of an iceberg that was set on a collision course with humanity.

Sitting on a chair with her hands tied behind her back was more than a little uncomfortable, but Tegan wasn't expecting kindness or luxury from her abductors. She eyed the conference room that she and Mariah were in. It seemed newly built and, except for paint and electrical fixtures, was nearly complete. A new hardwood floor was covered with thick plastic sheets, presumably to protect it from damage during construction. The girls were seated at the end of a long mahogany conference table, away from the door.

A few minutes prior, the pair had been hauled out of the storage area by Elvis and two other men and brought to this room. They'd then been left on their own but Tegan had a feeling that Elvis and the others weren't far from the other side of the door.

Two lamps hanging from the ceiling vaguely reminded Tegan of the interrogation rooms in old television shows. *Probably temporary until they install proper ceiling lights*, she supposed. The thought didn't ease her apprehension.

The door suddenly swung open. In walked a round-faced, bespectacled man no taller than five feet, with no eyebrows and greasy black hair plastered to his scalp. He held a mug of coffee in one hand and carried a large briefcase in the other. His dark trousers had prominent creases and his white poet shirt was tucked in loosely. The girls watched him as caged tigers would an unwelcome zookeeper.

The man completely ignored them as he set his briefcase down—the case being half his height—and pulled out three dark gray spheres the size of tennis balls. He clicked a button on one of them and rolled it to a corner of the room, then proceeded to do the same with the others. The spheres hummed faintly and hovered a few inches above the floor once they'd positioned themselves an equal distance from one another. Like the eyes of an alligator, shutters on the spheres opened, revealing curved green lenses.

A figure, over six feet in height, appeared. Mariah shrank closer to Tegan. *A hologram?* Tegan thought. Though the image was dark, as if the figure was standing in the shadows, the resolution was too perfect for her liking. It was as though the person was in the room with them. The figure was adorned in a knee-length black coat with a golden hood pulled low over the face.

The small man turned to the holographic image. He spoke strangely, as though there was sandpaper stuck in his vocal cords. "'Ello and good evening, Boss. I'm glad you could join us today."

The shadowed figure gave a short nod.

The man turned to Tegan and Mariah. He readjusted his glasses and flashed the girls a crooked-toothed smile. "I am Dr. Ian Nate. This will not take long, but only if you cooperate." He grabbed his briefcase and walked to the girls' end of the table. He sat across from them and rested his briefcase on the chair beside him. "Now," he said, "you must be wondering why you're 'ere. I'll keep it short and sweet. The memories you lost 'ave come back, and we are interested in those memories."

Tegan's legs trembled with fury and she cursed under her breath. "*Tony.*"

Dr. Nate didn't seem to hear her. "You can willingly give us those memories but, if not, we 'ave the means to *extract* them from you."

Blood drained from Tegan's face. Her eyes darted to the man's briefcase. *What else does he have in there?*

"So, dears, what 'appened after your plane crashed?" Dr. Nate asked, leaning over the table. His eyes bulged, frog-like, behind his glasses.

Tegan kept her mouth sealed, but Mariah spat, "We're not telling you anything. *You* tell us where we are and why we've been abducted."

"Eventually," Dr. Nate said, smiling again, "you will get your answers. But first, give me what I need."

Tegan lifted her chin. "No."

"As I mentioned, there are other ways for me to get the answers. But they will be excruciating."

Tegan glanced at the hologram. Though the eyes and most of the face weren't visible, she felt as though the figure's gaze was drilling holes into her mind.

She swallowed and turned back to Dr. Nate. "Fine, here's what we—I—recall. My friends and I were on our way to Dawson City in Yukon for our summer vacation. We got caught in a freak storm and our plane crashed. When we woke up, we found ourselves in a native village. We were nursed back to health. The next thing we remember, we were in some small hospital in Yukon."

The man slammed his fist down on the table with a bang. The girls jerked back, frightened.

"*You lie!*" Dr. Nate screamed, spittle flying from his mouth. He pulled his glasses off and his bulging eyes became bloodshot almost instantly. His face twisted into a hideous snarl that was as disturbing as it was terrifying.

"I'm not lying!" Tegan snapped, but her voice came out smaller than she'd have liked.

"Then you're not telling the 'ole truth! I want the *entire* story! We know you were involved in the attack on our mining operation! What were your roles? You were kept by the Elders for a reason—you were in Dema-Ki for many weeks!"

The room was dead silent save for the quiet humming of the holographic projectors. Tegan was flustered. *How does he know so much?*

"I will ask you one more time," Dr. Nate said. His eyes seemed to get redder by the minute. "What were you doing in the village?"

"I told you," Tegan answered. Again, her voice sounded too small for her liking. "We were being treated. The Elders and the villagers were kind enough to take care of us."

"Why were you involved in the attack, then?"

"They were like . . . like family. We wanted to help them because whatever you were doing in your operation, it made the people so sick they died. It was the least we could do to show our appreciation."

"What in 'ell made you think that five children could fend off dozens of men with weapons?"

The room went quiet again. Dr. Nate leaned farther over the table. Rancid breath reeked out of his mouth as he bellowed, "*Enough stalling! Tell me now!*"

He picked up his coffee mug and flung it across the table. The mug flew through the narrow gap between the girls and hit the wall behind them, shattering, its pieces spraying everywhere. Mariah shrieked as the pair flinched out of the way.

The holographic figure watched the proceedings, unfazed.

Tegan's heart was beating fast against her chest. *That could have hit us!* she screamed silently. *Fatheaded freak!*

Dr. Nate put his glasses back on, took a long, deep breath, and then smiled gently. He called for water and Elvis came through the door almost immediately with three bottles. Dr. Nate uncapped two and inserted drinking straws then placed them in front of the girls as Elvis left the room. Neither Tegan nor Mariah made a move.

Folding his hands over the table, Dr. Nate spoke in a calmer tone. "Something 'uge is 'appening, dears. The world is on the verge of collapse. The people in that valley, the Elders, know this, but they do not understand the extent of this cataclysm. Those of us 'ere—what we're doing, everything we're building—is for the future of mankind."

The girls listened guardedly while willing their heart rates to return to normal.

"You may think the people of Dema-Ki are nice—and you know, they probably are—but the problem lies in the fact that they are archaic in their solutions. We agree, them and us, that the world is in a very precarious situation. The solution *we* are creating is for the benefit of 'umanity and the Earth. We're out 'ere. We know what's going on. They are the ones who are hidden away from the rest of the world, so they are comparatively ignorant to what's happening. 'Owever, they are very capable of causing problems for us."

Tegan and Mariah continued to sit in silence, still snubbing the drinks in front of them.

Dr. Nate sighed. "This is why we need your 'elp. We need to know what the Elders are up to."

Ignoring the discomfort, Tegan leaned back against her chair. "How *do* you know about all this?"

"Your memories were lost," Dr. Nate said lightly, ignoring her question, "and then they returned. Why? The Elders are up to something and we need to figure out what."

Tegan and Mariah exchanged glances but neither spoke.

Dr. Nate took a sip from his bottle. "Look, there's a reason your memories were taken. And honestly speaking, would good people do such a thing, especially to kids? We're glad your memories 'ave returned. You can 'elp us figure out what they're doing."

"If you're the good guys," Tegan said, "then why abduct us? Why tie our hands behind our backs like this?"

"We weren't sure 'ow cooperative you'd be to strangers digging into your memories. We couldn't chance it. Plus, the information that you 'ave locked away is too important. We will get our answers one way or another. There's just too much at stake. This is bigger than either you or me."

The gears in Tegan's head kicked into overdrive. She had an idea, and hoped Mariah would catch on quickly

"Alright," she said. "I just need to stress that our memories aren't fully back yet. A little bit returns each day."

Dr. Nate's eyes lit up. "Of course, of course, but tell me everything you know." Taking a voice recorder out from his briefcase, he turned it on and waited attentively for Tegan to continue.

"Uh, well, as I said, we were taken in by the villagers after our crash. They tended to us and used some herbs and poultices for healing. Their village is . . . advanced, I guess you could say, seeing as they don't really have the tools that we do for construction and all that. They had these, like, greenhouses and stables and stuff. They had a beautiful temple as well, with a jar of crystals or something. Not sure what they were for, though. But all the villagers had one on them, so maybe it's a of passage thing. I dunno."

At that, Mariah caught on; the girls knew full well what the purpose of the crystals were. "Right," she jumped in. "And the villagers were really amazing. They had all these skills, like learning a language really quick, super hearing, telekinesis—pretty cool abilities."

"What else?" Dr. Nate prompted, checking the recorder to ensure it was capturing the conversation.

Tegan thought fast. Dr. Nate seemed to know a fair deal about Dema-Ki already, so sharing what she knew most likely wouldn't be an issue. But she feared that either she or Mariah would let slip more than what should be revealed. Still, they needed to give a little more to convince the short man that they weren't hiding anything. "There was also something about a prophecy, but I can't seem to remember it right now. Do you recall anything about a prophecy, 'Riah?"

Mariah puckered her face as she pretended to think. "No, not really. But I remember they taught us some of their self-defense techniques."

Tegan shrugged at Dr. Nate. "That's pretty much all we've got, I think. I'd tell you about the battle, but I don't remember very much about it." She looked up at the hologram again. It didn't seem to have moved at all since Dr. Nate had conjured it.

Logically, its presence shouldn't have bothered Tegan, but there was something unnerving about the way the figure stood immobile, staring at them from under its hood in complete silence. It was ludicrous, but Tegan could have sworn she felt cold air reaching toward them from the hologram's direction.

She faced Dr. Nate again. "I'm sorry, that's really all I remember right now."

Mariah nodded. "Me too."

Tegan braced herself as her next words left her mouth. "What we've noticed recently is that every time we get a good night's rest, we recover more memories the next day."

Dr. Nate looked over at the hologram and raised a brow. At least, that's what it looked like to Tegan; it was difficult to say as the man had no eyebrows to begin with.

The holographic figure remained statue-like for some moments. Then it dipped its head slightly.

Dr. Nate turned back to the girls. "Very well, we'll let you rest for tonight. But"—his words were sharp as a whip—"we will be back tomorrow to continue this. We are far from done." As he stood up, he added, "By the way, I 'ope you won't be foolish enough to try to escape again. If you do, the consequences will be severe."

Sausalito!

Of all the places they could have had dinner in the Bay Area, Adrian Black and Jerry Li had been invited to dine at The Spinnaker in Sausalito by Luigi Dattalo, the head of Phoenix Corporation's Quest Defense division. Dr. Albert Bertram, the company's Chief Scientific Officer, was supposed to join them but had asked for a rain check at the last minute to take care of private matters.

Dattalo held the door open for the other two and a hostess escorted them to their table. A well-dressed, olive-skinned man in his early forties, Dattalo was the son of Italian immigrants. Despite his heritage, he harbored none of the stereotypical tendencies except for his taste in fashion. Life as the head of Quest Defense, however, often deprived him the opportunity to flaunt his extravagant sartorial preferences.

The three men took their seats by the large windows and ordered a round of drinks. "Thank you, gentlemen, for dragging me out to this artsy-fartsy town," Black grumbled the moment their server had left.

"Hey," Dattalo said defensively, "it takes an open-minded person to be appreciative of the arts."

"Maybe so, but if your mind is too wide open, take care that what's in your head doesn't spill out."

The men ordered their meals, then leaned back to take in the view. Perched on wooden stilts over the water, the cozy restaurant provided a great view of the bay. Though it was dark outside, they could just make out Alcatraz Island in the distance against the backdrop of San Francisco's skyline.

Black and Li had stayed late at the office to go through some details regarding a couple of projects and, as a result both were now starving. Dattalo had called them and asked to meet over dinner, to which they'd readily agreed. The head of Quest Defense had been out of state for a while and needed to speak with them, though regarding what, neither Black nor Li knew.

The men exchanged small talk as they waited for their meals to arrive. Black took a sip from his drink. "It's good to see you again, Luigi. You're gone for months at a time now. It's so hard to catch a meal or drink with you once in a while."

Dattalo smiled and scratched his dark stubble. "That's a laugh and a half—even when I *was* here we barely had any downtime to enjoy something like this. But that's what the job requires." He lowered his voice. "Speaking of which, how are the Arcane Ventures coming along?"

"Fairly well," Black replied. "It's good to have all the projects running smoothly. Helps keep the stress level down, especially with what we have at stake."

He thought he saw Dattalo suppress an uncomfortable look, but it was gone so quickly that the notion left him. "The rate at which our plans are progressing gives me confidence," he added, "but more importantly it means the Boss is assured and might be more willing to extend a hand with regards to favors that we have requested."

Li nodded. "I got a confirmation email from the Boss a day ago assuring me that my parents in Hong Kong will be looked after once the next phases of the plan are in play."

Both Black and Dattalo lit up. "That's great news!" Dattalo exclaimed.

"Sure is." Li gulped down his drink. "My ex can freeze in the Arctic for all I care, though; she and that actor boyfriend that she dumped me for. If she hadn't left me, I could have made arrangements for her to be safe as well."

Dattalo chuckled. "Ah, women. Can't live with 'em, can't live without 'em."

Li grumbled as he ordered another drink for himself, then gave Black a grin that was as crooked as his candycane-striped bowtie. "You can live without 'em though, can't you, Adrian? This man is stuck in the office for ten to twelve hours a day. He hasn't got the time for socializing. Good thing you called, Luigi, or else he'd still be pounding away at his desk with me slaving alongside."

"I beg your pardon," Black said, eyeing them both sternly. "I'll have you know that I'm in a very committed relationship. At times she is incredibly demanding, but I love her nonetheless." After a theatrical pause, he said, "I am married to my job, gentlemen."

That earned a roar of laughter from his companions. "You nearly had me there for a second," Li said, taking off his thick-rimmed glasses to wipe them.

Black smiled, then looked back out the window. "I suspect that the transition may not be too hard for me as it may be for you guys, mainly because I have no family to deal with."

"Parents? Siblings?" Dattalo asked.

"Mom and Dad have both passed, and I'm the only kid they had." Black was contemplative. "I have to admit, the Boss gave me a reason to look past what I'm doing as just a job. Especially with the changes that will be happening soon, it really does feel as if I'm part of a family. Sure, a family with some members that maybe we can't stand, but a family nonetheless. And we're working together to create a better, brighter future. I couldn't be more blessed."

"Amen," Dattalo murmured.

"I think that should have been a toast," Li said wistfully.

Their meals arrived a few minutes later, much to Black and Li's elation. The men ate ravenously and continued chatting about trivial matters. Once they had finished their dinner, they sat back and enjoyed their drinks.

"So, Luigi," Black said, looking over at Dattalo, "how is the REAPR project doing?"

"The fenixium we mined last year in Canada and Siberia is working like a charm," Dattalo answered. "The components that our facility in Redding is producing are top-notch."

Li fixed his glasses higher up on his nose. "Glad to hear that. I hope there haven't been any more security breaches like the one a few months ago with the delivery guy. That was a horrible slip."

"Of course not. And you know we took care of that situation. The facility's guards are good at handling any problem thrown their way." Dattalo tapped his glass against his lips, eyes crinkling around the corners as he smiled—or forced a smile, rather, as that was what it seemed like to Black.

He studied Dattalo closely. "Is that all there is to report, Luigi?"

The Italian's glass-to-lip tapping stopped, then he slowly lowered his drink to the table. "Everything is running pretty much without a hitch. There are some limitations. As you know, the REAPRs can only operate at night due to the molecular structure of the nano-processors. That is, of course, something we have known and factored into the plan, as well as the fact that there are a few units lost each night. Negligible, really. But . . ." He looked from Black to Li, then back again. "But there's something else. After going through some numbers last evening and checking and re-checking them, I have come to the conclusion that we will need more resources for the global distribution of the REAPR pods."

"I thought that was all in place." Li said, fingers steepled over the table.

"It is, it is. It's nothing terrible, really. But we've noticed that the performance of some of the pods deployed in Asia is not as projected."

Black's grip on his glass tightened slightly. "Why?"

"That's what we're still trying to figure out. My engineers are working around the clock as we speak to get to the bottom of it. Now, what I recommend is increasing the number of pods in the Asian sector to make up for this deficit."

"What kind of increase?" Li asked, bringing his beverage to his mouth.

"Twenty percent."

Li nearly spat out his drink. "*Twenty!* Did you say twenty?"

Dattalo looked around self-consciously as people from other tables glanced over, frowning. "Yes, Jerry."

Black could tell that Li was doing everything in his power to calm down as the shorter man said, "Do you know how much that would *cost* us, Luigi?"

"I know, I know. That's why I'd really appreciate it if you could help me convince the Boss. You're the finance guy. You could maybe pull some numbers or something."

"Nothing gets past the Boss," Li fumed. "Playing with the numbers would likely cost me more than just my job!"

"Bring it back in, Jerry," Black warned, though he was upset as well. "Luigi, is there no other alternative? Can't we pull some pods from neighboring regions—maybe the ones from Russia?"

Dattalo had picked up his drink and resumed his glass-to-lip tapping. "I thought about that too, but as it is we have very, very few pods deployed in Russia. And you know why—it has to be in line with our strategy for the expected eventual response from the Chinese and Indian governments when the situation gets out of control with their populaces."

Black let out a long, conceding breath. "Alright. I'll speak with the Boss, see if we can't deploy more pods into the region. But please, you better make sure that there are no more surprises. I know I keep saying this, but there's a lot at stake here. This REAPR project needs to run like clockwork for the other phases to kick in."

Dattalo's tense demeanor visibly deflated as Black spoke. "Thank you, Adrian."

"What about the pods here in North America? How are they doing?"

The Italian let out a belch, then smiled his first truly relaxed smile of the night. "They're working just fine, don't worry. The news channels testify to that. Everything's on track here."

Black glanced out into the dark night, eyes raised to the heavens. "Good," he murmured. "At least that will give the Boss something to be pleased about."

Stars glittered brightly against the dark canvas of the cloudless sky, as if the cosmos was putting on a brilliant show for no one to see. The moonless night made constellations easy to trace with the naked eye as they twinkled and danced, reaching to the horizon where sky fused with earth.

Farmland stretched in every direction. The country air was crisp and the place was quiet except for a neigh or two from a horse in a stable somewhere. Farm folk were fast asleep in their beds, and, had anyone been awake to look, their clocks would read just past midnight.

If anyone *was* awake and stepped outside to look up at the serene sky, they would see nothing but the heavens winking down at them. Were they to look closer at a certain spot to the west, however, they might have noticed some stars vanishing briefly before reappearing, only to have other stars along a certain path disappear as well.

What no human eye would have been able to see was the entity that occulted the stars in the sky: an invisible shroud in the shape of a large bird of prey that descended slowly to a lower altitude. Closer and closer it glided downward, its sixty-foot wingspan partially obscuring the nightscape.

As the entity known as a REAPR—a Remote Autonomous Predator—approached the farmland, it would disintegrate into billions of particles, each no bigger than a red blood cell. The particles would disperse across entire wheat fields, descending onto the plants and devouring their way through the heads, destroying the harvestable part of the crops and leaving them barren, much like a tree without fruit.

Once they had ruined one stalk, the particles would move on to another and another as programmed, until they had devastated acres upon acres of crops. Then, well before sunrise, they would regroup and merge once again into the bird-shaped form and take flight, disappearing before the first rays peeked from the horizon.

The REAPR and its counterparts in fields across the country would return night after night like shadows of death, laying to waste wide swaths of farmland, until its purpose was achieved.

Devastator the pocket mouse sat in a corner of the office pantry, observing two men guarding the storage room where the girls were being held. One was Elvis—who sat on a chair right beside the door to the girls' room—and the other was a long-faced man with a potato for a nose, and eyes that were too close together.

Elvis and Potato Nose, Tegan thought, amused, as she observed the pair through her mindlink with the mouse. *What next? Dumbo and Clown Face?*

The wall-mounted clock in the office read two a.m. Tegan was out and about scouting for a way to get past the storage room door. Calling one of the guards over again wasn't going to work this time, that was for certain.

"Hey," Elvis suddenly called, startling Tegan. "Get me a cup of coffee, would you?"

Potato Nose sighed and ambled toward the counter where the appliances were. He checked the coffee machine, then the cupboards overhead. "Uh, I think we're outta coffee."

Elvis groaned. "Bloody—okay, hold on." He removed a key ring from his pocket and went through each key, muttering to himself. "First aid room, locker, storage room . . ."

Devastator's ears perked and Tegan noticed the keycard attached to the small silver hoop.

Elvis slid a key loose and held it up, tossing the ring with the remaining keys and keycard onto the small side table next to him. "Here, take this and go get some coffee."

Potato Nose gave him a wary look. "And where am I getting said coffee from?"

Elvis sniggered. "The main office."

"Are you joking? We're not allowed up at the mining site! I'm not going out there!"

"'Course you are. Come on, then." Elvis wiggled the key between his fingers.

"It's a ten-minute drive there and another ten minutes back," Potato Nose growled. "I'm not going. If you want your coffee so bad, you can go and get it yourself."

Tegan stared closely at Potato Nose. His eyes seemed to droop a little, and he continued to amble around like a sloth. *He's too lazy to go out*, Tegan thought. *What a bum.*

Elvis scowled at the other man. "I don't ask you to do much. Just wanted some coffee . . ." He got up and walked past Potato Nose, roughly hitting shoulders with him. Potato Nose wisely ignored that and walked over to take Elvis's seat, picking up the magazine the other man had been reading.

"Stay alert," Elvis warned him. "I know you pulled a double-shift for Tony yesterday but we still haven't caught the girls' accomplice. Whoever it is may come back to help again."

Potato Nose snorted. "Who'd want to help them?"

"How am I supposed to know? Either way, someone did, so be on your toes." Elvis absently touched the ping pong ball-sized lump at the back of his head as he checked the car key holder by the door that led to the cavern.

"Take one of the Hummers," Potato Nose said, opening up the magazine. "The truck's got some problems with the brakes."

"Cheers." With that, Elvis was gone.

Tegan watched the remaining man in the room from her spot under the pantry cabinet. He yawned loudly as he thumbed through the magazine, eyes drooping further. Tegan held her breath as he started to nod off. She took a few steps forward but froze when Potato Nose jerked and his eyes snapped open. He shook his head vigorously as if to keep himself awake, then got up and paced around.

"I hope that moron gets back with the coffee soon," he muttered.

What I'm hoping for is that you plunk your butt back down on that chair and fall asleep, Tegan grumbled.

She was in luck, for a minute later he settled down on the chair again, slumping deeply. He scooped up the magazine and opened it but Tegan could see he wasn't even reading. His eyelids slid low and his head started nodding slightly. With high hopes, Tegan watched him. Potato Nose tried for another minute or two to keep himself awake but eventually his head lolled forward until his chin rested on his chest.

Tegan waited for a bit, not daring to breathe, but the moment she heard the first snore, she tore out as fast as Devastator's little legs would allow. Upon reaching the coffee table where the key ring was laid, she stared up and contemplated how she'd reach the tabletop.

I wonder if...

The mouse bunched its hind legs and leapt up a good foot before digging its tiny claws into the wooden table leg and scurrying up the rest of the way. Tegan was exhilarated that her idea worked.

Loud snoring diverted her attention and she stared up at Potato Nose. A full-grown person was *huge!* It disconcerted her how everything that seemed normal to her as a human was grossly mammoth-like from a mouse's perspective.

Wow, what a honker, she thought as she took a closer look at the guard's nose, then shook herself. *Don't have time to waste!*

The mouse scampered over the table and grabbed the key ring in its small jaws. Surprisingly, it wasn't too heavy for the little creature. Tegan gazed at the card scanner by the storage room door.

How do I get it there without making any noise?

Tegan glanced at Potato Nose. Hoping that his snoring was noisy enough to cover any other sound, she pushed the keys toward the end of the table. They jangled against each other—louder than she had expected.

Potato Nose grunted and shifted in his chair. Tegan looked over, heart pounding. The man was still fast asleep. Not risking another moment, she grabbed the keycard between her teeth, braced herself, then launched off the table. She flew for a good two seconds, soaring high above the ground toward the scanner, though with the mouse's size it felt more like an eternity.

Then her flight ended abruptly as she smacked against the wall. As she plummeted to the floor, she was panic-stricken. *I missed the scanner!*

But no, the door quietly buzzed as she landed on her rump. So great was her excitement that the mouse let out a squeak. Potato Nose grunted again but didn't awaken. Tegan severed her connection with Devastator in the next heartbeat.

When she opened her eyes, she was startled by Mariah standing nearby, staring intently at her. "The door's unlocked, but I don't know for how long!" she whispered.

Mariah looked horrified. "What?"

"Shh! Just do what I do!" Tegan stood up and leaned forward so her tied wrists were past her bottom. She put one leg back through her arms, then the other. She straightened, her bound hands now in front of her.

Mariah followed her example. "Where'd you learn that?"

"Movies. You can actually pick up a thing or two. Get the box cutter."

Mariah retrieved the tool and cut Tegan loose before being freed herself. Tegan hurried to the door and, hoping that they weren't too late, pushed on it. It opened. The girls silently stepped out, sharing amazed glances as they tiptoed past Potato Nose.

They paused at the main entrance to gather themselves and took a few breaths to get rid of their jitters. Then, with a firm nod, Tegan tugged on the door and stepped out into the cavern.

The girls headed out, Mariah making sure to close the door behind them. Tegan paused to take Devastator out of her pocket and set him on the ground. The mouse twitched his nose up at her as if wondering what was going on. She gave him a small pat between his ears. "Thank you for your assistance," she whispered. "Stay safe, little buddy."

Devastator watched as Tegan took the lead and the girls ran from mound to mound. Breaths quick and short, they hurried around the steel building they'd seen earlier, giving it as wide a berth as possible. But even at this distance they could still hear a low, guttural growl.

"Teegs," Mariah whimpered, "why does that sound so familiar?"

Tegan didn't respond.

The growl sounded again, and Mariah reached out to grab Tegan's shoulder. "Oh, my God . . . is that—"

Tegan shushed her. "Don't even think about it! Stay focused on getting out of here."

Mariah swallowed and followed her friend as she led the way to the first of the three dirt roads they had to cross. They passed it without a problem but as soon as they reached the second, they heard a vehicle approaching from the main tunnel. They avoided detection by circling back around a large heap of dirt and rocks until the truck was out of sight. Leaning against the mound, they took a moment to catch their breaths.

The last road was about a hundred feet away from them, but fifty feet to their right several workers in orange coveralls were clustered around some kind of drilling machine. Two large work lights illuminated the area and their glow spilled in the girls' direction.

Tegan puffed her cheeks as they took stock of their situation. "Oh, boy."

"It doesn't look like the light reaches all the way here," Mariah said. "I think we may be in the clear."

"You wanna chance it?"

"Elvis will be back any minute. I'd like to be as far away from here as possible."

Tegan darted out, bent double with Mariah on her heels. It took less than ten seconds to reach a stack of wooden pallets, but it may as well have been an eternity. The girls knelt behind the pallets to catch their breaths again.

Tegan peeked across the dirt road. "There's an excavator on the other side," she informed Mariah, "but no one's in it."

Mariah gave Tegan a small but urgent push. The girls tore over the last dirt road and slid in front of the green excavator. "So far so good," Tegan whispered.

"Uh, might want to rethink that," Mariah gasped, peeping around the machine. "Dude headed this way, looks like the driver of this thing!"

"Shoot Follow me!"

The girls sidestepped around the excavator so they were on its right side when the worker was on its left. As soon as the driver was seated in the cab, they made a break for a stack of bricks a few feet away and dodged behind it. They peered around quickly, making sure they hadn't been spotted. No one else was around, and the man in the excavator was driving away.

Tegan wheezed. "Nearly there, 'Riah."

Mariah barely heard her. She pointed at a long, glassy teal building ahead of them. "What's that?"

Tegan took a look at the partially constructed edifice. "I saw a sign there earlier. It's an aquaponic facility or something."

To the girls' left was a small gray building with a sign on the door that read 'Water Treatment & Storage'. Tegan grinned.

"The power plant must be nearby, which means our escape tunnel isn't far either," she said.

"Um . . ." Mariah was looking over the bricks, toward the main tunnel. "Hate to be the bearer of bad news, Teegs, but I think Elvis is back in the building."

"What?!"

"I just saw an orange Hummer come out of the tunnel."

"For crying out loud—let's go, then!"

They sprang up and sprinted around the concrete building. "There," Tegan called out pointing ahead. "The hydro turbine!"

Just then, two young men emerged from the turbine building and paused to take a break. One of the workers removed his hardhat to reveal a head full of bright silver hair. The girls swept down, out of view.

"Move already!" Tegan growled. "We're wasting time!"

They waited impatiently until the workers moved away from the structure. Tegan took hold of Mariah's wrist. "Come on."

Just as she spoke, an amplified voice boomed through the cavern over the construction noise, raucous and angry. "You're in trouble now, you are!"

The girls stopped short and looked behind them. They saw no one, but they knew who the voice belonged to.

"*Elvis*," Mariah mouthed, panic shooting up her sides.

A terrible roar suddenly reverberated through the site. Goose bumps appeared all over Mariah's skin. Beside her, Tegan had lost all the color in her face.

"It *is* them," Mariah croaked. "Teegs, we need to go! We need to go! *Now!*"

Tegan would have remained rooted to the spot if her friend hadn't given her a forceful shove. They turned around and came face-to-face with the silver-haired worker they'd seen earlier. He appeared to be of Asian descent, maybe a year or two older than them. The girls were deadlocked, trapped between two enemies.

The worker met both their gazes. Then, with the tiniest and most earnest of smiles, he put a finger to his lips and stepped aside to let them pass. Mariah bolted ahead, hauling Tegan with her. Tegan looked behind her and watched the worker continue on his way as if nothing had happened.

The girls ran around the building that housed the hydroelectric power plant and followed the steel pipe that led into the small tunnel. Behind them, the sound of nasty snarling grew closer. There was definitely more than one of the creatures following the girls.

"You can't escape them!" Elvis's amplified voice boomed. "The Marauders will tear you limb from limb! Stop now and I'll pull them back!"

As terrified as the girls were, they weren't about to negotiate with him. Tegan ushered Mariah into the tunnel. "Right here! Go, go, go!"

The dark tunnel was barely five feet high and four feet wide, with the large pipe taking up most of the space. It was cooler and damper inside as well.

"You gotta move faster, 'Riah!" Tegan yelled as the sound of the beasts grew closer.

"I'm trying!" Mariah yelled back. "It's getting steeper! And muddier!"

They climbed the steep incline in a frenzy but kept slipping and falling in the mud. Now covered in filth, they dug their fingers into the ground and clawed upward. Another roar sounded. This time it filled up the entire tunnel.

"They're inside!" Tegan shrieked. "*Move!*"

They made it to the ladder mounted on the wall of the vertical shaft overhead. Mariah, glad that the ground had leveled off, leapt to catch bottom rung of the ladder and scuttled up, Tegan following close behind. The harsh breathing of the beasts echoed toward them.

They were at the top of the twenty-foot shaft, with Mariah trying to push open the manhole cover, when a chilling growl came from below them. Slowly looking down, she found a sight that made her heart jump to her throat. She tried to scream but horror stifled her voice.

Glaring up at her from the bottom of the ladder were two massive black-furred creatures with muscular frames—the Marauders. A third beast joined them, coming from behind. Their demonic, sulfur-colored eyes reflected a manic thirst for murder from under heavy brows, and their elongated jaws gnashed, revealing curved, gleaming fangs over three inches long.

Mariah had seen these creatures before—all five of the friends had, at the battle atop the Ayen'et, and more recently, in their nightmares. Below her, Tegan whimpered. "Mariah, get that cover open . . ."

"I'm trying, but the stupid thing's stuck!" she cried. "Mind-link with those monsters and send them away from us!"

"You know I can't! They're programmed deeply to kill!" Tegan shouldered past her, taking up half of the ladder while Mariah held onto the other half. Together, they pushed at the heavy steel cover with all their might, doing their best to ignore the monsters that leapt at them but kept sliding down the rungs.

"I—felt—it—move," Tegan puffed. Sure enough, when the girls pushed a little more, the heavy cover popped open, showering them with dirt and dust. They ignored it and shoved the cover away. Mariah scrambled out first into the open air. She reached down to pull Tegan up but at that moment, one of the Marauders managed to get a grip halfway up the ladder. It leapt and grazed one of its paws along the back of Tegan's calf, its blade-like claws slicing through her jeans. Tegan cried and twisted away before being pulled up by Mariah.

Together, the girls dragged the cover back to close the manhole just as the beast's jaws came snapping through. A loud *clang* resonated around them as the cover fell into place. Tegan stepped back, then winced and looked down at her leg through the torn jeans. Blood seeped from a single slash.

Mariah wiped the back of her dirty hands against her face. "Are you okay, Teegs?"

"I'll be fine, don't worry. It's not too deep."

"I'm shaking," Mariah confessed. "I'm shaking and I can't stop."

Tegan reached out and hugged her. Mariah wrapped her arms tightly around her friend in return, realizing the other girl was shaking too, and they drew on each other's remaining strength and courage.

"Why do you think that worker let us go?" Mariah whispered.

"I don't know," Tegan murmured. "But thank God he did. Come on."

The two of them took in their surroundings. They were facing a long, oval-shaped lake that looked manmade. Above them, the sky was filled with stars except for a few scattered clouds. Neither girl bothered about it as they ran around the body of water, but slowed when they reached a chain-link fence that stretched from the edge of the lake to a gigantic waste-rock dump, blocking their path.

All at once, there was a chaotic outburst. Deep roars and barks erupted, but from where they couldn't tell. There was frantic honking of vehicles and shouts, and someone yelled, "Get out of the way! The Marauders—they're loose!"

Without even glancing at each other, Tegan and Mariah ran toward the fence and scaled it just as the beasts came charging around the tumbled pile of rocks, hackles raised. They caught sight of the fleeing girls and gave chase, their dreadful brays splitting the night.

The girls clambered up the fence and jumped down onto the other side. "This way!" Tegan shouted, running toward a group of massive wheeled machines.

"Teegs, what are you doing?" Mariah cried.

"Getting us a ride out of here!"

"On *that?*"

"Go big or go home! There's nothing else here anyway!"

It wasn't until they'd come to a halt in front of the machine that Tegan realized just how truly colossal it was. The yellow Caterpillar mining truck was the height of a two-story building and had ladders attached to its front and side. She jumped onto one of the ladders and led the way up, leaving Mariah with no choice but to follow. Once they'd climbed onto the machine's railed platform, Tegan ran toward the crew cab to test the door.

"It's open!" she yelled as she slid into the driver's seat. "Get in!"

"The keys?" Mariah yelled back, taking shotgun.

"Right here in the ignition, thank goodness!"

"They just leave it *in* the cab?"

"This must be a secure site. Buckle up!"

Mariah clicked in, nearly hyperventilating. "What are you doing? You can drive a car, not one of these! Oh, jeez, we're toast! We're like twenty feet off the ground!"

"Look, look! It's all automatic! I can do this!" Tegan turned the key and a deep rumble came from the bowels of the giant vehicle, vibrating through the crew cab.

The beasts that were closing in on their position balked, taken aback by the roar of this new entity. With the precious few extra seconds, Tegan said a quick prayer, put the machine into drive, and stepped on the gas pedal.

A radio crackled, making both of them jump. Then Elvis' voice came on: *"Elias, the two girls are driving one of the bloody monsters!"*

Another man's voice came over the radio. *"What are you talking about? I don't see a thing on any of my monit—WHAT THE HELL?"*

"Stop them, Elias!"

The girls listened, wide-eyed, as the machine surged forward. Tegan was surprised at how responsive the massive truck was. She had fantastic visibility of everything around her as she skirted a gigantic open pit in the middle of the mining site. A huge sign dug into the ground read: 'QMI—Restricted Area'.

They heard metallic *thunks* at the back of the truck. Mariah glanced at her side mirror as more reports sounded. "They're shooting at us!"

Tegan checked her side mirror as well. "Ohmigosh, I did *not* sign up for this!"

A flash of bright lights caught her attention and she turned away from the mirror to eye the newcomer. She gasped.

Mariah leaned forward to look. "Agh!"

A gray pickup was hurtling toward them from their left. Kicking up a storm of dust, its driver was obviously intent on cutting off their escape route. The smaller vehicle missed them narrowly and came to a stop about fifty feet in front of the machine, not giving Tegan enough time to swerve or stop. The men in the pickup must have realized that they had cut in too close. They launched themselves out of the vehicle like rockets just as the thirteen-foot-high tires of the mining truck rolled over the gray pickup, flattening it without slowing. Tegan and Mariah both let out screams when they heard the vehicle crunch under their tires.

Tegan felt ill. *We could have killed those guys!*

About half a mile ahead, she saw floodlights on tall poles marking the main entrance to the mine site. A large security post stood in the middle with boom gates on either side.

No problem for this thing, she thought.

When she glanced into her side mirror, though, she realized they weren't out of trouble yet. An orange Hummer was barreling toward them. Elvis leaned out of the passenger's window with a shotgun in hand.

To make matters worse, she saw the Marauders tearing after the mining truck, closing the distance with each ten-foot bound. Mariah saw them coming, too, and let out a moan that quickly morphed into another scream.

The leading Marauder launched off the ground, then vanished from Tegan's sight. "Where did it go?" she hollered. "I can't see it!"

"That's not good," Mariah muttered. "It's on the truck!"

"How? That's a good twenty feet off the ground!"

The Marauder's head popped over the top edge of the front windshield. The girls screeched. It stared at them in a demented fervor, upside-down, then tried to descend onto the platform next to the crew cab.

Tegan turned the wheel sharply, hoping to fling the creature off the truck. It worked—somewhat. The beast was thrown off balance but instead of falling off the machine, it bounced and crashed against the railing. Its long, razor-like claws caught a bar and it hung precariously on the side of the truck. The girls watched, speechless. The angry Marauder let out a deep roar that rose above the noise of the truck's engine.

The radio crackled and the man, Elias, spoke. *"Alright, let's see them go through* this."

Tegan goggled when she saw what he meant. A quarter of a mile ahead of them, a long white tanker truck had pulled in front of the guard post, blocking both boom gates. On its side, painted in large red letters, was a single word: FUEL.

"Tegan!" Mariah yelped.

"I see it!"

The Marauder was still hanging onto the railing and just when it seemed to be slipping off, it hooked its other paws in place. Bunching its hindquarters, it pulled itself onto the platform and approached the girls in the cab. Its long snout was wrinkled in a snarl and saliva dripped from its jaws. Fangs bared, it slammed against Tegan's door again and again. The girls yelled curses as the safety glass began to crack.

Through the frenzy, Tegan saw that the exit was fast approaching. A giant man jumped out of the fuel truck. Tegan had a brief flash of a memory. Horrified, she recalled where she'd last seen that hulking shape. *He's supposed to be dead!*

"Hang on!" she said to Mariah. "I'm gonna try something!"

She gave the steering wheel a sudden turn to the left. The Marauder, its claws sheathed, lost traction and found itself thrown to the far end of the platform. It smashed into the railing, warping the metal, its back end falling halfway through the barriers.

Tegan yelled at Mariah to brace for impact. The big man realized what the girl was up to and he dove out of the way. The mammoth machine hit the smaller fuel truck, tearing open the body of the tanker, which burst into a tower of flames.

The Marauder that had been hanging precariously on the railing fell away burning and writhing, letting out an agonized screech.

Nearly blinded by the inferno, Tegan pointed the vehicle forward as she kept the gas pedal floored. The mining truck bulldozed past the fuel tanker, pushing the crushed vehicle aside, then continued on, obliterating the guard-house and the boom gates and spreading the blazing fuel onto the remains.

Her pulse rocketing, she steered the giant truck through the exit and out of the mining site. There was more gunfire but the vehicle picked up speed on the wide dirt road as it made its way downhill, putting more distance between the girls and their abductors by the second.

"We're out!" Mariah screamed, arms raised above her head victoriously. "We actually got out! I can't believe your harebrained plan worked!"

"Me neither!" Tegan screamed back, laughing. "Not your run-of-the-mill damsels in distress, huh?" She held up her hand and Mariah high-fived her.

Mariah powered down her window and stuck her head out of the cab. "Hey, stinkheads! How'd you like that, you—"

Whatever further words came out of her mouth were drowned out by Tegan exultantly hitting the truck's deafening air horn.

We're out!

"I don't recall being this dirty in my life," Mariah commented as she looked down and took stock of her mud-caked self.

Tegan giggled. "Me neither."

Mariah leaned back, willing her heart to return to its normal rate as Tegan drove along the dirt road. The path, flanked by tall pine trees, was wide enough for two mining trucks to pass side-by-side.

"What now?" she asked. "We've got no phone to call anyone, since those jerks apparently took them."

"We find the nearest payphone and call the guys," Tegan replied simply, eyes glued on the road.

Mariah frowned. "Shouldn't we call the cops?"

"Yes, right after we call the guys. We need to know if they're alright."

Mariah nodded and glanced at the mirror mounted on the far side of the vehicle to ensure that they weren't being followed.

"We clear?" Tegan asked.

"Looks like it. The fire should hold them for a while."

"Good, good."

Mariah rolled her shoulders and stretched out her feet. "I'm pretty sure we gave them a big shock back there."

Tegan smiled slightly. "There's no better way to leave that rotten hole than to make them wish they'd never taken us in the first place." Then, darkly, she added, "I hope Tony comes back to this mess and sees what a failure his plan was. I hope his boss crushes him like the roach he is."

"That would be nice," Mariah muttered as she peeled some dried mud from her arm. She glanced back at the mirror, then slowly sat up straight. "Oh, no."

A pair of headlights flashed to life some distance behind them, rapidly growing bigger. As Mariah watched, a second pair of headlights appeared from behind the first.

Tegan must have stolen a quick look at her own mirror, because an oath escaped her mouth. "This can't be happening! I thought they'd given up!"

Two loud thumps startled them. Adrenaline kicked in, coursing through Mariah's veins like acid. "They're shooting at us again! Drive faster!"

"I'm trying!"

Mariah held her seatbelt tightly as the mining truck sped down the dark, inclined road, leaving a tempest of dust in its wake. "Can't we go any faster?"

Tegan, hunched over the wheel, groaned. "I wish! We can barely do fifty with this thing!"

More gunshots rang out, unrelenting. "I think they're aiming for our tires," Mariah said, alarmed.

"This thing has four massive tires at the back—I don't think losing one or two would be a problem."

Mariah let go of her seatbelt and pulled at her hair instead.

A few small lights appeared a mile or so ahead. The girls squinted into the darkness, trying to make out what it was. Tegan gasped. "Town!"

Mariah covered her mouth, unable to believe their luck. Then her eyes caught a quick flash of something that reflected the truck headlights a few hundred yards away. "Phone booth!" she shouted. "There's a pay phone up ahead! Stop there!"

"Oh, yeah, let's just stop to make a phone call while they blow holes through us! Great idea!" Just as Tegan spoke, more bullets struck the back of their vehicle.

Mariah unbuckled herself and threw open her door. Paying no attention to Tegan's protests, she stepped out onto the platform and looked around the big body of the mining truck to get a proper view of their pursuers. "It's Elvis! He's shooting, and so's a guy in the other Hummer!"

Tegan completely disregarded her. "Are you dense? *Get in!*"

"Hold on, I wanna try something!" Mariah eyed the thirty-foot power poles that lined the road at intervals. A crazy idea budded in her mind. *Am I strong enough to do this?* she thought nervously, wrapping her fingers tightly around the cool railing. *Guess I'll find out . . . here goes nothing.*

She inhaled deeply and closed her eyes. The gunshots, engines, and background noises faded into oblivion, leaving her to listen to nothing but the steady flow of blood pulsing in her ears. A lightness overcame her and, for a brief moment, it was as if her feet had lifted off the platform.

Her eyes snapped open with newfound determination and she directed her entire focus onto a power pole ahead of their pursuers. It moved only a bit, remaining fixed in the dirt. She could already feel the wearying effect of uprooting the hefty post wedged six feet into the ground. Still, she would not give in. With all her might, she willed it upward. The pole slowly lifted out of the dirt, slanting toward the road.

Come on, come on . . .

Just as the Hummers came within feet of it, Mariah let the pole drop. She watched, transfixed, as it plummeted to the ground with a satisfying crash. The drivers of the Hummers slammed on their brakes but were too late. Running side by side, both vehicles collided with the fallen post. Flashes of electricity traveled down its length from the wires and leapt into the sparse bushes on either side of the road. A few small flames leapt to life in the foliage, slowly growing bigger and flicking upward like a serpent's tongue.

From inside the cab, Tegan let out a wild howl. "You crazy, amazing idiot—well done! Looks like you cut the lights to the town, though!"

Mariah was grinning from ear to ear so hard it hurt, and her trembling had eased. She stayed on the platform, keeping an eye on their pursuers. To her dismay, the Hummers were already backing up, exposing damaged bumpers and hoods. They turned and went off the road, rounding the pole through the scattered trees.

"They're still coming!" Mariah cautioned. Tegan let out a frustrated yell. Mariah quickly dug in her pockets and came up with a few coins. "We're close to the pay phone, slow down a bit!"

"We can't just stop here!"

"Look, we've got less than fifteen seconds before they're on us! I need two to see if the phone lines still work. If they do, I'll give you a thumbs-up and you just keep driving on." Even as Mariah spoke, she was startled by her own confidence.

Tegan shook her head defiantly. "No way. Not happening. I'm not leaving you."

"Too late." Mariah ran across to the ladder on the right side of the platform and descended. When her feet reached the bottom rung, she held on.

"Mariah!" Tegan bellowed. "No!"

"It has to be done! Do it, Tegan!"

The vehicle slowed just enough for Mariah to jump from the ladder. She hit the ground running, not once looking back. When she reached the pay phone, she snatched up the handset. There was a dial tone. She stuck her thumb up at Tegan, then frenziedly waved her away.

The machine picked up speed and rumbled on.

Mariah saw the Hummers bounce up the shoulder and back onto the main road. She dove behind thick bushes, blending into the shadows, and waited for the vehicles to pass, chest heaving.

The moment she was sure the Hummers were a good distance away, she hastened back to the pay phone and picked up the handset again. She slipped a quarter into the coin slot and called Jag's number. It went to voicemail right away.

She panicked again. Something had happened to them, she was sure of it. *I should call the cops right now.* As she reached up to enter the emergency number, she paused. Maybe she could try Aari's phone. If that didn't work, then she'd call the police.

She nearly broke the keypad while punching in her friend's number. This time, there was ringing. Mariah smacked the side of the pay phone repeatedly.

"Hello?"

She nearly burst out sobbing at the familiar voice. "Aari!"

"Wha—Mariah? Is that you?"

Mariah leaned heavily against the pay phone. "Y-yeah, it's me."

"Oh, my God! Hold on . . . Okay, you're on speaker now."

Jag's voice filled her earpiece. "'Riah?"

"I'm here," she said weakly.

"Where are you? Are you okay?"

"I . . ." Mariah steadied herself. "I'm fine. Tegan and I escaped. I'm somewhere . . . I'm on a road that leads up to a mining site where we were held, but I don't know where we are."

"A mine site?" Aari repeated.

"QMI. Some big open pit mine."

"QMI? You sure?"

"Yes. Why?"

Kody's voice cut in. "You're not gonna *believe* this. We're on our way to check around that place right now."

Mariah was so inexplicably relieved to hear their voices, it took her a few seconds to realize what Kody had just said. "Are you serious? How? Where are you?"

"Not far," Jag said. "Is Teegs okay?"

"Uh, I hope so . . ."

"You hope so?"

"She dropped me off at the pay phone so I could make the call. There are people after us."

"Wait, wait—what do you mean she dropped you off? And how many people are there?"

"Four or five, I think. They're in Hummers. And Tegan's in a really, really huge mining truck."

There was bewildered silence on the other end, then Jag said, "Okay, you're up on the road that leads to the mine, right? We'll get Tegan, then come for you. Hang tight."

"Be quick. Please." She glanced down the road toward the town. "There's so much we have to tell you."

Jag's tone grew gentle and reassuring. "We'll be there soon. Promise."

Mariah hung up the call. She fell to her knees then, and prayed that the guys would arrive in time to help Tegan.

"What if this is a trap?" Kody asked, leaning forward so his head was between Marshall and Jag. The Mustang was rolling on an empty road heading north. A sign beside the lane read 'Welcome to Pinos Altos—A Mining Ghost Town That Still Thrives! Altitude: 7,020 feet. Population: 206.'

"A trap?" Jag echoed.

"Yeah," Kody said. He questioned how he, of all people, was the only one to have this possibility come to mind. "What if the abductors are using Mariah and Tegan as bait and making them say stuff so they'd nab us when we come?"

The air seemed to have been sucked right out of the car.

"I got so worked up about finding the girls that it didn't even occur to me," Aari murmured.

"'Riah sounded genuinely relieved to hear us," Jag countered. "I don't think she'd fake something like that even under duress."

"We're still going in," Marshall said firmly. "Trap or no trap, we're getting your friends back."

The boys looked at one another and then nodded, resolute.

"How far are we from the mine site, Aari?" Jag asked.

The boy was staring down at his phone; Kody took a peek over his shoulder as Aari said, "If the location of the mine on QMI's website is right, then according to the map we're about fifteen minutes out."

Marshall stepped down on the gas pedal. "We'll be there sooner than that."

Kody was unable to sit still in the back of the car. No one in the vehicle had slept a wink in the past thirty hours but Mariah's call had erased any trace of fatigue. The guys had become discouraged after driving hundreds of streets and searching so many buildings. Now that the girls were nearby, they couldn't help but treat this moment as a miracle.

Trees and shrubs on the side of the road eventually thinned out until the car reached a rather derelict-looking town. As they made a left turn onto a street called Bear Creek Road, they noticed a handful of houses that appeared to have been recently renovated, but the further in they went, the more run-down the town became.

The Mustang's headlights illuminated the rough road ahead. Old brick houses bore tin roofs and were surrounded by short fences. The homes were spread out from each other. Except for a couple of timeworn cars parked on the side of the streets, the place looked abandoned.

"Welcome to Pinos Altos," Marshall said, voice low as he brought the Mustang to a stop.

"Where are all the lights?" Kody asked, checking the side and rear window. "I see street lamps, but nothing's on."

"Maybe this place wouldn't look so bad if there was some light," Aari said, looking up from his phone.

"Maybe. But it—" Kody's words were cut off by a series of bangs that caught them all off guard.

"Whoa—did you hear that?" Jag asked.

Kody focused his hearing, but he needn't have bothered because the second time the sounds rang out, the boys knew instantly what it was.

"Gunshots!" Aari hissed.

Marshall put the Mustang back into motion. "We're definitely in the right place."

Kody peered anxiously ahead. The road stretched out about two hundred yards in front of them, and everything was still. The quiet was almost unsettling.

Then the ground began to vibrate and a loud rumble followed. At the point where the Mustang's headlights merged with the darkness of the night, a yellow behemoth crested a small hill and rolled toward them, taking up the entire road. Kody's eyes were stuck wide open.

Jag pressed as far back into his seat as he could, watching the massive vehicle's advance. "What *is* that thing?"

Kody heard Aari wheeze beside him. "That's a mining dump truck."

"What is it doing all the way out here?" Jag gaped. "Look at those tires! They're huge! And it's heading *right for us!*"

The machine came to rest, as if the driver didn't want to run the Mustang over. The boys and the Sentry squinted against the glare of the truck's headlights.

Something nagged Kody as he remembered what Mariah had mentioned on her call. He leaned forward and squeezed his eyes shut for a few moments. When he opened them, everything appeared a few shades brighter, though there was a bluish tint around the edges of his vision. He narrowed his eyes and his view zoomed in on the cab of the mining truck. He studied the person at the wheel for only a second before gasping. As muddied and disheveled as she looked, he would recognize his friend anywhere.

"It's Tegan!" he yelled. "She's *driving* that beast!"

"You sure?" Jag asked, though even as he spoke he'd opened his door and gotten out. Kody followed, with Marshall and Aari catching up to them.

"Tegan!" Kody shouted, waving his arms about his head.

While Marshall hung back, Jag ran ahead. "Come down, Teegs!"

Kody saw the cabin door of the mining truck swing open. Tegan stepped onto the platform and hastened to the edge to take a look. When she saw them, she let out a yell and bolted down the ladder.

The boys picked up their pace, sprinting to Tegan as she ran toward them. Jag was the first to reach her and he grabbed her in a bear hug. Tegan slipped free and pulled him toward Aari and Kody, away from the direction she'd come, but when she saw Marshall, she backpedaled and lost her footing. She fell on her back end and scooted away from the Sentry, terrified.

Kody reached her and lifted her to her feet even as she struggled to get away. "Tegan—Teegs! Calm down! He's a Sentry!"

"But—"

He let her go when she stopped fighting against him and said calmingly, "He's with us, Teegs."

She looked at the Sentry with uncertainty, then said almost inaudibly, "We need to get Mariah and get out of here. They're after us."

Kody became aware of vehicles approaching. The newcomers' headlights lit the street on either side of the mining truck. He didn't take his eyes off the vehicles as they drew closer. Aari and Jag, wondering what he was staring at, went to look around the truck. In Kody's peripheral vision, he noticed Tegan backing away.

Zooming and brightening his vision again, he sized up the newcomers. As the image in front of him sharpened, he saw a man leaning out of one of the vehicles, lifting something in his hands.

"Tegan's right, it's them." Kody shrank from the sight. "And they're armed."

The men advanced, two of them training their weapons on the teens and Marshall. Kody recognized the giant who strolled calmly toward them and could hear the venom in the man's voice over the sound of the engines. "You really think you can get away? From here? From us?"

The orange-haired man holding the shotgun spoke, his Australian accent pronounced. "You've caused a damn lot of destruction, lass."

Kody glanced at Tegan, wondering what in the world she and Mariah had done.

"You better be well worth it," the Australian continued. "If not for the order to keep you alive, I'd gladly put a bullet between your eyes."

"Too bad we're not allowed to shoot to kill," the giant sighed, his tone thick with sarcasm.

The Australian smirked. "Can still shoot to maim, though."

Kody, Aari, Tegan and Jag backed up slowly but stopped when Marshall stepped forward to stand protectively in front of them. "What do you want with them?" he called. "They're just kids!"

"Kids!" The giant tossed his head back, letting out a humorless bark of laughter. "These girls probably caused us six figures in damage!"

The Australian lifted his head slightly, scanning Kody and the others. "Where is she?" he demanded. "Where is the other girl?"

"You have no right to take them," Marshall warned.

"We're talking about rights now, are we?" A wad of spit launched from the giant's mouth. "Hand them over."

The Sentry rolled his shoulders and snarled. "Over my dead body."

The giant shrugged. "Suit yourself." He signaled his cohort.

Kody saw the blast leave the Australian's shotgun before he heard the report. He opened his mouth to yell, watching in helpless horror as his heightened vision followed the cloud of pellets toward the Sentry.

The next thing he saw was Marshall being driven to the ground by a blur—Jag. Tegan dodged sharply as the bullets whizzed by.

Marshall landed roughly on the road, groaning. Jag leapt upright the instant he had Marshall out of harm's way, arms held up in surrender. "Don't shoot! Don't shoot! We'll come!"

"Hands up, all of you!" the Australian barked. "Now!"

Dazed and scared, Kody, Tegan and Aari did as they were told. They were ordered to move forward, which they did, slowly and with small steps. Then Kody heard Jag mutter under his breath, "A distraction would be awesome right about now, Aari . . ."

There was a tense moment of silence before the men let out startled exclamations. The mining truck beside them shimmered briefly and vanished from sight.

"What the hell?" the Australian cried.

Kody caught sight of Jag sprinting into a blur yet again. The armed Australian beside the mining truck was stunned when Jag appeared suddenly in front of him. The teenager grabbed his arms and delivered a knee between his legs before ripping the shotgun away from the winded man.

As the Australian fell to the ground, rolling in agony, Jag spun around with the speed of a striking snake and swung the shotgun at the unarmed man beside the Australian, smashing him in the face with the weapon's stock. The man, who'd barely had time to see Jag, let alone comprehend what was happening, was knocked to the ground, unconscious. Kody had to slow down his vision to capture it all.

As Jag spun again to face the third adversary—the giant—he was met with the man's massive fist. The shotgun fell, clattering on the gravel as Jag was sent sprawling backward. He rolled a couple of feet away before lying still in the dirt.

"Jag!" Kody shouted.

The giant pulled out a pistol from his holster and pointed it down at Jag. As his finger slid to the trigger, the mining truck suddenly appeared. Startled, the giant and the remaining adversary snapped their heads leftward to look. At that exact moment, Kody saw Jag disappear from sight like a specter.

Beside Kody, Aari mumbled pleadingly, "C'mon, Jag. Move it . . ."

Kody saw movement next to him; Marshall, seizing the moment of distraction, charged toward the two men left standing. He headed for the one holding an AR-15 rifle and kicked the weapon out of his adversary's hands. The Sentry swiftly slipped behind the man and grabbed him in a choke hold. With a heavy grunt, he lifted and flipped him over his shoulder, sending his opponent crashing onto his back. Marshall was upon him in an instant, delivering right and left hooks.

The giant calmly stepped behind Marshall and pressed his pistol to the Sentry's head, stopping him cold. "Here's the thing, hero. We need those kids. But you?" His finger slid to the trigger. "Not so much."

The bang was earsplitting, and the howl of agony that followed rattled Kody's ears. Then he realized Marshall was still crouched, unscathed, over the man he'd been hitting—the shot had gone wild. Kody rubbed his eyes and stared, barely able to take in what he was seeing.

The giant slowly sank to his knees, the gun in his now-limp hand pointed to the ground. Red dripped from a gash on the back of his head. The AR-15 that Marshall had kicked away now hung in the air as though suspended by invisible wires, its butt splashed with blood.

Marshall stood and grabbed the rifle. Lining up as a batter would, he swung the weapon around and nailed the giant in the gut. When the big man leaned forward in agony, Marshall struck out with a fist to the man's temple, knocking him out cold.

Kody would have watched him fall if not for Jag appearing out of the air in front of him, making him jump. He fist-bumped his confused-looking friend. "Nice work with the rifle."

Jag returned the gesture, looking even more confused now. "That wasn't my doing."

Kody was about to make a smart remark when a movement caught his eye and he stepped away from Jag.

Jag turned around to follow his gaze. Mariah was jogging toward them from behind the adversaries' Hummers; now the rifle hanging in the air made sense. She looked even worse than Tegan. When she got closer, she stopped and eyed Marshall with uncertainty.

Tegan bolted toward her, followed by Kody, then Jag and Aari. When she saw them approaching, she let out an elated cry and shot past Marshall to meet their open arms.

Kody grinned broadly. "You're all dirty!"

Mariah managed to punch him with one hand as tears left streaks down her mud-dried face. "Missed you too, brickhead."

The friends held onto each other for a while longer, unable to form words. The rapid beating of Kody's heart eventually eased. The silence was broken when Marshall came up to them and said gently, "I don't want to interrupt your reunion, but we've got a bit of work to do here."

Mariah pulled away and half-glared at Marshall. "You . . . you attacked us . . . and then you *followed*—"

"Mariah, it's not—" Jag began, but she held up her index finger.

"But then I just saw you," she continued warily, "and you were . . . you were *helping* us? Why? Who are you?"

Marshall wiped some blood from off his cheek with his t-shirt, then gave Mariah a remorseful smile. "I apologize for how this may all seem. My name is Marshall. We haven't got time for a chat right now, but I'm sure your friends will fill you in."

"He's a Sentry," Kody told Mariah. "*The* Sentry. It wasn't Tony after all."

At the mention of the name, a look of thunder and destruction descended in both girls' eyes. "That's one of the things we need to talk about," Tegan said bitingly.

"Later," Marshall said. He took out a switchblade from his pocket and tossed it to Aari. "Slash their tires. Be quick."

Aari caught the blade and ran toward the Hummers as Marshall went back to the four men on the ground. He saw that the one Jag had kneed was struggling to get up and quickly grabbed him in a chokehold to send him sliding into unconsciousness.

The Sentry and the friends found a box of zip ties in one of the Hummers and began securing the men's hands behind their backs. They then dragged them one by one and shoved them into some bushes about thirty feet away from the road.

The girls grew jumpy as Kody and Jag went to grab the last man. "What's wrong with you both?" Kody called.

"I think Mariah and I stirred the hornet's nest up there," Tegan said, her tone a few pitches higher than usual, "and I've got a feeling more of these guys will be coming down here soon. We really need to go."

By this time, Aari had finished his duty and handed the switchblade back to Marshall. "Are we all good over there?" the Sentry asked, watching as Kody and Jag finally got the last man into the bushes.

"Yeah," Jag replied. The group took one last look around, then packed into Marshall's Mustang.

"It's *really* crowded in here," Aari muttered.

"It's designed for two people in the back," Marshall said as he shut his door. "Hang in there, we'll try and get a rental once we're safe. Besides, we can't be driving this beauty anymore now that they've seen the car."

"Where are we going?" Tegan asked.

Marshall made a U-turn before tearing out of the small ghost town. "We'll figure that out as soon as we get out of here."

"This is so uncomfortable," Aari muttered. "Ow! Tegan, your elbow's in my ribs!"

"There's not enough room back here," Tegan protested.

"I'm getting dirt on me," Kody grumbled.

"Not our fault!" the girls chorused.

Marshall listened to the lot of them complain, entertained. They were driving through Deming and heading to Las Cruces with the teenagers crammed in the back as both sides recounted what had happened to them.

"Again, sorry about how cramped it is, guys," he said.

"Too bad the car rentals at Silver City weren't open," Kody sighed.

"It was four in the morning," Jag said. "And anyway, we needed to put as much distance as we can between those guys and us."

"You know," Aari said to the girls, "your escape sounds like something straight out of a movie."

"I was scared," Mariah confided. "Those beasts—the Marauders . . . it's the people from the mountain last year. It's them."

"What are they doing here?" Jag asked.

"It looked like two different projects," Tegan answered. "Above ground it was mining but underneath . . . I don't know. They had a whole lot of construction going on inside that cave."

"And aqua . . . aqua farms?" Mariah said. "No, wait. Aquaponic farms?"

Aari jumped in. "Hydroponic farms? You sure?"

"Yes," Tegan said.

Marshall frowned. "That's odd."

Tegan frowned in return. "Why?"

Marshall looked into his rearview mirror. "I think Aari might have the answer."

"Aquaponics is a way to grow plants with just water and light, essentially," Aari said. "There's no need for soil. And you can raise fish in harmony with the greens. Question is, why are they building an aquaponic farm underground?"

"Another maybe more relevant question is, who's behind all this?" Jag added.

"That Dr. Nate guy and the person in the hologram knew a lot about Dema-Ki," Mariah said.

"But how are they even aware of its existence?" Aari asked. "It's a fair assumption that it's someone from the inside. Maybe a rogue Sentry? So many questions that need answers. Jag, are you able to get in contact with Elder Nageau again?"

Jag folded his arms. "I don't know. He was the one who reached out to me last time. Marshall, can you?"

"Probably," the Sentry said. "Let's get away from here first."

"I'm so disgusted with Tony," Mariah said. "I have no words to describe how much I despise that . . . that mucus thing that blob fish secrete."

The friends erupted in peals of disgusted laughter.

"And this would be the same guy who said he went after me when he didn't, right?" Marshall asked over the ruckus.

"That's the one!" Tegan replied.

Kody clicked his tongue sourly. "He seemed like such a nice guy. I don't think I've given my trust away that quickly to anyone in ages."

"But that's the thing," Tegan said. "He didn't seem, you know, *evil.* He just looked like he genuinely believes in whatever he's a part of to a point where it's kind of scary."

Jag stretched out his legs as far as he could. "I'd like to know what it is that he's a part of."

"Whatever it is, I could feel the fanaticism simmering just below the surface."

"In any case," Mariah said, "if we see him again, I'll gladly set up his face on a date with a boulder." She yawned, setting off everyone else except Marshall.

The Sentry glanced back at the group sympathetically. "Just a while longer, guys," he said. "Hang in there."

The occupants of the car quieted down and it took a while for Marshall to realize that the teenagers had dozed off, even the four in the back who weren't settled comfortably. The Sentry glanced at the dashboard clock. It was a shame that it was only five in the morning; the car rental in Deming would not be open. Still, it was a good opportunity to drive on and put more miles between the abductors and the group.

It was just a little over an hour later when he pulled up in front of a car rental office near the Las Cruces airport. The moment he turned off the engine, the friends woke up, looking around blearily.

"Time for a new ride," Marshall murmured, unbuckling himself as the others groaned.

Getting out of the Mustang, he led the way into the rental company's building. The friends plopped down on the plastic chairs as he went up to the counter to speak with the clerk. He glanced back at them and grinned slightly when he saw them leaning against each other, trying to get a few more minutes of shuteye.

The Sentry's thoughts meandered as he passed the clerk his credit card. He still couldn't believe how young the five were, but he'd now witnessed some of them work their powers and heard about the girls' escape. As inexperienced as they may seem, they had skills and had proven that they could use them as a team.

Marshall got the keys to their new car. "Up and at 'em," he called to the others as he strode out the door. He heard the friends grumbling as they pulled each other up and followed him.

"Voila," he said, spreading his arms when he reached their vehicle. He turned to the teenagers. "What do you think?"

The friends, looking dead on their feet, stood in silence as they stared. Then, Kody spoke up groggily. "Marshall . . . that's a minivan."

"It sure is."

"We're trading a Mustang for a minivan?"

"Not just any minivan. It's an all-wheel-drive. We needed more room anyway and you know my car is too easy to spot if those guys come after you again. Pile in."

While the friends settled into the rental, Marshall jogged back to his car and gently pulled his backpack out of the trunk. When he returned to the minivan, he was not at all surprised to find the group reclined and looking considerably more comfortable than before. As he pulled onto the main road, Marshall glanced back at Kody. "So? How's our new ride?"

"Not answering that," Kody mumbled as he snuggled against his seat.

"Hey, Aari, you got your charger?" Jag asked. "The car's got a port and my phone's dead."

Aari fished his phone charger out of his bag and threw it to Jag. It was barely two minutes later when his phone rang. Jag answered the call. "Hey, Tristan."

Marshall could feel Jag's mood darken as the boy listened to his brother. The others sensed it as well as they sat up and leaned toward the front.

"Hey, Tris, hold on a moment." Jag muted the call and turned to the others; Marshall noticed that his eyes were moist. "My grandparents' crops have been hit. My . . . my grandmother was rushed to the hospital. She had a heart attack. Tristan is thinking of heading out there with Camilla."

Mariah rested a hand on his shoulder. "I'm so sorry, Jag. How is she holding up?"

"I'm not sure. But would it be alright if we drove out there? I know it's a long ways away, but . . ."

"No, no, it's a good idea," Aari said, leaning closer.

"How so?" Mariah asked.

"We can get a look at the destroyed crops firsthand and see if we can find any clues that may point us to the source of this scourge. And Jag can be there for his family."

Kody cocked his head. "That's a good point."

"So are we doing this?" Jag looked at all of them, a plea in his eyes.

Marshall nodded. "I think so."

"Thank you." Jag unmuted the call. "Tristan? Listen, you stay put. We'll head to Concordia ourselves. Yeah, we're sure. No, we *want* to do this. I'll call you when we get there." He hung up.

"Key in your grandparents' address on the GPS," Marshall said. Jag did as instructed, then rested back with a heavy exhale.

"We've got a ten-hour drive ahead of us," the Sentry told the friends. "Good time to catch up on sleep."

He received no argument and the cabin went silent until Kody started to snore from the third-row seat. When he stopped, Aari picked it up. Marshall had to suppress a tired chuckle.

It was early afternoon when Tegan coughed and sat up, her eyes closed.

"Sleepwalking?" Marshall asked.

"I can't open my eyes," she responded groggily. "I'm so tired. And so hungry. And dirty."

"Well, we're just coming into Dalhart, two hours from the Kansas state line. Let's see if we can find a place to get you guys cleaned up and grab some food."

"How long were we asleep?"

"Just about five hours."

"Five hours! Oh, man, I'd take another eight right now."

"Keep it down," Mariah moaned.

A sleepy-sounding Aari chimed in. "Too late."

Kody and Jag were roused as well, and the first words out of Kody's mouth were a complaint about his hunger. They hurried through a quick bite at a drive-thru and stopped at a mall. The girls grabbed the cheapest clothes they could find—and Mariah bought some makeup to conceal the bruise forming on her face where she'd been punched—while the boys and Marshall wandered around, grabbing other necessities. Once they'd gotten everything they needed, Marshall drove to a nearby public swimming pool.

Tegan peered out of her window. "Um, why are we stopping here?"

"You and Mariah need to clean up," Marshall said. "Can't have Jag's granddad wondering why you're all muddied. You can use the showers in the change room."

Mariah goggled. "You're kidding."

Marshall unlocked the doors. "Not at all."

With a grimace, the two left, their new clothes in a couple of backpacks. "We're gonna get such weird looks," Mariah grumped.

They returned twenty minutes later, looking fresh and clean in new t-shirts and shorts, and settled back into the middle seats of the minivan. "Okay, fine, that was a good call," Mariah said as she tied her hair back.

Marshall just smiled. "We have another five hours or so until we reach the farm, so what do you—"

"Nap!" Kody yelled. "See you all in a few hours!"

"I'm with the clown," Aari said, reclining his seat again.

In the end, Jag was the only one who decided to stay awake. "Would you like me to drive, Marshall?" he asked tentatively. "We've all slept a bit, but you haven't rested at all."

The Sentry was heartened by the offer. "I'm fine, Jag. But thank you."

A few hours on, open range began giving way to farmland. They were outside the town of Salina when they noticed pillars of smoke rising to the sky, as if many acres of crops were on fire. Jag hastily woke his friends who began murmuring when they caught sight of the smoke.

"Are the farmers burning their fields?" Tegan asked.

"I think so," Aari said, trying to get a better view. "They do that with spoiled crops."

"But the crops look okay from here . . ."

They spotted a few black vans on certain properties and television trucks parked on the shoulder of the highway. "This is unreal," Mariah whispered. "Are those government vehicles?"

"Seems like it." Marshall looked at the GPS. "We'll be at your grandfather's farm shortly, Jag."

He turned left, heading north to Concordia. Jag wound down the window to check the temperature outside but quickly put it back up. "Oh yeah, hot and humid. We're definitely in Kansas."

"Wanna take a dip in there?" Marshall laughed as he pointed at a water tank that sat atop a tower with 'Concordia Panthers' painted on it.

"Honestly, I wouldn't mind that."

On either side of the country road were more acres of farmland, along with barns and farmhouses. At some of the properties, horses and cattle glanced up to watch the minivan drive past. Mariah had her face against a window, whimpering quietly every time they passed a horse.

"You like horses, Mariah?" Marshall asked.

She faced him, eyes sparkling. "I *love* them. They give you unconditional affection, and riding one is almost like flying. It's amazing."

Jag was calling Tristan to let him know that they'd arrived when they finally turned onto a wide gravel path that led to a classic, wooden two-story home with a dark, pointed roof. A truck was parked off to the side and a barn sat stoutly some distance away.

"This is a really nice place," Marshall said as they got out of the vehicle.

Kody put on his ball cap as he contorted his face. "Yeah, except for the heat."

The front door of the house opened and a yellow Labrador retriever bounded toward them, ears flapping, barking loudly.

"Lady!" Jag dropped down, waving the dog over. "Lady! C'mere, pup!"

The Labrador ran into his open arms and snuffled his face, whining joyfully, her tail wagging. Marshall leaned down to pat Lady's head. The dog licked his fingers before turning her attention to the teenagers who swarmed her.

Marshall caught movement by the open door of the house and looked up. An older man was making his way out. He wore simple blue jeans, boots and a red checkered shirt.

Jag saw the newcomer as well and ran toward him. "Gramps!"

The man gathered Jag into a tight hug. As the others made their way over to them with Marshall at the rear, the two parted so the man could embrace the others. The Sentry could discern a vague South American accent as he called out to the five. "Aari! Tegan! Kody! Mariah! Look at you all!" He beamed at them, then fixed his gaze on Marshall. "Hm . . . don't believe I've met you before."

"Uh, this is Marshall," Jag said, glancing at the others. "He's a friend we met on the trip. Found out we were heading the same way, so we're all going together."

Marshall stuck out his hand. "Pleasure meeting you, sir."

"Call me Hugo, son." Hugo shook the Sentry's hand firmly. They locked eyes for a moment, and Marshall knew he'd just received a subtle warning: *I don't know who you are, but if the kids trust you, so do I. Don't screw it up.*

Marshall gave a short nod and dropped his hand back to his side. He followed the others into the house with Lady trotting in after them, her tail wagging nonstop.

"Tristan gave me a call and told me you were coming," Hugo said, leading the way into the dining room. A rustic pine table that sat eight was placed at the center. "Here, have a seat. Have you had dinner?"

"Not yet," Jag said.

"Good." Hugo went to the adjoining kitchen and came back with bowls of beef stew. They thanked him as he took his seat at the end of the table beside Jag, facing Marshall who sat at the opposite end. There was one empty seat at the table, and Marshall could only assume Jag's grandmother would have been sitting there if she weren't in a hospital.

As they took their first bites, Jag asked, "How are you, Gramps?"

Hugo reached out and patted Jag's shoulder. "I was doing well until all of this happened. I'm glad you're here, though. The last time your grandmother and I saw you was at Christmas."

"You know I love being here. How, uh . . . how's Gran doing?"

"She was in pretty bad shape, but thank goodness the paramedics arrived as quickly as they did. When the next town over got hit, she got really worried. And then when our crops got destroyed . . . it was just too much to take. She's in intensive care. They're giving her clot-busting medicine but are considering surgery once she stabilizes." Hugo took a spoonful of the stew. "I haven't left her side, but when I found out you were coming, I headed back. Good thing I did, too. The authorities were here for hours this morning."

"We saw them on our way over," Aari said. "What are they doing?"

"Asking questions," Hugo answered. "This is mind-boggling even to them. No one's ever seen this kind of thing before. Everyone was here, from the CDC to the USDA, and even the FBI."

"FBI?" Kody stammered, nearly spilling his stew. "I can understand why the others would be here, but why the FBI?"

"They have to look at it from all angles," Aari replied. "Including the possibility of this being a terror attack."

Hugo smiled at him. "Sharp as ever, hm?"

Aari turned a little red and continued eating. "This is really good, Mr. Sanchez."

"It's nothing fancy, but I'm happy you're enjoying it."

Jag stirred his meal. "Would we be able to go see Gran after dinner?"

"I don't see why not."

"If you don't mind, Mr. Sanchez, would it be alright if we took a look at your crops while you're away with Jag?" Aari asked.

"Sure. Don't know what you'll find, though. Authorities scanned dozens of acres but came up with nothing."

Mariah gazed out of the window. "It's strange. The crops look just fine."

Hugo nodded earnestly. "That's what I told Julia, too, when she came rushing in. But when you see it close up, it crushes you. The stalks are there, but it's as if someone has cut away every single wheat head. They're all gone." He lowered his eyes.

"Is there really no trace of anything?" Aari prodded. "No sign of what caused this?"

"None."

"Did you see anyone come by? Or hear anything funny?"

Hugo seemed mildly tickled by Aari's investigative queries. "I haven't. And no one else has, it seems. I checked my crops the evening before we lost them and they were fine. That seems to be the pattern. But if you want to hang around here, be my guest." Hugo wiped his mouth with a napkin. "So how was California?"

"The . . . beaches were nice," Tegan said, trading furtive looks with the others.

They finished the meal quickly after that. Aari and Mariah jumped up to gather the plates despite Hugo's protests, then went into the kitchen to wash the dishes.

Jag ran to get the keys to Hugo's truck. Hugo looked at Marshall and smiled slightly. There was something about the older man that was both inscrutable and comforting. "Guess we're off to the hospital."

Marshall returned the smile. "Thank you so much for dinner."

"It's nothing, really." Hugo stood up and joined Jag, who was waiting impatiently at the door. "We'll be back in a couple hours. If you're going to go outside, there are some flashlights in the closet to the left of the kitchen."

Marshall, Tegan and Kody watched as grandfather and grandson left the house. Aari and Mariah joined them as soon as the truck's taillights disappeared from sight.

Marshall slowly pushed his chair back and looked them all in the eyes. "Let's see if we can find out what we're dealing with here."

PART THREE

The Pendants

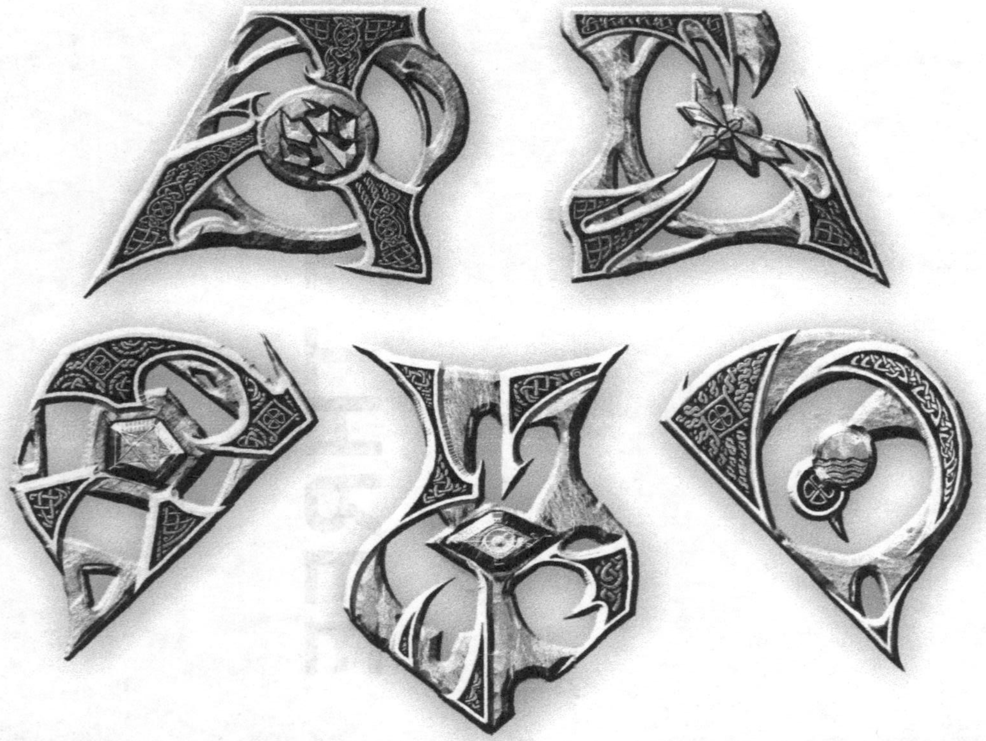

"One. Simple. Task. That's it. That's all the job required." The temperature in the conference room had plummeted the moment Tony stepped in. He observed the three men standing before him with icy disgust. He'd handpicked them himself for his unit, having seen them perform excellently many times in the past.

And yet, they'd been outsmarted by a couple of teenagers.

None of the three men would look him directly in the eye. Hajjar stood off to the side, thick arms folded over his equally thick chest, a bandage wrapped around his head and another around his hand. He appeared somber.

Tony hefted a four-foot length of steel pipe he'd picked up in the underground construction zone and arched his eyebrow at the red-haired Australian. "Liam."

The Australian briefly met Tony's gaze in acknowledgement. "Sir."

"You told me the girls escaped you once. You recaptured them, tied them up, and locked them up again. And you had an extra pair of eyes and hands to help guard the door. Right?" Tony spun the pipe like a staff, not expecting an answer. "Tell me, how did they manage to hoodwink you to escape the second time around?"

"They obviously had help, sir," the Australian said. "The first time they got out, someone hit me in the back of my head with a microwave oven."

"And did you find out who it was?"

"No, sir."

"Of course you didn't." Tony worked the pipe around his palm and over his knuckles. "This is incompetence. Stupidity. Ineffectiveness. Do I need to go on?"

The Australian shook his head.

"What am I going to do?" Tony's words dripped acid. "Losing the girls, colossal damages . . . I have to report all of this to my employer. I left you in charge, Liam, but I will be taking the flak for your ineptitude. I *despise* having my leadership and my judgment questioned. I've worked too hard for that."

The Australian stared over Tony's head at the wall behind him.

Tony shoved his free hand into the pocket of his skinny jeans. "And then, for reasons I will never comprehend, fortune brought *all five* of them right into your hands. And what do you do? You lose them, *again!* How? You were armed and had three other guards with you!"

"There was a man with them," the Australian responded weakly. "He wasn't much of a problem, but weird things happened."

"Yeah, I heard," Tony snapped. "Trucks disappearing and all that crap. What were you guys smoking?"

"I was with them," Hajjar interjected calmly. "I saw it, and I was completely sober."

Tony spun the pipe around his hand again. *Ohh, the half-blind guy thinks he can nullify this situation.* "And I'm supposed to tell my employer . . . what? That you got distracted by your hallucinations, thereby allowing these kids to escape? Who knows where they are by now!"

He jabbed one end of the pipe under the Australian's jaw. The man froze, eyes darting from the pipe to Tony.

"Careful, Cross," Hajjar sneered. "Keep that little demon inside you on a tight leash."

Tony turned to him sharply. Hajjar smiled. "I'm the head of security here, Tony. I don't have to stand here and watch this. Take it somewhere else, if you must entertain your sadistic urges."

Tony clucked his tongue and took a deep breath. “I’ve had it under control for a while now, Elias,” he said, “but I do have to dispense some sort of consequence for this unacceptable failure.” He looked back at the Australian, prodding the pipe against his throat. To his credit, the man didn’t budge.

“This is your mess,” Hajjar said indifferently. “Don’t leave me another pile to clean up here. I’ll be topside checking up on things.”

Tony waited until the giant had left the room before studying his three underlings. He was livid, yes; but even more so, he was disappointed. “The more I’m around all these ignoramuses,” he said to himself, though the others could still hear him, “the more I appreciate the Boss’s plan for the future. A world without fools. I really can’t wait.”

The men remained still.

“You two, out.” Tony nodded to the guards on either side of the Australian. “Liam and I need to have a chat.”

The Australian stiffened, eyeing the pipe under his chin. Tony noticed and tossed the pipe to one of the guards as they left the room.

The flame-haired man’s shoulders dropped in relief and he let out a small laugh. “I thought you were gonna hit me ’round the head with that.”

Tony turned so his back was to the Australian. “No,” he said, staring down at his penny loafers. “Of course not. That’s cheap.”

“Sir, I really don’t know what to say. I—”

“They were girls, teenagers. They were locked up in a room after being nabbed. You figured they’d be weak, knees knocking together and curled up in a corner. You figured they’d just sit and do as they’re told. Is that it, Liam?”

“Y-yes, sir. That was probably it.”

Tony leisurely turned around and stepped closer so he stood within six inches of the other man. “You most likely also thought, then, that since they looked like easy pickings, you could relax, drop your guard a little.”

The other man was ashen. "I—perhaps. I mean, quite likely."

Tony placed his hands on the Australian's shoulders, feeling him tense up again. "Do I pay you to slack off, Liam?"

"No, sir."

"Every assignment we've taken on prior to this demanded a high level of commitment. Why would this be any different?"

"It . . . it wasn't. It shouldn't have been."

"I've seen you, all of you, perform excellently before. This is why I depend on you."

"Thank you, sir."

"Will you be able to perform to my expectations again?"

"I can guarantee it, sir. This is one slip-up. We know our jobs and we do them well."

"I'm glad to hear it." Tony removed his hands from the Australian's shoulders. "You can go now. But before you leave, let me warn you that this is not over. If the Boss demands a pound of my flesh over this fiasco, I will tear two out of you."

Tegan traversed the wheat field with Mariah, shining her flashlight alternately at the ground and at the headless stalks. The sky overhead was speckled with bright stars and the moon cast an ethereal sheen over the six-hundred-acre farm. Every now and then an insect or some creature would emit a noise which kept the girls on their toes.

"This is depressing," Tegan said, running her fingers over the stalks. "I feel so bad for Jag's grandparents."

Mariah knelt to take a look at the dust-covered soil. "Me too."

Tegan looked around for Aari and Marshall and spotted their flashlight beams a couple of hundred feet away. Kody was on his own a little further down from them, using his night vision ability to scan the crops.

As they walked, a thought crossed Tegan's mind. "Are there snakes out here?" she asked.

"I sure hope not," Mariah mumbled.

"Let's check with our resident know-it-all. Hey, Aari!"

"Yeah?" Aari yelled. "You found something?"

"No! Just wondering if there are any snakes in Kansas!"

"Um . . . yeah! Lots! Mostly harmless, like gopher snakes, but some are pretty deadly!"

From somewhere in the depths of the field, they heard a scream from Kody. "*There are snakes here?*"

"Just be careful," Marshall called.

"Gah!"

They continued on, hoping to find something that the investigators from the government agencies might have missed.

Tegan was skeptical of that objective. *If the experts couldn't find anything, what are the chances we will?*

It was nearly an hour later when Kody suggested calling it quits. Tegan and the others readily agreed; they were still exhausted from the events of the past couple of days and, at this point, wanted nothing more than to put their feet up. They headed back to the house and fell onto the sofas in the living room just as the clock struck eleven.

Lady trotted in after them and lay by Marshall's feet. The Sentry reached down to pat her head warmly.

"Where's the remote?" Aari asked. "I want to see what's on the news."

Tegan located the remote between the sofa cushions and turned the television on, flipping through different channels until she came across a cable news station. An interviewer faced two people who appeared to be government officials. Judging from the sunlight outside the TV studio's wide windows, the panel was pre-recorded. Not surprisingly, the topic of discussion was the crop failures.

"We are still working on finding the cause of the outbreak," a woman identified on screen as a U.S. Department of Agriculture spokesperson was saying. "We have gathered samples from a large number of affected areas across the country, but test results remain inconclusive."

"So far we haven't identified any specific chemical or biological contaminants in the samples," the male official from the Environmental Protection Agency added.

"So is this a natural phenomenon, or is there something more insidious at play here?" the interviewer asked.

"Our test results remain inconclusive for now," the woman repeated. "What we do encourage, though, is that people in the affected areas remain vigilant, especially farmers."

The camera focused on the interviewer. "What do you want them to be vigilant of? What should they be looking for?"

"We don't feel that we should rule out anything at this point," the EPA man said. "Anything out of the ordinary that citizens observe may provide important information."

"That's really helpful," Kody remarked dryly. Tegan let out a snort.

"What we do know so far is that the effect on crops is very specific, as your viewers saw in the clips you ran earlier," the man continued.

"Turn it off," Aari said suddenly.

Tegan, though surprised, obliged. "What's up?"

Aari went to stand in front of the television. "I'll tell you what's up. The knee-jerk reaction to explain this whole crop failure phenomenon circles around the bug or disease theory. We can't blame people for thinking that way because we *are* dealing with crops here, so what they're naturally looking for is something biological or possibly chemical. You can tell from their conversations that they're searching for something organic, something that occurs in nature. But what if they're looking at it from a completely wrong angle?"

"Meaning?" Tegan asked.

"Think about this." Aari started to pace. "From what we've gathered from Marshall's account, there is clearly a human hand behind this. What if the destruction of the crops is being caused by something created in a lab?"

"Diseases can be created in labs," Mariah said, shrugging.

"True. But if I remember clearly—and Marshall, correct me if I'm wrong—when you were making that warehouse delivery you heard them talking about a Class One cleanroom and something they called fenixium, which, by the way, sounds like a kind of mineral to me." He stopped pacing and raised a finger. "Here's the thing. You don't need a Class One cleanroom—which is hundreds of times cleaner than a surgery room—and minerals to create bugs or diseases. You do that in a bio lab with bacteria and other organisms, not in a manufacturing facility. So the question becomes, what were they producing in there?"

Marshall rubbed his neck. "I do recall one of them mentioning that it was just one component that was being manufactured there. Whatever it is they were doing, the assembly of the final product was happening elsewhere."

"This a pretty big leap you're making, Aari," Tegan said.

Aari sat down on the coffee table, facing the others. "There's some conjecture, yeah, but it's based on actual info that we have."

Mariah tapped his ankle with her foot. "What do you think is doing it, then?"

"That's what we're here to find out," he answered. "We'll take a look at the crops again tomorrow and see if we can dig up anything."

Lady, who'd been dozing the entire time by Marshall's feet, suddenly leapt to her paws and hurried toward the front door just as it opened. Jag stepped in and greeted the Labrador affectionately before joining everyone in the living room. He sat down beside Marshall. "Hey."

"Hey, yourself," Mariah smiled. "Where's your granddad?"

"He decided to stay with Gran in the hospital. Those two are pretty much inseparable. Gramps asked me to drop by tomorrow."

"How's your grandma doing?"

Jag looked away. "She's still unconscious." He quickly shifted gears. "So did you guys find anything out there?"

"Nada," Tegan said. "We'll try again tomorrow when the sun's up. Aari's got an interesting hunch, though."

She listened as Aari gave Jag a quick rundown of their discussion. She had to admit that it was an interesting concept, but it still boiled down to the question of what exactly was destroying the crops. Jag's own response was much the same.

They sat around for another half hour until Tegan started to nod off on Mariah's shoulder.

"I think it's bedtime for Teegs," Kody teased.

"I'll show you guys to the guest rooms." Jag made a move to stand up, but Marshall held out a hand to stop him.

"Hold on a moment," the Sentry said as he picked up his bag. "I've been waiting for the right time for this. I would have done it earlier, but the circumstances ruled it out. Now that you're all together and we've got some room to take it easy for the first time since we met . . . Here."

He opened the bag with a degree of reverence and carefully removed a small, wooden chip-carved box. Tegan, her sleepiness gone, involuntarily leaned closer to Marshall, watching as he unlatched the box and pushed the cover back.

"Elder Nageau told me to give these to you when you were ready," he said. "I think now is as good a time as ever."

Tegan's inquisitiveness morphed into wonderment as the Sentry delicately held up five pendants, holding them by the black cords attached to them. He passed one to each of the friends, then put the box back inside his bag.

The pendant Tegan held was intricately carved from brushed metal; the detailed engravings were precisely made with admirable the skill. Her attention moved to the center of the pendant wherein a shiny gray crystal was placed. When she studied it closer, she gasped.

"I recognize this!" she said. "From . . . from Dema-Ki. Before we were trained, we were given a test. Remember? We were supposed to look into a crystal until we found an image. I saw an eagle's eye in mine and—and—"

Marshall beamed at her. "The Elders took note of what you saw within those crystals and had them carved into your pendants."

Tegan looked over her friends' shoulders as they gazed on in awe. Mariah's crystal was light bronze and shaped like the moon with the symbol of waves over it; Aari's blue crystal was fashioned into the silhouette of a dragonfly with half its body translucent; Kody's was a green pentagonal crystal with a five-pointed star woven from twigs at the center, and Jag's amber crystal was chiseled into the paw print of a wildcat.

"How did you get them?" Aari asked Marshall in amazement.

The Sentry just grinned. "Do you like 'em?"

The friends bobbed their heads enthusiastically as they slipped the pendants on letting them hang down their necks.

"As the Elders would have told you, these are not ordinary crystals," Marshall told them. "They help strengthen your spirit, which in turn strengthens your abilities."

"I remember Elder Nageau saying that the mind is able to channel a lot of power from the world of pure energy into the physical world," Aari said.

"A bridge," Tegan interjected. "He said that the mind was a bridge that connected the two planes."

Jag ran his fingers around the edges of his pendant. "Right. He used the analogy of a magnifying lens that focuses the sun's rays on an object. The sun's rays represent the world of pure energy and that the object symbolizes the physical world, while the lens is a mind that channels the sun's rays into our world."

"But for the lens to be effective," Aari said, "it needs to be clear of dust and impurities."

Mariah perked up. "I remember asking him how to keep our minds clear of 'dust'. It's easy enough to do it with an actual lens—just grab a cloth."

"And what was his reply?" Marshall asked, and Tegan could tell he was holding back a smile.

"His answer was twofold," she said. "On one hand, it's important for us to go through the different forms of training, like meditation, physical activities or just learning how to be still. On the other hand, he mentioned that it was about . . . um . . ." She trailed off, frowning as she tried to recall.

"It was about being vigilant in our day-to-day thoughts and actions," Aari finished for her.

Marshall looked at the red-haired teen. "And I'm assuming Elder Nageau mentioned why that's important?"

"It strengthens our spirit," Aari said.

Tegan added, "It's about doing the right thing, making the right choices, especially when it's the most difficult."

Marshall appeared pleased that they recalled these details. "Yes. Precisely."

"So what I'm gathering here," Kody grinned, "is that our crystals are basically rocket fuel for our powers."

"A lot of that depends on you, really," Marshall said. "The crystals have been assigned to you for life. The more you strengthen your spirit, the more effective the crystals will be."

Tegan held up her pendant and slowly closed her fingers over it, then met the Sentry's eyes. "Thank you, Marshall."

"I'm just a messenger. The Elders were the ones who wanted me to give this to you." He smiled a warm smile as he extended his arms over his head, stretching. "I think it's a good time to call it a night."

As Jag showed them to their rooms, Tegan held onto her pendant. She felt attached to it, like a kinship, as if it was an extension of her.

"You feel it too, huh?" Aari whispered. "It's like it fits just right."

"That's exactly it," she said. "But why? How?"

"I really have no idea. Then again, there are so many mysteries to this world. I just wish I knew the workings of it."

Tegan held her pendant tighter. "Me too."

The giant hamburger sat on the table, just waiting to be consumed. It was nearly the size of Kody's head and was layered with every delicious topping he ever wanted. The aroma of it turned him into a dribbling, jumbled mess. He basked in its presence for a moment longer, then reached out and grabbed it.

As he opened his mouth to chomp down, the burger suddenly gaped hugely and said in a high-pitched voice, "Outside, Kody! Go outside!"

Kody yowled and flung the talking food away before promptly falling off his chair. The burger landed with a splat on the floor but looked unharmed. It pushed itself toward him and continued urging, "Go outside! Outside!"

Kody's eyes flew open. He was staring up at the ceiling of the dark room he and Aari were sharing. Slowly, he sat up from where he lay on a small air mattress and pressed his hands to his head. *No more beef stew before bed,* he thought wearily.

He looked over at Aari on the guest bed. "Aari," he whispered. He received a snore in response. Rolling his eyes, he put on a pair of bunny slippers he'd found and tiptoed out to get some water. On his way to the kitchen, he passed by the other guest room, which the girls were sharing. He smiled to himself, glad to have the two back with the group.

Jag and Marshall were asleep on the sofas in the living room, and Lady had managed to wriggle her way under Marshall's arm; the Labrador seemed to have taken a liking to the Sentry.

Kody grabbed a mug and filled it. As he leaned against the kitchen counter and drank, he revisited his dream and shuddered.

Maybe he should have just eaten the burger to shut it up. It had looked rather appetizing.

He headed out of the kitchen and as he turned to head back to his room, he stopped.

Outside.

As if someone had taken control of his hands and feet, he found himself opening the front door of the farmhouse and stepping out onto the front porch. He gazed at the wheat field ahead and realized that, aside from the breeze that rustled the plants, it was completely silent. Then, in his slippers, he walked down the steps and headed into the nearest field without concern for what he was doing.

He heard a sound and turned to see Lady padding after him. He smiled and bent down to hug the dog as she snuffled and licked his hands and face.

"Aw, look at you!" he cooed. "You couldn't sleep either, huh? Did Marshall's snoring bug you?"

The Labrador looked up at him earnestly, tail ceaselessly wagging.

"Let's go for a walk, then," he said. "Holler if you see a snake."

Lady let out a sneeze and trotted along beside him.

Kody felt chatty. "You know what I dreamed about, Lady? A burger. A burger that spoke to me." He shook his head. "Hope no one snuck *you* bits from the stew. I wonder what kind of dreams you'd have. Would it be your owners meowing at you? Or maybe your tail barking at you each time you tried to catch it?"

Lady listened intently as they strolled through the field. Kody stroked her head. "You're such a good girl. When we go back in, I'll see if I can find you a treat."

The dog nosed his leg. He smiled at her, then looked up at the starlit heavens. It was really quite a beautiful night. They continued on for a while longer before Lady let out a yawn and a quiet whine.

"I hear you, I hear you," Kody said. "C'mon, back we go."

As he turned around to return to the house, he thought he saw motion in the sky. He squinted up but found nothing. *Probably just tired,* he reckoned, but there was a nagging in his mind and he scanned the sky again. Still nothing. He concentrated on his abilities so everything became brighter.

Man, you gotta love night vision.

Lady whined again and rubbed her head against him.

"Hold on, girl," he said, stroking her muzzle as he looked overhead. "I need to check something."

Then, in the distance, he saw it.

Is that a bird?

It seemed to disappear and reappear every few seconds, faintly blocking out some stars as it moved. He zoomed in and noticed that the silhouette had a large wingspan and was actually translucent.

Fascinated, he switched back to normal vision to see if he could spot it. Even though he knew where to look, the entity was invisible to him. He reactivated his night vision and zoomed in but his perception changed to one he'd never seen before; everything was a dark gray or black save for seemingly random white noise.

Confused, he looked down at Lady and screamed. He tripped over himself, landing on his backside as the dog approached him. She appeared light gray and white—much brighter than her surroundings. As she nuzzled him in concern, Kody's breathing began to slow. After the initial shock, he realized that his new vision looked familiar.

Oh, my God, he thought. *I've seen this before. From a video game. Is this... is this thermal imaging? Holy smokes, it is!* He jumped up and spun around, watching as some bright patches appeared in his line of sight and disappeared.

"Lady!" he hissed, astounded. "Lady, I've got something new!"

The Lab tilted her head, probably thinking he was crazy. Kody looked back to where he'd spotted the curious entity. It was a little farther away now, but instead of glowing white, it formed a dark grey shape against the black sky. He tracked it, watching as it descended onto the farm across the road from the Sanchez's. As it approached the crops, it seemed to disintegrate into countless particles before completely vanishing from his sight.

Kody spun around and sprinted through the headless stalks back to the house, his slippers kicking up dirt behind him. Lady, startled, ran after him. Inside, Kody woke everyone up, not caring about how loud he was. He gathered them in the living room and bent over to catch his breath.

"What is it, Kody?" Jag asked, rubbing his face.

Kody straightened with his hands on his hips. "I saw something," he said. "I went out for a walk and thought I saw something in the sky. I switched my vision a couple times and then this . . . this new ability kicked in."

Jag seemed to wake up at that. "New ability?"

"Yeah. It's thermal vision." Kody absently fiddled with the pendant around his neck. "I see the heat that things give off."

"Does this happen, Marshall?" Tegan asked, looking up at the Sentry beside her.

"It's not impossible," he responded carefully. "Your powers are obviously still developing. I wouldn't be too surprised if there were a few more layers to your innate abilities."

"What did you see, Kody?" Mariah asked.

"Something flew over to the farm across from us."

"A bird?" Tegan suggested.

"No. It was kind of transparent. Translucent. And it broke into millions of tiny bits before landing on the crops."

No one moved for a few seconds until Marshall went to get the keys to the minivan. "Let's go."

Kody kicked off his bunny slippers and pulled on his shoes. As the others walked out of the door, Lady whimpered, as if asking where they were going. Jag kissed her snout. "We'll be back soon. Be good."

Kody and the others scrambled into the minivan. Marshall turned the vehicle around and sped out of the property. "Where did you see it?" he asked Kody.

The teenager directed him straight down the road for a bit before instructing him to turn left. They parked on the shoulder some distance from the driveway that led to a neighboring farmhouse.

As they got out with their flashlights, Mariah peered around worriedly. "I hope we don't get shot for trespassing."

"Nah," Jag said. "I know Mr. Dale. He's too ahead in his years to be keeping an eye out at three in the morning."

They made their way through the crops. Kody touched the stalks lightly. "So Mr. Dale grows wheat too?"

"And corn. Way, way over there." Jag pointed to the right.

"I see some stalks without heads," Tegan called.

As Kody passed by a row of wheat, he saw movement and instantly turned to look. A head fell off and drifted to the ground in a pile of dust. Astonished, he informed the others and zoomed in on the stalk to see what was on it but found nothing.

"I don't get it," he said, puzzled.

Aari, who was shining his flashlight a few dozen feet away, whistled. "Oy, I saw one just drop, too . . . Whoa! More of them keep dropping as you head farther in!"

The friends and the Sentry hurried though the crops. Aari was right; heads were falling from stalk after stalk, as if a ghost was running unseen blades though them. Kody used his newfound thermal vision to find the source of the destruction but couldn't report anything. Whatever it was had become too widely dispersed for him to pick up.

"I can't see it," he told the others.

"Wait, I want to try something," Tegan, a few feet away, said. She knelt and closed her eyes. The rest of the group instinctively drew toward her, no one sharing a word.

Tegan opened her eyes a while later, frustrated. "I don't know what it is, but Aari's right. It has to be synthetic. I couldn't sense it in the novasphere the way I can with living things."

"So it's manmade but too small for even Kody to detect," Aari said quietly, swapping worried looks with Marshall, as if they had a hunch about what the entity was. Before Kody could ask, Tegan said, "Let me try something else. Find me an ant."

Kody quirked a brow. "What?"

"Find me an ant! Quick!"

They plunged to their knees and searched in the dark but Kody had the advantage with his night vision. He found an ant scuttling over the soil and very gently picked it up. "Here."

Tegan took it from him and placed it on a wheat stalk where everyone could see, then returned to her meditative state. The others saw the ant go still for a bit before it scurried up the plant. Kody, impatient, had to refrain from shifting around as the group watched the little creature move about in observation. Then, they saw the head of the stalk with the ant on it fall off. Tegan snapped back a moment later and gaped up at them.

"What is it?" Mariah asked. "What did you see?"

"I saw them! I can't believe . . ." Tegan slowly stood up. "They're unbelievably tiny, even to an ant. I've never seen anything like it. One was tearing away right under the wheat head with some kind of claw-blades? I don't know. And another was shredding the wheat into powder. They're definitely not natural. They move very quickly, too. The second the head falls, they're off to the next one."

"Where did you see them go?" Kody asked.

Tegan pointed at a stalk right beside them. Kody pushed past everyone else and leaned in so close his nose nearly touched the plant. He switched to thermal and zoomed in as much as he could. He moved around a bit until he found what Tegan had seen. She'd described it well; it was like a minuscule metallic bug with a long attachment at the end. "Houston, we have contact," he testified quietly.

"Can you grab it?" Jag asked.

"Sure, if we had—whoa! What the . . ."

"Kody?"

"It just glowed red and took off! Probably sensed how close I was." Kody got up, dusting his pants as he kept an eye on the bug. "We'll get them. Just find me containers."

"Oh, that's brilliant," Tegan said, applauding slowly. "We come out all the way here and have nothing to put these things in. Is there anything in the van?"

"Don't think so," Marshall said.

Kody scanned the next stalk. "Which one of us here has that super speed ability thing? Oh right, of course, that would be Jag! Could you be a dear and run back and grab a couple of small jars from the house?"

Jag did not look amused by the notion. "Is that what I've been reduced to? A gofer?"

"Yes," Kody answered. "Now go, Toto! Go!"

There was a grumble and a rush of wind beside Kody, which he figured was Jag taking off.

Tegan chuckled. "Toto?"

Kody kept track of the metallic bug as it moved on. "We're in Kansas. It seemed fitting."

Jag returned shortly after with three empty spice containers and passed one to Kody, who received it without taking his eyes off his target. He uncapped the container and held it in one hand while grasping the lid in the other. He brought them on either side of the bug; then, holding his breath, snapped the container and lid together, trapping the tiny entity inside with the stalk sticking out on either end.

"That thing's not happy," he said, clasping the glass jar tightly as he stared into it. "It's bouncing around like a rocket that's gone ballistic."

Marshall flicked out his switchblade and trimmed the ends off the stalk so Kody could twist the lid shut and secure the tiny bug. The teenager held up the jar, grinning. "Got it."

Mariah took it from him and pointed her flashlight into the clear container. "Wow. Can't see a thing."

"That's because it's probably a nanomite," Aari said. "A microscopic machine." He jerked his chin at Kody. "See if you can get more."

"Aye, aye." Kody grabbed another container from Jag and carefully put his nose up to several stalks until he found another nanomite. Together with Marshall, he caught it and passed it to Tegan. It took a little longer to find and seize a third one. As he capped the container, he chortled. "Look at me. I used to catch fireflies. Now I'm catching nanomites."

Tegan patted his back. "So, what now?" she asked. "Looks like we know what we're dealing with but we can't go to the cops for help."

"There is someone who may be able to help us," Marshall said slowly. "He's one of the few people I completely trust."

"Is he a Sentry too?"

"No, but he has some understanding of what we do."

"Who is he?" Aari asked.

"A good friend and a leading mind in the field of molecular science. If there's anyone who could help us figure this out, it's him."

Kody, hopeful yet skeptical, asked, "What's the catch?"

Marshall smirked drolly. "He's in California."

Kody tapped his fingers against his mouth and knew he'd been right to be cynical. "So we're going to go all the way back to California."

"Yes. We'll need to book a flight and leave first thing tomorrow. There's no time to lose."

"I don't want to leave my grandparents," Jag said quietly.

"And I won't ask you to. But it would be best if a couple of you could come with me."

Tegan passed the container she was holding back to Kody. "I'll go."

"I'm staying with Jag," Mariah said. "I'm sure Mr. Sanchez could use some extra help around the farm."

Kody went to stand beside Jag. "I'm staying, too."

They all looked at Aari, but Tegan answered for him. "Brainiac's coming with Marshall and me."

Jag put his arms around Mariah and Kody. "Sounds good, but we need to stay in close contact throughout. There's too much at stake."

Kody quickly shushed them and gestured to their left. The group wondered what he was pointing at.

"The nanomites are coming together," he whispered. "They're falling back into formation." He spun around to follow the movement of the entity as it rose into the sky. "There it goes. Looks kinda like a huge bird."

Jag started running back to the minivan. "If it's heading off, we should follow it!"

The others caught up with him and sprinted toward the vehicle. Marshall leapt into the driver's seat and took off in the direction that Kody was pointing. He was their eyes, keeping track of the entity's movement as best he could. "It comes and goes, guys! I'm losing it!"

"Drive faster!" Jag urged. "We need to find out where they're coming from!"

"Kody, do you still see them?" Marshall asked as he floored the gas pedal.

Kody didn't respond. He was craning his neck outside the window to scour the sky. Moments later he turned to his friends, disappointed. "I lost them."

The group let out a collective sigh. Jag placed his palms on his face. "That's alright, Kode-man. We know you tried your best. Besides, you caught three of them."

Marshall drove the now-quiet group back to the house and parked the car. They entered the house where Lady greeted them drowsily as if they'd interrupted her sleep.

Marshall turned to the five. "Alright. Tegan, Aari and I will leave tomorrow morning. Let's make sure we all have each other's numbers. Capeesh?"

"*Capito*," Jag replied.

They split off while Marshall went online to purchase flight tickets and returned to their beds, feet dragging. Kody, beyond spent, fell face-first onto his air mattress. As exhausted as he was, it took him a few minutes to fall asleep.

And all this because of a talking hamburger.

When Aari trudged out of the guest room a few hours later, he found Marshall at the dining table with a cup of coffee in one hand and his phone in the other. The Sentry smiled tiredly at him. "Good morning."

Aari helped himself to some coffee as well and joined Marshall. "Hi. You look really alert for someone who's had less sleep than the rest of us."

"Glad I look that way," Marshal said, then waved his phone. "I got the tickets. Our flight leaves in less than four hours. We'll arrive in California at about one and we're set to meet my contact at his house."

"You've been busy," Aari commented. "Maybe you can grab a catnap on the plane."

"Oh, I will."

The others joined them a while later. They chatted for a bit before Aari, Tegan and Marshall got ready to leave and headed out. The friends exchanged long hugs. After everything that had happened, they were reluctant to split up again, but they all knew what needed to be done.

"Take care, guys," Aari called as he and Tegan got into the vehicle after Marshall.

"You too," Jag said. He, Mariah and Kody waved as the Sentry maneuvered the minivan out of the driveway and onto the main road.

The drive to the airport was a short one and they were soon through the gate to board their flight. Marshall kept to his word and fell asleep before they took off, as did Tegan. Aari pulled his laptop out of his bag and, using the plane's Wi-Fi, checked the news. As he expected, the headlines were dominated by reports on the ever-widening crop failures. He shut down his laptop after a few minutes and closed his eyes, nodding off.

* * *

Jag cracked open a can of energy drink and took a swig. It was late in the afternoon and he, Mariah and Kody did not seem to be any closer to finding the origin of the nanomite swarm. Right after the others had left for the airport, he had driven out to purchase maps and a load of pens, then brought his grandfather's old computer down to the living room. As clunky as the thing was, it ran well enough and that was all they needed.

He sat down on the sofa and took a few more sips of his drink as he studied the map of the U.S. spread on the coffee table in front of him. Areas where there had been reports of destroyed crops were shaded in various patterns to indicate a timeline in hopes a pattern would emerge. Another map, this one of Kansas, was on the floor and being pored over by Mariah. Kody was plotting affected areas on a global map taped to a wall.

"Anything?" Jag asked him.

"No," Kody replied distractedly.

Jag sighed. They'd been watching news on the TV intermittently and doing research online, trying to work out the extent of the destruction. He glanced down at the Kansas map; Mariah was attempting to figure out where the nanomites would strike next. Once in a while she'd dip her hand into a container of Pringles, but for the most part remained intent on her task.

Jag helped himself to the chips as well. "No luck?"

"Not yet," she said. Lady, who was resting with her head on Mariah's lap, nuzzled the girl's arm. Mariah tore her eyes away from the map and snuggled the dog. "She's so precious. Aren't you, girl? I'm gonna keep you, yes I am, yes I am!"

Kody groaned. "You're doing the weird baby-voice thing, 'Riah."

"As if you don't do it either." Mariah kissed the dog on the nose. "Why must you be such a sweetheart?"

"I can't help it," Kody quipped. "I was just made this way."

"I was talking to Lady, you moron."

"Well, then."

"She's a distraction, that's what she is," Jag said, playing with the dog's ears. He took a quick look at the time; he'd have to leave in a couple of hours to buy some food for the three of them and deliver dinner to his grandfather at the hospital. Jag had visited him earlier in the day and found his grandmother to be in neither a better or worse condition. She was still unconscious, which Jag hoped wasn't a negative sign. He'd kissed her on the forehead and prayed for her recovery, then reluctantly left after keeping his grandfather company for a while.

Jag turned his attention back to the map in front of him and set his energy drink aside. Leaning forward, he clasped his hands under his chin while scanning the chart. It had become clear that the crop destruction was taking place in large areas of farmland in the Midwest. Another wave of destruction had laid waste to orchards and vegetable farms in California, centered in San Joaquin Valley.

Kody thumped the wall with another groan. "I wish something would just show up already. This—wait. What's that?"

The television showed seated journalists facing a podium in front of a blue backdrop crested with an official-looking emblem. Jag turned up the volume just as a skinny man in a suit walked on stage. He adjusted the mic, then addressed the journalists. "Good afternoon, ladies and gentlemen. The Secretary of Agriculture will be with us in a moment. He will make a brief statement and take questions afterward."

He then strode off stage and was replaced by a man thrice his size who took to the podium. The newcomer greeted the journalists, then said, "As you know, the nation has been hit by large-scale crop losses. Although isolated reports of these events began coming in three to four months ago, the situation has escalated over the past couple of weeks.

"While we have been unable to conclude the source of the crop damage as of yet, I give you my complete assurance that we have the best people from various agencies working to identify, isolate and neutralize this phenomenon—this scourge.

"We are also working with the United Nations and the governments of several countries who have been affected by this outbreak. The Secretary of State has been in close contact with the leaders of China, India, Australia, Canada, and our friends in Europe, South America and Africa. I too have been in touch with my counterparts in the aforementioned countries and regions. Working with them and the UN, we are trying to ascertain the state of global grain reserves.

"I would like to assure our citizens that we are doing everything we can to contain the effects that this phenomenon may have on U.S. agriculture production. We are, at present, taking all necessary measures to ensure sufficient grain supplies are available in areas hit hardest by the shortage.

"I am also asking the public, especially farmers and folks involved in supporting the farming industry, to report immediately if they notice anything suspicious or out of the ordinary occurring in their areas by calling the number at the bottom of the screen.

"With regards to the incidences of unrest reported in several cities across the country, I call on those involved to immediately cease these indictable activities. Adherence to the rule of law is crucial at times like this.

"Furthermore, I have been instructed by the Secretary of Homeland Security to remind you that looting will be not be tolerated. Law enforcement agencies around the country have been advised to take all necessary steps to maintain order.

"Once again, let me state that the government is doing everything possible to resolve this pressing situation and we ask for your full cooperation and support. Thank you. I'll now be taking a few questions."

Several reporters stood up and began shouting questions. An off-screen voice could be heard calling for one question at a time and the reporters quieted. A microphone was passed to a pretty, petite African-American woman in the front row. "Mr. Secretary, Naomi Shakur from CNN. You stated that you first heard about this disease around four months ago. What has your department done since then and how did things get so far out of control to reach this crisis point?"

"When the first reports came in they were, as I said, isolated," the Secretary replied. "We immediately dispatched teams to affected areas. Based on the findings at that time, there was no direct evidence of a connection between those regions. Since then, there has clearly been a significant increase in both the size and severity of the outbreak and I will admit that the rapid spread caught us by surprise."

The microphone was then passed to a balding, mustachioed man. "Good afternoon—Linden Sullivan, New York Times. There are all kinds of speculation going around. Is this a disease or some sort of bio-terror attack on our nation?"

"The results of our tests remain inconclusive," the Secretary repeated. "We have yet to discover the source, be it biological, chemical or some other cause. I am advised that no credible information exists to suggest this is part of a terror plot aimed at our nation and, in fact, the effects seem to be global in nature. Our view at this point is that no known terrorist group would have the capacity to mount an attack on this scale, nor has an of them made a claim."

The next journalist, a youngish fellow with a prominent jaw, spoke. "Trevor Romanov with Fox News. With all due respect, sir, your call for calm is not going to be enough for the growing number of individuals and families across the country who wake up in the morning wondering if they will have enough food on the table for the day. My question is: Does the United States have sufficient grain reserves, or have we depleted it since the implementation of the 1996 Freedom to Farm Act? And if so, how does the government plan to prevent mass starvation?"

"Whoa, easy, Trevor," the Secretary told him, stifling a chuckle. "You have more than one question there, the last one being rather hyperbolic but I'll address it anyway. To answer your first question, the United States used to stockpile grain but that practice was indeed discontinued after 1996. However, and let me be clear on this, supplies are being brought in from other nations with surplus grain, as global grain is largely a freely traded commodity. As we speak, arrangements are being made with our neighbors to the north in Canada, as well as Russia, to create a supply line. So let's take this a notch down and go easy on the doomsday scenarios."

Jag slapped his forehead. "If only they knew that this *will* lead to a doomsday scenario."

Another correspondent spoke up. "There have been reports of food riots in China and India, and rumors of mobilization of their armed forces along the borders. In light of the fact that Russia appears to be the only country mostly unaffected by this phenomenon, there is speculation in certain quarters that the Russians are behind this. Do you have any information on that?"

"To your question regarding alleged Russian involvement, that is simply a rogue theory and one I obviously have no information about. Specific questions about how other nations are responding to their own issues are better directed to the State Department, and you will have plenty of opportunities to do just that in the coming days."

Kody took the remote from Jag and muted the television. "So what do you think?"

"Lots of crazies out there but it looks like the guy from Fox had it right," Jag said, shaking his head. "If this thing isn't stopped, we're looking at starvation. Not for just the nation, but the entire world."

Mariah pulled up the collar of her t-shirt and gnawed at it, a murky expression stitched on her face. "We're the only ones who know what's really going on. That's kind of frightening."

Jag gently rubbed her back. "Keep at it, guys. We'll figure this out. I know we will."

***

Aari, Tegan and Marshall had gotten into a small rental car after touching down in California. Marshall, seeming to know exactly where they needed to go, drove through the streets of Goleta. He then exited the town and continued on until they reached a suburb with single-story bungalows on large plots of land. A few minutes later they arrived at the gates of a ranch-style home.

The Sentry picked up his phone. "And here we are. I just need to give him a call, and—"

Before he could finish his sentence, the gates opened. Aari saw Marshall glance at the security camera by the gate and give it a thumbs-up. They parked along the side of the house and, as they got out, were greeted by a neighing to their left. A striking silver horse was staring at them from a large paddock.

Tegan tugged on Aari's arm. "Look at it!" she whispered. "It's so handsome!"

"Too bad Mariah's not here," Aari said. "Or maybe it's for the best. We'd never be able to drag her away from it."

Marshall led the way to the back of the house. A sliding door to a deck opened and a tall, slim man wearing a light-colored polo shirt stepped out. His hair was slightly grayed at the sides but there was a boyish charm about him. "Marshall!" he called out.

"Josh!" Marshall hurried up the steps and grabbed the other man in a warm hug. "It's good to see you again!" He turned to the friends. "Aari, Tegan, this is Dr. Joshua Ferguson."

"Pleasure meeting you, Dr. Ferguson," Aari said, eagerly pumping the man's hand.

"Just call me Josh." From the bright light in the his eyes and the crispness in his enunciation, Aari knew he was going to enjoy getting to know the scientist.

Josh extended an arm, inviting the three of them inside. "I understand this is an urgent matter, Marshall, but Katherine has prepared lunch for all of us, so let's have a quick bite."

Inside the cozy dining room, two small dogs barked in welcome but were kindly hushed by Josh. As his guests took their seats, he mentioned they had a cat that was probably wandering around the property. Katherine Ferguson, her short straw-colored hair up in a ponytail, came out of the kitchen and smiled genially at the friends and the Sentry. Marshall got up to greet her and offered to help with lunch, but she declined and kissed his cheek before retreating.

The Sentry seemed exceptionally fond of Josh and Katherine, and Aari noticed that they reciprocated that affection as though Marshall was family. *Wonder what history he has with them*, Aari thought. It hit him then that the friends knew next to nothing about most of Marshall's life outside of his Sentry duties and his time with the Marines.

Josh served the first portion of their lunch, which consisted of artichokes, something Aari had never eaten before but found himself enjoying. They were served freshly baked swordfish next; Aari's and Tegan's jaws dropped.

Tegan took the first bite and wriggled in delight. "This is probably the best fish I've ever had. Kody's really missing out."

Aari took a picture of their meal with his phone and sent it to Kody, who immediately replied with incoherent capitalized typing and crying emoticons.

"Our boy's in a fit now," Aari told Tegan with a grin. She snickered.

Katherine brought out dessert once they had finished their meal and stayed around for a bit, then excused herself. "I need find that cat before it gets too late," she said with a sigh.

When she was out of the door, Marshall turned to Josh apologetically. "I'm sorry to take your time on a Sunday, Josh."

The older man patted the Sentry's arm. "Don't be. It's such a joy for Katherine and me to see you again after so long. Besides, I know you wouldn't have come here in such a hurry if it wasn't about something important." He pushed his empty dessert bowl aside. "Now, what is it I can do for you?"

Marshall pinched the edge of the table between his fingers. "Best if I start from the top. These two are with me on this, by the way. Their friends are in Kansas working on another aspect of this situation."

Josh laced his fingers over the table. "I am all ears."

Aari watched the man's reaction as Marshall explained everything concerning their hunch about the source of the crop failures, leaving out how the five had met him and their powers. When he finished, Josh let out a whistle. "So you're saying that the outbreak happening right now is *intentional?* Someone's actually behind this? None of the agencies investigating the crop failure so far have mentioned anything to indicate that. Why?"

Aari answered before Marshall could. "It's a question of paradigm."

"What makes you say that?"

"The government is working on an assumption based on past experience and training, which means they're instinctively looking for a biological or chemical cause. They're searching for the source in the obvious places, like soil, water, the crops, fertilizer, pesticides—anything else that the farmers may have used in the process." Aari made a square with his thumbs and index fingers. "They're locked in this box because that's where the source has traditionally been for crop failure."

Josh looked at Marshall, clearly impressed. The Sentry lightly thumped Aari's shoulder. "Probably should have introduced him to you as our mini Einstein."

"Probably," Josh said affably. "So what you're saying, then, Aari, is that they're looking at the ground when the destruction is actually . . ."

". . . Descending from the sky. Literally."

Josh absorbed this with round eyes. "That's unbelievable!" He sat still for a few moments, in a daze, then shook himself. "Alright, how can I be of help?"

"We need to find a way to destroy the nanomites—if that's what they really are," Marshall answered. "Doubt it could be anything else, really. Basically, we need to figure out what it's made of, what makes it work, and how we can eliminate it."

"We managed to catch three of them," Tegan added. "They're in my bag."

Josh was dubious. "You *caught* them? How? How could you possibly catch nanomites?"

Tegan gave a sheepish smile and looked to Aari for help, but he had no idea what to say either. Marshall came to their rescue. "Let's just say they lucked out," he told Josh simply.

Josh looked from Marshall to Aari and Tegan but smartly decided not to push the subject. "You mentioned that they come in the shape of a large bird at night?"

"We suspect that they travel fair distances from their source, wherever that is, and the form of a bird is the most efficient means of travel," Aari said. "There's definitely a significant level of programming involved here that allows these—I guess synthetic organisms?—to merge, dissolve and then remerge."

As he spoke, Tegan picked up her knapsack and brought out the three spice containers with bits of wheat stalk inside. Josh picked one up and put on his glasses to get a better look. "Hmm . . . I'll need some serious magnification to figure out if we have a nanomite after all."

Marshall picked up the other two containers and held them up. "Precisely. Which is why we came looking for your help."

"I'll take them down to my lab," Josh assured them. "I have all the equipment I need there to study it and run some tests.

Why don't you guys drop by tomorrow afternoon? Marshall, you know where I work."

Marshall nodded. "Sounds good."

Josh was still looking at the container in his hand when Katherine returned, worried. "Josh, have you seen the cat?"

Josh removed his glasses and sat straight. "Isn't she outside?"

"No. I've been calling her and she usually comes, but she hasn't this time around."

Just then, they heard a quiet meow. Aari leaned back in time to see a tortoiseshell cat walk in light-footedly from the study. Katherine groaned, then reluctantly beamed and picked up the cat. "She was inside the whole time!"

Her husband chuckled. "That sneaky feline . . ."

Marshall slowly got up, Aari and Tegan following suit. The Sentry passed Josh the two other containers and hugged the couple again. "Thank you for the wonderful lunch, guys."

Katherine put the cat down so she could give him a proper hug in return. "It was our pleasure, Marshall. You and your friends are welcome here any time."

Aari and Tegan said goodbye to her and headed back to their car with Marshall and Josh. The two were ahead of the friends, talking quietly but still audible to Aari and Tegan.

"This is really crucial, Josh. No one in the League has ever seen anything like this. It has a global reach and it's destructive. We don't know what the ultimate purpose behind this attack is yet, but we're working on it."

"I understand," Josh responded quietly.

As they reached the car, Aari's phone vibrated in short bursts inside his pocket. Frowning, he pulled it out to see what was causing the alerts. His eyes widened. "My Twitter feed is blowing up," he said. "There've been more riots in major metropolitan areas across the country."

Josh looked down at the containers in his hands. "Maybe I ought to go to the lab and get started this evening."

Aari barely heard him as he scrolled through the app. He was about to put it away when a passing headline caught his attention. He quickly clicked the link. “Looks like things are getting out of control in India and China. There are confirmed reports that China has started mobilizing its military.”

“What for?” Tegan asked.

“Looks like it’s to quell the unrest there.”

Marshall leaned against the car. “I’m not so sure about that,” he murmured, and his next words disturbed Aari. “My gut feeling says there’s something else brewing.”

Mariah and Jag hopped out of the pickup and exchanged puzzled looks. The Walmart parking lot was ridiculously full for a late Sunday afternoon, yet the grocery stores they'd visited in the last half hour were all devoid of customers. They'd managed to get dinner for Jag's grandfather and were searching for bread for themselves and Kody, who'd remained at the house.

Jag made sure the truck's doors were locked, then walked with Mariah toward the store's entrance. They had to traverse the entire length of the parking lot since they'd only managed to find a spot at the very far end. As they approached the front of the store, they were met with the sight of a long lineup outside the building. Groups of people were hurrying through the entrance, but the rest were in line.

Mariah nudged Jag and indicated at the waiting crowd. "What in the world?"

Jag fiddled with his pendant. "I don't know . . ."

They passed the lineup to the doors where two uniformed security personnel were standing. Mariah paused when she saw a sign taped to the wall beside the guards. "Are you kidding me?" she sputtered. "We have to get in line if we want to buy bread or grain products?"

With a resigned sigh, Jag steered her to the back of the line. As they passed by the men and women, they noticed that the people seemed restless; some even appeared downright agitated. There was a group of three men standing in the middle of the lineup; a couple of them wore sleeveless shirts that showed off tattoos and rippling biceps. They were drinking from soda cans, but Mariah caught a whiff of alcohol.

Impatient people and booze, she noted silently. *Not a good mix.*

"There are so many people here," she said as they took a place behind a small, kindly-looking elderly woman. "Maybe a hundred or so. Do we really want to stand in line for bread, Jag?"

"We need something for breakfast tomorrow," he replied, weary.

"Can't we just get eggs or something for now?"

He seemed to be considering it when the woman in front of them turned around and smiled. "This is happening in grocery stores everywhere, sweetie. We're here because every other store in town has run out of bread. If you want to get something else, though, you'd better be quick." She nodded at the people exiting the store. "Those folks are clearing the shelves in a hurry. But these ones here, including the out of town types," she added, lowering her voice as she looked down the line at the men who were drinking, "decided that they would stay in line to get bread regardless."

"If this is the only place with bread, the prices must be really jacked up, huh?" Jag asked.

"Oh, yes. It's nearly tripled now."

Mariah winced. *That's crazy.* She shook Jag's arm slightly. "We should get something else, then."

At that moment, the line moved forward a bit. As if that was a signal for Jag, he replied, "Let's just wait it out."

Mariah grumbled and folded her arms. A woman several spots ahead of them was struggling to keep her children under control. Three of them were milling around her legs while the youngest was in her arms, wriggling and getting loud.

"I wanna go home, Mommy!" he howled. "Hoooome!"

The woman tried desperately to shush him but that only made it worse. The child started wailing and screaming. Mariah and Jag politely looked away as the woman blushed, clearly not wanting any attention drawn to her.

"Hey!" a rough voice called. "Shut your mouth, you little punk!"

Appalled, Mariah searched to see who it was that was being so uncouth. She wasn't entirely surprised to find that it was one of the three muscled men. He had a thick beard and wore a baseball jersey. Gulping down the rest of his drink, he crushed the soda can in his meaty hand and tossed it aside, belching.

"Disgusting," Mariah hissed.

Jag rubbed her arm to calm her. "Shh, ignore him."

"He yelled at a child!"

"I know, but I'm not sure you want to be confronting him, especially since he's looking pretty plastered right now."

Mariah, tempted to gesture rudely at the drunk, kept her peace as more people joined the line. Men and women walked out of the store at the far end of the building with bags. It occurred to her that most others in the lineup were observing those shoppers, too.

A man spoke up behind her, jolting her out of her trance. "What is this, the Soviet Union? I can't believe we're lining up *for bread!* This is the United States of America, for god's sakes!"

A few people muttered in agreement. Mariah could sense the restlessness growing in the crowd. All she wanted was to get the bread and leave the area but the line was moving very slowly. Forty minutes later, she and Jag were twenty people away from the store entrance.

"Nearly there," she said, pleased.

Jag grimaced. "Not quite." He motioned her over to his side so she could see what he meant.

Through the automatic glass doors at the entrance, the line of people didn't magically dissipate as it entered the store. Stanchions had been placed inside the doors, with chains snaking deep into the building. People were still lined up between the stanchions, some talking to each other and others looking down at their phones.

Mariah snorted. "Sure hope they'll have enough left for us."

As if waiting for Mariah's words, a woman's voice, cloaked in a Kansas twang, came over the store's exterior speaker. "Dear Walmart customers! As we have a limited supply of bread and other baked products at this time, we regret to inform you that the lineup to the bakery section is now closed. You are welcome to shop for our other low-priced items in store."

She continued speaking but her words were drowned out by the uproar from the waiting crowd.

"No!" the woman with four children cried. "I've got no bread left and I've been to six other stores!" Holding onto her youngest with one arm, she grabbed the hand of another child and hurried past everyone else to the front of the line with her two other kids running to keep up. Those behind her protested and hastened after her.

"To hell with it," the man wearing the baseball jersey barked. "I ain't havin' none of this!" He and his friends ploughed past the guards, knocking them to the ground on their way into the store.

Others started to run after them, trampling the guards as they rushed in. Mariah stared at the scene unfolding before her, horrified. Jag grabbed her around the waist and pulled her off to the side as more people pushed forward, shouting at each other to move out of the way, not bothering to stop for anyone who was knocked down in the fracas.

A scream reached their ears, followed by the shriek of a child. "*Mommy!*"

Mariah pulled away from Jag and caught sight of the woman with the four children. She lay on the ground not far from the guards and was being trodden on. Her wailing kids tried to reach her, all of them with tears streaking down their faces. A couple of them were forcefully pushed aside as people continued rushing into the store.

Mariah started to run toward the commotion but Jag held onto her tightly. "What are you doing?" he demanded. "It's a free-for-all over there!"

"That woman is being trampled!" she shouted. "And I think one of the guards got knocked out!"

Jag let go of her and looked toward the turmoil. As the screams from the children grew louder, a fire lit in his eyes. "Okay, okay—I'll clear a path to them. You get the lady and her kids, I'll get the guards. Ready?"

Mariah grasped her pendant and nodded. Jag hunched forward, as if preparing to ram the crowd with his head, and charged. Mariah followed close behind as he pushed and heaved both men and women out of the way. There were yells of protest but Jag didn't stop. He ran through them, forging a path like a bull until he and Mariah reached the fallen mother and the security guards.

Mariah pulled the semi-conscious woman to her feet, struggling against the crowd that had resumed its course into the store. Holding the woman tightly, she managed to force her way through to safety. The four children, seeing Mariah guiding their mother away from the mob, tottered after her, arms out as they sobbed.

Mariah sat the woman down against a wall and checked to see how badly she was injured. One hand was hanging limp and there was a gash along her forehead. She had several unsightly welts on her face and arms, and she could barely open her eyes. Mariah did her best to stem the blood coming from the biggest wound before realizing that she was trembling herself. She saw the four little ones trying to get close to their mother and made way for them.

The youngest whimpered as he shook his mother. "Mommy? Are you okay? Mommy?"

The woman let out a weak acknowledgement. The boy looked at Mariah, scared, wide eyes pleading. Mariah wasn't even able to fake a smile but she gave the boy a protective half-hug. "It's okay. Your mommy will be fine."

Jag appeared beside her, one guard slung across his shoulders, awkwardly half-carrying and half-dragging the other. He got them both into sitting positions next to the injured woman and fell onto his back end beside Mariah, sweating. "It's a mess in there," he said, panting for breath. "I took a look inside and it's . . . it's terrible. This turned nasty really fast."

Sirens could be heard in the distance. Mariah went to see if she could spot the police cruisers. As she did, a family of four rushed out of the store at the other end of the building, carrying full shopping bags.

A man shouted nearby, "There! They have it! They've got bread!"

The mob started toward the family like a pack of wolves closing on their prey, hurrying until they broke into a run. Mariah searched around wildly for anything that could be used to shield the family from the horde. Her eyes fell on a line of shopping carts along the edge of the parking lot nearest to the store.

Perfect. She narrowed her focus on the last cart in the line. Within the next second, the entire train rocketed toward the mob. The man leading the pack stopped only just in time as the carts rumbled past him and smashed into a retaining wall with a deafening crash, sending broken pieces of the wall and metal parts flying.

There was a collective gasp as the mob came to a halt. Mariah looked toward the family on the other side of the pile of mangled shopping carts. Seizing the reprieve, they were fleeing to their vehicle. Relief threatened to weaken Mariah's knees as they sped out of the parking lot.

When she made her way back to Jag, she found him eyeing her, stunned. "You smashed the wall," he said.

She wrapped her arms around herself. "Yeah. Sorry."

"Don't be. That was great."

The wails of sirens grew louder. Bright, flashing lights lit up the store grounds as police vehicles swerved into the parking lot. Armed cops rushed into position to reinstate order. A policewoman spotted Mariah and Jag and hurried over to them. She took a quick look at the injured mother and guards before pulling out her radio to call for medical assistance.

Ambulances arrived not long after along with more police vehicles. The EMTs assessed the situation and began treating the injured. Mariah and Jag watched for a few minutes before he took her by the arm and they melted away from the scene. Once back in the pickup truck, Jag drove out without a word, leaving the scene of the riot behind.

Mariah leaned against the door and blankly watched the town go by her window. She had stopped shaking but her body felt frail as the adrenaline subsided.

The entire scene involuntarily replayed in her mind. *How did that happen? Aren't we more civilized than that? This shouldn't . . . none of this should've . . . oh my God, they just trampled that woman. They stepped on her while her kids were watching. No one tried to stop them. I don't . . . I . . .*

Jag broke her line of thought. "Hey, 'Riah?"

"Huh? Yeah?"

"You look pretty shaken up."

Her fright turned to vehemence. "Obviously I'm shaken up! Didn't you see what just happened? What *was* that, Jag? Everyone suddenly flipped out and turned into animals!"

He slowed to a halt at a red light and rubbed the back of his neck with both hands. "Aari's predictions were right, I guess. He said that this would happen."

"But we're supposed to be civil and looking out for one another!"

"That was devastating. I still can't believe it even happened. But we need to stay strong, okay? You're tough, Mariah. You were abducted by brutes and you handled that."

"It's one thing to be captives in the hands of thugs. You expect them to be ruthless. You know who the bad guys are. But what we saw . . . everyday folk turning into something else, something so inhuman . . . that's what bothers me." Mariah could feel her wits leaving her. "Why can't we go to the police? We have enough evidence about what's going on. We can go right now and talk to them. I know they'll listen if we present proof."

"I get that you're upset. Believe me, I am too. That was beyond deplorable. But Marshall said—"

"I know what Marshall said," she snapped.

Jag looked as if he would retort but the car behind them honked; the light had turned green. He accelerated away, clenching and unclenching the steering wheel. Mariah kept looking at him insistently.

His lips tightened. "Tell you what. I'll see if I can connect with Elder Nageau. I'll talk to him and find out what the best course of action is."

"You told us that he said to trust Marshall. That means the authorities are definitely out of the question as far as Dema-Ki is concerned."

"Let me speak with him anyway. Let's see what he has to say this time. Now come on, we'll buy eggs for breakfast like we should've, then we'll make a quick stop by the hospital and give Gramps his dinner."

There was nothing more that could be said. Mariah rested against her door again and closed her eyes, trying to get the violent images out of her mind, but she knew she wouldn't be sleeping well that night.

It seemed that all the attendees in the boardroom were tense. Adrian Black fidgeted with his tie as he sat at the head of the large mahogany table, facing the screen on the curved wall at the opposite end. With him were Jerry Li and Luigi Dattalo, along with Dr. Albert Bertram. Although Phoenix Corporation's chief science officer was a rather rotund fellow whose bearded face could easily qualify him as shopping mall Santa, he was not to be trifled with. Black knew all too well how ruthless the man could be when incensed.

Hanging from ceiling mounts on either side of the room were two big display screens that hid the windows behind them. The screen on Black's right was split to accommodate images of three women and two men; five of the six people who headed the Sanctuary projects in various locations around the world. The left-hand screen showed Tony Cross, Dr. Nate and Vladimir Ajajdif. The three of them were seated in the partially finished boardroom of the Sanctuary beneath the Quest Mining site in New Mexico. The two screens were muted for the time being.

Black tapped his fingers together and counted twelve present, including him. The first Inner Circle meeting in months . . . *boy, has the group ever grown.*

"What's with the surprise meeting?" Dattalo murmured to Black, fixing the collar of his impeccably pressed white shirt.

"No idea," Black said. "The Boss called for it."

"Any agenda given?"

"None."

"Must be something urgent."

"We'll have to wait and see."

Li pushed back his chair to look past the screen on the right and out the big windows. "What I'm more curious about at the moment is, what's up with the weather?"

Black was wondering the same thing. San Francisco had been getting a lot of bad weather as of late. Thunder boomed and lightning cracked blindingly over the cityscape, casting an eerie blanket of gloom over the usually lively metropolis.

Dr. Bertram didn't seem bothered and nodded almost imperceptibly at the left screen. "I see Mr. Cross and Dr. Nate are joining us. I was under the impression that it would be just Vlad. Those two are seldom in our meetings. Why are they here now?"

"I guess they were invited by the Boss," Black said impassively, though his gaze lingered on the young man and the doctor for a while longer. He knew what Dr. Nate did and greatly admired him for it. Dr. Nate was the chief advocate for their cause and was unofficially dubbed the organization's "preacher and enforcer." Black knew that the diminutive man was ironfisted with his methods, which was how their cause had gotten so far; he could make believers of skeptics.

Tony Cross was someone Black knew very little about. The young man did the Boss's bidding and the scope of his work was outside the operations of the company. He was the one who would get his hands dirty with the Boss's personal errands. Although he was well aware of the company's business, he exhibited very little interest in it. In fact, he didn't seem at all keen to take part in the meeting.

A woman's voice came over the intercom. "Mr. Black, it's ready. Projecting through in ten."

"Thanks, Linda." Black unmuted the conference call. "Stand by, the Boss has dialed in. Connecting in five seconds."

Every man and woman present, even Tony, sat upright as though simultaneously experiencing a sudden chill. A buzzing reached their ears. Black watched as an image at the other end of the table flickered into existence. The image steadied after a few short seconds, revealing a tall figure that appeared to be seated in the room with them.

Black let a small breath escape from his lips. Seeing the Boss's hologram appear was something he could never get used to even though the figure always looked the same; garbed in a long, dark coat with the hood pulled up so that the shadows blocked out every facial feature.

He noticed that the Boss was holding a violet sphere the size of a golf ball. *Without fail, there it is*, he thought. He'd never seen the Boss without the sphere at any Inner Circle meeting, and though he was curious, he never ventured to ask about it.

In a deep voice modulated by a digital voice changer, the Boss spoke in an almost inhuman, metallic tone. "Good day, ladies and gentlemen. Thank you for being here on such short notice. I know you're all busy with your projects as there is much to be done, so I will keep this meeting brief."

The figure paused, as though studying their individual responses.

"I have called you here, first, to express my appreciation for your hard work and dedication to the cause, and second, to impress upon you that we cannot afford any slipups, especially as we move into this critical phase of our mission. It is imperative that we be extra vigilant now. The greatest risk we face when things are going well is that we lose our focus. Again, let me make this clear: No mistakes. No excuses."

Black dared a quick look at the left-hand screen. None of the three men there blinked, but Tony's face turned a light shade of red.

"I am disturbed by the events at the New Mexico site," the Boss continued, the metallic voice turning frosty. "I will not tolerate any more of such incompetence. I do not need to remind you about the importance of what we're doing here."

Black watched silently, taking note of how the holographic image seemed to look directly at each member of the inner circle. It was as if the Boss had a hand on the pulse of the organization and could extrapolate whatever needed to be known just by observing the body language.

Shaking his pen between his fingers, Black thought, *Maybe that's the real purpose of this meeting; to sense the group . . . here's hoping no one present gets caught in something they can't fix.*

"The crucial role we are all playing in the future of humankind, the future of the planet . . . the vital purpose of our cause . . ." The Boss lifted the small sphere and gazed at it. "You are here because you are believers, so I don't intend to preach to the choir."

A flash of lightning illuminated the boardroom, followed closely by the crack of thunder. The office lights blinked several times and the hologram flickered. Black and the others watched, transfixed, as the distorted image took on the semblance of something otherworldly. The Boss was speaking again but what came out of the speakers was a long, high-pitched crackle and screech that made those present flinch.

Then the lights stopped blinking and the hologram came back into perfect focus. Black realized he'd been gripping his pen tightly and dropped it.

The Boss regarded them from under the golden hood. "As promised, I've kept the meeting short. I will now open to the floor. Questions?"

That's it? Black cleared his throat quietly. "Thank you for impressing upon us the importance of vigilance as we move forward with our plans, Boss. For the benefit of everyone here, could we perhaps ask you to share some insights on the big-picture status of our projects?"

"I was planning on updating all of you at a later time, but since you asked . . ." The sphere rolled between the Boss's fingers. "The Sanctuaries are coming along well, save for that ignominy I mentioned earlier."

Black didn't have to look at Ajajdif or Tony to know that each of the men had probably shrunk in his chair.

If the Boss took notice, it didn't show. "Except for some minor tweaking and requests for additional resources, I think Mr. Dattalo's team has done a great job with the REAPR project. The incursion is going according to plan. The global distribution of the REAPR units is coming along as scheduled and is showing great results.

"We expect to pass the midway point of our projected worldwide target in about two weeks. If things continue at this pace, the mobilization of forces we've seen in China and now, according to the news, India, will move to the next phase as chaos within their borders gets worse.

"We need to ensure that the remaining Russian crops are unscathed. Also, even as this project moves along, we mustn't lose sight of the other endeavors we have in the pipeline. They will need to be rolled out in the proper sequence.

"That said, I am pleased to inform you that two major undertakings in that area are coming along well. As you know, Dr. Bertram is heading one of them. I trust the specimens of your two projects are replicating as anticipated, Albert?"

"Yes," Dr. Bertram said, daring a quick smile. "They're actually progressing better than expected."

One of the women on the five-way split screen coughed politely. A blonde who looked to be in her early forties and whom Black found to be very attractive, noted that those present were waiting for her to speak and said, "This is all good and fine, but we know this is just one half of the equation. The other is our strategy on a key resource for the cause—the future guardians of the planet. How are we doing on that front?"

Black was certain the Boss was smiling under the hood. The metallic voice reached out from the speakers once again. "Why don't I let Dr. Nate bring us up to speed? This is, after all, his area of expertise."

The small man took off his glasses and gave them a good wipe before placing them back on his nose. He made sure his greasy black hair was still sticking flat to his scalp, then addressed the group. "Thank you, Boss. I will try to be brief. The program for selecting the Stewards is coming along remarkably well. Across the globe, I might add." He seemed to puff out in pride at this. "The reprogramming methods of these young minds 'ave proven rather effective. 'owever, for reasons unknown, several candidates rejected assimilation, thus making them unviable for our purpose. I 'ave made some improvements to our methods and they will be implemented soon. The new approach will drastically improve the yield we are seeing from the procedure. We expect to attain close to an 'undred percent success rate from this point on."

"Thank you, Dr. Nate," the Boss said. "Good job with the work you've done so far. Any more questions? No? Very well, then. We shall adjourn."

As Black reached to terminate the conference call, the Boss raised a hand. "Dr. Nate, please remain seated. And Tony . . ."

Black glanced at the left screen. Tony, who was halfway out of his chair, paused uncertainly.

Despite the electronic distortion, disdain was clear in the Boss's voice. "I will speak with you tomorrow."

* * *

Dr. Nate sat alone in the New Mexico boardroom, facing the hologram that was also projected there. Tony had left quickly after Ajajdif, and Dr. Nate couldn't blame him. At the same time, he was also thankful that he wasn't the one on the Boss's bad side.

"Good progress on the reprogramming method, please keep me informed as the results come in," the Boss said, then stood. "Moving on to something that's been a thorn on my side. Dema-Ki. I need to find out what the Elders are plotting. The only way to obtain that information is to extract it from the two girls—whom you *lost*."

Dr. Nate shrugged helplessly. It wasn't his fault the pair had escaped, but he supposed the Boss's anger toward Tony would have to spill over to him eventually. He watched as his superior tucked the violet sphere away into a pocket.

"We cannot afford to have the Elders interfering with our plans," the distorted voice growled.

Running his thumbs over where his eyebrows should have been, Dr. Nate said, "You yourself 'ave said they're isolated. 'ow much damage can they cause?"

"You have no idea!" the Boss snapped. "We must be at least two steps ahead of them."

"If they're that much of a threat, why don't we simply go in and take them out? We 'ave the resources for that. All three Ospreys are back stateside, aren't they? I'm sure we can be in and out of that village within an hour. By the time they realize what's 'it them, it will be too late."

"If only it were so. You're forgetting what they're capable of, Doctor. More importantly, there are certain individuals there whom we will need alive to complete the final phases of our plan. But most of all, there is an object of great importance which is under the protection and safekeeping of one of the Elders. Without this relic, our final solution cannot be fulfilled. Even if we go in, it would be prudent to do so knowing what they're up to. A shock and awe operation from the air will not work. It'll have to be boots on the ground. And even *then* I wouldn't authorize the mission without knowing what the Elders have planned."

"Yes, I suppose that makes sense." Dr. Nate wavered, unsure if it would be smart to voice what was on his mind, then said, "I find it rather odd that the fenixium was only available to be mined in two places on this planet and of those places, one just 'ad to be near that bloody valley. If it wasn't for that, they would 'ave remained oblivious of us."

"I've been thinking about that as well, Doctor, ever since the day we discovered it. Why was the most concentrated source of supply so close to that cursed place? We'll never know, I suppose. Fate has a strange way of dealing her cards. Regardless, I make my own destiny. That is the key to what we do here."

Dr. Nate stared, not wanting to interrupt.

The Boss looked down and readjusted the black coat. "I'll be instructing Tony once again to bring me the children. Once we have them, I expect you to extract the information needed." The hologram looked at him directly and the ambient temperature in the room seemed to plummet. "I can count on your expertise, yes?"

"Of course."

"Good. One last thing before we part. I think it's time for me to address our Stewards in all six Sanctuaries. They are our future, after all, and they need to know that we are getting closer to our destination."

Though Nageau had studied the sculpture of the island in miniature for years, he was still fascinated by the amount of detail evident in the work of art that sat upon the wooden table. Dozens of tiny shopping stalls had been delicately placed in an open-air marketplace near a golden beach with a sheltered turquoise harbor where large trading vessels were tied alongside a pier. Numerous homes dotted the island and at the center of it all was a majestic volcano. Even though it was merely a model, Nageau had to stifle a shudder at the story he'd been told since he was a child—a story that everyone knew.

The people of Dema-Ki were a hybrid race. Over two thousand years ago, a group of fifty-one survivors had barely managed to escape their home when a once-dormant volcano erupted with a cataclysmic force. Many residents were killed by the sulfurous ash and lava, and many more died as the island slowly collapsed in on itself and vanished into the depths of the ocean.

The survivors, who had boarded a trading vessel at the last possible moment, watched with tear-filled eyes as their home disappeared in front of them, unable to comprehend or accept what had happened. Each of them had lost some, if not all, of their family.

The Islanders were a peaceful people and extraordinarily advanced for their time. They had learned to harness the hidden potential of the human mind and powers inherent in nature, allowing them to exercise a range of skills, including healing, omnilinguism, telekinesis, extreme agility, strength, speed and many other abilities that varied from person to person. Though such skills would appear mind-boggling to others, they were as natural as breathing to the islanders.

The survivors journeyed across raging seas and through vicious storms for nearly four moon cycles before arriving on the rocky coast of a new land. After a brief skirmish, and with some trepidation, the indigenous inhabitants of the land welcomed the newcomers. It wasn't until the Islanders shared some of their healing abilities, their history and their tradition that the strangers were truly accepted.

Over time, the two races became one; the Islanders showing their new family how to unlock their innate abilities, while the indigenous tribe demonstrated how they lived in harmony with nature on the coast of what would, to the modern world, be referred to as the Pacific Northwest. Eventually, the new hybrid race moved northward and inland, establishing their community in a remote place and naming it Dema-Ki, the hidden valley.

A woman called to Nageau. "Shall we begin?"

Nageau blinked and straightened, then turned to face the other four Elders. They were seated around a small fire pit inside their comfortable assembly shelter. The flames crackled invitingly as Nageau took his place between his mate and a bearded, red-haired man.

"I apologize, dear friends," he said, pushing his cloak out so it wouldn't fold under him. "I called for this early morning meeting but sidetracked myself. That miniature display simply never ceases to astound me."

"Fine workmanship indeed," the flame-haired man agreed. "So what news have you regarding Mariah and Tegan?"

"I am glad to say that the girls have been found and are in safe hands," Nageau reassured him. "If what the Sentry has told me is accurate, the two caused quite a bit of havoc for their abductors while escaping."

Tikina's eyes flashed. Pride for her apprentice, Tegan, shone through a brilliant smile. Another woman, wearing a royal purple headband, bore the same look as her—Mariah had been her apprentice. "They are spirited, that is for certain," she said.

"This is, unquestionably, fantastic news," her mate cut in gruffly. He had muscular arms and thick black locks. "But Nageau, you seem . . . troubled."

Nageau threw some kindling onto the fire. "Sharp as always, Ashack. Sharp as always. Yes, you are right. There is the matter of the girls having been interrogated while they were held captive."

The woman with the purple bandana went rigid. "They were not harmed, were they?"

"No, Saiyu. It is just . . . The girls told the Sentry that whoever was interrogating them knew of our existence here in the valley."

For a long minute, the only sound to be heard was the popping of the fire from the pit.

"Are you sure?" the flame-haired man asked. "Do you suppose they could have misunderstood—"

"The girls say that our valley was mentioned by name, Tayoka."

"Who was it that asked the question?" Tikina queried.

"Some fellow whom they did not know. But what the girls did say was that another person was present. Hidden and silent, but watching and listening. The interrogator kept referring to them as a superior."

Ashack subconsciously rubbed his exposed arms. "What did they want to know?"

"Mainly what and how much we knew about *them*, and what we are planning to do," Nageau answered. "The girls gave away very little and managed to delay the interrogation until the next day. They escaped before that, of course."

"Peculiar," Saiyu muttered. "There are very few possibilities as to who would demand to know about us."

"None of which I am overly fond of," Ashack grunted; gruffness seemed to be sowed into the very fiber of his being.

Nageau held up a hand. "I know this is a sorely pressing issue that will require further discussion, but there is one more thing I would like to share first."

The other Elders hesitated before nodding.

"The five discovered something important about the source of the scourge faced by the outside world," Nageau said. "Thanks to Kody's intuitiveness and sharp eyes, they have found an entity that may be at the root of this affliction."

Tayoka rested a hand on Nageau's shoulder. "You trained him well, Nageau."

"Apparently he couldn't sleep well after the Sentry had given the five their pendants and decided to take a walk outside. As fate would have it, it was then that he observed the entity. It also seems he has uncovered another layer to his abilities."

The others brightened slightly.

"Wonderful." Tikina cast her eyes toward the fire. "I only wish we could have had more time to train them before sending them back to their homes."

Saiyu took Tikina's hand in hers. "We did what we could with the time we had, my friend."

"What are the five doing with this evidence they now have?" Ashack asked.

"Tegan and Aari have left to meet with the Sentry's contact," Nageau said. "The others are staying back at the home of Jag's grandfather to try and identify the location where the entities are coming from."

"Speaking of his grandfather," Tikina said, "or rather, family in general . . . how long will the younglings have to keep this part of their lives away from their parents? I understand the importance of maintaining our existence here a secret, but is it not only right for their families to be informed? Especially since more will be asked of them as time goes on."

Nageau looked around the fire at the other Elders and could see that they were torn on the subject.

"I agree that the families have a right to know," Ashack ventured slowly, "but there is no telling what the consequences of revealing our presence might have on our people here and those in the outside world."

Tayoka shook his head. "My question is, with all the recent developments, do you suppose the time for us to shed our veil is nigh?"

"No," Ashack snapped. "The world is not ready. They are yet to arrive at a stage of their collective evolution that would make them receptive to what we have to offer."

"I suppose this is a matter to be deliberated at a later date," Nageau said calmly.

Saiyu waited for a break in the discussion before asking, "I take it there is still no news about our two deserters?"

Tikina tugged at the sleeve of her shirt. "None. There is no trace of them. Hutar and Aesròn have somehow managed to slip past the Guardians. They are long gone."

Ashack's arms tightened. "What is our course of action, then? Can we not locate them in the novasphere?"

"I was unable to sense either of them," Tikina answered. "And that worries me greatly. It seems as if they have somehow learned to . . . mask their presence."

"Are you sure?" Saiyu asked. "That is an incredibly difficult skill to master. Nearly impossible, even. Perhaps they have . . . perished."

"Those two are fighters," Ashack said darkly, "and they are very keen. Besides, they know the forest well."

Tayoka was quiet when he spoke. "Something tells me that they have crossed into the outside world."

Nageau raised his fingers to the fire. The flames licked toward his hand but were just out of reach. "Tikina?"

"I . . ." His mate clearly didn't want to utter the words she was about to. ". . . I fear Ashack and Tayoka may be right."

Saiyu closed her eyes and turned away. Nageau swallowed his disappointment. "Then, regrettably," he said, "there is little else we can do. We have sent out search groups and scoured the novasphere. If they truly are nowhere to be found, then we must let this go and move on. The best we can manage now is to let the Sentries know so that they can keep an eye out."

"I am not sure if that is prudent," Ashack warned. "Need I remind you all of Hutar's lineage?"

"We are not to judge a person by the deeds of his ancestors," Nageau said firmly. He lowered his hand from the flames. "Let us get back to our earlier discussion about who is so anxious to learn what Mariah and Tegan know about us. As you mentioned, Saiyu, the list is a dramatically short one."

"Yes," Saiyu murmured, "and the two that come to mind are either a rogue Sentry, or . . ."

"Or Reyor."

The others recoiled at the name and the fire in the pit dimmed momentarily of its own accord.

"Do you believe that?" Tayoka asked, hushed, his eyebrows swept upward. "You have been unable to sense . . . Reyor . . . in the novasphere since the banishment."

"I am aware of that," Nageau said, his voice thick, "but we cannot rule this out as a possibility."

The conversation that followed was neither pleasant nor helpful and the meeting didn't take long to come to a close. As they emerged from their assembly shelter, they noticed the sun was fully risen and shining down upon them. After bidding the other Elders a subdued goodbye, Tikina and Nageau strolled back to their living quarters—which the villagers called *neyra*—with their arms linked. Tikina pushed open the door and stepped in but Nageau hung back outside.

"There is something I feel like I should do," he said softly.

Tikina leaned against the open door with a knowing look. "If it will help ease your mind . . ."

He gave her a peck on the forehead. "Thank you for understanding, Tikina."

She righted his cloak and gave him a loving smile. "Do not thank me, beloved. You do not need my permission. Now go. I will have our midday meal ready when you return."

* * *

Nageau emerged from the densely packed trees and gazed up at the stunning waterfall that stretched high above him. The cascading waters ended in a pool at the base that was calm around the edges. The whole environment carried with it a therapeutic effect, but it still wasn't enough to completely soothe the Elder.

He closed his eyes and took deep breaths for several minutes. A tingle seeped through his body as he basked in the fine mist from the waterfall. It cooled his skin and allowed him to relax, but his posture remained intact.

He opened his eyes and deliberately rotated on his heel to observe what was behind him. The forest thinned out slightly to create a crescent-shaped tree-line a dozen yards from the edge of the pool. The greenery at first seemed insignificant, but if one were to look closer, five trees would stand out at the brink of the crescent. They were tall, gorgeous pines, all of them many hundreds of years old.

Nageau quietly made his way over to the middle tree. Its richly textured bark was several shades darker than the rest. He pressed a hand to the rough trunk, feeling the notches against his palm and the life in the tree. "Hello, old friend," he whispered.

Though there was hardly any wind, the tree's branches swayed and rustled leisurely, as if sighing a greeting. Everything else in the forest seemed to have gone silent. To the Elder, it was as though the tree had drawn every spirit into its being.

He kept his hand on the trunk, thinking. He'd visited this place less than a handful of times, the last being years ago when he'd had to make a difficult decision. He'd been racked with doubts and fears, but sitting under this very tree aided in soothing his qualms. Now, he rested against it and allowed his worries to trickle away once more.

You have been here for nearly a millennium. You have seen my ancestors come and go. You have remained a strong and vigilant warden, and we thank you for that.

The darkened tree rustled again, seemingly breathing its acknowledgement.

Nageau recouped in tranquility before a strange sensation crept upon his mind, as if something, or someone, were tapping his consciousness. He opened up and reached out to the presence. When he sensed it, he laughed in delight. *Jag! Is that you, youngling?*

Elder Nageau? It was indeed Jag—a little faint, but most definitely him.

Yes, youngling. I see that you have managed to find me.

Ah, yeah. I thought it would be difficult, but it turns out that it's not too bad. So many people seem to be . . . dormant, I guess? It's like their consciousness is inactive in the novasphere, but yours is bright. Like, the sun kind of bright. I'm confused, though. I tried reaching out to Marshall to see if I could connect with him but I can't.

The Elder chuckled. *Telepathy is a strange gift, and one that can take some a lifetime to master. Do not fret. There will be some people with whom you cannot connect for the time being.*

Okay . . .

I had actually intended to reach out to you, Jag. I am relieved to know that Mariah and Tegan are safely back with you. I tried many times to reach them while they were being held, but their consciousness was not yet receptive.

That's alright. At least you tried, and I really appreciate that. Jag paused, as though wavering. *Uh, Elder Nageau, I'm happy I found you and all, but something's been bothering me. It's become obvious that whoever we're dealing with out here is powerful and has the means to carry out whatever it is they intend to do, and . . .*

Yes?

I just don't know how our small group can stop this. We've accepted—well, re-accepted—our responsibility but... we've seen things, Elder Nageau. While we may not have a lot of evidence, I'm sure we have enough information that we could help the authorities fight back this darkness, whatever it is. He paused again, waiting for Nageau to respond. When he received no answer, he continued. *Mariah and I saw an incident earlier. Actually, we were there as it happened. It was regular people going at each other, trampling one another just to get some bread. We were—we were really shaken up.*

Nageau gazed up at the tree that loomed protectively over him. *I hear you, youngling. It is rather serendipitous that you chose to reach me when I am at a very special place in the forest. I have not ventured to this hallowed spot for many years. But that is a story for another time.*

He clasped his hands. *Jag, the most important thing we are trying to do now is find out who exactly is behind this. Having looked at recent events and the evidence from Mariah and Tegan, the Elders and I have come to the conclusion that there are only two possibilities. While the authorities may be able to stop the one, the other—if indeed this is the person behind this cataclysmic scheme—will most likely be impervious to their methods. But far worse, if cornered, the devastation that could be unleashed by this person will have irreversible consequences. Only those mentioned in the prophecy have the ability to put an end to this. You must trust me, youngling. I cannot stress this enough.*

Though Nageau couldn't read them, he could feel Jag's tumultuous thoughts roiling. Then the boy said, *Yes, Elder Nageau.*

Nageau ran his fingers absently through the grooves in the tree's bark. Go, Jag. *Continue with what you are doing. You are on the right path.*

Alright. Take care, Elder Nageau.

You too, youngling.

Jag severed the connection between them.

Nageau pushed himself away from the tree and drew back his shoulders. He took one last look at the waterfall before whirling around and striding back into the forest, vanishing into its green embrace.

Aari, Tegan and Marshall hurried toward the single-story rectangular building, eager to see what Josh and the new day would bring them. It was a rare overcast morning in California that loomed over them.

Aari's phone rang just as they reached the door of the laboratory. The other two continued into the building but he stayed outside when he saw Kody's name on his phone.

"Be right in," he told Tegan and Marshall as he answered the call. "Hey."

"Hey, Brainiac. How's it going?"

"It's fine. We met Marshall's contact yesterday and we're about to step into his lab right now. Everything alright there?"

"Yeah. We're searching for more information, trying to figure out where the nanomites are coming from and how far they've spread. We're hoping to find a pattern or some other clue."

"We have vital info that the authorities don't, Kode-man. These things, they come out from a central point somewhere, arrive at the target zone, destroy the crops, then either return to where they came from or go to their next target. If you guys can figure out the pattern for a given area, the focal point will be the epicenter. That would be where these things are originating from."

"We'll gather more data and let you know if we find anything. It's hunting season, buddy."

"Okay. And I'll fill you in later on what we learn from here."

As Aari was about to hang up, Kody said, "Uh, Aari?"

"Hm?"

"Things are actually getting bad pretty quickly over here. Jag and Mariah got caught up in a riot that broke out at the local Walmart yesterday."

"*What?*"

"They were pretty shaken up," Kody said. "But they're doing better today."

Aari leaned heavily against the door to the building. "Oh, man . . ."

"I really hope we find a solution soon."

"You and me both."

"There's one more thing. My dad called last night on behalf of all our parents. They think we're all in Kansas right now with Jag's granddad but they're getting worried about us, what with the riots and all. My dad said they're asking if we could cut our trip short and head back home."

"And what did you say?"

"Being the man with the golden tongue—hey!"

Jag's voice came on suddenly. "Golden tongue, my foot! He was sweating the whole time."

Aari laughed as Kody returned on the other end after apparently snatching the phone back from Jag. "*As* I was saying, being the man with the golden tongue, I told him that we were already halfway into our trip and would like to complete our *adventure* before returning."

"Did he agree?"

"I guess. It was a reluctant agreement. But yeah, that's all the news I've got."

"Alright. Call me if anything else crops up."

"Yep. Bye, dude."

As Aari ended the call, Tegan emerged with a strange look on her face. She held the door open. "Come on, Aari. We've been waiting for you."

"Sorry. It was Kody." Aari followed her inside. "You okay?"

"Yeah, I just thought I heard . . . never mind. They're waiting for us."

They entered a reception area with a few chairs and found Marshall already seated. Aari filled his companions in on his call with Kody. Just as he got comfortable in his chair, Josh emerged in his lab coat and glasses to greet them in his characteristically youthful and energetic way. "Good morning!"

Marshall rose to meet him. "Morning."

Aari took stock of the Josh's bloodshot eyes and noted a layer of disquiet behind his genuine smile.

This can't be good, he thought as the man led them down a corridor with spotless linoleum flooring. There were doors on either side of the passageway, each with a window that gave a view of workers handling a variety of equipment. Some workers operated in dim amber light and were covered in cleanroom suits that left only their eyes exposed. Others went about their business in brightly lit rooms while wearing civilian clothes or lab coats.

Josh led them to a medium-sized meeting room with a round table at its center. An open laptop rested on the table. As Aari took a seat, the bright ceiling lights reminded him of a doctor's office but the notion instantly disappeared when he saw an image on a flat screen mounted on one wall.

"What is that?" Marshall asked as he and Tegan sat down on either side of Aari.

"That, Marshall," Josh said, "would be one of the three specimens you brought to me yesterday."

Aari shuddered. "That's a disturbing-looking thing."

Josh dimmed the overhead lights so the image could be seen better. "You're not wrong."

The main body of the specimen was dark gray with a black hexagonal core. Attached to it was a long, ribbed appendage, at the end of which were four blades arranged like pincers. To Aari, it looked like either a tail or an extremely long neck.

Josh gestured at the image. "Let me start by saying that whatever this thing is that you found, I've never, in all my years of working with MEMS and nanotech, seen anything like it."

"MEMS?" Tegan asked.

"Micro-electro-mechanical systems," Aari replied without missing a beat.

Josh smiled his approval. "That's right. They're essentially really, really tiny machines but a level removed from nano. Nano is a way smaller scale.

"I've been here all night, studying this thing and subjecting the specimens to a range of tests. Here's what we know. We'll begin with the structure of the nanomite. It's completely unique. It's made of a material that I have never seen before, which in itself is amazing. It's a special semi-conductor, like silicon, but it runs much cooler. It's special because it's capable of receiving optical signals. And here's the clincher: It's able to transform itself mechanically, moving the bonds that hold it together in order to rearrange and create new bonds with other nanomites."

Josh looked at them excitedly but only saw blank stares, though Aari was feverishly trying to piece together what he'd just heard.

Marshall rested his cheek against his fist. "Wanna say that again in English?"

"Basically, what we have here is a nanomite that receives instructions—or programming—through optical radiation. In other words, digitally encoded light bursts. And because it's cooler than silicon, it leaves practically no heat signature."

"Which means it's not observable on infrared or thermal imaging systems?" Marshall asked.

"Yes, unless you had an extremely sensitive system and knew exactly when and where to point the sensors."

Aari, Tegan and Marshall looked at each other.

"One other advantage of its ability to rearrange its bonds," Josh said, motioning in awe at the image on the screen, "is that it can deflect light or let it pass and make itself virtually invisible to the naked eye."

Aari could see the man was dying to learn how they had found and captured the specimens in the first place. He cringed inwardly; neither he nor the others were in a position to offer an answer to the unasked question.

"What you're telling us is, we're dealing with something that is pretty much undetectable by any kind of sensor," Tegan said.

Josh nodded. "I'm afraid so. And the news gets worse. I've tested one of the nanomites under extreme conditions of heat, pressure and shock. This *thing* came out unscathed."

"What are you saying?"

"I'm saying that it's pretty much indestructible."

"How can we stop it, then?" Aari asked. "How do you stop something that can't be detected or destroyed?"

"I don't know. It's just . . . *too* perfectly designed."

Marshall tilted his chair on its two back legs as he pondered. "What about EMP?"

Josh took off his glasses and rubbed his eyes. "As I said, it functions on a basis of optical radiation and as such is impervious to bursts of electromagnetic pulse."

"If it's optical-based, couldn't we use light against them?" Aari pressed. "Like a laser beam?"

"Possibly. It depends on the type of laser that is employed. But more importantly, you'd have to find them first. They probably come out at night and leave before dawn because that makes the most efficient use of their stealth capabilities. My assumption is that going stealth during the day would drain a considerable amount of their energy."

Tegan tapped the table with a finger. "Where do they get their energy from?"

"They're designed with extreme efficiency in mind," Josh said, "which explains the formation they assume to get to and from their destination."

"You're talking about the bird-shaped swarm," Aari said.

"Yes. It would be a highly efficient mode of transporting the nanomites."

"I get it," Tegan said. "It's like geese flying in formation. It allows them to fly seventy percent farther and longer without tiring."

"Bingo. And another way that they're efficient is right here." Josh walked up to the screen and pointed at the nanomite. "The claws you see here double as a propulsion system when in flight."

"That still doesn't answer where they get their energy from," Marshall said.

"Of course, sorry. Our little friends here get their energy from background radiation, like dim light and radio waves which, by the way, completely permeate our environment."

Josh rested his hands on the table and leaned in. "There's something else. I believe these things operate at two levels of protocols. One is for them to carry out their primary function from the instructions they receive, probably on a daily basis to keep their targets current. But it's the second protocol that troubles me. They seem to have a set of self-defense instructions built in. When I did the extreme testing on the nanomite, its attitude changed. It turned into a berserk red micro-rocket that bounced around the test container. Looks as though if it senses a threat, it will fight back. It does so by disengaging its stealth mode to conserve energy for the fight. And that was just a single nanomite. I shudder to think how an entire swarm of these things would react if directly threatened."

Marshall stared up at the ceiling in frustration. "How would anyone even create these things?"

"With cutting-edge expertise and lots of money," Josh said. He sat on the edge of the table, shaking his head. His excitement had waned and he looked as dejected as Aari and the others felt.

"It sounds like they're unstoppable," Tegan growled. "Whoever created them covered every single angle."

A forlorn pause hung like a cloud in the small room until Aari broke it with a thump of his palm on the table. "I don't believe that. There's *got* to be something we're missing."

The rest considered his comment in silence until Josh's enthusiasm picked up slightly. "You know what, Aari? You're probably right. Everything ever created by man can be undone by man. Let me take another look."

"You should rest first, Josh," Marshall said. "A fresher mind might open some locked doors."

Josh closed his laptop and turned off the projector. "That's true."

They left the room and returned to the waiting area. Josh shook the teenagers' hands again. "I'll take a few hours' nap then get right back on it, don't you worry."

Marshall shook his hand lastly. "We'll be hanging around here, so if you find anything, give me a call and we'll be right over. And thank you, Josh."

The scientist smiled. "Don't even mention it. There has to be an Achilles' heel somewhere on these things. We'll find it."

Kody, Jag and Mariah sat in the living room, quickly gulping down their lunch so they could get back to work. Lady was curled up on a dog bed beside them, dozing. Kody had taken her out for a quick run that morning and she was now tuckered out. All the windows in the house were open to allow as much air circulation as possible. Concordia was too blistering for the trio this day, even with the fans Jag had found that didn't do much other than blow hot air back at them.

They returned to the computer and maps within a few minutes. Mariah had been jotting down all the reports she'd found in chronological order and passing them to the boys, who would then shade in the map of the country. They'd tuned Jag's grandfather's radio to a news station while the television remained muted.

Going by Aari's hunch, they were working on the assumption that there had to be an epicenter to the crop destruction for each region. They fervently tried to search, identify and chart every farm area that had been destroyed. No set pattern had emerged as of yet but they carried on, resolute.

Kody and Jag stood back to study the affected areas and noticed that six distinct zones had begun to appear. These were massive and stretched from Texas all the way to North Dakota, west into Montana, and reaching as far as Washington State. Some of the crop destruction spilled over the border into Canada from the northernmost zones. There was also a distinctly affected area in central California.

This is pretty extensive, Kody thought. *They're hitting our key crop-growing regions.*

"We need more data, 'Riah," Jag said, sticking his pencil behind his ear.

"Got a new batch, hold on." Mariah quickly scrawled on a sticky note and passed it to Kody. "Here."

Kody took it, pressing it down on the table between him and Jag. "Thanks."

Together, they shaded the new locations onto the map but a clearer pattern remained elusive. "Still nothing," Kody sighed once they'd finished.

"Yeah, but look at this." Jag ran his fingers over the chart. "The rate of destruction at each of the six zones we've ID'd seems to be the same over time. It's not like one zone gets hit one day then another zone gets hit the next, or that it spreads faster in one zone than another. Each day, about equal amounts are getting destroyed all over the country."

"That's something the authorities really should have noticed," Mariah muttered, scrolling through a website.

"Maybe they have, but they're looking at the wrong place for the cause," Jag reminded her. "We're the only ones who know that."

They worked for another hour, shuffling between online reports and what they gathered from the radio and TV. Kody pressed his forehead against the map and stared at the state of Kansas where he was shading. His eyes began to hurt after a few seconds due to the close proximity, forcing him to sit up again. That was when he noticed something. He tapped Jag's arm repeatedly. "Hey, hey, take a look. You see it?"

Mariah shuffled away from the computer and scanned the map with Jag, emitting a little sound of surprise. "Yeah. It's like a rough circle with wedges here and there that haven't been destroyed."

"Yet," Jag added.

"Exactly," Kody enthused. "It's like a pizza with a few slices missing."

Mariah and Jag quirked their eyebrows at him before Jag jabbed at the map with his pencil. "Nice job, Kody. See if you can find what's at the center of this."

Kody picked up a ruler. He bent over the map for a minute, reviewing the roughly hundred-fifty-mile radius of Kansas farmland where crops had been destroyed. He made several lines extending from the tips of the pizza slices, then stabbed his finger at a spot. "Ransom."

"A town called Ransom?" Jag asked.

"Yep. Wonder who named it. And why."

"How far is it from here?"

Kody glared at him. "Ugh, *math*."

The click-clacking of the old keyboard interrupted the inevitable banter as Mariah typed. "Got it," she said. "It's about a three-hour drive from here, but if we drive fast . . ."

Jag slapped his knee. "Wonderful. What's the weather like tonight?"

The keyboard click-clacked again. Mariah smiled. "It's actually gonna be pretty cool."

Kody jumped up and pranced around, arms flailing, startling Lady awake. "I can't wait!" he whooped. "I've been sweating like a turkey that knows it's Thanksgiving!"

Jag grabbed Kody by his shirt and pulled him back down beside him. "Great, good to know."

Lady got to her paws. She trotted to Kody and rested her head on his knee, yawning. He beamed down at her and patted her between her shoulders.

Jag stood up and arched his back. "Alright, you two. Dress warm." He slowly broke into a victorious smile. "We leave for Ransom this evening."

It was eight o'clock that night when the call came. Aari, Tegan and Marshall were sitting on a park bench drinking slushies, watching Californians go about with a spring in their steps, as if nothing in the world was wrong. Aari had to admit that he envied their obliviousness.

Marshall answered his phone. "Hey, Josh."

Aari's attention turned to the Sentry immediately.

"Really? You sure? Holy—that was fast. No, we're not too far out. We'll be right over." Marshall hung up, tossed his empty cup into a trash can and windmilled his arms at Aari and Tegan. "Come on, you two! We may have a breakthrough on our hands!"

The pair chugged the rest of their slushies, inevitably getting a brief but intense headache, then piled into the car. Marshall took every shortcut through Goleta that he knew and they found themselves back at Josh's lab building twenty minutes later. Inside, Josh steered them into the same meeting room. The jubilant scientist had bags under his eyes.

"Sit, sit," he told them breathlessly. As they took their respective chairs, he added, "I think I've found the Achilles' heel we're searching for. We know the nanomites' molecular structure is quite similar to that of silicon, but it is a very distinct material. Still, I believe the process that was used to create the nanomites is not terribly different from the process for creating silicon chips, which is one of the things we do in this facility.

"You may have noticed that the suits we use in our cleanrooms leave little to no skin exposed. That's to reduce the chances of contamination in the semi-conducting wafers. But sometimes, during production, tiny amounts of certain contaminants—we call them dopants—are intentionally introduced into the process. For example, a little bit of boron can give the silicon certain electrical properties, or a bit of phosphorous can make it act differently. I've been trying to figure out if we can take the same approach with the nanomites. In other words, to see if we can contaminate them by introducing a dopant into their matrix to render them harmless." He paused for effect.

Marshall idly rubbed his tattoo. "What did you find?"

"Some good news and some bad news. First, let's get the bad news out of the way. There is no known or readily available element that will fit into the matrix of the nanomite structure. So we can't simply run out to a store or a lab somewhere and purchase a bagful of dopants." He paused again, then said, "But—and here's the potential good news—such an element might be available in a most unlikely place. It's a long shot, but it may be the only chance we have."

Tegan rested her forearms on the table and leaned toward the scientist. "Which would be . . .?"

Josh sat on a chair facing the three of them. "Back in the spring of '88, I met a brilliant scientist at a material science symposium in Reno. It was an interesting time because we knew the Cold War was coming to an end, and the Soviet Union was on the verge of collapse. Anyway, the scientist I met, Dr. Branson, worked for the government during and after the Second World War. He was in his early eighties but, boy, was he sharp as a tack.

"He was interested in the work I was doing at the time and we kept up a friendship that lasted until he passed away four years later. Before he did, he called me and asked to meet him. He was living in Arizona at the time and I flew out to see him the next morning. What he told me that day seemed far-fetched. At the time I dismissed it as maybe the ramblings of a dying man."

The light in Josh's eyes faded, as if he were reliving the moment. Tegan quietly prompted him on. "What did he say?"

"He said . . . he said that he had been involved in a project to create an element that didn't exist in nature. Of course, that in itself isn't unique. If you remember your high school science, several of the so-called trans-uranium elements such as neptunium and lawrencium were created in labs. But the purpose of creating this element was what blew me away. See, back in the day, with the end of World War Two, the expedient relationship between the Allies and the Soviet Union began to fall apart. The Cold War followed.

"According to Dr. Branson, a group of German scientists working on a secret semi-conductor project was abducted by the Russians. The project they were working on would have given the Soviets a very significant advantage over the U.S. in accuracy for their ballistic missiles. Dr. Branson and his team were asked by the Department of Defense, which back then was known as the Department of War, to come up with a means to counter that.

"This team quickly set out to find a solution and, building on some work that was done earlier in that field by scientists at Bell Labs, created an element that could act as a dopant to all forms of semi-conductors or semi-conductor-like material. Only five kilograms of the material was ever produced but it proved to be successful in a range of initial tests."

"Seriously?" Aari exclaimed, throwing up his arms in jubilance.

"Where do we find it?" Marshall asked.

Joshua pinched his lips together. "That's where the challenge comes in. During its final test, which was intended to assess its atmospheric reliability, the element was placed in a canister aboard a specially modified B-29. Unfortunately, on the final leg of the test flight, the aircraft crashed into Lake Mead. That was in the summer of 1948."

Tegan slapped her hands over her face, groaning. Aari was as devastated as she was, and by the looks of it, so was Marshall.

The Sentry, pressing his fingers against his forehead, asked, "Why did Dr. Branson tell you all this, Josh?"

"Because he was extremely passionate about the discovery he'd made," Josh answered. "He was totally crestfallen when the government pulled the plug on the project after failing to recover the canister from the bottom of the lake. The agency responsible had since moved on to other projects that met their objective. Dr. Branson wanted to pass the torch of his invention to me, hoping that, with my background in this field, I would find some revolutionary application for it today. I regret not pursuing it. I regret having dropped his torch."

Marshall patted the older man's arm. "There's a time and place for everything. Maybe this element remaining lost was not an accident. It could still prove its usefulness now."

"Wait a minute," Tegan said, drawing her hand back through her hair. "How is this material supposed to help us if it's been at the bottom of a lake all these years? The water would have destroyed it, even if it was in a canister."

"Maybe not," Josh replied. "Dr. Branson told me that the canister was specially designed and made of stainless steel, and all three feet of it was double-shelled."

Tegan rested her cheek against her shoulder and scrutinized the scientist. "Are you saying this thing may still be in that wreckage?"

"I believe it to be."

"The government didn't search for it?"

"They did, but they never found the plane. It wasn't until about a decade ago that a private dive team using side-scan sonar found the wreckage in the northern arm of the lake. Because it lies inside a national recreation area, the divers couldn't really do much. The national park services were the ones who had to take on the responsibility for the site."

"Wait, they found it?" Aari asked. "Wouldn't the government have tried to retrieve it?"

"It's been over sixty years since they terminated the project. The government probably no longer considers it of any value since the world has changed so much in that field of science. The wreck site was closed off to public access to preserve the plane's remaining integrity. And so, like a lot of other government projects that fall out of favor, this is likely locked away in the bowels of bureaucracy. Whoever was in charge of this whole thing back then is long gone."

Aari blew out a long breath. "If it's still in that wreckage at the bottom of the lake, how do we get to it?"

"Very carefully, I'd say," Tegan mused, "seeing that it's closed to the public."

Aari gently thumped her arm, then looked at Josh. "What do we do if we find it?"

"*If* you retrieve it, bring it directly to me," the scientist said, energy easing back into him at the prospect of holding his old friend's work after all these years. "I'll have to test it and design a delivery mechanism so it can be deployed."

Tegan clapped once. "Where would we deploy it?"

"That," Marshall said, "is where Jag and the others come in."

Jag parked the pickup on the side of a road at a point he presumed to be the center of Ransom, Kansas. Though he knew from additional research that the town was small, it seemed even more so in reality. There were supposedly three hundred residents living in a hundred-and-thirty homes but it was hard to credit even that modest figure from what could be seen in their immediate vicinity. He, Kody and Mariah walked swiftly up and down the streets searching for any site that could possibly house the nanomites.

The town was quiet, with only a few homes still showing lights. Mariah jogged ahead of the guys, scanning each house.

Jag looked at his phone. "Nearly midnight," he told the others.

"Man, it's really quiet here," Kody said as they passed a tired-looking brick building, the town's hospital.

"Well, yeah. Small town, plus it's a work day tomorrow. I don't think people usually walk around this late at night here, but try to stay out of sight anyway."

Mariah returned within a few minutes. "I'm not seeing anything that could be a potential base. It's mostly residential."

"Let's check out the other streets, then," Jag suggested. "Kody, you scanning?"

"I am, but I'm not picking up anything except snoring or television chatter," Kody said, "and I don't see anything in the sky."

"Keep trying. We should be able to pin down the nanomites' base here."

They roamed the town, genuinely amazed at how tiny it was—Jag estimated that it only covered seven square blocks—and noticed that most of the streets proudly bore names of states: Kansas, Delaware, Kentucky and Rhode Island.

"Duck!" Kody hissed. "Someone's looking out their window!"

Jag dove behind a bush, Mariah doing the same a few yards away. They remained hidden until they heard Kody signal they were clear to prowl the streets again. Jag checked the time once more and saw that it was a few minutes into the new day. He tilted his head back to look up at the sky, worried. *I hope we didn't miss them leaving . . .*

There was a short whistle from Kody, who stood at an intersection a block away. Jag and Mariah loped over. He pointed into the distance. "Right there," he said, voice soft. "The whole swarm. I can only just see it. It's heading away from us."

"Where did they take off from?" Jag asked, straining to get a sight of the nanomites.

"I'm not sure. I was just scanning the sky and I saw them already in flight. It looks like they may have come from somewhere to the east. Or it might have been south."

"Shoot," Mariah spat. "Do you still see it?"

"It's kind of floating in and out of my—ah, nope. There it goes. Lost it."

"That's fine," Jag said. "They'll return."

Kody scowled. "Hopefully. What now?"

"Let's think. The crop failure began not too long ago. If these nanomites are being launched from locations all across the country, they would need secure bases, places where no one can find them. Why would they use a small town with mostly residential buildings? No family in their right mind would willingly let their home be used."

"It would be easier to just rent or buy a house and set up the base there," Mariah said.

Jag snapped around. "Yes! Exactly! Come on, we need to call Aari!" He turned and ran back to his grandfather's pickup, not waiting for the others to get inside before dialing Aari's number.

Aari's voice came on the other end. "Jag, I was just about to call! Are Mariah and Kody with you?"

"Yeah," Jag answered as his friends climbed into the truck. "You're on speaker, by the way. We can all hear you."

"Great. So this is a long story but the short version is that we think there may be a way to stop the nanomites."

The pickup truck resonated with cheers before Mariah shushed the boys and looked out the window to make sure no one had heard them.

"One small detail about the material we'll need to stop them, though. It's inside an old airplane. And the plane's at the bottom of a lake. In Nevada."

There was dead silence after that, then Kody shrugged and said, "Honestly, I think we've dealt with worse."

"That's true," Jag agreed. "What's the plan?"

"Marshall, Tegan and I will drive to Nevada to get the anti-nanomite. We've already picked up the diving gear. I'm actually really excited about it."

"I'll bet you are. You can finally put that diver certification of yours to good use."

There was a smile in Aari's voice as he spoke. "Yeah. Marshall's an expert diver, apparently. He hasn't gotten his gear yet, though. Dunno why. Anyway, what's up with you guys?"

"We're at the place where the nanomites are being deployed from," Mariah said. "It's a small town."

"Is that confirmed?"

"Yeah, Kody saw them leave. The problem is, we don't know which house is being used as their base."

"You sure they're launched from a house?"

"It's all they have here, except for a few farms at the edge of the town. And a hospital."

"Alright. How can I help?"

Jag flicked his fingers on his armrest. "We need you to check the realtor sites for Ransom—that's the name of the town. See if you can find any houses that were sold or listed for rent within the last six months. Maybe twelve months, but I doubt it."

"The house wouldn't be rented," Aari said. "It would make more sense to buy it. Whoever's setting off the nanomites might've done some modifications to the interior of the house to use it as a base. They wouldn't want a landlord showing up to check on them, and they would have wanted to put in some heavy-duty security systems as well. I think we can safely rule out renting."

"Good point. Think you can find what we need?"

"Sure thing. I'll get back to you in a bit."

The call ended and Jag put his phone in the cup holder. "We'll just wait, I guess," he said.

They passed the time by mulling over the notion that the others might have found a way to bring an end to the nanomites' reign of devastation. As elated as Jag was, he wished they'd made the discovery earlier; his grandmother was in the hospital as a result of the shock from the Sanchez farm losing its crops. Though he never told the others, when he'd first received the news that she'd been hospitalized, it was if a stake had been plunged into his chest.

As children, Jag and his siblings were often at the farm during the summers when their parents' work would take them away for weeks at a time. He had many fond memories there. His grandfather showed the siblings the ropes behind running the farm, and his grandmother would bake and sing for them. One incident that Jag would always keep in his heart took place when he was six years old.

A fierce storm had been brewing outside during the night. While the entire household slept through the tempest, Jag remained awake, frightened by the roar of the wind, the claps of deafening thunder and the groaning of tree branches just outside his window. At one point, the thunder was so loud it sounded as if it was right over the ranch. Jag had let out a terrified cry and, in his haste to run to his grandparents' room, got his legs tangled in the covers and fell.

His grandmother was by his side in what felt like an instant, lovingly helping him up and guiding him to the kitchen. She poured him a glass of warm milk and made him sit on her lap by the large living room window to watch the storm. He was frightened at first, but then she began singing a quiet lullaby. Her soothing voice eventually eased his mind and he fell asleep to the sights and sound of that howling night. Since then, not only had he ceased to be afraid of storms, but his trepidation had transformed into a sense of wonder for nature's powerful forces.

Jag was jarred out of his memory by his phone ringing. Scooping it up, he answered the call. "Got anything?" he asked.

"Yes," Aari said. "There are two houses that were sold in the last few months."

"Where are they?" Mariah asked.

When Aari gave them the address to both homes, Jag's hopes fell. "No, that's not it. I remember walking by those roads. They're in the north end of town. Kody said he was sure the nanomites came from the southeast."

"I'm not seeing any sales from there. Nothing rented, either."

"Check again."

"I did, and I've checked other realtor websites. There's nothing except for the two houses I mentioned."

Jag was tempted to hurl his phone out of the car. "Could it have been a private sale, then?"

"It's possible, but that means it won't be listed online. We won't know."

"There has to be a way, Aari."

Aari sighed loudly on the other end of the line. "I don't know, man." The sound of typing came from the phone's speakers. "Actually, hold on. I can check the town's utility company's database to see if there's been any changes in account ownership for billing."

Kody's eyes narrowed. "They'd put a record like that online for anyone to see?"

"Eh, not exactly, but given the situation we're in . . . Leave me to it. I'll call again if I find anything. Might take a while."

Jag put the phone back into the cup holder after hanging up. "I have a funny feeling El Hacker is at it again. First that recalled video game last year, now this. Hope he doesn't get into trouble."

Mariah grinned mischievously. "He must have picked up more tricks with all that free time he had while we weren't hanging out."

It was nearly three-thirty in the morning when Aari rang them back. "I may have found what you're looking for. It's in the southeast quadrant, too. Turns out there were three homes sold, not two. There was a change of utility accounts but nothing for that location on any realtor database. It must have been a private sale just like you said, Jag." He recited the address and Mariah wrote it down on a small piece of paper.

"You are magnificent, El Hacker," Kody cooed.

"Shut that pie hole of yours, Captain Knucklehead."

"How rude. But as you wish, *Colonel Dweeb*."

"Dweeb? You better watch it, Lieutenant Lint-Licker."

"Or what, Sergeant Smart—"

"That's enough," Mariah cut in, grinning through a sigh.

"Great job, Aari," Jag added.

Aari laughed. "What? For the insults? I could have done way better but it's late and I'm tired."

Mariah blew a raspberry. "No, you dunce. For finding the house. We'll go check it out."

"Yeah, no problem. Good luck, guys. And be safe."

The trip to the southeast corner of town took only a few minutes. Jag let the pickup roll to a stop a few houses away from the address Aari had given them. They got out and stealthily made their way over to an old, pale blue building. It was the last house on the street, at the very edge of town, and surrounded by a new, high-privacy fence with a securely padlocked gate.

Kody reported that he could hear nothing from within the property. Jag peered through the gate and the other two joined him, doing the best they could to remain unseen by any watchers inside.

"Oh, man," Kody whispered. "This place is wired with cameras. They're really small, like spy cams, but they're there."

Jag felt fierce satisfaction. "We're in the right place, then."

"That garage beside the house looks pretty new. Why would they get a completely new garage and fence but do nothing to the house?"

"Better question is, why is there a chimney sticking out of the roof of the garage?" Mariah asked.

Jag peered closer. She was right. A slim metal cylinder rose up from the small building. "Weird."

"The rain cap looks funny," Kody said, pointing at the odd-shaped cone at the top of the chimney. He moved back from the fence. "My Spidey senses are tingling."

"Same." Jag scratched under his jaw. "Should we wait in the truck to see if the swarm comes back?"

"It's nice and cool out here," Mariah said. Tugging the boys along, she crossed the street and plopped down on a patch of grass under a tree. "I vote we sit and wait."

The boys sat down beside her. Jag picked up a twig and poked it at the ground. "You know, I thought we'd be sleepy by now."

Mariah stretched out one leg with the other tucked under it. "It's hard to be tired when we're so close to finding the thing we've been looking for."

An hour later, Jag saw Kody perk up, back straight as an arrow. "I see them," he said.

Jag and Mariah crept over to the gate, again keeping out of sight, and peered through while Kody kept his eyes on the swarm. "Yeah, they're definitely heading this way," he confirmed. "They'll be here in a few seconds."

Try as they might, Jag and Mariah couldn't see a thing so Kody narrated what he observed. The nanomites came to a microsecond halt over the garage, then plunged downward in a thin streak into the chimney. Kody nearly yelled out in delight. "We've got it!" He held out both his hands and his friends slapped them gleefully.

"Should we try going in?" Mariah asked.

"No," Jag answered. "They probably have more security inside. We should head back to the farm and talk with the others before doing anything."

Kody put his arms around both of them as they headed back to the truck. "Let's celebrate this excellently successful and sleepless night with an early breakfast!"

Aari gazed out at the sparkling blue waters of Lake Mead from behind his sunglasses. A soft breeze caressed his face. His fatigue had dissipated the moment Marshall drove into Overton, Nevada half an hour earlier. Impatience and zeal now seized him; he could hardly wait to dive into the depths of the manmade lake in search of Dr. Branson's canister, which hopefully held the key to preventing a global catastrophe. It didn't hurt that he would be seeing a B-29 Superfortress that had sunk many decades ago, either.

"Aari!" Tegan called.

He found his friend eagerly scrambling around a deserted two-story building that had once been a lakefront resort. Carrying a fishing rod in one hand and a tackle box in the other, he strode up to her as she ran up a set of spiral stairs that ended a couple of feet away from the flat roof. She jumped the small gap without hesitation.

Aari smiled up at her. "Having fun?"

"I'm roaming around an abandoned building that would probably be spooky at night," she raved. "Of course I'm having fun!"

He watched as she danced a little jig on the roof, entertained. "You get happy with the strangest things, you know that?"

She laughed. "My parents say the same thing."

Aari turned back to the lake and saw Marshall coming up the long concrete boat ramp that led to a comically small dock. The Sentry noticed Tegan as he approached and waved. Tegan returned the gesture and leapt back onto the stairs to make her way down to them.

"So can we rent a boat?" she asked.

Marshall nodded. "I told the two guys who run the marina that we'll be out for a couple of hours. Why don't you get down there? I'll grab the scuba gear."

"Sure," Aari said.

It was a long walk in the blazing sun, and Tegan complained nonstop under her breath. They hopped off the ramp once they reached the end and turned left toward the marina office. A man with a beer belly greeted them. "Hello! You with that Marshall fella?"

"Yep," Tegan replied.

Aari motioned at the two red-and-white speedboats that were tied up at a dock. "Had a lot of people come by today?"

The man's mustache quivered as he gave an awkward giggle. "Actually, we only have four boats. Two of them are out on the water now. We don't really get many people coming to this place since the Echo Bay Resort went out of business." He pointed at the building Tegan had explored earlier. "My friend and I figured we would lease the marina from them and try to turn that around at the very least, then maybe tackle the resort later. At the rate we're going, it might take some time."

Marshall appeared a minute later beside Aari and Tegan. The owner of the marina eyed the scuba gear he was carrying. "Going diving, I see," he said, then jokingly added, "You're not gonna pay the old B-29 a visit, are you? Park rangers won't take much of a liking if you do."

"Nah," Marshall said. "There are other interesting dive sites. Plus, we've got some fishing to do."

The man relaxed. "Only one of you diving today?"

"Um, yeah," Aari said. "Me."

"I'm not particularly fond of being deep underwater," Tegan told the man, blushing. "And I don't like relying on a can of compressed air to keep me alive."

The man's beer belly jiggled as he chuckled. "Fair enough." He showed the three to their boat and wished them well before heading back to the office.

Aari put the fishing equipment down as Marshall stowed the scuba gear, then stopped the Sentry. "I don't get it. You said you're going down to the wreck, too. Why don't you have anything other than your dry suit and mask?"

"You'll see," Marshall answered as he and Tegan untied the boat from the dock. He then punched coordinates into a GPS; he'd explained earlier that he got the location of the wreck site from a diver friend who'd visited it several times before public access was prohibited.

Once everything was set to go, the Sentry expertly maneuvered the eighteen-foot craft out of the marina and onto the lake. It would be twenty to thirty minutes before they reached their destination. Marshall pushed the throttle, sending the speedboat flying over the calm surface of the water. Aari stuck his face over the side, letting the wind and spray from the water keep the heat at bay before Tegan pulled him back.

The lake was surrounded by mountains, though some might consider them hills. It was a typical sunbaked Nevada scene and yet Aari found himself loving the atmosphere. Maybe the magic was there because he knew that the lake had held onto its prize—the wreckage of the B-29 bomber—for so long and soon he would be able to see it for himself, see the old plane as it slumbered in the depths of the dark blue water. *This is going to be amazing*, he thought, tapping his feet impatiently as the boat raced toward the wreck.

The first thing he pointed out when they reached the site was that the buoy and down-line they were expecting to tie the boat to were not painted as brightly as was normal.

"They don't want it to be an easy find," Marshall explained. "It's meant to be off-limits to the public, remember?"

Tegan got the fishing equipment ready; she was to remain on the boat and act as if she were fishing while the other two went for their dive. "Why don't they just remove it, then?" she asked.

Marshall shrugged and turned off the engine so he could secure the boat to the buoy. "It's a permanent setup. They don't want boaters dropping anchors and damaging the plane. Aari, you ready?"

Aari laid out his diving gear and suited up. After donning his own suit, Marshall helped him adjust his regulator and face mask. Aari and Tegan spent a few minutes testing the underwater transceiver that would let them communicate with each other during the dive.

"The plane used to be over two hundred feet below the surface," Marshall told them. "But the lake's water level dropped over the years so it's around a hundred feet below us right now, which means what we're doing can be classified as a recreational dive. After you reach the bottom on the main down line, there's another line to the wreck itself. You'll only have fifteen minutes of air before you need to head up and do your decompression stops. Remember, when you come up, stop at the fifty-foot mark for two minutes, then go to forty feet and stay there for one minute. Thirty feet, one minute. Twenty feet, two minutes. Ten feet, two to five minutes. Got it?"

Aari recited the stages back to Marshall. When the Sentry was content, he passed Aari a powerful HID light and gave him a pat on the back. "You're good. Head in."

"What about you?" Aari asked.

Marshall put his flippers on, then fitted a scuba mask that only covered his eyes. "Right. About that. I'm gonna jump in after you. I'll look like I'm drowning for a bit—which I will be—but don't worry. Now go."

Aari was flustered by the Sentry's words but was gently pushed into the lake before he could say anything. He bobbed for a bit, getting himself used to the water, then dove. He saw right away that there were two hefty-looking concrete blocks that anchored the main down line.

A muffled splash made him look to his right; Marshall was now in the water beside him. The Sentry pinched his thumb and forefinger together in an 'OK' sign. He paused for a bit—then inhaled deeply. Aari watched in shock as the man took in as much water through his nose as he could. He started to swim over but Marshall waved him away.

He's filling his lungs with water! Aari thought, heart pounding. *What is he* doing?

Marshall's body went limp as he lost consciousness and began sinking. Aari switched on his light, kicked his flippers and went after the Sentry. Just before he reached him, Marshall's body jerked and his eyes opened. He moved each limb in turn, then nodded at Aari. The teenager looked at him wide-eyed, unable to comprehend what he'd just witnessed. By all accounts, Marshall shouldn't be alive. Yet here he was, leading the way into the depths as if nothing had happened.

Though still shaken, a thrill pulsed through Aari when he saw the tail of the B-29 appear ahead of him. He swam after Marshall, following the smaller line that led from the massive concrete anchor of the down line to a metal stake beside the tail of the old plane.

He scanned the decades-old aircraft with a degree of reverence. The fabric-covered control surfaces would be delicate, so he kept clear of them. They already looked to have been damaged by previous divers who'd either touched or stood on them.

Looking away from the wreck, Aari spotted an oxygen cylinder that sat on the lake's muddy floor, a sign that the plane had been fitted for high-altitude work. Even though they were here to retrieve the anti-nanomite, Aari wished he'd brought a waterproof camera along.

Tegan's voice filled his ear. "Hey, Aari, I see a boat . . ."

"How far is it?" he asked. "Is it a park ranger? Is it heading toward you?"

"I don't think so. It looks like some locals."

"If they come closer, let me know."

"Sure."

Aari and Marshall headed to the nose of the aircraft; Aari could see jets of bubbles occasionally escaping from Marshall's nostrils before the Sentry inhaled again. *Is he sustaining himself on dissolved oxygen molecules in the water?*

The pair noticed that there was only one engine left on the plane, its propeller blades bent from the force of the impact with the lake. It was massive and covered in silt, as was the rest of the aircraft. At the cockpit, they found the pilot's window missing. Aari gestured at the opening. Marshall tapped his temple with a finger, signing to keep this area in mind as an option for entry, then swam around to the front of the plane. The aircraft's nose was heavily damaged, a second possible entrance.

Aari stayed near the Sentry as they did a complete lap around the plane. The co-pilot's window was also knocked out and there was a tear by the tail, but neither were large enough to swim through.

"Aari, the boaters are heading this way," Tegan warned through his earpiece.

"We're not inside the plane yet!"

"They better not stop to ask me questions, then."

"Keep fishing, Teegs. Make them believe you're alone."

"Yeah . . . hopefully they buy it. Will let you know."

Aari and Marshall headed back to the pilot's escape hatch. The hatch itself was broken off, leaving just the stump of a hinge. The Sentry, muscled as he was, nimbly swam through the access, careful not to touch the corroded frame around the opening. Aari made his own entry more cautiously, wincing as his air tank lightly scraped the top of the hatch frame. Hoping he hadn't done too much damage, he eased the rest of his body through.

There were two parachutes lying in the cockpit and, strangely, a pair of pants as well. The pilot's seat was mostly concealed under a thick layer of deposit, as was almost everything else.

The co-pilot's controls were totaled but the instruments seemed relatively unscathed. Aari and Marshall swam carefully to avoid stirring up silt and compromising their visibility.

The two continued their search for the box. Josh had been certain that it would be somewhere in the crew compartment in the aft section of the plane, so they began working their way in that direction. Aari swung his flashlight around, feeling as if he were a police chopper scanning the ground for fugitives.

The beam passed over an odd protrusion under some equipment racks in the science station. He drew closer to the object and reached out to wipe the silt off, but hesitated. Then, excitement surged through him. The container perfectly matched the description Josh had given them.

Steadying himself, he lightly wiped the corner of the object clean. A small cloud of silt disrupted his view as it wafted in front of his face. He waited for it to clear and waved his flashlight at Marshall to get the man's attention. The Sentry reached his side within moments and tried to open the box but it remained sealed. Aari put his flashlight down and together they managed to pry the top open. An explosion of bubbles and dirt met them, stirring up the water so much that their visibility was gone for a full minute.

When the murk finally cleared, Aari picked up his flashlight and pointed it into the box. He was wobbly, ready to rejoice. They were one step closer to ending the nanomites' destructive run.

The pair peered into the container, and Aari screamed silently.

No!

The box was empty. The canister containing the anti-nanomite was nowhere to be seen. Aari stuck his arm into the box and slapped around hysterically. He looked to Marshall but the Sentry's dismayed expression gave him no reassurance.

It has to be here! This is where it's supposed to be! Aari spun around and swam back and forth, shining his light around so incoherently it may as well have been a strobe. *This can't be happening!* He didn't care now if he destroyed the wreckage in his panicked search—they needed to find that canister. That was all that mattered.

Marshall caught Aari and held him firmly by the shoulders. When he was sure he had the teenager's attention, he pointed to his wristwatch and then upward. Aari's mood plummeted further. He didn't want to leave the site but had no other choice unless he wanted to run out of air during his ascent. As he passed Marshall the flashlight, the Sentry assured him through a series of hand signals that he would comb through the plane for a while longer.

Unenthused, Aari swam out of the B-29 and began his ascent. In his preoccupied state, he nearly forgot to make his decompression stops. As he halted at his first break, he heard Tegan's voice in his ear once again, this time sounding distressed.

"The locals on the boat stopped and asked me what I was doing, Aari," she said. "I waved my fishing rod at them but I don't think they believed I was here on my own."

"Are they still there?"

"No, they left. I'm worried that they've gone to call the rangers. They looked *really* suspicious of me."

Aari muttered a curse under his breath. "Be up in a bit."

Ten minutes later he broke the surface of the lake. He pulled himself into the boat and removed his mask and scuba gear. Tegan had a towel ready for him. "Where's Marshall?" she asked. "Is he alright? I saw him earlier and that was the creepiest and stupidest—"

"He's still in the wreckage," Aari said, removing his flippers and dry suit.

"Why?"

He threw his flippers aside angrily. "Because the damn canister wasn't in the box like it was supposed to be!"

Tegan's face fell. "You're kidding."

"Do you think I'd joke about that?" Aari snapped. "Come on, Tegan."

Tegan tossed him the towel without saying anything. She kept her expression neutral, which Aari knew was her way of staving off hurt. He dried off his face, hair, hands and feet before folding the towel and putting it aside. They sat together, both looking out over the water. He knew he'd been unfair in lashing out at her, but the distress was eating at him.

He fingered his pendant, feeling its edges and the blue crystal in the middle, then bumped elbows with her. "I'm sorry, Teegs."

"It's fine."

"No, it's not. That's not how we talk to each other. I'm just . . . really upset right now."

"It's fine."

"Teegs—"

"Really, I get it. Truthfully, I probably would've reacted the same way." Tegan in turn bumped her elbow against his, then glanced over the side of the boat. "I just hope Marshall finds that canister before those locals come back with an unwanted surprise—and, oh, speaking of whom . . ."

The Sentry popped to the surface. He pulled off his mask, tossing it into the boat, then hauled himself onto the craft. Leaning over the side, he threw up what was most likely half a bucket of water. Both Aari and Tegan cringed.

"It's not there," the Sentry said, teeth gritted.

Tegan sucked in her cheeks, arms crossed. "Someone must have removed it."

"The box looked like it'd been shut for ages," Aari said. "I'm thinking probably since the plane went down."

Tegan sat down heavily on one of the seats. "That doesn't make sense. Josh said the government couldn't find the canister, which was why they scrapped the project."

Marshall untied the boat from the down line. "We're gonna have to delve further into this."

"I just can't believe we came all the way out here to return empty-handed," Aari said. The rumbling of a distant motor wafted to his ears. A red-and-white speedboat, just like theirs, was coming from the direction of the marina. "That's not the locals you were talking about, right, Tegan?"

"No. Those guys were in a silver boat." Tegan wouldn't take her eyes off the vessel. "It's going through the water pretty fast. Looks like it's coming right at us, too."

"Do we have a pair of binoculars on board, by any slim chance?" Aari asked.

"Nope," Marshall responded from where he was securing the fishing and scuba gear at the back of the boat.

Aari cast an eye up at the sky. Maybe if he found a bird, Tegan could use it to check out who it was that seemed to be heading their way. A lone, red-tailed hawk was circling not too far away from them. "Hey," he began.

"Already on it," Tegan said, closing her eyes.

Aari watched as the hawk abandoned its circling and flew toward the oncoming vessel. It lowered its altitude, which he figured was to allow Tegan to get a better view of the occupants. As he waited, he shook more water out of his hair with his hands. Just as he was finishing up, Tegan snapped back violently, startling him into smacking himself. She shoved her knuckles into her mouth to stop herself from yelling out.

Aari grabbed her wrist. "What?"

"Tony!" she yelped. "He has another guy with him, and he's got a gun!"

"Marshall!" Aari yelled. "We need to go!"

The boat's engine rumbled to life. "They're between us and the marina," Marshall said. "We won't be able to go back just yet."

Tegan eyed the approaching vessel. "What do we do?"

"Sit tight, both of you," the Sentry ordered. He pushed the throttle and their boat took off, bouncing over the lake away from the direction of the marina. The wind had picked up, turning the calm water choppy. The engine was loud to the trio's ears and the gusts blew into their faces. Tegan held onto her seat, tensing with each impact, her hair flying wildly behind her. She turned to look at their pursuers, who were slowly but surely getting closer.

"Where are we gonna go?" Aari shouted, but Marshall didn't hear him over all the noise.

Tegan was shaking her head quickly. "They have binoculars! It doesn't matter where we go, we'll be in their sights!"

Aari kicked his heel repeatedly into the bottom of his seat. "Great! Just what we needed!"

Tegan kept watch on Tony and his cohort as Marshall pushed the boat up to full speed. They soared over the waves for another minute. As they approached a rocky islet to the left, the Sentry pulled back on the throttle.

"Why are we slowing down?" Tegan demanded over the motor.

"Just trust me," he said.

Biting the tip of her thumb, she eyed their pursuers as they got nearer. *Marshall, I hope you know what you're doing . . .*

As Tony's boat continued at top speed and came within a couple of hundred yards of theirs, Marshall opened the throttle and made a tight turn around the islet, forcing Tony to overshoot. Their pursuer would have to make a wide turn to re-engage in the chase. They pulled away from the rocky outcrop and sped back down the arm of the lake toward the marina. As they passed the area where the B-29 lay, Marshall called over his shoulder to Aari and Tegan. "I need you to throw all of our gear overboard!"

Aari gaped. "You can't be serious!"

"We've got to get rid of the excess weight! You need to dump everything!"

Tegan dove for the anchor, cut off the rope and heaved it into the lake without a second thought. She saw Aari shake his head in remorse as he picked up the scuba tank and leaned over the side of the boat. He hesitated, then threw the equipment over.

Marshall kept the throttle pushed all the way forward and the vessel started to pull away from their pursuers. Tegan threw her fists in the air. "Yes!" Her confidence was short-lived, though, as a second later, the sound of gunfire traveled across the lake.

"They're shooting at us?" Aari demanded. "I thought they want us alive!"

"They're shooting at the boat," Marshall corrected. Another shot sounded as the last word left his lips. Tegan was sure she'd felt the projectile strike something and the Sentry confirmed it. "They hit us! I've lost throttle control! We're stuck on full speed!"

"I don't think that's a problem right now!" Tegan rubbernecked around Marshall. "There's the marina! We're gonna make it!"

Bang!

Tegan nearly bit through her lip when a second, more resounding impact hit the boat just as Marshall started turning into the bay. *Nice going,* she berated herself. *You just had to open your big mouth and jinx it, didn't you?*

Marshall was battling with the controls of the boat. "They got the steering system! I have no control!"

"Just keep going, we're nearly there!" Tegan yelled.

"But we're heading right for the fuel dock!" Aari yelled back.

Marshall smacked the wheel, giving up his fight. "We're gonna have to jump!"

Aari looked at the sky, then held up his hands. "Wait! If we take away their ability to see us, we can jump out right before the boat hits the fuel dock. Maybe they'll lose sight of us in the commotion!"

Tegan wasn't particularly thrilled with the idea. "I've had my share of exploding fuel tanks, thank you. Besides, how are you gonna hide us from them? You can't cover animate and inanimate objects simultaneously, in case you forgot the last time you tried that."

"I'm not planning another battle-on-the-mountain routine." Aari pointed up to where he had been looking. "Teegs, if you could hop into the hawk again and go after their binoculars, we—"

"Ah. Think I got it." Tegan located the bird then closed her eyes. Reaching out with her mind, she easily took over the creature's consciousness. The next thing she saw was a literal bird's-eye view of Lake Mead. Just ahead of her, Tony and his goon were turning into the bay, about five hundred feet behind Marshall and the teenagers. She dove toward them, feeling the wind zip through the hawk's feathers. The man beside Tony had his binoculars pointed at Tegan and the others, and was yelling.

The hawk careened into him, wings flapping into his face and talons raking his skin. He let out a shout and waved his arms wildly, trying to smack the aerial attacker. "What the—"

Without wasting time, Tegan grabbed the binoculars in her talons and shot away. She smirked when she heard Tony and his cohort bellowing. Dropping the binoculars into the water, she let go of her connection with the bird and snapped herself back in the boat with Aari and Marshall.

"It's done!" she said. "What now?"

Aari held onto the side of the boat. "I think we're far enough away . . ."

"Far enough away for *what?*"

"Far enough that they won't see us jumping into the water. All they'll see is our boat colliding with the dock. They'll think we went down in the explosion."

"You actually meant it? You're nuts!"

"I'm liking that idea!" Marshall yelled as he grabbed a small waterproof bag that held their most important belongings. "Get ready! On my count!"

I need to hire someone to do these stunts for me, Tegan griped. She readied herself with Aari and Marshall on either side of her. Tony's boat was still a good distance from them. The three watched, waiting until they were only several dozen yards from the fuel pumps.

"Now!" the Sentry barked. "Jump!"

Tegan dove headfirst off the boat and into the cool water. She surfaced to look around for the others and heard Aari shout, "Keep going! Don't stop!"

Not needing to be told twice, she kicked forward. She wasn't sure how much breadth they'd given the fuel dock but a moment later an explosion sent a shockwave through the water, temporarily deafening her. The waves thrust her closer to shore. She took a quick glance to her left and saw the marina engulfed in a fiery orange glow with a tower of black smoke rising from its center; thankfully the office was still intact.

"Nearly there," Marshall encouraged from somewhere to her right. His words were partially inaudible to her abused ears. "Just a little farther."

When they reached the shore, the Sentry helped the teenagers to their feet. "We'll have to walk up through the bushes beside the ramp to get to the parking lot. Don't want to be seen by anyone."

"That's quite a hill," Tegan said as she wrung out her clothes, exhausted and still shaken from the explosion.

They'd trekked from bush to bush and were nearly at the top when Tegan saw a familiar man with an even more familiar honker running down the concrete ramp, calling out to Tony. "Potato Nose," she notified the others. "That means they're up here too."

As they reached the top, Marshall signaled the friends to remain hidden behind a mound of brush. He then began crawling toward a large boulder about ten yards from the edge of the parking lot and took a quick look. The next second, there was a loud bang and he fell back, tumbling down the hill. Tegan covered her mouth with her hands. She followed Aari as they ran to Marshall, who was dazedly attempting, and failing, to sit up. He ordered them to stay down as two more shots rang out. They ducked instinctively but continued toward him until they were by his side.

"You're bleeding," Tegan whispered, gently lifting the Sentry's head. A puncture wound bigger than her thumb was present on his upper arm. A thick scarlet streak tainted his gray t-shirt and trickled down his arm to the dirt. If the man was in pain, he was refusing to show it.

"I'm fine. It went right through." With only a little difficulty the Sentry removed his top and tore it into strips before tying them tightly around the wound.

Troubled and impressed, Tegan asked, "Will that do it?"

"For now." Marshall pulled the teenagers behind a bush just as an orange-haired man came into view at the top of the incline.

So there's Elvis, Tegan thought. Seeing her former jailer standing there with his pistol pointed at where they'd been only moments ago infuriated her.

"Aari," Marshall said. "You're able to bend light, aren't you? I want you to cover me. I'll take care of the goon up there but he has the advantage of elevation, and he has a weapon."

The boy looked at him worriedly. "Are you sure? You just got shot. There should be another way—"

"No time. I want you both to keep moving up through the bushes while I deal with the problem. You with me?"

"Y-yeah."

"Good. Do it."

The Sentry shimmered from one side to the other before disappearing right in front of Tegan. Aari took hold of her arm and together they snaked through the undergrowth. He kept a constant focus on Marshall to maintain the screen around the Sentry. They were a few feet from the top when Elvis, still peering over the edge, grasped at something invisible around his neck, choking. He struck out in every direction in hopes of bringing down his unseen attacker. His face turned pale before he weakened and lost his grip on consciousness altogether and let go of his gun.

As he was being lowered to the ground, Tegan heard yelling and fast footfalls. Potato Nose was sprinting back up the ramp.

"He must have heard the shot when Marshall was hit!" Aari whispered.

"Marshall's got it under control," Tegan said.

The pair saw Elvis' gun abruptly rise from where it had fallen and right itself. It was pointed straight at Potato Nose as he approached the start of the ramp. The gun fired twice and Potato Nose screamed and staggered, clutching his thigh before falling onto his wounded side. Unable to stave off the shock and pain, he remained sprawled.

Tegan towed Aari to the parking lot where a Cadillac SUV was parked beside their rental. Marshall reappeared before them and pulled his tactical switchblade from the waterproof bag. Tossing the knife to Aari, he said, "You know the drill."

As the boy destroyed their pursuers' tires, Tegan took the bag from the Sentry. "I should drive, Marshall. You're hurt. We need to get you to a doctor."

He smiled at her, his gaze calm and soulful. She couldn't understand how he could possibly be so placid about his condition and their situation. "No, I know, and no," he said as he dropped into the driver's seat. "But thank you for looking out for me, Tegan."

Tegan closed the door for him as Aari returned and the two leapt into the car. Marshall wasted no time hightailing it out of there and left the marina, the abandoned resort and the pursuers in their dust.

"I should have known," the Sentry berated himself. "I was stupid. The only way they could have followed us here was through the credit card I used to rent the boat. I thought those thugs wouldn't have the capability to do something like that. They must be well-connected."

"It doesn't matter," Tegan said, though inwardly she wondered how in the world the Sentry was driving with a bullet wound in his arm. "Marshall, I know you don't want to, but we should really get you to a hospital. Let me or Aari drive."

"No."

Fed up with his stubbornness, she demanded, "Then what?"

"Get my bag, please."

"Um, sure . . . where is it?"

"It should be by Aari's feet in the back."

Aari passed the bag to Tegan, who opened it. "What am I looking for?"

"A small green bottle with silver powder in it," Marshall answered.

She rummaged around until she found the item. She held it up for the Sentry to see. "This it?"

"Yes. I need to know, are you squeamish when it comes to blood?"

"Uh, not really. Why?"

"What you're holding is an old Dema-Ki healing compound. Or at least a knockoff version that I made. It still does the trick, but it takes a little longer to work. I need you to untie the bandage and pour a quarter of the contents of the bottle directly into the wound."

"While you're driving?"

"Yeah. The sooner we get this done, the better it will be."

Tegan pulled off the bloodied strips that were tied around his upper arm, popped the cap of the bottle open, and tilted it until the dust trickled into the wound. Marshall winced, causing Tegan to worry that she'd done something wrong. "Is it supposed to hurt?"

"Just for a bit. It'll be okay soon. Thanks."

Tegan put the bottle back into the bag. Marshall passed her his phone. "Go into my contacts and call Josh. Put him on speaker, please."

Tegan found the scientist's name and tapped it. Josh picked up the call. "Marshall!"

"Hey, Josh," Marshall said. "I need to cut to the chase. Tegan, Aari and I went to the B-29 wreckage and—"

"You found it!"

"We did, but the canister wasn't there."

"That can't be right. Are you absolutely certain?"

"As certain as I'll ever be."

Josh sounded devastated. "No, no. That's impossible. It has to be there. You must have missed it."

"Josh, listen . . . Dr. Branson was up there in age when he told you all this. Maybe he wasn't able to recall things as they happened exactly."

"No. That man was as alert as I ever saw him. Maybe even more so. These were not the ramblings of a dying man. I'm sure of it now."

"I didn't say that. But maybe his memory had gone a little fuzzy."

"Perhaps, but not on this subject. I'm telling you, Marshall, that man was completely lucid."

"I don't know what to say, Josh. All I know is that the canister wasn't down there. Aari went with me. He can vouch for that as well."

"I don't understand," Josh mumbled.

Marshall tried jogging the scientist's memory in hopes that there would be some information that he might have missed. Tegan, paranoid that Tony and his men might have repaired their vehicle and were already giving chase, tuned out of the conversation and scanned the road behind them. For a fleeting moment she thought she saw a black SUV but it turned out to be a delivery van. She was lost in anxiety for several moments until she heard Josh exclaim, "Wait! Wait, wait, wait. Wait."

"Remembering something?" Marshall asked sanguinely.

"Yes. Well, maybe. Dr. Branson did mention something else. At that time it didn't seem significant . . ."

"What was it?"

"After the plane crashed, they scrambled out onto their life boats. Dr. Branson recalled arguing with a crew member about retrieving the canister but the other man was opposed to it because the aircraft was sinking. The crew member said a lot of the equipment on board had been ejected from the plane when it hit the water and he wasn't going to risk his life searching for something that might already be gone. It so happened that there was another person in the vicinity, a young man in a canoe who called out to them to make sure they were alright, then rowed away to get help."

"What happened then?"

"They paddled over to the floating debris but found nothing. He was sure that the canister had gone down with the plane and that they could have retrieved it. Here's what I'm thinking. That young man with the canoe was the only witness to the entire incident. Maybe, just maybe, he might know something about the canister."

Tegan turned to Aari; a little bit of hope had crawled back in.

"Do you have any info on this witness?" the Sentry asked. "Did Dr. Branson see him again after that?"

"Sadly, no. It made the news back in the day, though. I'm sure local newspapers ran the story, and small town papers would have included the names of those who were present. You should be able to find information at one of the libraries around there. They usually maintain collections of stuff like that."

Marshall looked at his watch. "Pretty sure the libraries are closed right now."

"If we could find a place with Wi-Fi," Aari said from the backseat, "I can check to see if they've digitized their newspaper archive."

"Good idea, Aari," Josh said.

Marshall exhaled heavily. "It's yet another long shot, though. And I mean really long. What's there to say this kid—or man, now—would know anything about the canister?"

"He's the best lead we have, Marshall. None of the crew members are alive today."

Marshall bobbed his head slowly in agreement. "We'll call back and let you know if we find anything."

"Please do."

Tegan ended the call and passed the phone back to Marshall. "Where are we going?"

"I remember seeing a motel around here," he replied. "The sign said free Wi-Fi, so Aari can use his laptop there. We haven't picked up a tail, have we?"

"Nope, nothing of concern," she said.

"That's a relief."

They reached the motel half an hour later. As they headed toward the entrance, Marshall tied another strip of cloth around the wound. "Would you look at that. It's starting to close up now."

"Sorcery," Tegan whispered jokingly, but both she and Aari were blown away.

Dema-Ki is amazing, she thought. *I really miss that place.*

The woman behind the check-in desk eyed the Sentry's bloodstained bandage. He shrugged. "Hiking accident with my niece and nephew."

While he got a room for them, the teenagers stood back and repressed their snickers as the woman had to force herself to continuously draw her eyes away from Marshall's fit, bare chest. The Sentry didn't seem to notice, or if he did, he made a point to ignore it. He paid with cash, took the keycard and led Tegan and Aari to their room. It was small inside, with two beds, a round table, and a couch.

"I'll take the couch," Marshall said.

Aari fell onto one of the beds, connected his laptop to the motel's Wi-Fi and soon all that was to be heard from him was the patter of his keyboard and some muttering. "Maybe Boulder City newspapers. And Overton. Hmm . . ."

Tegan kept vigil by the windows in case their pursuers turned up but as time wore on, she calmed down and paid more attention to Aari as he spoke to himself.

"Okay, forget local newspapers . . . How about high school papers? Maybe he was still in school at the time . . ."

Tegan lurched toward the window as a car pulled into the premises. When she saw the occupants get out, she relaxed. *Just a couple. Good.*

Aari was still muttering. "So not Boulder City, then. Back to Overton?" He went quiet for a few minutes, then yelled out, startling Tegan and Marshall. "Got it! Right here in the school newspaper, they ran a small article about the B-29 crash and the student who went for help!"

Tegan forgot about her vigil and practically cannonballed onto the bed beside him. Marshall peeped over her shoulder. Aari pointed at a black-and-white photo of a thin but athletic-looking teenager on the screen.

"His name is Elwood McAllister," Aari said. "Let's see if we can find out where he lives."

He typed the name into the search bar and included the state and county. He scrolled down a few links before one in particular caught their eyes. Marshall rested his forehead against the edge of the bed as Tegan fell back and clawed at her face.

"Are you *kidding* me?" she cried. "He's *dead?*"

Aari clicked on the link. "It says in the obituary here that he served in the Vietnam War as a pilot. His jet was shot down, so he was KIA. They mention his loved ones here . . ."

Marshall looked at the laptop again. "Does he have any kids?"

"No kids, no. Uh, it does mention that he was survived by his wife who . . ."

"Where does she live? Wait, better question—is she still alive?"

"I'll check." More taps on the keyboard. "Yes, she is! She remarried. And you're not going to believe this. She's right here in Overton. Looks like she's lived most of her life in this town."

"Get the address," Marshall instructed. "We'll see her first thing tomorrow morning."

"You really think she'd know anything about the canister?" Tegan asked doubtfully.

"As long as we have some kind of lead, we need to pursue it."

Aari keyed the address into his phone, then shut his laptop down with an air of success and called Jag to tell him of the day's events. After completing the call, he relayed what Jag had told him to Tegan and Marshall over a takeout dinner the Sentry had paid for, again using cash. Then, exhausted, they bade each other good night and turned off the lights. Despite Tegan's fear of Tony finding them, she fell into a night of restful sleep.

Jag parked the pickup truck in front of the Sanchez farmhouse just as the sun was setting and hopped out, mulling over his conversation with Aari. He picked up three shopping bags from the back and walked toward the front door. He'd been relieved to hear that his friends and the Sentry were okay, but it bothered him that Tony had been able to track them to Lake Mead so quickly.

Does that mean they know the rest of us are in Kansas?

Jag stepped into the house and passed the living room on the way to the kitchen. As he was putting away the groceries, Kody trotted in. "Yo. What did you get for dinner?"

"Tuna salad. There wasn't much else available."

"Oh." Kody peered into the two bags that Jag had left untouched. "I see the gizmo and hardware stores were open. Got everything you need for your plan?"

"Mmhm." Jag put away the last of the groceries. "You know, I never figured we'd use our vacation money to buy these things."

"Hey, if it all goes well, these could be considered souvenirs."

They headed to the living room where Mariah was sitting beside Lady on a large throw rug, hugging her. She looked up at the boys as they walked in. "Hey. Got everything?"

Jag stretched out on one of the couches. "Yes, ma'am."

"You okay? You seem a little preoccupied."

"I was on the phone with Aari on my way here. They had a pretty big incident."

"What happened?"

"Tony and his men came after them but they managed to escape. Marshall suspects that they traced his credit card transactions somehow. But that's not the only thing. Marshall was . . . shot."

Mariah, horrorstruck, pulled away from Lady. "What—how bad is he hurt?"

"It went right through his arm so it's a clean wound, but he's refusing to go to a hospital. Says he can patch himself up for now. According to Aari, he doesn't look anywhere near out of the game, which is good."

"Good Lord, he's crazy."

"Are they safe now?" Kody fretted. "Away from Tony? I'm telling you, when I get my hands on that piece of—"

"They booked it out of there, yeah." Jag traced the contour of his pendant. "They're lying low in a motel some ways away from Lake Mead."

Kody sat down heavily on the other couch. "Did they at least find the canister?"

Jag's face tightened. "No. It wasn't there."

Kody seemed to teeter on the edge of a fit. "Oh, great! *Great!* What are we gonna do now, then? Can Marshall's friend in Goleta create some kind of explosive that we can toss into the nanomites' hideout?"

"About that . . . . Aari says that the nanomites are nearly indestructible. That's kind of why they went searching for that canister. There's an extremely rare material inside that may act as an anti-nanomite. But"—Jag sat up—"just because we can't destroy them doesn't mean we can't figure out a way to at least disrupt them."

Mariah pushed her copper-blonde hair over her shoulders as Lady sniffed at it. "Not sure I understand what you're saying."

Jag picked up a pencil and a small sketchpad from the coffee table. "We said we were gonna figure out a plan to get into the nanomites' base. Look, I've had an idea in mind and I've already got the tools we'll need tonight. Come up here."

His friends joined him on the couch and watched with growing curiosity as he drew out his plan on the sketchpad. "Awesome art skills," Kody said.

Jag hit him on the arm with his pencil. "I get it, I'm not Tegan. Bear with me here. I think we'll be able to get into that garage tonight."

* * *

The three of them trooped up the street toward the blue house at the end of the road. It had been a restless drive to Ransom and the friends were glad to have finally arrived at their destination. They carefully peeked through the narrow-barred gate. The property looked as vacant as it had the night before.

"You ready?" Jag asked Mariah.

She removed her knapsack and pulled out a heavy black cloth. "All I need are Kody's eyes."

The aim was to render blind the middle of the three cameras that watched over the garage. Once Kody had recalled what make and model they were, it only took a few quick keystrokes to find out that the cameras had a viewing angle of a hundred-and-thirty degrees. Taking out the camera in the center would create a narrow blind spot for the friends to slip through. The trick was for Mariah to drop the black cloth over the camera fast enough so it would seem to anyone monitoring that the camera had a malfunction.

Once Kody pointed out exactly where the camera was attached on the garage's crossbeam, Mariah took over and Jag watched in wonderment as she levitated the cloth high above them and guided it, lowering the fabric over the camera with the precision of a surgeon.

Jag gave her a small grin. "I didn't know you could move things that accurately."

"Neither did I," she said. "I guess the crystal's really helping."

Kody tapped their shoulders. "The cam's covered. You're up, Jag."

Jag nodded and backed up to the opposite side of the road. He bounced on his toes a couple of times, then ran toward the gate. When he was a few steps away, he leapt and sailed over the eight-foot tall obstacle, landing lightly on the other side with a roll. Turning around, he saw Kody and Mariah staring openmouthed.

He jogged back to the gate. "You two are gonna let flies into your mouths."

Kody picked up his jaw. "Sorry. It's just neat seeing you jump like ten feet in the air."

Jag cracked his knuckles as he assessed the chain that held the gate closed. "This is a huge padlock . . ." Taking the lock in his hands, he placed his thumbs within the shackle's gap and gave a mighty tug. The lock didn't give. He tried again without any success.

"C'mon, Jag," Kody murmured. "It's just a lock."

"It's a pretty strong one," Jag grunted. He tugged with all his strength a few more times before letting it go in defeat. "I can't do it. It won't break. It's built too tough."

Mariah looked at him firmly through the gate. "Speed. Agility. Strength. Those are your gifts, Jag. You're not going to be stopped by a petty lock. Try again."

Jag massaged his hands. His fingers hurt from pulling but Mariah had a point. He needed to concentrate.

He touched his crystal, letting his fingers linger on it, before clamping onto the heavy metal. Then he gave one sharp tug and the shackle suddenly snapped, popping open without breaking completely. He quickly unwrapped the chain securing the gate, letting his friends onto the property. As they walked in, Mariah gave him a rub on the back. "That wasn't too hard, right?"

"Quiet, you." Jag smiled, taking the lead. "Stay in a single line right behind me. We need to keep inside the blind spot."

The friends wasted no time getting to the regular-looking door right next to the main garage door. Before Jag could stop him, Kody put his hand on the knob. He was instantly thrown off his feet and landed on his back. He let out a shaky groan and remained on the dirt, gasping for breath.

Jag was by his side in an instant and looked over him worriedly. "Kody. Hey, buddy, can you hear me?"

"The door . . . it . . . it's charged." Kody trailed off, muttering a jumble of curses.

Mariah knelt on his other side. "You were electrocuted!"

"Seems . . . seems like it. I'll be f-fine."

Jag slid an arm behind Kody's back and helped the other teenager up. "I think it was a warning shock. Not meant to cause serious harm but enough to make you think twice about trying to go inside."

"Which means they would have the inside rigged as well," Mariah concluded.

"And that," Kody said, tapping Jag's head with an unsteady finger, "is why you were right to create Plan B. Well done, sir."

Jag let go of his friend when he saw that he could stand, albeit unsteadily. "You sure you're okay to go on?"

"I'm good. Let's go." Kody rubbed his shoulders and nodded at Jag, emerald eyes shining once again.

The trio pressed themselves to the wall and shimmied along to the back of the garage. Kody saw no cameras, which gave Jag a boost in confidence. He chose a spot on the wall and dropped to his knees as Mariah took out the tool he'd bought from the hardware store—a cordless reciprocating saw.

"This saw isn't too loud. Still, I'd like to get this done quickly." Jag squeezed its trigger and let the blade into the wood siding with a plunge cut, quickly slicing out a two-foot square opening at the base of the wall. He pulled the loose section free as Mariah brought out a remote-control toy car; it was another gadget Jag had picked up earlier. Fixed to the car's roof was a wireless camera made to attach to a car's rear license plate and display a rear view on a dash-mounted smartphone.

Mariah looked troubled. "What if there are motion detectors inside? Won't this thing trigger an alarm?"

Jag powered the car on with an app on his phone and did a quick test run on the grass. "If I did the research right, no. Motion detectors are usually set to ignore anything less than a foot or so above the ground. They've got the tolerance built in so that they don't pick up pets or pests. Otherwise if there was a mouse running around, it would set off the alarm constantly."

Happy with the way the RC car was handling, he used his phone to guide it into the garage through the hole he'd cut. He moved the car judiciously, spinning it to give the camera a view from every angle. "It's really dim inside," he said. "But looks like we lucked out. This hole we just cut is hidden under a row of shelves and, from what I can see, there are only two things to be worried about. There's a camera on the left corner of this end of the garage but it's pointed away from us, and there's a motion sensor across from us, facing our way. It doesn't seem like an alarm's gone off, so I think we're still good."

Mariah produced two more black cloths. "Guess I'm up again."

She went down onto her stomach and looked through the hole. Jag shifted his weight from one foot to the other, praying that neither the sensor nor the camera would activate a warning system. It felt like too many minutes had passed but he understood that she was taking her time to avoid mistakes.

"Done." Mariah sat back and wiped some perspiration off her brow. "That was stressful."

"You're doing good." Jag brought their spy car back out and tucked it back into the bag. Then, together with Mariah, he crawled through the hole and into the garage while Kody stood watch outside. Jag cleared the metal shelves above their small entrance and gave Mariah a hand up.

The garage wasn't too big. There was another row of shelves to their right but what piqued their interest was a ten-foot long table at the center of the building. A bank of computers sat on its stainless-steel top and three LCD monitors cast a bluish glow onto the wall.

Mariah toyed with the mini flashlight attached to the belt hoop of her jeans. "Is there someone in here?"

"I don't think so." Jag called softly to Kody, whose head emerged through the hole. "Kode-man, can you tell if anyone's been in here recently?"

Kody shook his head as he scented the area. "It's stale. No one's been here in a while."

"Good to know. Thanks."

Kody wiggled back out. Mariah unclipped her flashlight and shone it around, then walked to the long steel table to study what was on the monitors. "These look like they're running something." She pointed the light under the table to see where the cables led but all that was to be seen was a mess of wires. "What's that humming sound?"

"A generator, I think," Jag answered. "They'd probably want their own source of power that isn't connected to the grid." He'd taken out his flashlight as well and traced it around the garage. "Bingo." He strode over to the corner where both of the shelves met. What appeared to be a cap for a fuel tank was sticking out from the ground. Jag unscrewed it and took a small whiff before covering it back up. "Yep, definitely fuel down there."

Mariah waved her light under one of the shelves. "Bet that manhole under there leads to the generator."

"Seems like a good guess to me." Jag wandered around the garage. "I don't see anything that could house the nanomites. Unless they just roam free in here . . ."

"Doubt it," Mariah said. "Take a look at this."

Jag found her staring up at the pipe that connected to the chimney outside. His forehead pinched. "I wonder why it's not attached to anything? It's just sticking out a few inches from the ceiling."

"It's probably just an open passage for the nanomites." The beam from Mariah's flashlight bounced off something at the back corner of the garage. "Hey, look. Another pipe. It leads right into the floor."

Jag followed her to it. The opening of the pipe was shaped like a funnel and covered by a metal cap that didn't budge when he tried to pry it open. "What in the . . .?" Then his flashlight illuminated a thin black wire that linked to the cap. "Oh, I see. It's like a valve or shutter. When it's time for the nanomites to leave, it slides open automatically."

Right beside the pipe was another manhole; it was larger than the one they'd found earlier. It looked heavy and had a recessed locking handle on it. Jag twisted the handle, then pulled open the cover and looked down. A ladder descended into a separate space below.

"Are we looking into the underworld?" Mariah wondered.

While it was obviously not so, Jag had to admit that it was a fitting question. The lower chamber was dimly lit just like the garage but was tinted an eerie red. It also seemed to be the source of a humming sound that reminded him of the drone of a dishwasher.

He swung his legs down. "Shall we?"

"Take it away," Mariah replied.

He climbed down and Mariah landed shortly after him. A structure stood at the center of the chamber, taking up nearly all the space of the eight-by-eight room; a dark, five-foot-tall sphere that rested on a concrete pedestal. The stainless-steel pipe that pierced the ceiling beside the access cover connected near the base of the sphere.

"The nanomites' hive," Jag breathed.

Mariah made herself as small as possible so she could maneuver through the tight space around the sphere. "There's a hatch here with writing on it—P.O.D. 003-16", she said. "I think they call these things pods."

Jag was barely able to fit in after her. He directed his flashlight at the hatch Mariah had found. It was hardly larger than the size of his head. "Looks like a maintenance access." He took out his phone and snapped photos of different angles of the sphere, as well as the serial number.

"We found it, finally." Mariah pointed her light upward, strobing it as if they were at a rave, and did a little dance.

Jag grinned lopsidedly. "Yeah. Now let's get out of here."

They scurried up the ladder and closed the cover behind them. Jag took a few more pictures of the garage and the equipment before heading out. Mariah levitated the cloths off the devices she'd covered and Jag shoved the section of siding he'd sawn out back into place.

Then, retracing their steps, Kody and Mariah ran out so Jag could shut the gate and chain it back up. He clicked the padlock back in place, though it closed a little loosely, then jumped back over the gate. Mariah was removing the fabric that covered the middle camera when Jag heard Kody whisper. "Guys, the nanomites are coming back . . . and they're glowing red."

"What?" Mariah squeaked. "They didn't return till almost dawn the last time we were here!"

Jag lifted his head and noted a faint red cloud approaching the garage in the shape of a bird. *That's not right . . . I'm not supposed to see them!*

The nanomite swarm was expanding, extending the wingspan of the formation from six feet to an intimidating sixty.

"Run." Jag backed toward the pickup, fear finally setting in. "Run!"

They turned and made it to the vehicle at breakneck speed. Jag could hear an incensed metallic buzzing like angry bees behind him. The buzzing grew louder too quickly for his liking. He dared a glance back. *They'll be on us in seconds!*

The friends crashed against the truck, peeled themselves off, and dove inside. Just as they slammed their doors, the nanomites struck the side of the vehicle like countless minute missiles. Jag brought the truck to life as the bird shape reformed and banked like a fighter jet, turning to attack them from the front. The teenagers screamed.

The oncoming assailants smashed into the pickup before scattering into angry glowing particles, leaving behind countless pits on the windshield. Jag didn't wait for them to regroup. He hit the gas and sped out of Ransom as the nanomites returned to formation and pursued the friends.

"Everyone okay?" Jag asked. "Did any of those things get in?"

"No," Kody said, checking himself over. "I think we're fine—"

Mariah cut him off with a shriek. "Something's biting me! They're on my arms!"

Kody unbuckled himself and climbed into the backseat. Jag heard Mariah slapping at her arms while Kody was telling her to stay still so he could help her get the nanomites off.

Jag kept his foot on the gas pedal and looked into the rear-view mirror to check on the swarm. He was startled by how quickly they were closing the gap. *Are they gonna chase us all the way back to Concordia?*

The swarm was only yards behind them. As Jag came into the next town, streetlights began to appear. Mariah and Kody were still struggling to get the nanomites off. "They're moving too fast!" Kody exploded. "I can see them drilling into her with their blades! We need to open the windows, Jag! It's the only way we can get them off her!"

Jag drove past the first set of streetlights. "We can't do that! They'll be on us any moment now!"

But to his astonishment, when he checked his mirror once more, he saw that the swarm had hung back before reaching the first lights. The nanomites hovered, as if staring at the truck. Then, with a perfect barrel roll, the entire swarm turned as one and headed back in the direction it had come from. The menacing glow faded.

"They're leaving," Jag said breathlessly, easing off the accelerator. "They're gone. We're safe."

"Then we can open the windows!" Kody rolled down the screen next to him. Jag couldn't see what they were doing, but he figured that Kody was holding Mariah's arm out the window and swatting the nanomites away with his vision magnified.

"Are they gone?" Jag asked.

"One second . . ." Jag heard two taps, then Kody's triumphant voice. "Peace out, jerks! I found a new use for my debit card!"

"Thanks, Kody," Mariah said, relieved. "Is there a Kleenex or something? I've got blood on my arms."

Jag, taken aback, demanded, "What? How bad is it?"

"It hurt a lot when I was getting bit, but it only stings a little now. It's like I was poked with sewing needles."

Jag passed her some spare napkins from the cup holder. "Sooo . . . I guess we set off an alarm somehow."

Kody wound up the window. "You don't say?"

"I still think we managed to waltz in and waltz out pretty easily, disregarding what just happened," Mariah said.

"I'm guessing the strategy of their security setup is to be nondescript," Jag told her. "All the cameras and stuff are most likely there to act as a failsafe. It's possible that we missed other sensors they had because the nanomites came back with their attack mode engaged, just like Marshall's contact said they would if they were threatened. I'll have to send the photos we took so they can figure out an alternative to the anti-nanomite. Then hopefully we may still be able to find the means to put an end to the crop destruction."

Tegan, Aari and Marshall gazed at the elegant Victorian house. Its pointed roofs and multiple stone chimneys, along with the many carved facets, made the violet home seem truly one-of-a-kind. A well-maintained lawn with a few small, gurgling fountains welcomed them as they walked up the cobblestone path to the house. There was a fragrant aroma of flowers and herbs from gardens on either side of the path which Tegan found to be pleasing.

A golden lion-head door knocker shone in greeting as they approached. Tegan marveled at the artwork and how lifelike it seemed, then reached for the metal ring and knocked a few times.

The door opened partway and an elderly, curly-haired woman peered out. She was small and wore her makeup lightly, but something in her watchful manner bespoke a spirited edge. Her voice was strong yet gentle when she said, "Yes?"

Marshall smiled kindly at her. "Good morning—Mrs. McDowell?"

"That would be me . . . do I know you?"

"No, ma'am, you don't. I'm Marshall Sawyer. This is Aari and that's Tegan." Tegan and Aari tried to make themselves look as sweet and charming as they could while Marshall continued. "We were wondering if you would be able to spare us a few moments of your time. We would like to speak with you about an important person. Someone we believe is very special to you."

"And who might that be?" she asked, curiosity lifting her brows.

"Elwood McAllister."

As soon as the words left his mouth, the woman's ocean-blue eyes widened in surprise. "Who are you and what is it about Elwood that you want to know?"

"We're people who are very concerned about the crop failures affecting the country. I'm sure you know of it. We have done some extensive research and believe that you may be able to help."

"Me? What makes you think an old lady like myself, content in my quiet corner of the world, can possibly be of any help?"

"There was an event that happened a long time ago, when Elwood was a teenager. We think he may have seen something that could help us stop this horrific attack on crops across the country."

Tegan noted how carefully the woman tried to guard her expression; it was easy to see that she was uncertain of what to make of this encounter.

"It was the summer of '48," Marshall ventured. "There was a plane crash at the lake. Elwood was there."

The woman opened the door a little wider and signaled for the Sentry to go on.

"We're hoping—well, we were at the end of our rope when we found out about Elwood. We're hoping you might know about an object he may have seen at the wreck site that day; a metal container about this big. Silver colored." He held his hands apart, describing the shape of the canister. When she hesitated, Marshall added imploringly, "Please, ma'am, this is incredibly important. You may have the key to stopping the destruction we are seeing across our country and now, around the world."

"But how?" she asked, confused.

"What is inside the canister could put an end to the crop failures."

She exhaled and opened the door the rest of the way. "Come in."

Tegan, jittery, crossed the threshold and was instantly taken by the interior of the house. To her left was the kitchen and to the right was a parlor. The woman led them toward the parlor and invited them to sit on the wooden-legged, floral-patterned sofas. The curtains were drawn back from the large windows to provide a view of the garden and street. A tall cabinet sat in a corner, filled with china dolls and dishes. There were a couple of bookcases on one side of the room and countless framed pictures hung on the walls or sat on corner tables.

"You have a beautiful home," Tegan told their host.

The woman smiled graciously. "Thank you, dear. My late husband used to build houses, so everything you see here is his work. Of course, I did help with the decorating. He passed away a year ago, may his soul rest in peace." She sat on the sofa across from them and rested her hands on her lap, one on top of the other. "Now, tell me what you need to know."

Marshall tapped the tips of his fingers together. "Before I begin, Mrs. McDowell, I have to say that it is crucial that this stays between us. There are some bad people out there who will stop at nothing to halt our progress."

"Why in the world would they want to do that?"

"I really don't have a clue, but one thing we do know is that they intend for this crop failure to lead to a global catastrophe. Nations could be pitted against each other in a desperate fight for food."

The woman's eyes widened. "Don't the authorities know about this?"

Tegan and Aari shot Marshall a look. *You're handling this.*

Marshall glanced at them for a microsecond before addressing their host again. "They do to some extent, but they aren't equipped to handle this scourge. I will provide you with the complete explanation, I promise, but not today. I really need you to trust me, Mrs. McDowell. I know I'm asking a lot of you but my plea is not for myself. There are malevolent forces at work. The circle of trust is very small . . . and it needs to stay that way for now."

Tegan couldn't tell if it was the earnest note in the Sentry's voice or the sincerity in his eyes, but a sense of calm filled the room as soon as those words were spoken.

The elderly woman slowly rose from the sofa and smoothed out her long beige skirt. "Well . . . alright. But we cannot begin without some tea first. And please, do call me Rose."

Tegan looked at Aari, who in turn stared at Marshall in wonder. The Sentry smiled and simply shrugged at the positive turn of events.

Rose returned with a lacquered tray and set it down on the table between the two sofas. "Help yourselves, dears. Use as much sugar and milk as you'd like."

They thanked her and picked up their teacups. She poured for herself as well and took a sip before asking, "So how can I help?"

"As I mentioned earlier," Marshall said, "we need to know if Elwood revealed anything to you about a canister he may have seen after the crash at the lake all those years ago."

Rose took a few more sips from her cup before setting it down and picking up a small photograph from the side table. "Oh, Elwood, you beloved fool." She held up the photo for Tegan and the others to see.

It showed a young couple standing with their arms around each other and wide smiles of utter joy on their faces. "This was us just over six decades ago," Rose said. "I loved him dearly. Still do. And I know he certainly loved me. You know, as a young man he imagined buying a motorcycle and traveling across the country with me. And he actually made it happen! We covered every state in the lower forty-eight on that bike of his. It was an amazing time." Her face softened as she reminisced. "A dreamer he was, too. Always looking for a big break, some kind of fortune that would make him rich so he and I could live lives of adventure.

"That morning of the plane crash, he was supposed to be doing chores at the farm. I still remember how his eyes lit up when he told me about it. How astounded he was! It was a clear blue summer day and he was fishing in his canoe when this huge plane flew right over his head, so close that he thought it was going to hit him. The waves from the crash toppled Elwood out of the canoe and into the water amongst all the debris from the plane. He managed to right his boat and got in, only to find it half-filled with water! The men from the plane were clambering into lifeboats and seemed to be having an argument. He called out to them to ask if they were alright, then paddled to shore to get help.

"Elwood wanted to stay, but he knew his parents would be furious with him for missing his chores so he headed back to the farm. When he emptied water from the canoe, though . . ."

Tegan leaned forward, toes curled. "What?"

"He found something—that silver container you're looking for. Of course the silly boy thought it was some kind of treasure and took it with him back to his house. It was sealed, so it took him ages to get the thing opened. When he did, all he found was silvery-blue dust. Still, he took a sample to the nearest pawn shop to see if it was worth anything. Obviously, the pawnbroker said it wasn't. Around that time—this was a couple of weeks later—we heard stories about men in black suits going around town asking questions about the crash. Elwood panicked." She giggled. "He thought he would be in trouble for taking the container, so my adorable dunce took it and hid it where he was certain no one would be able to find it."

"Where is it?" Marshall asked, his tea forgotten in his hand.

Rose put the photograph back on the table and picked up her cup. "There used to be an old Mormon missionary town that was settled in 1865 on the Colorado River. Over time the town grew into a sizable community. When the work on the Hoover Dam started, that would be 1931 or so, the valley started to flood and the townsfolk were forced to leave. The story they tell around here is that the last resident reluctantly left in his rowboat as water reached his front door. That was in 1938. Eventually the Colorado completely filled the valley and became Lake Mead. The name of the town that was doomed to this watery death," she paused, "was St. Thomas." She looked her guests in their eyes. "That was where Elwood hid the canister."

Aari was astounded. "He dove underwater to hide it?"

"Yes," Rose said, nodding her head firmly, then beamed. "The water in that part of the lake wasn't too deep and Elwood was an excellent swimmer. The settlers had dug a few wells in the town. It was inside one of those that Elwood dropped the canister, weighted with heavy rocks so it would stay down. That was the last we ever spoke about it." Rose lifted her gaze skyward and took a deep breath. "If only Elwood were here. If you're right and the dust in that canister will help stop this scourge . . . then he really did find treasure after all."

Tegan felt a tug in her heart, an ache for the woman who now lived alone. Though she wasn't much for physical contact, she reached over and took the woman's hands. "Thank you for sharing this with us."

Rose was misty-eyed. "No. Thank you for what you are trying to do, and for making Elwood a hero all over again in my heart."

There was a silent pause as the visitors respectfully gave space for their host to collect herself. Finally, Marshall broke the stillness. "How do we find this town?" he asked.

Rose stroked the side of her cup, thinking. "I believe it's about twenty or so minutes from here."

Aari, sitting in between Tegan and Marshall, scrunched his face. "How are we going to get to the canister? We don't have any of our diving gear. Or I guess Marshall can—"

"Diving gear?" Rose chuckled. "I'd think sunscreen and some water bottles would be a better idea."

Aari slowly un-scrunched his face. "Pardon?"

"The lake's water level has dropped in the last decade, dear. St. Thomas is no longer underwater, at least what's left of it. A few people visit the area sometimes but I must warn you, it gets very hot out there this time of the year. Take lots of water, and a hat, too!"

Tegan, Aari and Marshall stared at each other, unable to register their luck. *This is unbelievable!* Tegan thought. *We need to go! Right now!*

"Thank you so much, Rose," Marshall said softly. "You have been so incredibly helpful. This is the break we've been hoping for."

Their host merely dipped her head. "I normally don't let complete strangers into my home, dear, but there is something about the three of you that resonates well with me. You can feel that about some people sometimes, a purity, and it erases all doubt. I see it in all of you."

Tegan was pleasantly taken aback by the woman's words, as was Aari. Marshall recovered quickly and smoothly as he finished his tea. "That's very kind of you to say. I can see why Elwood fell in love with you."

"Oh, pish posh," Rose said, but she looked happy to hear it. "Go now, dears! You have work to do."

As the three left the house, the woman called to Marshall. "You take good care of those kids, young man! If not, I'll be coming after you with my umbrella! And don't forget the sunscreen!"

Marshall laughed and waved at her as they got into the car. "She's an interesting mix of sweet and spunky, isn't she?" he asked.

"Kinda felt like I was looking at an older Mariah," Tegan said from the backseat as Marshall pulled onto the road.

Aari buckled his seatbelt. "So I'm not the only one who thought that!"

"Alright, kiddos, this is it," Marshall said. "We're nearly there. Aari, could you locate St. Thomas?"

Aari's phone went off just then and he picked up. Tegan tried to get him to put the call on speakerphone by flicking his head with her fingers but he was too intent on the conversation. He flailed at her for a minute while conversing; she knew it had to be either Jag, Mariah or Kody on the other end.

Aari hung up and lightly hit his forehead with his fist. "That was Jag. He and the others infiltrated the nanomites' base in Ransom last night and got attacked by the things. The nanomites returned earlier than usual, so Jag thinks that they may have triggered some kind of silent alarm. Apparently the nanomites went nuts, just like Josh said they would when their second protocol kicks in. Mariah got a few small chunks of skin taken out but they managed to get away, and she's doing fine."

Tegan knocked her knees together, rolling her eyes. "We really can't have one day when nothing happens to any of us, huh?"

"Apparently not. I'm hoping that this won't be a pattern."

"As long as you five are okay, we're good," Marshall said encouragingly. "Aari, you got the location on your phone?"

"Yep, right here."

Tegan cracked her knuckles as they sped toward the abandoned town that hid the prize they'd been searching for. "Here we go."

Marshall winced each time the tires of the vehicle dipped into a hole in the road. The asphalt had long since given way to gravel and then to dirt, neither of which their rental car was designed to traverse over smoothly.

Scattered around them was a vista of dry plateaus, barren hills and a rocky mountain range in the distance. Brush and bushes seemingly made of sticks and dried twigs stuck out in plentiful clumps on either side of the road and rolled into the flat land ahead of them. The sky overhead was bright with some clouds that grew a little thicker just behind the mountains.

"This is a cool place," Tegan said. "It's surreal."

Aari had his phone out and was snapping pictures. "I can't believe we're going to see a town that was submerged for *decades* and then just reappeared ten years ago . . . I have no words for this. It's strange. I mean, here we are in the midst of a growing catastrophe, investigating historic places we probably never would have otherwise."

"The universe has a mysterious way of working," Marshall agreed. "Thing is, even in the most challenging of times, there's always a blessing to be found. We just either need to push past the darkness to appreciate it, or adopt a different mindset to find it."

"Is it a Dema-Ki thing to impart wisdom whenever an opportunity presents itself?" Tegan asked brightly.

Marshall gave a lopsided smile. He turned the car off the winding track and onto what was supposedly a parking area, but was really just a small patch of level ground comprised of more crushed rock and sand. A wooden visitor sign bore a few posters with information and images of St. Thomas. There were no other vehicles around.

The intensity of the environment didn't hit them until they got out into the blazing heat and began the trek down to the valley not far below. It was as if they were truly the only people on the planet; there was no city noise, no sound of cars. The world had simply dropped off into a void and all that was left was this shallow and arid valley.

Marshall let Tegan lead him and Aari through the narrow, winding path, avoiding small animal droppings that speckled the ground. Up ahead, Tegan jogged between two of the stick bushes that had spread onto their path. "Gah! Spider webs! *Noooo!*"

"Thanks for clearing that for us, Teegs," Aari called.

"Shut it, Barnes!"

Marshall laughed quietly and pulled the brim of his cap down. He could already feel the sweat rolling down his neck and arms. Taking gulps from his water bottle, he thought, *Rose wasn't kidding about the heat.*

A few small notices on wooden posts cropped up here and there to remind visitors not to touch or remove anything from the soon-to-appear historical sites. Marshall patted the signs as they walked past, lips pressed tight together.

It took nearly half an hour to reach the first trace of human settlement at the edge of the once-submerged town of St. Thomas, Nevada. While it may not have been much to look at, it was still intriguing to see the remains of a building that had probably been a house made of clay and stone. Aari and Tegan both ran ahead, phones in hand as they eagerly explored. Marshall watched them fondly and allowed them to wander for a few minutes before advising them to continue onward.

"Keep an eye out for wells," he reminded them as they passed the remnants of another building.

"Right," Tegan said. "Whoa, check that out! The roof is still kinda intact!"

She took off toward the building, leaving Aari and Marshall to hasten after her. While the teenagers crouched and peeked through a hole in the wall where a window to the basement used to be, a circular clay-brick protrusion about a foot high caught Marshall's attention. He walked over to it and looked down into a yawning hole with gray dirt at the bottom. *Here we are*...

He whistled to the others and they loped over. "We've found well number one," he said. "Let's hope the canister is in there."

Bending down, he grasped the rusty iron grate that had been placed over the opening and pulled at it until it came loose. He tossed it away and wiped his hands on his pants. Tegan took a rope, peg and hammer from her bag while Aari produced a collapsible shovel from his. Tegan hammered the iron peg deep into the dirt and tied one end of the rope securely around it as Marshall looped the other end around his waist. He grabbed the shovel from Aari and lowered himself into the well. It wasn't until he reached the bottom that he realized how narrow the space was.

He held the end of his flashlight in his mouth and began pushing the dirt to either side of him. It took a few minutes of shoveling before he hit hard ground. Shaking his head, he folded the shovel and climbed back up the rope to the surface where the teens helped him out.

"Nothing in that one," he said, then sneezed the dust from his nose. "On to the next." As he walked, he noticed that Tegan and Aari seemed amused. "What's so funny? We haven't found the canister, you know."

"Er . . ." Tegan held her hand to her mouth, eyes crinkling. "Anyone ever told you that you've got an interesting sneeze?"

Marshall knew his cheeks were blooming rose-red.

"Not that it's weird," Aari said quickly.

"Just . . . unique," Tegan chimed in, giggling.

Marshall pulled the brim of his hat lower and avoided speaking until they reached the next well. It was bigger than the first one but not as deep. Marshall rubbed his hands together, yanked the iron covering loose, and put it aside. He tested the pegged end of the rope, drank what was left of his water and then descended into the hole.

Reaching the bottom, he cleared the drifted leaves and twigs before shoveling away at the dirt. Noticing that it had suddenly become dark, he glanced up and saw the teenagers peering down at him intensely. He pulled the flashlight from his mouth. "Hey, Thing One and Thing Two, you're blocking my sunlight!"

"Oops! Sorry!" Tegan pulled Aari aside, letting the light shine down again.

Marshall grinned to himself as he gripped the flashlight in his mouth once more and dug deeper into the well. He'd been working for just over ten minutes when his shovel hit something much harder than dirt. He put the tool aside and knelt down, running his fingers over the obstruction.

Rocks.

Hadn't Rose mentioned that Elwood had weighted the canister down with rocks?

Marshall picked up his shovel and cleared the rest of the dirt away before pushing aside the football-sized slabs. He removed three of them before his hand brushed against something. His heart began to race and he dug until his fingers touched what felt like rotted canvas. Pangs of doubt crept in. *The canister's supposed to be made of metal . . .?*

He continued to dig and brush away the dirt. When the bottom of the well was sufficiently cleared, he paused to point the flashlight at the object. The canvas had been a bag with strap handles. He tore at the material, paying no attention to the clouds of dust it gave off. The light reflected off a shiny surface half-buried in the remains of the bag and loose dirt. He reached in, sensing a smooth, rounded object against his palms, and lifted it from its resting place—tenderly, as if it was a gem—and yelled from around his flashlight. "*We got it!*"

The teenagers whooped and hollered and begged him to hurry back up so they could see the canister for themselves. Marshall gingerly dusted off the silver capsule and placed it into his duffel bag, then clenched the rope in both hands and climbed out of the well. Aari and Tegan closed in on him while he opened the bag just enough for them to see inside.

"I can't believe it!" Aari exclaimed, hands resting on top of his hat as his feet tapped out a little jig. "We actually found it! It's real and we *found* it!"

"In the nick of time, too," Tegan said. "Look over there, by the mountains. The clouds are rolling in pretty fast."

Marshall heard a rumbling in the distance. "We're done here. Let's move it!"

Tegan and Aari ran ahead, still hollering in joy. Marshall jogged behind them, feeling the weight of the canister against his back.

Unbelievable. We did it.

The wind came up without warning, nearly blowing Marshall's cap off. He could feel a few drops of water pattering onto him.

"This is ridiculous!" Aari called. "The one day we come out into a desert where it never rains, it actually *does?*"

"Doesn't matter, we got the canister!" Tegan shouted.

Marshall slid a hand into his pocket to check the time on his phone, but found that it wasn't there. *Come on, Marshall,* he groaned.

By this time they were nearly at the incline that led to the parking area. Marshall raised the car keys and called to get Aari's attention. Aari turned back and caught the keys as the Sentry tossed them. "You two go ahead and get to the car—I dropped my phone somewhere and I don't want you getting caught in the rain!"

"Alright! We'll save a bottle of water for you!" The teenager lengthened his strides and caught up with Tegan.

Marshall turned around and rushed to retrace his steps. "It better not have fallen while I was getting out of the well," he muttered.

After some searching, he found his phone lying face-down on the path . . . right beside some animal droppings. He sighed. *At least it didn't land* in *that mess.*

He checked the screen to ensure that it wasn't cracked and ran back up the path, looking forward to the bottle of water the teens had promised him. Raindrops were falling faster now but he managed to keep just a little ahead of the storm clouds. Fifteen minutes after recovering his phone, he topped the last incline. The sight that welcomed him brought his high spirits to a jarring crash.

The doors on the right side of the car were wide open. Tegan's and Aari's bags lay haphazardly on the ground but the teenagers were nowhere in sight.

No. No. No.

Marshall stumbled forward. Right beside the car, he saw fresh marks in the dirt where a vehicle had spun its wheels. The sand and gravel of the parking lot had been disturbed, indicating signs of a struggle.

The Sentry threw his duffel bag into the backseat of the car, letting out a roar of anguish. *How did they find us?*

As soon as the thought crossed his mind, a hunch struck him. He went on all fours and searched underneath the vehicle. Stuck under the trunk, behind the right tire, was a small black box—a tracking device. Marshall cussed himself out as he tore off the tracker and raised it over his head. Just as he was about to smash it on the ground, he stopped himself. If he left the device in the parking area, Tegan's and Aari's abductors would think the car hadn't moved and that they were home-free.

As he rolled the device off his palm and let it fall into the bushes, he caught sight of something glinting in the sand: the car keys. Aari must have dropped them.

Marshall clung onto the keyset tightly, got into the car and raced onto the uneven road. *I should have taken care of the threat when I had the chance . . .*

The storm caught up with him; rain beat down on his roof, a wild tribal drumming. Flashes of lightning behind him lit up the road. All he could think of was how he had botched his duty so horribly. He'd let Aari and Tegan out of his sight and now they were gone.

What kind of Sentry am I?

PART FOUR

US Regions Afftected by Crop Failure

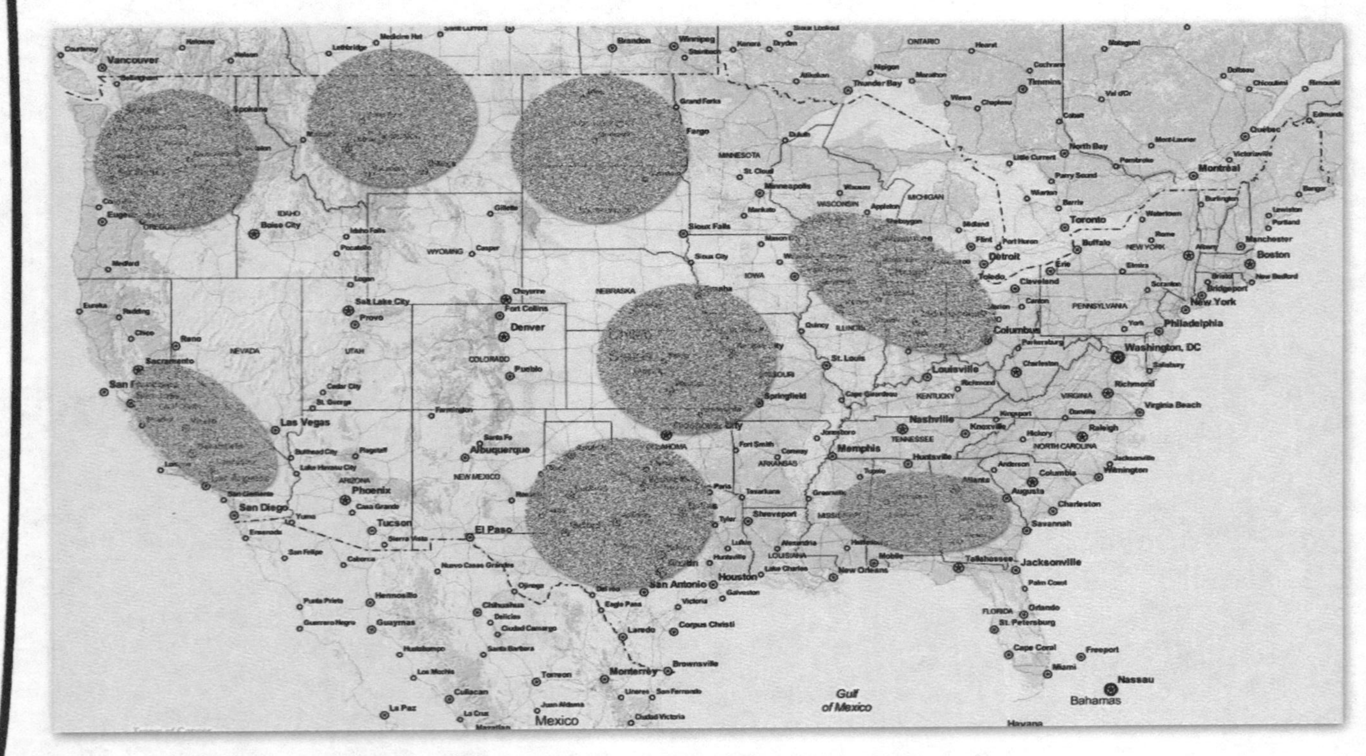

"Where are the others?"

"We're not telling you jack," Tegan spat. Her world had turned black the moment her captors slid a bag over her head. "Why don't you just bug off, Tony, and let us out!"

She knew she was sitting in a speeding vehicle by the way it handled every turn and lane change. A rough hand had a death grip on her right arm—each time she attempted to move, the hold would tighten to the point where she was sure her humerus would snap.

"We're not the bad guys!" Tony said from somewhere up front, sounding exasperated.

Just ahead of her, she heard Aari launch a torrent of choice words at Tony. "That's rich. What do you call this, then? Surprise adoption?"

"Good Lord, you two . . ." From the volume of his voice, Tegan assumed Tony was leaning toward them from the front seat. "I like you kids, okay? But this is my job and it's bigger than you or me. A lot bigger. So if you're not going to cooperate, I will do whatever I must to make you talk. You just need to tell me where Jag, Mariah and Kody are."

Aari growled. "They're not with us."

"Don't sass me, Aari."

"You're not getting anything out of us, sleazeball."

A flurry of thuds and muffled sounds of struggle followed. Tegan, blind, didn't know what was going on. Aari's yells were abruptly cut short.

"Aari?" Tegan called, worry creeping in. "Aari? Answer me! Why isn't he answering? What did you do to him?"

"He's just having a nap right now," the captor holding her said, speaking with a familiar accent. "The lad won't be a bother for a while."

Elvis! Now the hand that held her felt like that of a rotted corpse.

"Tegan, please," Tony said. "Where are the others?"

"Where are you taking us?"

"Somewhere. Not far now."

"Where?"

"*Tegan!*" Tony bellowed. "Tell me where your friends are!"

Elvis squeezed her arm without mercy. She clenched her teeth, not wanting to let out any sound of pain.

"Don't make this difficult, Tegan. Liam, take that thing off her and show her your hand."

The sack over Tegan's head was pulled off. She impulsively inhaled fresh air—or at least, it was fresher than what was circulating through the sack. Elvis turned her head toward him, though not before she saw that she was sitting in the rear seat of a seven-passenger vehicle. Aari lolled in the middle row with a brute of a man beside him. Tony was in the front passenger seat watching her, and Potato Nose was driving. Through the front windshield Tegan could see low-hanging gray clouds.

"Look here." Elvis grinned; *grimaced, more like*, Tegan thought. He brought his free hand to her eye-level and she jerked back. The Australian's pinkie had been cut off and unevenly stitched up. The skin around the wound was red and inflamed.

Elvis wiggled his remaining fingers. "Mr. Cross had that digit removed because I failed to keep you and the other girl locked up. Best cooperate with him 'less you want to lose a pretty pinkie, too."

"Well done, Liam," Tony praised acerbically. "A little pain is sometimes all it takes to motivate performance. I'm impressed with how quickly you located our . . . guests. Bag her again."

Elvis—or Liam, as Tony called him—already had the bag over Tegan's head before Tony finished. The last thing she saw before darkness wrapped around her again was a cross-street through the tinted side window. She quickly committed the street's name to memory.

In spite of what Elvis had shown her, she remained resistant. "I'm still not talking."

"We'll try again in a few minutes," Tony said, "when we have more room to work."

No one addressed her after that. She'd given up her efforts at pulling away from the Australian and could do nothing but wait. The vehicle came to a stop and she heard a window roll down. A voice from outside asked, "What's your business here?"

Potato Nose fumbled for words as Tony said, "It's me."

"Oh! It's Mr. Cross! Open the gate!"

The vehicle rolled forward and made a turn before halting again. The engine shut off and Tegan was wrenched out and guided inside a building; she could tell from the blast of cool air that greeted her. She was taken to an elevator and then around a few corners before being suddenly forced down onto a hard chair. Someone tied her hands behind her back.

Finally, the sack was pulled off her head. She blinked in annoyance as harsh fluorescent light assaulted her eyes, and found herself seated at one end of a small table in the middle of a bare room. Tony sat across from her, with the Australian standing behind him. Tegan wanted so badly to swing a bat at their faces.

"Where's Aari?" she asked.

Tony lazily rocked his head to the side. "If you would look right there . . ."

She glanced to where he indicated and saw her friend lying still on the tile floor, wrists bound and a sack still over his head. "Aari? Aari! What did you do to him, Tony?"

"He's still napping," Tony said. "Relax, he'll come around sooner or later. Right now, you have something bigger to deal with. Look, we know the others are in Kansas, so if you could just tell us where exactly—"

"They're not in Kansas."

Tony stood up, hands spread apart on the table, and glared. "They *are* there. Someone by the name of Marshall Sawyer purchased only three tickets for a flight from an airport in Kansas to California. I'm gonna go out on a limb and say Sawyer is the fellow who was with you at Lake Mead. This means your friends are still in Kansas. What were you doing there?"

Tegan flicked the tip of her tongue derisively at him. "Get out of my face."

Tony lashed out, delivering a hard slap to her cheek. She gasped, spittle flying out of her mouth. Her eyes watered slightly but she looked back at him defiantly.

Tony met her gaze and the coldness edged out of him. He slowly sat back down and skimmed his hands over his honey-colored hair. "Please, Tegan. I don't want to hurt you, any of you. God knows I really, really don't. But you need to tell me where the others are or you'll leave me no choice." When Tegan only glowered at him, he hit the table with his fist. "Liam, get the others. And make sure they bring the tools."

"Yes, sir." The Australian exited the room.

"You're gonna cut off my finger?" Tegan asked. "Is that it?"

"You forced my hand!" he barked. "I need to do what needs to be done. You *will* talk one way or another!"

She stared at him, hatred and, strangely, pity welling up inside her. "You're out of your mind. I don't know what it is you're a part of, but you're nuts."

"It may seem a bit out of this world right now, but in the end it will be worth it."

"Right. The end justifies the means. Except I'm not so sure it actually does."

Tony ignored her. The Australian returned, followed by Potato Nose and the brute who had been beside Aari in the vehicle. The brute was holding a hammer, a chisel, and a roll of rags. He set them down in front of Tegan. She sized up the tools, her mouth dry. *They wouldn't.* She glanced at the Australian's severed digit as he freed one of her arms to rest it on the table, and stifled back a whimper.

"Which one shall we take off today, sir?" the brute asked, tenderly rubbing a thumb along the edge of the chisel while Elvis held Tegan's hand down.

"Whichever one you like," Tony said. "Tegan, I'm begging you. I don't give a damn when it comes to getting my guys in line, but you kids—you haven't really done anything wrong. I'm giving you one last chance." He fixed her with an imploring look. "Where are Jag, Mariah and Kody?"

As the reality sank in that she couldn't escape what was about to happen, Tegan tried to appeal to him. "Tony, please . . . please, don't do this."

"Where are they?" he repeated. Their gazes were locked, both beseeching the other to concede but neither wanting to surrender.

Tegan's lower lip trembled and she fought to stiffen it. The brute moved to place the blade of the chisel against the first knuckle of her little finger. The hammer hovered just above it. Tegan breathed out shakily and, with a feeling that she'd locked in an answer she could never retract, shook her head at Tony.

The young man looked defeated. With a pained expression, he murmured, "Do it."

The brute aligned the chisel properly and raised the hammer. Tegan screamed as it swung down.

"I found something!"

The hammer halted an inch from the head of the chisel. Tegan forced herself to swallow back her scream when she realized she could still move her finger. She looked away, silent tears sliding down her cheeks.

"What is it, David?" Tony asked.

Potato Nose, who'd been crouched by Aari while the events were proceeding, showed Tony the boy's phone. "The girl didn't have hers, but he did. It's password-locked but I can crack it no problem."

Tony's posture relaxed immensely. He quickly waved the brute away from Tegan. "Will we be able to trace the location of all the numbers on the phone?" he asked.

"Yes. I have some contacts who could lend a hand there."

"Great. Get on with it."

"Yes, sir."

Potato Nose and the brute cleared out of the room as the Australian secured Tegan's arm behind her back before returning to his position behind Tony. Tegan was emptied of tears but she still sniffled here and there.

Tony moved the hammer and chisel far away from her. "You were lucky. Extremely lucky."

"There wouldn't have been a need for me to be 'lucky' if you'd just let Aari and me go."

"I can't do that."

"Why not?"

"I do what's expected of me. I don't ask questions. If you five are what my superior wants, my job is to deliver. It's that simple. I trust the Boss completely."

"You're not telling me anything!"

"Yeah, feel my frustration now?" he shot back.

"If you expect us to cooperate, we have the right to know what's going on!"

"It's not my place to tell you. I'm sure you'll soon learn what we're all about, though."

"Fine. At least tell me how you found us."

"Tracking device on your car. We put it in place as a failsafe back at Lake Mead yesterday. Good thing we did."

"If that's the case, how come you didn't pick us up until now?"

"When that friend of yours shot my guy in the leg, the GPS tracker in his pocket took most of the bullets. We only got it fixed this morning. Who is your friend, by the way? We got his name, but why is he with you?"

Tegan shrugged indifferently.

The room washed into silence after that. Tony busied himself with his phone. He turned his device sideways and rapidly tapped the screen.

Tegan was both dumbfounded and offended. *Is he legitimately playing a game right now?*

The door opened and Potato Nose entered with an exultant smile. "We got them, Mr. Cross. Concordia, Kansas."

A fifty-pound chain dragged Tegan's heart down. There was nothing she could say or do to deter them from hunting her friends. The only thing left now was to pray that Jag and the others would be able to fend for themselves. Maybe Marshall, by an extremely long shot, could reach them in time to help.

"Where in Concordia?" Tony asked.

"We'll have to wait till tomorrow morning. My girl on the inside won't be back in the office till then."

"*Tomorrow?*"

"She's not on our payroll, Tony. This is a favor for us. It has to be on her terms."

Tony looked back at Tegan. Though her hands were out of view behind her, she slowly curled all her fingers to hide them from him.

"Fine," he said, getting up. "Tomorrow. Make sure she's tied tight."

Aari stretched out his legs and let out a long groan as the Australian tautened the cords holding Tegan's arms behind her back.

Tony headed toward the door. "Don't go anywhere now, you two. An acquaintance of yours is coming to see you tomorrow. And he has ways to extract more information out of you than I ever will."

"I lost them, Josh. I lost them."

"I understand how you must be feeling, Marshall, but let's keep exasperation at bay. Stay focused on finding the kids. Send me the canister and I'll start working on the dopant right away. That's one worry I can take off your mind."

The Sentry was waiting in a short lineup at an express courier office. He'd been on the phone with Josh for the past few minutes. The other man was shocked to hear about Tegan's and Aari's abduction but still extended what comfort he could.

Compartmentalizing his stress, Marshall asked, "How long will you need to get the dopant ready for use?"

"At the fastest I'd say anywhere between twenty-four and forty-eight hours for the first batch," Josh answered. "I'll arrange for a quick way to get it back to you."

"Actually, when you're done, send the prototype to the other three in Kansas. I'll text you the address in a bit."

"Will do. Don't worry, Marshall. Leave this in my hands from now on and you can channel your energy into finding the kids."

The Sentry wiped away some water droplets from his jaw. How it was that the scientist could impart calmness over the distance astounded him, and for that he was deeply appreciative. "Thank you," he said heavily.

"I'm here to help," Josh said. "Listen, I have to check on one of my projects. Keep me posted on the kids, okay?"

"Yeah."

Marshall hung up just as he reached the service counter. He placed the duffel bag in a shipping box, packing it tightly with bubble wrap and Styrofoam, then sealed it and paid the extra cash for overnight delivery. As he rushed out to his car, he was mauled by fast, heavy raindrops and swore at the downpour.

Driving back onto the main road, he silently begged Aari and Tegan to forgive him and prayed for a sign to guide him back to them.

***

The constant pounding in Aari's skull was at last starting to ebb. He'd felt the ache as soon as he came around and wondered if he'd taken a baseball bat to the head. Now he sat across from Tegan in the barren, windowless room. There wasn't much to discuss. They were both weary and had it up to their eyeballs with their so-called vacation, and he had no idea how she was dealing with it all. *Being nabbed twice in a week. That's not right.*

He tapped her foot with the toe of his shoe. "Teegs? What happened when I was knocked out? I don't feel my phone in my pocket anymore."

"They took it," she said blankly. "They managed to trace the others down. They're waiting to pinpoint their exact location right now."

Aari rested his forehead on the table, closing his eyes halfway. "What are they gonna do with us?"

"I don't know."

"So we're just stuck here, then?"

"Seems like it."

He raised his head. "Did something happen, Tegan?"

She began to quiver slightly. "They . . ."

He straightened. "They what?"

"They nearly cut off my finger. The only thing that stopped them was one of Tony's men finding your phone."

Aari was burning under his collar. "Tony ordered your finger to be cut off? Why?"

"I wouldn't tell him where the others were."

He was angry to the point of speechlessness. Though now glad that his phone had been found, if only because it saved his friend from losing a finger, he feared for Jag, Mariah and Kody.

"He was begging me to tell him so he wouldn't have to hurt me," Tegan said; it sounded as if she was forcing her voice to work.

Aari scowled. "Who? Tony?"

"Yeah. He said he likes us all and doesn't want to put us through pain, but whatever he's part of is bigger than any of us."

"That's a load of bull. What *is* he a part of, anyway?"

"He didn't say. All we know is what Dr. Nate told Mariah and me."

Aari kicked one of the table legs. "Is he going to come back for us?"

"Doubt it. When he left, Tony said that we should expect a visitor tomorrow evening."

"Tomorrow evening?"

"Yes, Aari," she replied, impatient. "That's exactly what he said. And something tells me that our visitor might be Dr. Nate."

"For what? More interrogation?"

"Probably. He's not going to play as nice this time around, I don't think."

"Then we'd better get out of here. Doesn't matter if it's really him coming or someone else; either way, I'm not keen on finding out."

"You do know we're being kept behind a solid metal door that is most likely guarded, yeah? And that we have no idea what or where this place is?"

"Can you find a creature, some animal to be your eyes like you did at the cavern?"

"I tried. There aren't any close enough."

Aari rested his head on the table again. "Ugh. How long was the drive from St. Thomas to here? That might give us a general idea of our location."

Tegan coughed. "Actually, I may have an idea. They took the sack off my head for a bit when we were in the car. I saw the name of a street we passed."

"Great. Now what we need is to find a way to get that information out."

"I think I can try something. Remember when we were at Josh's lab, and you stayed outside to take a call from Kody?"

"Yes . . .?"

"Jag took the phone from Kody for a moment, didn't he?"

Aari inched upright and scrutinized her. "I thought Kodeman was the only one with super hearing."

"He is," she said. "But what I heard—or what I think I heard—were Jag's thoughts."

"No way."

"It was like a badly-tuned radio, with words cutting in and out, but it was his voice. This is a long shot, but maybe I can reach out to him."

"How is it you could hear him?"

"Most of my training with Elder Tikina was spent in the novasphere, remember? That's how I locate the animals I take control of. Maybe telepathic communication is just the next step in the development of my abilities. The Elders did say it could happen to us."

Aari was too excited to sit. He hopped up and circled the table. "If you can reach him and get him to tell Marshall about the street you saw . . ."

". . . then we can still try to escape," Tegan finished, grinning.

"Precisely." Aari sat on the edge of the table and winked at her. "And I think I've got an idea how we can go about doing that."

Despite his diminutive stature, Dr. Nate enjoyed driving big cars. His Chevy Suburban trailed easily over the dirt roads that led to the mine site in New Mexico. He'd just finished a call with Tony and now spoke to the Boss to relay the good news. "Tony recaptured two of the five!" he said gleefully. "And 'is men are working to locate the other three."

"It's a start." The Boss's voice carried the characteristic unemotional tones of a vocal distorter. "Are all sites ready for the speech in a couple of hours?"

"They are all 'ooked up and ready to go, just like you wanted."

"Good. I want you to call Tony back."

"And tell him what?"

"I want the two young ones to watch my address to the Sanctuaries. Have him arrange for that."

Dr. Nate admired the Boss's perceptiveness. "I see . . . I will inform him of this right away."

"Thank you. I hope you enjoy tonight's speech, Doctor."

"I'm sure I will, Boss. I'm sure I will."

***

The view was nothing to be sneezed at. Snowcapped peaks glistened in the setting orange sun. One mountain stood taller than its brothers to the right. Though stunning, it seemed ancient, as if it had watched the world since its beginning.

A warning buzz sounded.

Kenzo Igarashi sighed. *Looks like it's time.* He clicked the remote he was holding and the striking scenery in front of him vanished. Most of the living quarters weren't properly set up yet, but he was one of the lucky few in the New Mexico Sanctuary who'd gotten a functioning ultra-high-definition LED screen.

He pushed off from his bed and checked himself in the mirror. His silver hair, a genetic oddity he quite liked, was sticking up at the back so he combed it down, then left his room to walk along a hallway lined with doors behind which other workers of the Sanctuary resided. A few others, dressed as he was in bright orange coveralls, were making their way out of the honeycomb-shaped dormitories at the eastern corner of the cavern. Most of the other occupants were already assembled.

A black-haired girl, Kenzo's cousin, caught up with him and linked her arm through his. Her coveralls were dirty and she had dust all over her face but she still smiled radiantly. "Hey! Where were you?"

"Taking my break in my room," he said, patting her hand.

"This is so exciting!" she gushed. "We're finally going to hear from the Paterfamilias! I've been waiting for this moment for a long time!"

"You sound like we've been here for years, Ren."

She laughed. "Sixteen months. It does feel like it's been ages, though. It's been an incredible ride, hasn't it? Eye-opening, even. Thank goodness we were found—we've been given a new chance."

Kenzo patted her hand again and forced a laugh. *Found? New chance? We were kidnapped, Ren. And now we're nothing but slaves.* He could never understand how it was that he was the only one, or so it seemed to him, who was able to resist Dr. Nate's cerebral reprogramming. For over a year and a half he'd had to pretend that he was one of the youths who'd been inducted into the organization.

A twinge of sadness pierced his heart as he gazed at Ren. She had been transformed into a drone for the cause and was completely unaware of the chain that had been wrapped around her soul.

She pulled him into the amassing crowd and he found himself at the center, staring at a massive screen that had been erected. Most of the lights in the cavern had been turned off with the exception of a few at the outer edges of the work area, and those were dimmed.

Kenzo saw Dr. Nate sitting up front with Vladimir Ajajdif, facing the crowd and looking proud of himself.

Mind warper, he thought disgustedly. He'd trained himself to plaster on a neutral expression to blend in with the others who seemed so keen in their cause. For the billionth time, he found himself wondering if there were any others who'd managed to fool Dr. Nate and were playing possum, pretending to be one of the masses to save their neck.

Everyone knew the consequences of trying to escape the Sanctuary. They'd seen it. When Kenzo and his cousin were first plunked into the Sanctuary with a batch of other kids, a few had tried to escape but were taken down by the Marauders and ripped apart. Gruesome photos of their remnants were circulated and videos depicting the attacks were on loop for weeks. Kenzo had heard what the other youths had to say about the would-be escapees—stupid, idiots, why would anyone even want to go back to the atrocious world they'd been saved from?

His thoughts meandered to the two girls who'd escaped a few days ago. They weren't part of the youths residing in the Sanctuary, that was for sure. He hoped they'd managed to survive the beasts that had been unleashed on them, and wished he could have done more than just stepping aside and letting them past him.

A crackle from the speakers behind the big screen quieted the crowd. The screen flickered for a few seconds before an image appeared of a figure with a golden hood pulled down over its face. A ripple of whispers traveled through the ranks.

"Greetings." The voice was digitally distorted and pitched low. "I'm pleased to speak to all of you tonight. Thank you for joining me from different time zones across the planet. This is my first address to you since we began building our future together. As such, not only is this moment special—it is historic."

Kenzo risked a quick glance around him. Every other youth present had their attention fixed on the Paterfamilias.

"Since the dawn of our species, humanity has possessed the freedom of choice—the choice to live in accord with the planet or not.

"But the choices that were made over the last few centuries have led us down a path of destruction fed by greed, corruption and arrogance. Mankind has taken the planet and all that she has to offer for granted, and this has led us to where we are today.

"Soulless corporations and spineless politicians have duped the mindless masses to voraciously consume resources without a thought to what their self-indulgence can lead to. Sadly, this abuse is not the sole domain of the rich nations of the world. This greed and venality is prevalent across the globe, driven by a sense of entitlement." The metallic voice grew coarse with disgust. "Popular culture and its vile disregard for human decency. Its obscene self-obsession and exploitation of young minds. You have all seen this. The garbage that pollutes human consciousness.

"With haughtiness they have trampled under their feet the values that have been the safeguard of our species and the planet. This breakdown of society began long before you and I came into the picture. Day by day, it worsens."

Whispers broke through the crowd again before being subdued.

"As you have learned in the time you've been at your respective Sanctuaries, the cause we stand for is nothing short of the salvation of our planet. Your unwavering commitment to our purpose is the foundation for a new world, a new future. You are the precious pioneers who will lead the way.

"As the world outside collapses into a heap of dust, the world you have begun to build will rise in its stead. The Sanctuaries you are constructing are in anticipation of the coming downfall and the evisceration of humanity.

"The end for the old world is close at hand, my friends, and what I am doing in hastening its demise is simply a matter of mercy. Soon enough, we will replace it with a new order.

"Though we may be confined here for a time, we will patiently wait for the day where we can return to the surface. That day will mark the birth of a new Earth and a new race of man, shorn of the imperfections of our forefathers."

A rousing cheer shot up from the massed youths. Kenzo joined in, howling and clapping, but he wanted to smite them all. *Hastening humanity's demise? No sane person would follow a leader who's bent on burning the world. Why won't these guys wake up?*

When the cheering died down, the Paterfamilias continued, abstractedly rolling a small violet sphere in one hand. "Stewards of New Earth. Most of you have grown up being told that the way to govern ourselves is through self-determination and a government that serves its people through the separation of powers between law of the state and the law of morality. How has that worked out?"

The crowd jeered and catcalled.

"When you learn to be in tune with your new purpose, you will free yourselves from the strangling grip of the old ways. In the coming weeks, I will be revealing to you how we'll organize ourselves as curators of the new future. With that, I call upon each and every one of you to redouble your efforts in building what must be built right here, right now, for the world that we will soon hail. To you, and to New Earth."

The crowd roared as the screen went blank. "New Earth! New Earth! New Earth!"

* * *

Tegan and Aari were dumbstruck at what they'd just witnessed on Tony's tablet.

Tony grinned broadly as he pulled the device away from them. "Hope you enjoyed that crash course on our cause," he said reverently. "And I know what you're thinking. However, what we're doing to speed up the end of the old world is not for you to be concerned with." As he walked out of the room, he added, "I'm looking forward to possibly welcoming the five of you into our fold. You will help create a new and lasting future for the betterment of both mankind and the planet."

With a population of thirteen million, Mumbai is by far the largest city in India and probably its most westernized. It amalgamates flavors from the bygone British Era with twenty-first century trappings—lavish hotels and a booming film industry. Yet this is a place where one can find wealth and extreme poverty co-existing; it isn't uncommon to find tin-roofed shacks erected haphazardly beside opulent mansions.

The Sentry was perched at the top of a radio tower, granting him an ample view of the bustling city below. He'd been restless since the night before. It was as if his spirit sensed an impending disturbance. Listening to his intuition, he'd let his feet guide him to a street with closely-packed shops on either side and scaled the communication tower at its center.

Strange looks were initially thrown his way but people soon moved on, busy as they were with their own problems and trying to make a living. The chatter of Hindi and occasional English fell away as the disconcerted Sentry waited for a sign that, in spite of him wishing otherwise, might prove his hunch right. With his heightened senses, he began scanning below for potential trouble.

At a large grocery store nearby, dozens of customers stood restlessly in a long line under the sweltering heat of the midday sun. Several other stores that sold food had similar lines of shoppers waiting impatiently to get their hands on essential items like rice and wheat.

Security guards were posted at the doors of the shops and policemen patrolled the neighborhood, watching for signs of unrest. Imposing green military trucks chugged along their designated routes, belching black smoke into the already polluted air. It appeared that the presence of police and armed troops was succeeding at keeping potential troublemakers at bay.

A thought crossed the Sentry's mind: *What if the agitators have it all planned? What if all they're waiting for is a distraction—*

No sooner had the notion cropped up than a loud explosion rocked the city. The Sentry held onto the tower as he turned to see a home appliance store consumed by flames. Shockwaves from the explosion shook the tower, forcing the observer to tighten his hold on its steel frame. There was a brief moment of stunned silence followed by a flood of screams from the multitude below. The Sentry hurriedly surveyed the scene.

Fire shot through the roof of the ruined store and bodies of shoppers lay sprawled at its entrance. Many survivors huddled, bloodied and weeping, while others, obviously in shock, wandered around, seemingly lost. Police and troops ran toward the devastated shop, shouting into their radios for assistance. Even the guards posted at the grocery stores nearby ran to help.

And that opened the floodgates.

The people who'd been in long lines outside the stores grabbed the opportunity and rushed in to seize what they needed. They jostled one another away and ganged upon those who'd managed to obtain the products they wanted. Men and women flew from the shop with looted food only to have it snatched away by other desperate and hungry people.

Even though his intuition had turned out to be dead right, the Sentry wished it hadn't been so. Riots like these tore at the very fabric of society and it hurt to see his fellow citizens reduced to such a state. He watched the enraged, frantic people below for a while longer until additional police arrived on the scene. He then vaulted from the radio tower and landed on the ground like a cat. Perfectly unharmed, he slunk away. He knew the time had come to inform the League of the darkness that was descending on his country.

* * *

From the top of a knoll overlooking the district of Tongshan in the southern part of Hubei Province, China, a tall young woman with lustrous black hair gazed out at the scenery of rolling hills interspersed with expansive stretches of rice fields.

The place was famous for its beautiful mountains that attracted tourists in large numbers from all over the world. On a normal day it would be a serene sight to behold, a vista little changed from the time Chinese farmers began cultivating rice in paddies nearly four thousand years ago. Today, though, the countryside was a scene of devastation. Pillars of dusky smoke rose into dark clouds that hung over the fields. From a distance, the landscape could have been mistaken for a tableau of quietude blackened by menacing tornadoes.

The rice fields had been hit with the same scourge that was sweeping much of the world. Overseen by government troops, farmers were clearing their fields and burning their dead paddies.

Reports that Australia, one of the country's major suppliers of wheat, had also been hit by crop failure caused major concerns for the government. It was especially troubling since the United States and Canada were not in a position to fill the vacuum as they too had been badly affected by crop losses.

The young woman was a third-generation Chinese Sentry who'd driven to the countryside to escape the pain of having to witness the growing number of riots breaking out in the cities. *And then I see this out here,* she thought bitterly.

Rice was the staple diet for more than half of the nearly one-and-a-half billion citizens of the country. It was considered part of China's cultural heritage—comparable to the Irish and their potatoes. In fact, the word for 'rice' in Chinese *meant* food. The devastation of this crop could tear down the entire country, especially with rumors that the grain reserve figures the government had touted all these years were grossly inflated.

But what worried her just as much, if not more, was the information she'd received earlier in the day through her contact in the government. China had mobilized its military forces along its border with Russia and its operatives were preparing to hack into the Russian power grid system to take it down. That could only mean one thing: an invasion.

Russia, as it turned out, was the only country to have been mostly spared by the scourge. There was even speculation that the Russians were behind the attack on global grain production. Of course, there was no evidence of it but that didn't stop the hardliners in the government from using it as justification for their desperate maneuver. The informant had also told the Sentry that China had covertly established a pact with India to secure Russian grain supplies following the invasion.

Turning her back on the burning crops, she thought, *Nothing like a calamity and fear of the loss of power to bring former enemies together . . . time to reach out to the League.*

60

Aari was being prodded awake. He opened his eyes and raised his head from the ground where he'd slumped off his chair. Tegan stood over him, a thin layer of amusement beneath her morose stare.

"So," she said, "I woke up and found you in a weird yoga position in your sleep. How'd you even fall off like that?"

With Tegan's help, Aari pushed himself back into the chair and shook off his grogginess. "Beats me."

Tegan paced from one corner of the room to the other and back again, head down. "Well, I've been trying to reach Jag."

"Did you get him?"

"Not yet. It's hard. The first time I did it was completely by accident."

"You still managed to do it. Keep trying."

"I am. That thing we saw last night, though . . . that's bothering me."

Aari shuddered. "At least now we know what this is all about."

"That can't be the full picture. What reason would they have for wanting us to join them?"

"We *were* in Dema-Ki for a while, and we were trained by the Elders. It's like, if you had the opportunity to take someone who's been on the other side and have them under your control, wouldn't that be valuable?"

"There has to be more to it. I don't believe they'd go through all this trouble just to secure a few pawns."

"I'm just shooting in the dark. But you may be right. It makes me shudder to think what they've got in mind for us."

Tegan joined him back at the table. "Did you see the way they cheered last night after the speech? It . . . it was mob mentality, wasn't it? How can anyone be so thrilled about tearing down the world?"

"It's a cult, that's what it is."

"I'm gonna try contacting Jag again. I want no part of this." She slouched down and closed her eyes.

Aari respectfully gave her silence. His thoughts wandered as he reflected on all that had happened to the friends. *Never in a hundred lifetimes would I have thought we'd be involved in something like this. This is surreal. What the Elders said about the prophecy's warning . . . It's happening. How are we going to tell our parents about all this when we get out of here—if we get out of here?*

Tegan knocked on the table rapidly. Aari shook away his thoughts and saw her staring at him. "Did you get him?" he questioned softly.

She put a finger to her lips and nodded. Then she startled Aari by pounding on the table. "Shoot! Lost the link. I'll try again."

Aari tapped his shoes together as he waited. The room was quiet for several minutes until Tegan said, "It's done. I told him all I could and he's calling Marshall as we speak. He'll keep me updated on Marshall's progress."

"Nice, Teegs! Didn't I say you could do it?"

"Yes, Brainiac, you did."

"What's it like, by the way? Conversing through thoughts?"

"It's . . . well, if the connection's strong, you can kind of feel their presence in your mind, like a gentle hand. Or a hug. I don't know how else to explain it. Other than that, it's really no different than thinking to yourself."

Will I ever be able to do that? Aari wondered. *It would be pretty cool to communicate with the others without needing to speak. We could probably achieve a lot more, too.*

"What are you thinking about?" Tegan asked.

"Eh, nothing," Aari said. "I just hope we get out of here soon."

"Marshall will find us. It's just a matter of time."

***

It was midday when Marshall parked near an industrial complex consisting of four linked buildings. According to a discreet sign, the facility belonged to Quest Defense. Marshall surmised that Quest Defense and Quest Mining, which ran the mining site that had held Mariah and Tegan, were part of the same operation. The complex was surrounded by a tall fence topped with razor wire and the Sentry wouldn't have been surprised if it was electrified, except there were no warning signs to indicate so. The site was flanked by streets on two sides and by an empty plot of land on the third.

Through the fence he could see a large parking lot in front of a two-story glass structure that he assumed housed offices. To his right, at the center of a wide double-lane entrance was a security post. The road split, with one branch presumably leading to the back of the complex for warehouse deliveries and the other ending at the parking lot at the front. A small traffic circle was located near the guard post just outside the fence.

He noticed a few security personnel patrolling the area. Though he couldn't tell the exact number, he guessed that there were at least six men on duty with two at the post at all times. The Sentry thought it odd that a couple of guards wore black uniforms while the rest were in blue. He also noted a building about twice the size of the security post, tucked away to the left of the entrance, and wondered what it was.

He was anxious to locate where Tegan and Aari were being held inside the sprawling complex. There was also the challenge of his being completely blind to the interior layout of the buildings. He would need eyes on the inside but the only pairs he could count on were locked away.

Marshall mulled about it for a while longer and a plan soon began to form. He slowly smiled as he picked up his phone to call Jag.

* * *

Tegan!

Tegan, who had been pacing again, stopped abruptly. *Jag!*

Hey. Okay. I'm on the phone with Marshall. He studied the facility as best he could from the outside. It's under heavy security but he thinks he's figured out a way to get you and Aari out of there. He'll need your help, though.

Great! What does he want us to do?

There was a pause, then he said, *To begin, he wants you to stay put.*

Tegan couldn't comprehend what she was hearing. *Come again?*

He's working out a plan. Since you guys are already inside, it gives us an advantage. You can help take down that facility. He wants to know if you have any idea about the layout of the building and where exactly you're being held.

We were blindfolded when they brought us here, Jag.

Oh.

If only I had Devastator with me . . . I suppose I could try to link with an animal around here.

Another pause. Then, *Marshall's relieved to hear that. You're okay with this, right? You'll have to endure maybe another day there.*

As long as Marshall has a plan, I guess we'll hang tight.

Thatagirl.

Tegan severed the connection and rested heavily against the wall as she filled Aari in. "So we've got to stay put for another night."

"Let's hope Marshall knows what he's doing," Aari said resignedly. "I really don't want to deal with these people anymore."

The magnificent pentagonal temple sat atop an exquisitely landscaped terrace at the western end of Dema-Ki. Five wooden columns, finely carved, rose thirty feet from the ground. Resting on top of the columns were statues of slender human figures that supported the dome of the building with their arms. At the center of the temple's open foyer was a marble cauldron from which streamed dazzling, iridescent flames. The colorful plumes of fire would dance day and night. No matter how many times one passed it by, it would still fascinate and transfix the observer.

Nageau sat with Tikina, Saiyu and Ashack upon three comfortable, curved benches that formed a semi-circle in an alcove within the grand hall. The benches were surrounded with ornamental rocks and plants, flanking two small fountains that bubbled quietly. The whole temple exuded a meditative and serene aura. Many Dema-Ki residents visited this place for contemplation and spiritual healing.

The Elders spoke softly for a time so as not to disturb the villagers who were already inside. When Nageau spotted Tayoka making his way over with quick steps, he waved a greeting. "And so our friend arrives at last."

Tayoka took a seat on the only free bench. "Ah, I am terribly sorry for my tardiness. I had been called to tend to something at the other end of the valley."

"Nothing worrisome, I hope?" Saiyu asked.

"No, no. Now, Nageau, is it true? Has the Sentry located Tegan and Aari?"

"Yes," Nageau answered. "He mentioned that Tegan managed to connect with Jag telepathically and she was able to pass on some useful information."

"The crystals must be helping," Tikina said. "I am glad of the progress the younglings are making in spite of the challenges they face."

"As am I," Saiyu agreed. "Rejoice, Nageau! There seems to be a cloud hanging over your head. Are you not pleased with how our apprentices are advancing?"

"I *am* thankful for this," Nageau said, "but the Sentry also revealed to me that Tegan and Aari had witnessed a speech delivered by the leader of these people."

"And?" Tayoka prompted.

"It was apparently a rousing speech about a vision for the planet, and it confirms our fears. Even worse, the younglings mentioned that this person was in possession of a . . . small violet sphere."

The faces of the other Elders turned pale.

"The *lathe'ad*," Saiyu whispered.

Ashack shakily pushed himself to his feet and treaded with uneven strides out into the grand hall. Tikina took Nageau's hand in hers. "Are you certain that is what they saw?"

"Yes," Nageau murmured heavily. "I am convinced. Reyor is alive."

"So we can rule out the notion of a rogue Sentry, then," Saiyu said despondently.

"This is far, far worse than a rogue Sentry. I am thankful, though, for the guiding hand of the universe that has helped us keep the authorities out of this blight, especially now that we know who possesses the last of the five *lathe'ad*."

Saiyu rose from her seat. "Allow me a minute to bring Ashack back."

"Of course."

The Elder returned shortly with her mate, whom she bade to sit beside her again. Ashack resettled himself and sighed. "Fine. We know it is Reyor. What now?"

"The outbreak must be stopped," Nageau said. "That is the first priority. The Sentry's contact, Joshua, has been sent the canister that was found. He is devising a means to deliver the material which they believe will destroy the source of the epidemic."

"Are they certain it will work?"

"Joshua is quite confident, having tested it on the specimen he received from Aari and Tegan."

"But even if it does work, it is just one canister," Ashack persisted. "Would there be enough material for the entire world?"

"I have no answers at the moment," Nageau said. "All I can say is, if there is a time the world needs prayers, it is now. I have received word from Sentries in several countries that the situation is worsening. Patience is wearing dangerously thin in countless communities and whole nations. We are facing a ticking time bomb. The Sentries are doing what they can but this is beyond them. We need to eliminate this scourge at its source."

Ashack gestured impatiently. "It will only get worse as it comes down to survival of the most ruthless. The intrinsic need to live will overpower everything else."

The gentle gurgling of the fountains behind them provided a stark contrast to the Elders' strained discussion. Saiyu clasped her hands over her lap, her bracelets clinking, and said, "Perhaps we should connect with our Sentries in all the affected areas. The time to organize a more direct response to this scourge has arrived."

Nageau concurred. "We can start by reaching out to Sentries we have linked with in the past and directing them to connect with the others we have yet to locate and communicate with. The first task will be for them to identify the location of these pods, as they are called, by employing the method used by the younglings or any other means available to them."

"I will help coordinate this," Tayoka volunteered.

"Thank you."

"That sounds like a step in the right direction. However . . ." Tikina hesitated. "I do not mean to turn this conversation back to Reyor, but now with the five exposed, do you suppose their families might be in danger?"

"That notion has been concerning me," Nageau answered. "I had hoped it was my overactive mind acting up, but now that you have voiced it, I see a need for us to give this question serious consideration. We may need to act on this matter sooner rather than later."

"Are you suggesting that we bring them here, to Dema-Ki?" Ashack asked, eyes narrowing slightly.

"As I said, we will need to study this carefully before making any decision. Though Reyor's intent for their families is unknown as of now, I think that, yes, that may be an option. I take it that you do not favor this?"

"You mean well, Nageau, and we are all aware of that. But now that we know Reyor is alive and could very well pose a threat to Dema-Ki, it may be prudent to keep the five's families away from here."

"This is something that will need further contemplation," Saiyu asserted. "It is a delicate matter."

Nageau nodded. "Tayoka, if you could please connect with the Sentries immediately, that would be good."

Tayoka dipped his head. "I shall."

"If that is all, I believe we may adjourn."

Nageau and Tikina were the last to leave. The pair walked together into the foyer and gazed at the flames that streamed from the cauldron. Tikina gave him a light squeeze as she said, "Our foe is a dangerous one. Cunning, too. Each step we take after this will have to be thought out with painstaking care. Whatever disagreements may arise amongst us, the Elders will always stand by you and we will never fail to act as one. But that you already know."

Nageau took her hand and led her past the cauldron and down the steps of the temple. "Yes, as sure as I know the sun will rise tomorrow. I have never doubted for a moment the loyalty and commitment of the Elders to our people and our faith. My real concern however, is for the five. They have been on my mind constantly with the knowledge that"—a sense of guilt tightened around his throat like a noose and his voice was choked—"they will have to grow up faster than anyone their age ever should."

The metal door opened and a short man with greasy black hair and bulging eyes framed by glasses stepped in. Aari had no doubt that this was Dr. Nate. Tegan, across the table from him, looked like she was ready to stomp on the diminutive man with a pair of heavy boots.

Dr. Nate carried his briefcase, which was half as tall as he was. He smiled like a weasel as the door shut behind him with a heavy and definitive boom. "Ah, this is much more secure than the last place. Very nice." He stared pointedly at Tegan. "I'd like to see you try to get out of this one, young lady."

Tegan didn't move a muscle and stared blankly in return.

Dr. Nate set his briefcase down by the table and stood between the teenagers. "Young man, I don't believe we've 'ad the pleasure of meeting before. I am Dr. Nate."

Aari kept his lips together and glanced at Tegan. She flared her nostrils slightly in loathing.

"Tegan," Dr. Nate said. "I tried so 'ard to convince you and Mariah that we aren't the bad guys, but you both foolishly refused to believe that and caused us nearly one million dollars in damage on your way out our door."

Aari goggled. *A million bucks?*

"Now, then. If I am to assume correctly, neither of you are willing to cooperate, yes? Well, alright." Dr. Nate opened the briefcase and pulled out a rugged, military-grade laptop which he placed on the table. The next thing he produced from the case was a pair of big wraparound glasses, painted black with a thin cable attached. Aari eyeballed the glasses with growing unease.

The last thing Dr. Nate pulled out of his briefcase was a gel-like helmet, its blue surface studded with a dense field of electrodes and micro-LED lights. Now Aari was really worried.

"What's all that?" he asked.

Dr. Nate stroked the helmet in a manner that made Aari half expect it to purr. "An advanced wireless optogenetics controller unit. It is my newest creation. These devices 'ave multiple uses, young man. Right now, they will 'elp make you more, let's say, cooperative, so we can finally get some answers out of you."

Aari did a quick deduction. *Optical manipulation of the brain by the helmet and who knows what the glasses will do . . . Oh boy.* He looked at Tegan and she gave him an imperceptible nod. *Right. Game time.*

"That thing uses light to manipulate neuron cells, doesn't it?" he asked, driving his tone a notch higher.

The weasel smile returned to Dr. Nate's face. "Smart boy. Yes, it does indeed."

"Why do you have that? That's gonna mess up our minds!"

"Calm down, it won't hurt at all."

"*Liar!*" Aari screamed. "You could completely fry our brains with that thing! Don't put that on me!"

"I won't have to if you'll tell me what I want to know."

"No!"

"One last time, Aari."

"Drop dead!"

Dr. Nate picked up the helmet. "I gave you a chance and you completely blew it."

Aari shrank away from the approaching man. "No, no, wait! *Wait!*"

"Too late, boy." Dr. Nate raised the helmet.

"I'll tell you! I'll tell you what you want!"

"What are you doing, Aari?" Tegan snarled.

"We can't let him put that on us—God knows what it could do!"

"We can't betray the Elders! I swear, if you talk—"

"Tell me, do you recall anything about a prophecy?" Dr. Nate interrupted.

"Yes," Aari answered hurriedly. "It was a really big thing to them. When they first took us in and healed us, they—"

Tegan jumped up and lunged at him. He ducked, but mistimed it. She crashed into him, knocking him out of his chair and sending him sprawling to the floor.

"Guards!" Dr. Nate shouted frantically.

Tegan stood over Aari, teeth bared, dark hair falling into her face. "Traitor! Don't you *dare* talk!"

Yeesh, she's a good actor, Aari thought as he cowered, head tucked between his knees. *This is terrifying.*

Two armed men burst into the room and pulled Tegan away. She bucked and yelled at them, all the while threatening Aari to keep his mouth shut. Dr. Nate helped Aari up and sat him back down on the chair, then addressed the guards. "I want you to take 'er away until I'm done chatting with this young man."

Aari watched as the guards dragged Tegan from the room. She was putting up a real fight and throwing all into her performance. Hoping that he could be as convincing for Dr. Nate's interrogation, he sat back and thought, *Real test begins.*

* * *

She's not looking too good, Jag.

Those words were what drove Jag to dive into the pickup truck and tear toward the hospital. His grandfather had called him to speak about his grandmother's condition. When Jag heard she wasn't faring well, he dropped everything without a moment's thought.

He arrived at the hospital shortly afterward, found his way to the Intensive Care Unit, and stepped lightly into the room. He went to join his grandfather by the bedside and slung his arms around the elderly man in greeting. Looking over at his grandmother, he was pleasantly surprised to see her eyes were half-open. Her face lit up from behind her oxygen mask and she weakly lifted a finger, beckoning him closer.

Jag sat beside her on the bed, softly stroking her hair, and gave her the happiest smile he could manage. "Hey, Gran."

She pulled the mask off, much to the alarm of her husband and grandson. Jag wanted her to put it back on but she shook her head. "Let me talk, *meu neto*," she said, coughing.

Jag hesitated, then put the mask down and kissed her forehead. She caressed his cheek with her thumb, smiling. "It's lovely to see you again, Jag. We've missed you, your grandfather and I."

"I've missed you, too," Jag said softly. "How are you feeling?"

"You know, I've seen better days." She laughed, but it came out as a painful wheeze.

As Jag gazed down at her, he found himself having to fight back tears. "I love you. And Tristan loves you, and Camilla, and Mom and Dad, and—"

"Shh, dear. I love you all too."

"Stay strong, alright? Keep fighting. Keep fighting, okay?"

She just continued to smile up at him. "You have a good heart, Jag. I know you'll do amazing things in your life." She coughed again. "You are a light, a beacon. Never let anyone take that away from you, and don't lose who you are." She stroked his cheek again. "I am so, so proud of you."

Jag blinked rapidly. He tilted his head so he could nuzzle her palm. She started to sing, then, softly and at first uneven, but he recognized the tune immediately and was brought right back to that night of the terrible storm. As his grandmother continued to sing, a sense of peace came over him like it had when they'd watched the tempest together all those years ago.

Her voice eventually ebbed as she fell asleep. Jag picked up her mask and adjusted it for her, then got off the bed and hugged his grandfather again.

"I thought she wasn't doing well," he said, "but she looks alert."

His grandfather wiped his eyes with the sleeve of his shirt. "She's been conscious, yes, but her heart muscle isn't healing. The doctors have determined that the damage is . . . is irreparable. Maybe—maybe we'd want to get the rest of the family here within the next few days."

Jag was stunned. His grandfather had not divulged that information to him over the phone. He was at a loss for words. A tear slid down his cheek as he reached for his phone and he hurriedly brushed it away. "I'll call Tristan."

His brother answered his phone on the first ring. "Hey. How's everything?"

"Not good. Gran's not doing well. Gramps thinks it'd be best if we got the family down here."

"Oh, God, no."

"She was conscious just a short while ago but she's weakening, Tristan. The doctors said that the damage to her heart isn't getting better."

"Okay—okay. We'll be there as soon as we can, promise. Camilla's in Seattle on a short business trip."

"And Mom and Dad?"

"I told them about Gran. They're cutting their trip short and catching the earliest flight out of Zurich tomorrow. How's Gramps?"

"I'm not sure. You know how inseparable they are. Add that to the crop loss and I don't know how anyone in his position could be doing too well."

"Give him a hug from us and tell him we'll be over soon."

"Yeah."

"Take care of yourself, Jag."

"You too."

Jag slid the phone back into his jeans and went to put an arm around his grandfather. "Tristan and Camilla say they love you, and they'll try to come as soon as they can. Mom and Dad are in Switzerland right now, but they're catching the first flight out tomorrow."

The old man acknowledged him. They sat quietly for a while, feeding off each other's strength, until Jag's phone rang. He quickly picked up when he saw that it was Kody.

"Hey, man," Kody said, sounding as though he was uncomfortable. "I really, really don't want to do this, but we need you back for the plan."

"Right, sorry. I'll be there soon."

"I didn't want to pull you away from your family, but—"

"It's fine. See you in a bit." Jag hung up and turned to his grandfather. "I'm really sorry, Gramps, but there's something I have to do. I'll be back as soon as I can, I promise."

He hugged his grandfather one last time before stepping out and running to the pickup. It hurt him to leave the two of them in the hospital but the plan needed to be executed flawlessly and he had to be with his friends to see it through.

The sun had almost set when he pulled into the driveway at the farm. He got out and met Kody and Mariah, who informed him that everything was in place. "I just need your phone," Kody said.

Jag passed it to him and the other teenager ran into the barn with the device.

* * *

"A car just pulled up," Kody whispered into an old walkie-talkie two hours later. "Everyone good to go?"

Inside the dimly lit barn, Jag nodded at Mariah, who dashed up the stairs to the dark hayloft. He then placed himself against the wall opposite the barn door before clicking his own walkie-talkie and answering. "We're ready. You holding out okay on the roof?"

"They parked right in front of the house but they haven't seen me, so yeah. They're getting out now; four of them. Tegan was right on the money about these guys tracking us—oh. Oh, jeez."

"What?"

"I see Tony. He just got out, that actual pile of—"

"Focus, Kody. Weapons?"

"Tony has some kind of an automatic weapon. I think the others have tranquilizer guns. They're going toward the house now. No, wait. They've turned. They're heading to the barn. One of them's on the phone—looks like they're getting directions from whoever's on the other end."

"Good thing we put both our phones in here, huh?" Jag said, lifting up a rake.

"Yeah. Alright, Tony just told the other three to go in. He's staying outside. Get ready. They'll be there in three, two—"

The barn door directly ahead of him creaked as it slowly opened. Whoever wanted to get in was trying to be stealthy. Jag looked up from where he stood and saw three armed men enter with their weapons aimed at him. He dropped his rake and raised his hands over his head. "Whoa—whoa! What are you doing here? Please, don't shoot!"

As one of the men prepared to squeeze the trigger of his gun, a sixty-pound bale of hay dropped onto him, knocking him to the ground. His head hit the floor and he didn't get up. Another bale landed on the second man before he could react. He fell in a heap, still gripping his weapon.

The third man didn't dawdle. He pointed his gun at Jag and squeezed the trigger. Jag anticipated the shot and jumped into hyper-mode. He saw the dart leave the barrel in apparent slow-motion and easily sidestepped the projectile. As the dart traveled leisurely past him, he reached out and grabbed it before it hit the wall, then spun around and charged at the shooter.

A look of horror formed on the man's face when he realized he'd been jabbed between his collarbones. The world returned to normal speed as Jag watched the weakening man drop his gun and fall, lying spread-eagled on the ground. He kicked the gun away as Mariah ran down the stairs with ropes in hand. She moved the bales of hay from the two men once Jag had properly knocked them out with their own tranquilizers.

As she relieved the trio of their possessions and tied them up, Jag picked up his radio. "We're all clear down here, Kode-man. Tony still out there?"

He waited for a response but heard nothing. "Kody? Can you hear me?"

Someone from outside the barn called out angrily. "You want to talk to your friend? Come out of there!"

Mariah gasped, then mouthed, "*Tony*!"

Together, she and Jag exited the barn and peeked around the corner. They saw Tony walking backward toward his vehicle, dragging Kody with him. The muzzle of his gun was pressed against the teenager's head and he had an arm around Kody's neck.

"I see you!" Tony shouted. "Step out slowly with your hands up!"

"Don't hurt him," Jag snapped as he and Mariah walked toward the young man. "We're coming out."

"Keep moving! Don't try anything funny or I'll shoot him!"

"You want us alive," Mariah yelled. "You're not gonna kill any of us!"

"Maybe not, but I sure as hell can make this extremely painful for him! Want proof?"

As Tony lowered his arm to take aim at Kody's knee, a streak of gold appeared from behind Tony's car. Mariah cried out. "Lady!"

The Labrador leapt and dug her jaws into Tony's upper arm. He threw his head back and roared in pain, but he didn't let go of his weapon while trying to shake the dog off.

Kody moved fast, jabbing an elbow right below his assailant's ribs. Tony dropped the gun as he gasped for air but lashed out with his free arm in retaliation. Kody ducked and Tony's swing went wild. In spite of being winded, the young man regained his balance, grabbed Kody and mercilessly flipped him over his shoulder. Kody landed hard on the ground and lay there, sprawled. Tony reached for his gun and picked it up. As he brought the barrel around toward the teenager, the enraged Labrador clamped down hard into his calf.

Tony screamed a curse. He pointed the gun at Lady, fuming, and was set to pull the trigger when Kody forced himself up and swung around, delivering a powerful kick to the side of Tony's face. With his attacker dazed, Kody rushed to grab Lady and bolted unsteadily to the safety of the wheat field. That was the cue Jag needed.

He moved into action and covered the distance between him and Tony in less than a second; with Tony's background in martial arts, he knew he had to be quick. Tony had no idea what hit him as he was bowled to the ground before being grabbed by his shirt front and hauled up. Before he could react, a fist slammed into his face.

"That's for kidnapping my friends," Jag snarled. He landed another right hook and heard Tony's nose crack. "And that's for trying to shoot Kody."

Mariah appeared beside him and, with a queasy look, shot a tranquilizer dart point-blank into Tony's abdomen. Jag let go and Tony went limp at their feet. Mariah bound the young man up with a rope she'd brought out, grimacing in distaste as she got some blood on her hand.

Lady trotted up to them, Kody just behind her. Jag picked up the dog and snuggled her. "You're a crazy girl, you know that?"

"How'd she get out?" Mariah asked. "I was so sure Kody closed the front door."

"Maybe she's learned to open doors or something. Either way, I'm glad she came." Kody went around Tony, wrapped his arms under the man's armpits, and pulled him toward the back of the barn where an old shipping container was being used to store spare parts for farm equipment. Mariah and Jag retrieved the two men in the barn, leaving Kody to take care of the last one.

Once the friends had the men bound and placed in the container, Jag shut the doors and secured the locking bar with wire. “They’re not going anywhere,” he said, grim. “We’ll deal with them later.”

Tegan stumbled,having been roughly shoved into the room by a guard. She straightened and marched back to her chair opposite Aari. Her friend blinked tiredly at her as she took her seat.

"Where were you all night?" he asked.

She brought her shoulder to her ear to take care of an itch. "They put me in a room not far from this one."

"I'm guessing you didn't get a good look at this place, then."

"Nope."

"That's a bummer."

"How long was Dr. Nate with you?"

"I don't know. A couple of hours, maybe more."

"What did you tell him?"

"I gave him enough misinformation to keep him busy."

"Did he buy it?"

"Oh, I'm fairly sure he did. I told him that the Elders are plotting to take them down, and that they seem to know what's going on. I said that they'd planted spies inside his organization, too." Aari laughed wearily. "He looked spooked by that and went into a gratuitously long ramble trying to convince me why he and his people are the good guys."

Tegan relaxed back against her chair. "That was a good move."

"Thank you. He asked if I knew who the spy was but I told him I had no idea, and that was all that came back with my memory. He told me to try to find out who the spy is. I agreed. I think he and I are good friends now."

"Let's make sure he continues to believe that."

"Right. Coming back to our present situation . . ."

"I've been trying to find an animal around here that could help me check out the area, but I can't seem to find any to connect with."

"Have you tried searching for something smaller, like an insect?"

"An insect?"

"Yeah. Something that has wings, like a butterfly. Or, you know, just a fly."

"Ech, I guess I can give that a shot." She closed her eyes and opened her mind, probing the novasphere. It took a while but she finally felt a peculiar presence touching her mind. She hopped into the creature without hesitating and was instantly overwhelmed by its visual capabilities.

Her new perspective offered a wraparound view of her surroundings. The three-hundred-and-sixty-degree vision was initially disorienting but also intriguing. There were no blind spots; a big advantage for her mission, though she would have loved getting rid of the nausea caused by the creature's erratic flying and raucous speed. But soon she gained a level of comfort that allowed her to navigate the creature with confidence. *Time to check out what my crazy ride is.*

She flew to the nearest reflective surface she could find—a glass panel on the exterior of a building—and brought her host right up to the surface. When she saw what the insect was, she pulled the connection, opened her eyes and croaked, "Yeow."

Aari looked at her as though he'd been eagerly awaiting for her to return. "Did you find something?"

"Yeah," she answered. "A dragonfly."

"A *dragonfly?* Seriously? That's so cool. And perfect for recon. Did you know their eyes are freakishly advanced? Pretty much all insects have multifaceted eyes, but dragonflies have *thirty thousand* individual facets! And each one creates its own image but they have, like, enough visual neurons to compile all those into *one* picture."

"Thank you for the biology lesson, Aari. I figured that out all on my own. Matter of fact, I know it so well that I think I may just need a bucket to throw up in."

"Uh, why?"

"It's too much! My brain can't handle all that visual input!"

"I'm sure you'll be fine once you spend a little more time linked with it."

"I did manage to get some degree of control but I'm not sure I really want to go back to it."

"You have to, Teegs. We don't have a choice. I know you can do it."

Reluctantly, she nodded and readied herself, then jumped back into the dragonfly. Rather than synchronize with the insect's abilities all at once, she decided to take things in increments this time. The dragonfly was quite the speedster and had the ability to move each of its four wings separately for greater maneuverability. Another thing she learned quickly was that the creature was always hungry. *Is this what Kody feels every day? Gosh, no wonder he eats so much.*

Lastly, she revisited the dragonfly's vision. Aari was right; it took a bit of time but eventually she became used to its incredible panoramic perspective, which included more than just the human-limited color spectrum she was accustomed to.

Time to get to work. She guided the dragonfly until it was high enough to see the complex in its entirety. *Mmkay . . . four buildings, all rectangular and linked with two covered walkways. Total length . . . erm . . . a thousand feet? Sure. Width . . . I'll say about four hundred.*

She flew to the front of the building nearest to the street and hovered above a well-filled parking lot until she found the entrance. Stealthily, she followed a worker through the sliding glass doors. *Definitely admin*, she thought, using her multidirectional vision to gather information about the main lobby. There were two receptionists tending to people in business suits but nothing else of interest, so she continued further into the building. As she made her way into the second building via one of the linking corridors, she wondered where she and Aari were being held.

The next building was clearly a laboratory. There were rows of long tables where dozens of men and women worked vigorously over banks of computers and various lab equipment. Tegan perched the dragonfly on a security camera to have a good look. *Nothing out of the ordinary here, but why does it feel like I'm near . . . myself? Hey, hold up.*

She flew in the direction of that strange sensation until she reached a wide passageway that ended with a blue door. As she flew closer, the sensation grew stronger.

Looks like there's a sign posted on here . . . Blah, blah restricted area, elevator use for authorized personnel only—hey! We took an elevator down, right? So it must be behind this door. Agh, could someone open this stupid thing, please?

Long minutes passed and it was clear that no one was going down or coming up. Peeved, Tegan continued her reconnaissance. The next building was labeled as a production facility but she saw nothing that indicated nanomites were being manufactured there. She wasn't sure what she was looking for; perhaps some signage to indicate the type of operation that was going on inside the building. *But that would be too easy, wouldn't it?*

Tegan flew to the last structure at the far end of the complex and discovered that it was a large warehouse. She returned to the lab and waited by the elevator again but no one appeared to grant her underground access. Giving up, she went back outside and circled the complex. She took note of the number of guards patrolling the premises as she flew above them, marveling that she could see them even though the dragonfly was moving in the opposite direction.

To the right of the complex was a security post where guards inspected incoming and outgoing traffic. She noticed another building not too far from it and made a note to revisit it later as she continued on. She turned left to the other side of the building. An Olympic-sized pool lay serenely next to the production facility. Curious, she flew toward a signpost. *This is a test pool?*

That would have held Tegan's attention if her outstanding vision hadn't picked up a small shipping bay beside the lab building she had been in earlier. The sensation that she was getting closer to her human self grew stronger as she drew nearer to it. A door with a keypad above the handle stood at the entrance, bearing a warning similar to the one inside the building. *This must be another entrance that leads to the elevator.*

She cut the link with the dragonfly again and was jarred into the room with Aari. It was strange going back to her limited vision. "Aari?"

"You've been gone for a while," he said. "Guess you got used to the dragonfly, huh? Found anything?"

She described to him everything that she'd seen. "Do you think we're being held under the laboratory building?"

"Considering these people tend to have their operations underground, it's entirely possible. But we won't know for sure until you can visually confirm that."

"I can't do that unless someone opens the door that leads to the elevator."

"That could take some time. Got anymore sightseeing to do while you wait for your knight with the door's access code?"

"Just a bit, yeah."

"Have fun."

Tegan was back in the dragonfly a few seconds later. The insect, left to its own devices, had wandered back to the guard post. She led it to the curious structure beside the post and waited for someone to open the door. Unlike the lab elevator, she didn't have to hang around long for someone to step out. The man, wearing a black uniform, did not look like the average security guard. His crew-cut and beefed up physique gave him an intimidating appearance.

Tegan slipped past and saw the door shut behind her just as she processed the many computer screens in front of her. They displayed live camera feeds from around the complex. As she moved toward a shelf, she was stunned to see it was filled with ammunition and other military-type equipment.

Not your regular security service, she thought as she flew to the top of the shelf. She noticed some kind of remote-control device resting on one of the racks as she passed by. Underneath the many buttons were engraved letters.

M.C.U.

Flashbacks erupted. *Aari saw this on the mountain after the battle, didn't he? That's the Marauder Control Unit! The beasts are here? But . . . no, that can't be it. If they were, I would have seen their kennel somewhere out there.*

Turning back to the screens, she observed the feed for a few moments, then her vision picked up something else. *Hello, what's this?*

A second set of monitors was arranged together on another wall. Another guard, just as menacing as the one who had walked out the door, was sitting in front of it. He glanced at the screens from time to time but for the most part was writing on a notepad; it didn't seem as if he was too concerned with the images displayed in front of him.

Tegan brought the dragonfly closer to the monitors. The images displayed were of areas she hadn't seen during her excursion inside. She hovered closer. *This has to be underground. That metal door with the guards standing by it must be for the room Aari and I are in.*

As she moved her attention to all the different monitors, she grinned to herself. *Well would you look at that . . . they do have a secret lab down there after all.*

Mariah trudged out of her room, hair in a messy bun. She found Jag and Kody in the kitchen in animated conversation.

Jag grinned at her as she sat down with them. "Look at you, sleeping past lunch."

She stretched. "Mmph."

"Guess what came just a few minutes ago," Kody said, displaying a black, football-shaped object in his hands.

She stopped mid-stretch and gawked. "It's here? Josh got it done?"

"Yeah." Jag passed her a sheet of paper. "Apparently he had someone on standby to personally fly this out to us the moment he was done putting it together."

Mariah took the paper from him. "This is a note from him."

"Uh huh."

"Mild explosive designed to disperse powderized anti-nanomite . . . confirmed powder works on the nano specimen . . . device designed to explode ten seconds after activation . . . created the 'football' in a hurry . . . not enough time to test reliability . . ." She put the note down and assessed the palm-sized device. "Really? It looks pretty professionally done."

"It does, doesn't it?" Jag said. "He sent us two of these in case one fails."

Kody held the device up to inspect it. "What I'm worried about is that we may have tripped an alarm the last time we were there, which was why the nanomites came back way before sunrise and attacked us. Since we don't know what triggered it, we're probably gonna set it off again."

"We'll have to be quick, then, because the nanomites will be in their pod when we go this time."

"By doing what we're gonna do, won't we alert the people behind all this?" Mariah asked.

"That's why we're doing a test run on this site first. Hopefully they'll see it as a random malfunction of the pod and not necessarily part of a larger takedown. Marshall called this morning and said that he has connected with other Sentries in the League. They're using the method we worked out to figure where the rest of the pods are located. Tonight's outcome will determine how we move forward. If we succeed, the League can replicate this across the country and later, hopefully, the world."

A sense of pride budded in Mariah as she listened to Jag. *He's changed. He's no longer the kid who just a year ago wouldn't take the lead on anything and instead got into trouble for stupid fights in school.*

"Are we just gonna leave Tony and his guys in the container when we head out?" Kody asked.

"Unless anyone has any objection," Jag answered, "then yes."

Mariah smirked. She had no problem with that.

***

Walking single file to stay once more inside the security cameras' narrow blind spot, Jag, Mariah and Kody rounded the garage that housed the nanomite pod. Jag knelt and pulled away the section of the wall they'd cut earlier while Mariah readied the black cloths to place over the cameras.

Jag went on his stomach and took a cautionary look inside, then hurriedly pulled back. "There's someone in there! A woman's sitting at one of the computers!"

Kody crouched beside him. "Oh, man, I should've checked to see if I could hear anything inside. Did she notice you?"

"No." Jag bit his lip, jaw moving side to side rapidly as he searched for a solution.

Mariah shooed them away. She lay down by the hole and looked into the garage. A woman with short blue hair and stretched earlobes was perched on a stool, facing the bank of computer monitors. A lunch bag lay on the tabletop on one side of her and a bottle of water stood on the other.

I wonder if I can get the cloths past her without her seeing . . . agh, probably not. Can I take her out?

There was a hefty toolbox on the shelf behind the woman. *Would that be too obvious if anyone views the footage? The box just randomly falling on her? Hmm . . . what if it looked like an accident? It's gonna be touch-and-go.*

Mariah forced the stool out from under the unsuspecting woman. Her fall wasn't graceful and she ended up on her backside, stunned. Before she could recover, Mariah brought the toolbox down on her. The woman sprawled back, arms and legs splayed, out cold.

Taking the black cloths, Mariah hung them over the cameras and motion detector, then crawled into the garage. Behind her, the boys—unaware of what she'd accomplished but having heard the commotion—were beside themselves.

"What are you doing?" Jag demanded.

"Don't worry, it's clear," she called once she was on the other side.

There was a delay, then Jag appeared through the low opening; Kody stayed outside to stand guard like before. When Jag saw the woman on the ground, he said, "You and Tegan sure know how to do some damage, don't you?"

"Don't have time for compliments, buddy boy." Mariah ran to the steel pipe that led to the pod in the chamber below. "Okay, here's the wire. Jag, you wanna—Jag? What are you doing?"

Her friend was holding a rectangular black device. "Would you look at this?" he said. "This remote controls all the alarms and motion detectors around here. She probably disarmed them when she came in."

"You said alarms and motion detectors. Anything there for the cameras?"

"There's no label for that here . . ."

"Then they're still functioning, so there *was* still a need for stealth." She marched toward the steel pipe with the automated cap—the nanomite conduit—that stuck out of the floor. "See if you can locate the circuit that powers the cap. Once the power is off, you should be able to work it manually."

Jag walked briskly around the garage as he traced the thin wire. "It's not connected to any of those computers. It goes underground for some reason. Moving on, then." He took a wire cutter from his bag and snipped the wire, then knelt next to the cap atop the pipe. "You ready?"

Mariah had taken out the football-shaped charge. "Yep."

He forcibly slid the cap open. "Go, go, go!"

She worked the switch to start the timer and dropped the device down the pipe. Jag shut the cap firmly and they ran to the other side of the room. They hunkered down, counting down the last seconds.

Five one-thousand, four one-thousand, three one-thousand, two one-thousand, one . . .

Nothing.

They peeked at each other through their arms, quizzical, then got up. Jag headed back to the pipe. "Was there supposed to be a blast, or . . .?"

Kody stuck his head through the hole in the wall and yelled at them. "What the heck did you do?! It sounds like crazed bees down there! I can hear 'em going nuts!"

"The football didn't go off!" Jag yelped. "Get the second one ready!"

Hundreds of clinking impacts were audible to Mariah's ears now. "They're trying to get out!"

Jag put his hand on the cap. "When I pull this, you've only got a second to get that in there! Alright? *Now!*"

He slid the cap open once more and Mariah lobbed the device into the pipe. He jerked the cap shut and then bounced away, slapping at his arms as minuscule red dots appeared before them. "Some of them got out . . . Ow! Let's get out of here!"

All at once, Mariah felt like she was being bitten by fire ants. She thrashed, trying to shake the nanomites off her. They were angrily tearing at her; pinpricks of blood appeared on her arms, and she knew they'd bitten under her t-shirt.

A muffled *boom* came from under their feet and rattled the pipe. The metallic buzzing and clanking petered out and, at the same time, the nanomites hounding Mariah and Jag ceased their attack.

Jag slowly raised his arms and observed them. "Lovely. It looks like I have bloodied freckles." He beamed at Mariah. "I think we did it! I guess if enough of them are taken out, the rest are affected as well."

Mariah blew out a breath. "I think you're right. Mission accomplished."

"Let's get back to the truck so we can clean up and head home." He started crawling back outside, humming happily to himself at their success.

"Jag," Mariah complained. "Aren't you forgetting something?"

"What?" Jag called, already halfway out.

"This poor lady's lying all splayed out on the floor! Shouldn't we do something about her?"

"No, leave her be. It'll look like she fell from her stool and was hurt by the toolbox when it fell—which is actually what happened, might I remind you."

Mariah huffed, grabbed the wire cutters they'd used, and exited the building. Outside, she laid prone by the hole in the wall and removed the cloths from the monitoring devices. Kody pushed the wall section into place and the three of them strolled off the property, taking care to return everything to normal.

As they drove back to Concordia, Kody said, "Now that we know it works, we can report to Marshall and Josh, and the

Sentries can handle the other pods. Should be smooth sailing from here."

Mariah exchanged high-fives with him, grinning. "I sure hope so."

* * *

"Mr. Dattalo?"

"Nngh . . . speaking. It's two a.m., this had better be important."

"Sir, I'm sorry to wake you up but I thought you should know that the pod at Ransom is not responding."

The head of Quest Defense sat up in his bed, covers falling around his waist. "Not responding?"

"Remember I called you a couple nights ago about the REAPR going on the offensive?"

"You said that was a false alarm."

"Yes, but now I'm not so sure. It looks like we've lost connection with the pod's systems."

"Who's in charge there?"

"Katie. I actually tasked her to be there day and night since the last incident."

"Ah, good. I like that you've taken the initiative. So what's the problem?"

"I've been trying to reach her. The cameras blacked out for a couple of minutes, but they came back on just now. I see her lying on the floor like she'd had some kind of accident."

"Get someone there to check on her."

"Yes, sir. Already on it."

"Wait a moment. You said this was the Ransom pod?"

"That's right."

"Alright. At least it's not the Texas one."

"You mean in Vernon? Yeah, I heard they're the new version."

"They're second-generation nanomites. We wanted to up their capabilities. In any case, make sure you see to Katie and fix the pod issue."

"Yes, sir. Again, so sorry to wake you."

Dattalo put his phone on the nightstand and lay back down. He tried counting sheep but after a hundred, knew he'd lost his need to sleep.

The Elders were alone in the temple, save for an older woman who sat at the opposite end of the hall with a leather-bound book in hand. It was late in the night but none of them had been able to sleep until they'd heard from Jag. When the boy had contacted Nageau with the news, they thought it best to hold a meeting straightaway.

"So," Nageau said, spreading his arms, "the method to end this plague has been proven successful. The material given by the Sentry's friend works."

Saiyu smiled broadly. "It is certainly encouraging."

"My only concern is that the first device Jag and Mariah used failed to work," Ashack grunted.

"But the second one did," Tayoka reminded him. "And the devices were put together in haste. The new ones will be more reliable, no doubt."

"Now that we know the material works and how best to deliver it," Nageau said, "we need to move quickly. We have been afforded a very small window of opportunity wherein we have the element of surprise. It will only be a matter of time before the enemy becomes aware that their tools of destruction have been neutralized."

"How much time do you reckon we have?" Tikina asked.

"Less than two days."

"Can we rally the League on such short notice?"

"Yes, thanks to Tayoka. Things are already in motion. From what the Sentry and the five have gleaned, there are two sites involved in creating this scourge. One is in a place called Redding and the other in Boulder City, which is where Aari and Tegan are. They have now assumed the role of infiltrators rather than prisoners and have given the Sentry useful information about the site.

"In addition to the bases that produce these devices of destruction, there are six—well, five now—major locations that house them in their pods, a kind of nest. I have reached out to and carefully selected the Sentries for this mission. Marshall has also contacted them and they have been assigned to their respective targets. There will be two Sentries assigned to each pod and four to the site in Redding. Tegan, Aari and Marshall will take care of the one in Boulder City."

"Who do we have in the other areas?" Saiyu asked.

"There are the lads Marshall suggested—twins—who traveled some distance to be at Redding with two other Sentries. Jag, Mariah and Kody will be heading to a place called Vernon in Texas where another pod is located, and a couple of Sentries are now positioned in Montana."

Tayoka raised his hand partway. "Is that not where the five are from?"

"It is," Nageau answered. "More Sentries are on their way to the other three places in the states of California, Washington and North Dakota and will be in position shortly to strike on our signal. They have done the groundwork. All they are waiting for is the delivery of the material to destroy the pods and their orders."

"With the wind of destiny at our backs, this mission will hopefully be successful," Ashack said, perking up slightly, "but what does this mean for the rest of the world? How do we put an end to the scourge elsewhere?"

"The Sentry's friend can produce more of the material within a moon cycle."

Ashack frowned and crossed his arms over his chest. "Is that the best he can do?"

"It is difficult to produce as it does not exist in nature. It must be created."

Saiyu fiddled with the bracelets on her arm. "So much damage will be done by that time, Nageau."

"I know. But this is the best situation we have, my friend. Sentries in different parts of the world have searched for alternate means to produce this material. It seems Marshall's contact is the only one right now with the capability to deliver the needed quantity in the shortest time."

"By then," Ashack said heatedly, "we will have lost our element of surprise. Knowing they are under attack, the enemy will increase their security measures, making it far more challenging to destroy the pods."

Nageau placed a hand on the dark-haired man's back. "Take heart, Ashack. The Sentries are keeping a very close eye and will be prepared."

"I think we have momentarily forgotten an important question," Tikina said. "Now that we know who the puppet master is, what do you suppose . . . Reyor's . . . reaction will be?"

An uncomfortable chill came over the Elders. Nageau pulled a thread from his cloak. "I understand that the last thing we want to do is infuriate the person who is the living embodiment of what the ancient prophecy warns of, but this is something that can no longer be avoided. We must be prepared for retaliation. I will need to meet with Magèo to inform him about this and see what he can do to prepare to defend the village should the need arise."

"If anyone, that batty inventor of ours should be able to devise some means of defense," Tayoka chimed in.

"You really think Rey—that harbinger of darkness would dare attack us?" Saiyu asked. "Here?"

"I doubt Reyor would bear any love for our home anymore," Tikina said. "It is a worst-case scenario, but I suggest that we ought to be ready so we are not taken by surprise."

The other Elders agreed, all of them quiet and somber. Nageau stood up and brushed his cloak. "Come, my friends!" he said in a resonant voice. "Cast aside your masks of solemnity!

We have received an encouraging sign this night. These are the times spoken of in the prophecy. This is when we must stand strong with the Bearers of Light against the dark storm. The five have arisen to fulfill their role as ordained, thus we must fulfill ours. The League stands ready. Let the incursion begin!"

This is serious déjà vu right here.

Hijacking the delivery truck as it headed to Quest Defense had proven easier than expected. The driver had stopped for a "stranded" motorist and seconds later found himself pulled from the cab and rendered unconscious. Now, wearing a black-and-red uniform jacket that was slightly too tight, Marshall felt the eerie familiarity of driving the medium-sized box vehicle. His cap had the shipping company's name, ZappEx, stitched on the front. He'd assumed that Quest Defense would not have wanted just any courier company handling their cargo and had intercepted the vehicle he'd seen making other deliveries.

He'd spent the previous two nights observing the afterhours routine. The workers in the labs worked two shifts, the later one ending an hour before midnight. He planned to arrive at the complex between eleven-fifteen and eleven-thirty and park at the smaller shipping bay on the left side of the lab/R&D building. If Tegan's late-night dragonfly snooping was accurate, batches of yet-to-be-activated nanomites in steel canisters and their empty pods would be ready for pick-up from this bay.

Tegan had been a great help. Using Jag as intermediary, she'd described the interior layout of the complex and the nanomite lab. She'd also taken note of the guard's patrol schedules and provided Marshall with the keypad code he would need to enter the building. The girl was a natural when it came to covert reconnaissance; it was almost alarming.

Marshall made a right turn into the entry and stopped at the guard post as workers drove through the exit, their late shift completed. His watch read eleven-twenty. *Good timing.*

The guards were in some kind of heated argument. As he rolled down his window, Marshall caught the exchange, "Then you handle that! It's none of my business!"

Marshall lowered the brim of his cap a second before the guard turned to him, face glossed in irritability. When he took stock of the Sentry, his petulance increased. "Who are you? Where's Charlie?"

Currently taking a snooze behind a bush in his Iron Man boxers, Marshall thought. The words that actually left his mouth were, "He had a family emergency. Called in at the last minute."

The guard was suspicious. As he began to ask another question, his partner yelled something inaudible to Marshall's ears. The guard turned his head and barked crudely in response before waving Marshall through and continuing the squabble.

The Sentry wasted no time putting distance between him and the guard post. As he drove to the back of the complex, he glanced at his bag that lay on the floor by the passenger's seat. Proceeding past the main shipping bay and the submersion test pool, he quickly parked the truck at the smaller bay. Grabbing his bag, he sprang out, unloaded a dolly from the back and wheeled it to a door. The keypad was just as Tegan had described it.

He punched in the required four digits. The door buzzed, accepting the code. Marshall straightened the dolly, opened the door, and walked through.

Near the main entrance to the complex, a man in a black uniform strode toward the security post. A wide scar crossed the bridge of his crooked nose and his jaw jutted out slightly, giving him the appearance of being constantly displeased. He waited for the last few cars to file out of the facility, then walked to the door of the enclosure. The guards inside let him in.

"Who was driving that delivery truck?" he asked, calculating eyes boring into the pair.

"Charlie called in sick," one of the guards answered. "That was his replacement."

"Did you get his I.D.?"

"Jeez! The guy's from ZappEx. They wouldn't send in just anyone, you know. Pretty sure he's qualified for the job."

"So you did *not* verify," the man in black said frostily as he exited the post. "I'll call the company to confirm this. If anything is amiss, you'll be sorry."

The drive to Vernon, Texas, was mostly silent as Jag seemed preoccupied during the entire ride. Kody sat quietly for once; Mariah figured he must have been too nervous to chatter away. She stretched out her legs, then glanced at Jag. "You've been awfully silent. What's got your gears spinning?"

Jag looked as if he'd been startled out of a reverie. "What? Oh, umm . . . nothing. Just feel bad for leaving my grandparents without telling them what's going on."

Mariah faltered, then said encouragingly, "We'll be there and back before you know it, Jag."

He nodded, though they shared no further words.

After a few hours of travel they arrived at Vernon. It wasn't a big town but it was certainly more populous than Ransom. Most of the houses in town were single-story properties built on large plots of land. At its outskirts, the town rapidly gave way to farmland. Mariah thought the place seemed relatively lifeless considering its size. "Where is everyone?" she wondered. "It's too early on a summer vacation night for it to be this quiet."

The answer manifested before them a few minutes later when the truck turned down a street and came upon a scene of colorful bright lights, blaring music and a large crowd of people enjoying themselves.

Mariah gasped. "*A fair!*"

"This place is far from dead," Kody noted. "Man, look at all the rides! Look at how *huge* that Ferris wheel is back there! I didn't know they could have all this stuff for a county fair—I want in!"

"Sure looks inviting," Jag said, driving past the festivities. "Duty calls, though. We're here for a reason."

"Ugh, I know." Kody tapped the windshield; it was new, since the nanomite-pockmarked one had to be removed. "Good thing we got this replaced, huh?"

"Good thing the replacement was quick."

They found the house they'd been assigned to. Marshall's friend, one of the Welsh twins, had taken over using Aari's tactics in locating nanomite pod sites and had provided them with specific directions. The house lay at the edge of town and nearly every aspect of it mirrored the appearance of the one in Ransom. As the friends got out of the truck, Mariah asked, "Are all the locations like this? Tall gates and fences . . . Look! Even the garage looks exactly like the other one, with the chimney and everything."

"Maybe they were looking for a certain type of design that met their requirements," Jag supposed. "Would make it easier to modify it to their means."

Mariah took a step forward but Jag held her and Kody back, then gathered them in a small huddle. As they rested their heads against each other's, Mariah saw a gleam in Jag's eyes.

"It goes down tonight," he said. "All the nanomite pods across the country, and the manufacturing sites, will be taken out by the League, with the Elders at the helm. Tonight, we take a stand against an enemy bent on destroying life as we know it." He breathed out slowly. "Tonight, we take the first step in fulfilling our roles in the prophecy . . . fulfilling our roles in this world."

The little impromptu speech reverberated through Mariah's ears and fused into her blood, sending an invigorating rush through her entire being. She beamed and couldn't help but press a quick peck to each of the boy's foreheads. "Let's get started, then."

It didn't take long before the friends reached the back of the garage. After Kody assured them that he could hear no movement inside, Jag used the cordless saw to cut a hole in the wall. Once that was done, he said, "Assume the layout and security setup inside is the same as Ransom's. 'Riah, you know the drill. Kode-man, you too."

Mariah effortlessly covered the cameras and the motion detector inside the garage, then she and Jag made their way through the hole. She pointed her flashlight around, taking note of the setup. "Built exactly like the one in Ransom."

Jag jogged to the steel pipe protruding up through the garage floor. "I ain't complaining. Makes it easier for us."

She tossed him the wire cutters. As Jag went to work with the tool, she carefully took one of the anti-nanomite footballs out of her bag and cradled it. Jag cut through the wire easily and pried the cap on the pipe open. "Drop it."

Mariah activated the device and slid it in; the teenagers heard it whistle down the chute, then a thud as it landed. Jag made to close the cap, but it wouldn't budge. "Uh . . ."

"Use your strength, Jag! Hurry!"

"I can't use too much or I'll—"

There was a loud scrape and a *clank*. The cap had been torn off and fell onto the floor.

Jag looked on in abject horror. "—break it."

An all too familiar sound echoed up the pipe. *The football didn't detonate*, Mariah realized, aghast. She fumbled getting the second device out. The metallic buzzing grew louder as it approached the mouth of the pipe.

Jag grabbed her arms and swung her toward the hole in the wall. "Get out! Get Kody and get to the truck!"

"But you—"

"Now, Mariah!"

Mariah spun around and dove through to the other side. Kody, who'd heard everything, pulled her up the moment she was out and the two took off. "We can't leave Jag!" Mariah screamed.

"He said to get to the truck!" Kody yelled back as they raced out of the property. Just then, a muffled boom sounded.

"Oh, so *now* it goes off?" Mariah cried.

They scrambled into the vehicle, keeping the back door open and waiting for Jag to emerge from the house and jump in.

Mariah shook Kody's arm hysterically. "Where is he?"

The electrified door next to the main garage entrance burst off its hinges and landed on the ground, emitting a corona of sparks. Jag rocketed from the exit and somersaulted over the ten-foot gate. Hot on his trail, the nanomite swarm glowed a threatening red. Jag stopped for a brief moment to look directly at the truck, then turned and bolted away from them toward an empty plot of land adjacent to the house. The nanomites pursued him, ignoring Mariah and Kody.

Kody, already in the driver's seat, engaged the gears, stepped on the gas pedal and took off after Jag. "What is he *doing?* Trying to get himself killed?"

"No," Mariah choked. "He's leading them away from us."

Aari looked up warily when he heard the door to the room open. To his astonishment, he saw Marshall come through the door backward, dragging an unconscious guard. The teenagers scrambled to their feet so quickly that both their chairs toppled over. "Marshall!"

Marshall winked at them before stepping back out the door. "Hey, kiddos."

"About time you showed up," Tegan said with mock gruffness.

The Sentry entered again, dragging a second unconscious guard. "Nice to see you too, sheesh." He placed the guards in a corner of the room and brought out his switchblade to cut the friends loose from their bindings. Aari and Tegan gave him a quick hug. Though Marshall seemed surprised, he hugged them back and smiled. "You two alright?"

"Yeah," Tegan said. "I guess you got in without a hitch?"

"You guessed right. There's a camera just outside the elevator pointed along the passageway. I took it out, so that hallway is safe."

"How'd you take it out?" Aari asked.

"I climbed through the ceiling panel, found the cable and cut it. But that's only one camera down; there are others that are still functioning. It won't be long before the guards come to investigate, so we don't have much time." He opened his bag. "I trust that you're familiar with these?"

Snug inside the bag were several green cubes and pyramid-shaped gels. With wide eyes, Aari stuttered, "Aren't these the explosives from Dema-Ki?"

"The pyramid ones, they're incendiary, right?" Tegan asked. "I remember Mariah telling me about them."

"Yes," Marshall said. "The cubes contain high explosives but the pyramid ones will erupt in an intense flame and incinerate any object they're placed on, even the toughest metals."

"How did you get your hands on these?"

"All Sentries receive knowledge and skills from Dema-Ki that are essential for us to carry out our duties. That includes producing things we need from available materials." He zipped up the bag. "There's a room right across from the elevator where they've stored the pods and the unactivated nanomites waiting to be shipped out. I'll load them into the truck. That'll probably take a few trips. In the meantime, could I task you guys to rig this place up?" He held out the bag.

Aari took it and passed it to Tegan. "Leave it to us. I can cover Tegan so the cameras don't spot her."

Tegan slung the bag over her shoulders. "Oh, okay, so I'll be the one walking around with the explosives, then."

"You know the place better than I do *and* where the cameras are. You'll know the best places to plant these."

"True."

"Thanks," Marshall said as he smoothed his shirt. "Before you go . . . you'll see three indents on one side of the explosives."

"Those are timers," Aari recalled. "Longest one is set for two hours, that's all I know."

"Yes, that would be the third one. Avoid the first one, it will leave you with mere seconds. Use the middle setting. That will set the explosives to go off in half an hour. That should give us enough time to rig the whole place up and get out."

"Got it," Tegan said, then dragged Aari out of the room. "Come on, Brainiac, we've got work to do."

Marshall followed and shut the door behind him, then tossed Tegan a hefty multi-tool. "Good luck, you two. Try not to take out any more cameras unless it's absolutely necessary. We don't want to alert the guards more than I already have."

The friends nodded at him as he directed a dolly into the room opposite the elevator. Tegan twirled the tool around her fingers. "Cover me."

Aari fixed his attention on her. After a few seconds of shimmering, she disappeared. "You're good to go," he said. "If you take a few steps down the hallway, you'll see a corridor to your right. There may be a camera there."

Tegan's disembodied voice sighed. "I'm invisible, Aari, not blind."

"I forgot. Sorry."

"It's fine. You're right, by the way. There is a camera. There's no way you'll get through without being seen. I'll have to take it out but I think I can make it look like a routine malfunction."

Aari lay on the ground and peered around the corner so he could continue bending the light around Tegan while minimizing the risk of detection. It didn't take long before the camera was hanging loosely from its mount with the lens pointing downward.

"I don't think that looks like a routine malfunction," Aari hissed.

"From their end, it will," she responded haughtily.

Once she'd returned, they continued down the main hallway. They passed a room to their left, which Tegan didn't bother to check.

Probably sensing Aari's impending question, she said, "That was the room where they held me. Nothing to blow up in there." She opened a door on the right. "What do we have here? Ah, nice. It's where the nanomites are tested before being packed and transferred to the storage area."

We're in the belly of the beast. The notion sent a cold and unpleasant tingle through Aari's body. *The world is being brought to its knees and this is where the scourge begins.*

Clearly not impeded by such thoughts, Tegan continued on, focused as she was on the task at hand. "Right, so . . ."

"What do you see?" he asked.

"It's mostly long lab tables and shelves in here, but there are three steel barrels at the far end of the room."

"What's in them?"

"If I really had to guess, having seen them with the dragonfly, some chemical used in the final stages of producing the nanomites. Speaking of which, that critter's still around here somewhere."

"You just left it in here?"

"I forgot to guide it back out."

"Okay, well, that's not a big worry right now. I guess we should use the incendiary gels on the barrels?"

"My thought exactly." As she ran over and positioned the gels, she asked, "I've been wondering, Aari. When you bend light away from something, you can't see it, but somehow you never lose track of where it is. How?"

Aari mulled over the question; it wasn't something he'd ever thought about before. "I'm not too sure, but you could say it's just like having a sixth sense. Once I've covered an object—or person—I can feel where it's located at any given moment."

"Interesting. Alright, I've planted a couple of cubes around the room as well."

"I can see them. We're good here?"

"We're good."

They jogged down the main hallway, hearing the elevator open as Marshall returned from loading the truck. Ahead, they came upon a second corridor and continued until they noticed a long rectangular room with a half-glass wall to their right.

Tegan observed the inside. "I remember this room. I thought it looked awfully familiar when I first saw it."

"That's probably because it's like one of the rooms at Josh's facility in Goleta," Aari said.

"That's it! It's where they cut these thin sheets from a circular block . . ."

"Wafers," he said instantly. "That's the first process in creating the nanomites. We'll definitely need to plant explosives here."

"There are cameras in there. They'll see the door open by itself."

"You'll make them believe in ghosts, then. Go on, Teegs."

Tegan opened the door and ran in, quickly placing the green cubes out of the camera's direct view, then ran back out. She hurried down the third corridor, leaving Aari to crawl in her wake to avoid detection by the cameras inside the wafer production room. They passed by a conference room but opted not to rig it.

Tegan came to a halt. "Everything here is set. Two more rooms to take care of and we can skedaddle."

Aari ceased bending the light around her and she appeared ahead of him, bouncing on her toes. At the end of the corridor they noticed a conveyor belt that ran between two rooms on either side of the passageway. Through the large glass windows of the room on their right, they could see a stainless-steel sphere that took up most of the space in the chamber. The conveyor belt ran through the sphere and continued into an adjacent room.

Aari read the stenciled markings on the glass. "REAPR Fortifier . . . what in the—!" He pulled Tegan down so they were crouched under the window. "There's a camera in that room pointed our way! I think we've been spotted!"

Tegan reached into the bag and pulled out a pyramid-shaped incendiary. "Then we need to make quick work of this."

Aari stopped her before she could move. "Why has it been so quiet?"

"Huh?"

"I haven't heard the elevator in a while. Marshall should be using it to make his trips to load up the truck."

Just then, they heard the hum of the elevator's descent followed by the clanking of its metal door opening. Tegan gave Aari a hard enough knock on the arm. "There, see? He's here. Don't scare me like that!"

A deep, thunderous growl rolled toward the friends like a wave intent on submerging them. It was an all too familiar and a very unwelcome sound.

"Cover me," Tegan requested quietly. "I want to see what it is."

Aari, bewildered, wavered, then complied and walked behind her as he silently screamed, *I don't think we need to confirm what kind of creature makes a noise like that!*

He pressed against the corner of the wall before Tegan grabbed his arm. "There's a Marauder sniffing around," she breathed. "A guard in a black uniform is controlling it—yikes, that's a nasty scar on his nose—and they're blocking our only exit out of here."

Aari brought Tegan back to visibility. "We have to get around them somehow."

A roar suddenly filled the entire lab, sending tremors through the floor and morphing into shivers up Aari's spine. The guard spoke up. "I know you're in here, kids. We've captured the man who helped you out. Turn yourselves in now and I won't let this beast loose."

"Not happening," Tegan hissed so only Aari could hear. She scanned around, then reached out to open the nearest door. Scampering in, the friends found themselves in the conference room they'd passed by earlier. There was no other way out but Aari figured that if they could climb up and fit through the ceiling panels, they might be able to hide. They quickly got onto the table and Aari jumped up, knocking a panel loose and pulling himself up into the opening in the ceiling.

"Not this again!" Tegan moaned.

Aari extended his hands down from the ceiling. "Hurry! The Marauder's gonna pick up our trail!"

Tegan raised her arms above her head and Aari grabbed her hands. As he started pulling her up, she shrieked. "It's seen me! It's staring through the window!"

The glass beside the table shattered as the Marauder crashed through it. Without meaning to, Tegan let go of Aari and, in her fright, stumbled backward and fell off the table. The muscular black beast leapt onto the tabletop, taking her place, and stared the girl down. Saliva dripped from behind its bared fangs; its dark yellow eyes burned into her.

Something creaked. Aari's eyes were about to pop out of his head—the framework supporting the ceiling panels had begun to warp under his weight. He searched madly something to grab on to but it was too late. The entire frame came down an instant later, bringing him with it. Ceiling panels and the not-so-intrepid teen crashed onto the Marauder, momentarily knocking it off balance.

Aari rolled off the table instinctively and got to his feet, pulling Tegan up. They ran out of the room, leaving the stunned beast to recover. They turned down the hallway toward the elevator but when they saw the beefy guard eyeballing them from the other end the corridor, they spun around and darted into a room across from the one they'd been in. It was lit in dim amber light that gave it an ethereal atmosphere. Large glass beakers lined shelves that spanned the walls.

They raced for a door at the other end of the room. Aari turned the knob but the door remained stuck. "It won't open!" he barked. "It won't bloody open!"

Tegan jiggled the knob violently but got no better result. They turned back toward the door they'd come through and saw the ghastly shape of the Marauder silhouetted in the doorway. Its ears were erect and the mane-like fur on the back of its neck and shoulders bristled. *This thing looks different from the ones on the mountain*, Aari thought as he looked around for something to use as a weapon. *Why isn't there anything here?!*

The Marauder skulked through the open door a few steps then rocketed toward them, its long legs extending with each stride. In desperation, Aari grabbed a beaker off the shelf beside him. As the Marauder crouched to make its final leap toward the friends, he flung the viscous content onto the floor in front of the creature. The beast's paws slid out from under it as it lost traction and fell, smashing its jaw to the ground.

Aari and Tegan wasted no time running past the flailing Marauder. As they did, the beast managed to get partial grip with its hind legs and lashed out. The long claws on its forepaws caught Aari, tearing the back of his shirt and leaving two lengthy crimson lacerations on his skin. Aari bellowed as white-hot pain seared up his body. He staggered but Tegan rushed to hold him upright and helped him out into the hallway. They saw the guard still blocking the elevator; he laughed in wicked delight but didn't make a move.

He's letting that thing play cat and mouse with us! He's sick! In spite of the stinging pain, Aari retained the presence of mind to pull Tegan back down the third passageway toward the REAPR Fortifier chamber.

"Why are we coming back here?" Tegan demanded as they ran into the room.

Aari located a large hatch in the spherical structure and tugged at it. "Because I think I have an idea how we can get rid of that monster, but we gotta be quick. Give me a hand!"

Moments later the Marauder prowled into the room with its nose to the ground. It lifted its massive head to the open hatch and caught sight of Aari inside the sphere. Letting out another ear-splitting roar, it prepared to leap at the boy but stopped at the last moment. It turned away from Aari and sniffed the air right in front of it.

Tegan, invisible thanks to Aari, was nauseated with dread and adrenalin. The beast's nose twitched an inch from her shoulder. She could see each hair on its muzzle, every wrinkle in its protruding brow, and could almost taste the putrid, hot breath. Its lips retracted slightly and its tongue slid snake-like between its fangs. Tentatively, she reached out to it in the novasphere even though she knew it would be in vain, and she was right. The creature's overpowering urge to kill could not be overridden. She pulled back before she was swept away in its bloodlust.

Aari yelled out to get the Marauder's attention but the beast purposely ignored him and continued sniffing around. Tegan attempted to stealthily maneuver away from the hellish creature.

Beads of sweat ran down her forehead; she tilted her head back to keep them from falling on the Marauder.

The beast growled and finally whipped around to face Aari. He yelped and climbed onto the conveyor belt that ran through the sphere and into the next room. It was a tight fit but he managed to squeeze through just as the Marauder pulled itself into the sphere. When he lost line of sight with Tegan, she became visible again. In a single breath, she activated an explosive cube using the shortest setting available and tossed it in after the Marauder.

The beast couldn't fit through the smaller opening of the conveyor belt and snapped its head around just as Tegan slammed the hatch shut. The beast battered against the metal door, bellowing. Not wanting to stick around for the fireworks, Tegan left the room only to run into Aari as he exited a smaller passageway between the conference room and the REAPR Fortifier chamber.

"We need to get away from here," Tegan said, taking him by the arm. "That thing's gonna—"

The explosion in the metal sphere rocked the entire lab. The friends stumbled and were thrown against the floor. They slowly picked themselves up and tried to shake off the intense ringing in their ears.

"Tegan," Aari gasped, the cuts in his back making it hard for him to think. "The guard . . . we need to get past him."

"Yeah," she said, teeth clenched as she helped him up. "I need you to cover me. Can you do that?"

"I . . . I think so. But you have to stay in my LOS or else he'll see you."

"That's fine. I want you to walk toward him as if you're surrendering. I'll be right in front of you."

"Smart," he said, grimacing. "Let's do it."

It took Aari a few tries before he could bend all the light around Tegan. They rounded the corner toward the guard, who was hurrying down the long hallway with his pistol drawn.

Aari held his arms up. "I'm coming out! Please, just don't . . . don't shoot. I'm hurt."

The guard kept his gun level with Aari's chest and stopped walking. "Where's the girl? And what the hell exploded?"

Aari didn't answer. As soon as Tegan was behind the guard, he dropped the cover. Tegan grabbed a fire extinguisher from the wall and raised it high above her head before bringing it down on the man's dome. The guard turned around woozily to see what had hit him. Tegan swung at him again, catching him on the side of the head. He collapsed, falling over backward.

"You're a menace, Tegan," Aari called. "Get that elevator open!"

Tegan picked up the guard by his feet. "As much as I don't want to say it, we can't leave this guy down here."

"Bring him up with us, then."

"But we can't leave the other two imbeciles that Marshall took out, either."

"Argh! Okay, we'll take them all! Just hurry up—the bombs are gonna go off in a few minutes!" Forcing his pain aside, Aari dragged one of the guards out of the vault where he and Tegan had been held.

Tegan retrieved the last man and lugged him to the elevator. "Wait a sec!"

"What now?"

She cupped one hand over another, leaving some space between them, and closed her eyes. The dragonfly she used for reconnaissance buzzed into the elevator, flew through her hands and landed on her palm. She returned to herself and closed her fingers gently around the little creature. "I don't want it getting caught in the explosion. Not after all it did for us."

Aari pressed the up button and they ascended. "We'll have to help Marshall," he said. "They better not have hurt him badly. Who knows how many guards are holding him down."

The doors slid open and they pulled the men out of the elevator, through another pair of metal doors, and out past the open loading door of the small shipping bay. They dropped their human cargo when they beheld the scene laid out in front of them.

Six men in uniform lay on the ground. The friends couldn't tell whether they were dead or alive.

Marshall was several dozen yards away, grappling with a black-garbed man. The Sentry's back was to the friends, denying them a proper view, but the guard dropped to the ground and remained there. Tegan and Aari could hardly process the astonishing scene; one man victorious against seven armed adversaries.

"Marshall!" Tegan called. She opened her hand and the dragonfly winged away. "It's done! The place is rigged, but Aari's hurt!"

The Sentry turned around and located the source of the voice. He started to respond when he froze, eyes wide. "Move!" he shouted. "It's coming for you!"

The friends, bewildered, turned to see what he was yelling about. A yelp tore from Aari's throat. Another Marauder was bolting toward them, closing the gap by ten feet with each stride.

Marshall somersaulted over the friends' heads and landed between them and the Marauder. Striking out with his foot, he caught the beast squarely on the muzzle. He pushed Aari and Tegan out of the way and delivered another kick but missed. Turning, he ran toward the submersion test pool. The enraged Marauder careened after him. The Sentry dove into the pool, disturbing the stillness of the surface. The Marauder splashed in right after him and both man and beast disappeared underwater.

Aari and Tegan ran over and dropped to their knees by the pool, screaming out to the Sentry. "*Marshall!*"

Their cries were met with dead silence.

Jag sprinted along the street away from Kody and Mariah, shooting glances over his shoulder. The nanomite swarm was less than twenty yards behind him; its nightmarish red glow and terrifying bird of prey silhouette making it seem as if he was being chased by a creature straight from the depths of the underworld.

House after house passed by in a blur, all of them devoid of lights. An open plot of land appeared some distance away and he made a break for it. With the speed that he'd built up, he leapt headfirst and flew the remaining distance into the tall, dry grass, sliding into a prone position as he landed. Spitting out bits of soil, he turned to steal a quick look at the nanomites. Spread out into their intimidating sixty-foot span, they dove for him as one.

Well that didn't work, Jag thought, taking off toward an office building across a narrow street to his right. Bright light emanated from behind the structure and music filled his ears as he got nearer. *The fair! It's right behind the building!*

He scanned the two-story office block as he ran, searching for a way up. *Agh, no time to climb—have to jump for it!*

The nanomites' glow reflected in the office windows, appearing as though he was rushing straight toward the swarm. Rejecting the disturbing illusion, he bent his knees and launched off the asphalt, soaring higher than the building. He landed on the flat roof, rolling to break his fall. Shaking slightly from the exertion, he scrambled upright. When he saw the nanomite swarm rising up to meet him, he balked. *Crap.*

Vaulting over two air conditioning units and an electrical access box, Jag recalled how the Ransom swarm had broken off its pursuit as it approached a streetlight. Hoping the bright lights of the fair would also be a deterrent, he looked over the edge at an empty, fenced parking lot that lay twenty-five feet below him. Taking a few steps back, he dashed toward the edge, leaping far enough to clear the fence and landing on the street in a cat-like crouch.

The nanomites plunged after him and just narrowly missed engulfing the teenager as he reeled out of the way. *I can't shake them off,* he thought, blood pumping in his ears. *Looks like the fairground option is out—don't want to put the townsfolk in harm's way. Oh, man, what am I gonna do?*

He changed course, going left along the street rather than crossing to the fairgrounds. At an intersecting road ahead, a large semi-truck was chugging along with its windows down. Instead of taking time to go around, Jag boosted his speed and leapt over the hood of the truck. The driver, shocked by the sudden phantom blur that had sailed by his windshield, hit the horn in confusion but kept moving. Jag swiveled around to check if the nanomites had stopped.

They hadn't.

Hot in pursuit, the swarm broke formation and swirled past the truck. Some swelled like waves over the vehicle, others rolled under, and still more flew through the open windows. Startled by the nanomites, the driver shouted and lost control of the truck. The massive vehicle swerved toward a corner of the fairground parking lot where a mobile crane held aloft a dazzling illuminated sign that read "Welcome to the Vernon County Fair!"

Jag gasped as the truck hit the crane full on and was brought to a nasty halt. The billboard on the crane broke loose from its sling and plummeted to the ground, breaking into pieces and sending sparks flying everywhere.

The terrified driver dropped out of the truck and crawled away, still yelling, but didn't seem badly hurt. Jag's relief didn't last long; the nanomites were closing in on him. He leaned forward, preparing to run, but then saw that the crane, recoiling from the impact of the truck, was beginning to swing—over the fence and directly toward the colorful Ferris wheel loaded with people.

The tip of the crane struck the edge of the large wheel. Fairgoers, mostly children, shrieked as the ride started to tilt off its axis.

Jag took off toward the fair, arcing away from the nanomites. "*No!*"

He bounded over the fence and was nothing but a blur as he dashed through the shocked crowd. The wheel leaned in his direction, wobbling precariously. He took a few more steps then sprang over the shouting mass of people. As he flew toward the wheel, he saw young, sobbing children on the verge of slipping from their seats as they held onto the safety rails for dear life.

Using his momentum combined with a burst of his activated strength, he forced the wheel back upright. The cries didn't cease but parents were able to pull their children back into the protection of the cars. He maintained his speed as he tumbled off onto the other side of the wheel, moving too rapidly for the crowd to form a picture of what had just transpired.

As he made a break for the fence, the nanomites—still in their colossal bird of prey formation—intercepted him, cutting off his escape route. He skidded, wheeled around and charged into the heart of the crowded fair.

The nanomites swirled through the spokes of the Ferris wheel like translucent red flames, flying right by the faces of startled fairgoers. The swarm ignored them and remained locked onto Jag. Jag picked up speed, maneuvering through the crowd until he was once more nothing but a blur. The nanomites followed, weaving through the throng of people. The townspeople took notice; confusion turning to panic as fingers pointed at the otherworldly entity streaking through their midst.

Jag, stealing a split second to turn back and check on the swarm, accidentally knocked into a performing unicyclist. The unicyclist yowled as he rolled in reverse and crashed into a clown, who in turn barreled backward into a juggler juggling fire torches; the torches fell to the ground in a cascade of flames and were quickly stomped out by the juggler. Jag continued running but yelled "Sorry!" to the performers, who couldn't see where the apology had come from.

This place is way too crowded, Jag thought. *If I keep up this speed I could end up seriously hurting people.*

Halfway across the fairground, he came upon a row of game and food stalls. He bounded up onto the plywood roof of the first stall and gap-jumped the rest of them, not once losing his footing even at his speed. The nanomites clung stubbornly to their pursuit but he was able to stay a few yards ahead of them. He reached the last stall and propelled off, landing on a porta-potty by the fence at the other end of the fair. He nearly slid off but swiftly crouched to regain his balance. A woman inside screamed as the moveable toilet rocked back before settling down again. Jag shouted another apology and jumped over the fence and onto the road.

The sixty-foot wide swarm was upon him. He bobbed and weaved but could already feel a few of the nanomites biting the back of his neck. As he slapped them away, a truck roared up the road toward him. The driver's window was rolled down and a voice yelled at him to get in.

Kody! Jag burst away from the nanomites toward the vehicle, slid over the truck's hood and landed on the other side. He pulled the door open and jumped in. Kody did a skidding U-turn and raced back down the road.

"You're crazy, Jag!" Mariah scolded, hugging him from the backseat.

Jag put a hand on one of her arms. "I had to do it! I didn't want to bring them to you and—"

Kody screamed, cutting him off. "They got in! Some of 'em got in! They're on me!"

Jag unbuckled Kody's seatbelt. "Switch!"

"Are you nuts?"

"I think we've established that I am! Switch, Kody!"

"Alright—ow! They won't stop biting! *Ow!*"

Jag slid a foot over and put it on the accelerator just as Kody moved his leg. He took the steering wheel from his friend and got into the driver's seat as Kody wriggled into the backseat of the truck, still trying to remove the nanomites.

"That thing's still coming after us!" Mariah informed them as she attempted to help Kody.

Jag peeled down Main Street through the middle of the town. "Of course they are."

Kody was smacking away at himself, too busy to even remotely care about the exchange.

"Hey," Mariah said, "the freeway! Don't miss it!"

Jag stomped on the brakes but the truck slid forward, overshooting the exit that led to possible safety. He accelerated again, not wanting to be caught in the storm of glowing red nanomites. The truck went under an overpass and over railway tracks, then passed a brightly lit intersection on the road.

"Why aren't they stopping?" Mariah snapped. "The Ransom swarm gave up eventually!"

"I think these ones are different," Jag answered, holding onto the wheel tightly. "They chased me through the fair and didn't give two hangs about being seen."

"What are we gonna do now? How do we get rid of them?"

"I . . . I don't know," Jag said, the words like acid on his tongue. This was supposed to have been an easy task; get in, drop the anti-nanomite bomb, get out. Nothing to it. Now because of his mistake, they were in a perilous situation with no solution present. The swarm hunting them wasn't going to give in until they'd taken down the teenage threats.

Nice going, Jag. You messed this up big time.

Marshall inhaled the water of the test pool and thousands of daggers punctured his nose, throat and lungs. The searing pain was always present with these intakes. For the first few seconds he would have to fight the urge to get his head out of the water until, eventually, his lungs would switch to aquatic respiration and metabolize the oxygen in the pool. He saw the Marauder swimming toward him even as his vision went dark around the edges until only a small disk of light filled his view. His body heavy, he sank further into the deep pool.

It was only seconds later when his body started to course with energy again, but it may as well have been an eternity. He jerked back to life and his eyes snapped open. The Marauder was mere feet away from him, its narrowed pupils holding his complete attention.

With a burst of power, Marshall flipped around and swam away as if he was naturally a creature of the water. He maneuvered smartly, always staying ahead of the beast. It was a competition now—which one of them would succumb to the need for air first. It would never get to that, Marshall knew, because the Marauder would eventually pop to the surface while he could survive in the water indefinitely.

The beast paddled its lion-like paws, enraged that the man had dared to abuse it and take the teenagers away from its grasp. Though it didn't belong in the water, it was apparently programmed to be relentless in the pursuit of its prey. Marshall twisted away to keep a safe distance but was an instant too slow. The Marauder dug its claws deep into the Sentry's thigh. Marshall wrenched his head back, fighting the impulse to open his mouth and bellow in agony. With his free leg, he delivered a savage kick to the beast and lucked out when the tip of his boot struck the creature's left eye. With a tormented growl muffled by a cloud of bubbles, the creature let him go and remained motionless as it tried to regain its bearings.

Marshall seized the moment and shot away as quickly as he could, leaving a crimson trail in the water. Its equilibrium recovered, the Marauder swung around and immediately re-engaged its prey. With powerful strokes it pushed its massive, muscular frame toward the Sentry, intent on a kill.

Marshall swam into the deeper end of the pool and reached for the switchblade in his pocket. He hoped that the Marauder, driven by rage and the scent of blood in the water, was ignoring the depleting air in its lungs to maintain pursuit. As he reached the bottom of the thirty-foot-deep pool, he slowed down, partly to draw the creature nearer and partly to reserve some strength for what was to come.

He glanced back to gauge the distance only to see the beast's massive head inches from his feet. Ignoring the pain from his wound, he pulled his legs in and flipped around just as he reached the bottom. Using the pool floor as his springboard, he propelled himself toward the startled creature, the six-inch knife in hand. He stabbed at the Marauder's face, hoping to blind the creature; instead the blade plunged into the side of the beast's neck. A veil of bubbles rushed out from the creature's snout as it screamed, losing what little air it had left. It started to paddle furiously to the surface.

Sensing the animal's desperation, Marshall rushed toward it and locked both of his arms around its neck. He used the full weight of his body to try and drag the creature down. Even in its weakened state, the beast kept swimming toward the surface.

For a brief moment Marshall thought he had the edge in the furious tug-of-war. Then with a last burst of its remaining energy, the Marauder clawed its way upward with Marshall in tow. The Sentry, still holding onto the beast, soared out into the open air as the creature broke the surface.

"Marshall! *Catch!*"

The Sentry had a mere moment to react to Tegan's voice. He blindly reached out at the height of his trajectory. A green cube landed in his hands. With no time to think, he twisted toward the Marauder as it heaved for air and plunged the explosive into its open jaws, deep into its throat.

He fell back into the water and kicked his legs vigorously, diving deep as pain flowed like venom up his limbs. Just as his feet touched the bottom, he heard a muffled *boom* above him. Even at his distance from the surface, shockwaves from the explosion threw him violently against the side of the pool. Tossed about like a rag doll, he quickly shook off his disorientation and swam slowly toward fresh air.

Breaking the still-churning surface, he dragged himself over the concrete edge and proceeded to purge his lungs of water. Feeling better almost immediately, he looked across the massive pool. Bits of the Marauder's carcass floated on the water saturated with the creature's blood—a sorry tribute to an undeniably formidable but cruel adversary.

Two pairs of hands helped the Sentry up. Aari grimaced at the wound on Marshall's thigh. "That thing did a number on you, huh?"

"You could say that," Marshall offered, "but I think we did a bigger one on it."

"So you knew I'd already armed the device with the shortest time?" Tegan asked.

He smiled through a twitch of pain. "No. I was just betting on it."

"You're crazy. Like, really crazy."

"We should leave," Aari said urgently. "This place is gonna go up any second."

Limping, Marshall led the way to the courier truck and over the guards that lay on the ground. Fortunately, he'd finished loading the vehicle with the inactive nanomites and empty pods when he was jumped by the guards.

The three of them crammed into the cab—Marshall and Aari wincing in pain—and the Sentry swerved around the complex. As they barreled through the exit, they heard the first explosions in the underground lab. They held on tightly to their seats as detonations rocked the vehicle. Marshall maintained a firm grip on the wheel, keeping the truck on course.

As they drove past the security post, they saw the second of the four buildings collapse in on itself. Marshall slowed down to get a good look at their handiwork. The juddering of blasts sent his teeth into an involuntary chatter.

"Ka-boom," Aari murmured. "We did it. Somehow . . . we did it."

Soon all that was left of the building was a massive pile of rubble and debris. A stout column of gray dust swirled into the starry night. Though they felt thoroughly satisfied, an adrenalin crash dropped onto the little group.

"I think we're done here," Marshall said. Aari and Tegan slumped against each other without argument.

The Sentry changed gears and drove away from the scene, leaving the complex to stand watch over the conquered laboratory for the rest of the night.

* * *

"They're not letting up," Mariah warned from the backseat, looking through the rear window of the truck. The nanomite swarm kept pace as the trio sped past the freeway exit and entered a long, lonely farm road.

Kody flopped around beside her; he hadn't stopped slapping at himself. "I'm being bitten in places I can't see! I can't get them off!"

"'Riah, can you help him?" Jag asked.

"I've been trying to!" she exclaimed, swatting the back of Kody's neck as the pickup swayed left onto a narrow dirt road.

When she looked behind again, she noticed that the nanomites had fallen back. "Uh, Jag? I think they've stopped chasing us."

"What? Just like that?"

"Seems so." She watched the swarm hover for a time before the red glare faded and the nanomites could no longer be seen. "Looks like they only wanted to chase us out of town."

"We're definitely far enough out of Vernon, plus I think they know they can't get to us as long as we stay in the truck. Kody, how you doing back there?"

Kody rubbed his arms, face and neck. "I'm not being attacked anymore, if that's what you're asking. They just stopped. Got some pieces taken out of me, though."

Mariah fished out napkins from a door pocket and handed them to him. "Here."

"Thanks." He dabbed at his skin. "So, what now?"

Mariah stared out at the darkness; the area didn't seem inhabited. A small wooden structure stood in the distance, but even from afar it appeared run down. *This feels eerie . . . wish we had more than just these headlights out here.*

"We have to finish what we started," Jag muttered. "Safe to say that the nanomites will be going back to their pod, so we can try again with our last football."

"Is there enough time for that?" Kody asked. "Wouldn't they be on their way to ruin more crops?"

"If we hurry, maybe we can still catch them. If not, we'll have no choice but to wait until they return."

"Then I would suggest finding a way to turn around, my good sir. I'm not overly fond of this route we're taking. Gives me the heebie-jeebies."

Jag slowed and, with some tight maneuvering, got the truck into a U-turn and headed down the narrow path to the road that led back to Vernon. Mariah toyed with the football, then placed it on the seat between her and Kody. As she did, Kody began slapping his calves, looking startled and annoyed. "They're biting me again! What's with that?"

Mariah smacked him anywhere that he wasn't covered to get the nanomites off, but her efforts were in vain. "Why are they only attracted to you?"

"How on earth am I supposed to kn—*augh!* Come *on!*"

"Mariah!" Jag yelled.

"I can't see or do anything!" she cried.

Kody threw himself against the door and the backrest, thrashing. Mariah sat back, powerless, as her friend battled the invisible assailants. If the nanomites were bigger or at least glowed red, she could locate them and get rid of them instead of having Kody flounder about like a fish out of water.

Jag braked suddenly, catching Kody and Mariah by surprise as they slammed into the backs of the seats in front of them. Mariah pushed herself away furiously. "What was that about?"

"There's some dude in the middle of the road," Jag growled. "He's not walking straight. Might be drunk." He honked the horn. "Great. He's not moving out of the way, either."

Kody resumed his fanatical self-slapping and scratching. "Help him move, then! Ow! Noooo! Get off!"

Through the windshield, Mariah saw the man's outline in the truck's headlights. He appeared to be garbed in a dark coat. She watched mutely as the fuzzy figure tottered forward before stumbling and falling face-down to the ground. Jag groaned and jumped out of the truck, Mariah following him out of instinct. The man lay still, his body was shaking.

"Sir?" Jag called as he approached. The impatience had ebbed just slightly from his voice.

The man didn't respond. Mariah heard cursing behind her and turned to see Kody hopping hurriedly through the shadows toward them, still fighting the nanomites. He was calling out to her but she was unable to decipher what he was saying through the yelps and angry oaths escaping him. It didn't help that the truck's headlights and the noise of its engine filled the space between them. He reached them, eyes wide in terror, just as she and Jag got closer to the fallen drunk. About five feet from him, Mariah finally understood what Kody had been trying to tell them.

But it was too late.

The man in black started dissolving right in front of their eyes and dispersed into a cloud of particles that glowed a deep blood-red. The friends stared in growing horror as the nanomites rose from the ground in front of them, forming into their massive bird of prey silhouette. Jag started to yell for them to run but before they could move a muscle, the ghastly form morphed into a pulsing sphere that began to engulf them, trapping the teenagers as if they were inside a snow globe crafted by a devil.

Mariah thought she was screaming but the sound did not leave her throat; the nanomites' glow burned bright in her eyes. She tried to maneuver away but they stuck on her like a layer of new skin, pressing down on her and gnawing away. With a screech, she writhed violently in an unsuccessful attempt to get the nanomites off her body. She could feel them tearing away the smallest bits of her flesh and thrashed harder.

Jag's muffled voice reached her through the blinding swarm. "'Riah! The football!"

I can't see anything but red! she wailed silently. *I need to see it before I can move it!*

The device was in the truck, far out of her sight. Try as she might, she wasn't able to push against the thrust of the swarm and run to the vehicle. Jag shouted at her again, and this time he sounded more desperate than ever. "*Mariah! Football! Please!*"

Stretching out one arm, Mariah let out a roar so powerful that she stunned herself amidst the onslaught. The nanomites fully covered her exposed skin and closed in over her eyes, drowning her in blackness. She fell onto the road, screaming.

Kody was the one who caught sight of the football hovering out of the open back door of the truck and rocketing toward them. It was just a fleeting view through a minuscule window in the swarm. But that was all he needed.

"Football!" he cried.

Jag, with the layer of nanomites weighing him down, pushed forward to grab the football as it flew toward him. As though sensing the threat, the swarm furiously converged on him, blocking his vision altogether.

Kody heard Jag let out a sickening scream. With no realization of what he was doing, he dove—with his new layer of skin consuming him—into the path of the approaching football. It zoomed over his head but with quick reflexes he brought his hand back and caught it. As the nanomites swarmed over his eyes, he activated the football and released it. A loud bang was instantly followed by a thick cloud of blue dust, blanketing the friends.

Kody found himself with his cheek pressed against rough gravel, looking down the road toward the truck. *Did I do it?* he wondered groggily, slowly lifting his head. When his eyes readjusted to the headlights from the vehicle, he realized that he was not, in fact, looking at the surface of the road itself, but a carpet of inert nanomites that were no longer glowing red.

Someone helped him up; he had a vague sense that it was Mariah and her voice, hoarse from screaming, confirmed his impression. "They're dead."

Kody searched sluggishly for something comical to say but all he could manage was, "No, just doped."

"You know what I mean." Mariah made sure Kody was able to stand without swaying, then went to Jag's aid but he was already halfway up. The trio scanned their surroundings. Kody turned to the others and saw for the first time that his friends were covered head to toe in red dots and streams of blood. He thought he'd gotten numb from the pain, but looking at their innumerable minute incisions, he felt the agony kick in tenfold.

"We're done here," Jag said hoarsely. He was stone-faced for a few moments, then cracked a smile. "We did it." He turned to Mariah. "*You* did it."

Mariah started kicking the nanomite dust onto the side of the road. "Powers are growing is all," she muttered modestly. "Kody was the one who set the football off anyway."

Jag and Kody swapped amused grins and joined in, then the three of them headed back toward the truck, moving stiffly from the pain. When they reached the vehicle, they worked on cleaning themselves as best they could. Once they were done, they slammed the doors shut with a sense of triumph. Jag pulled away from the deserted road and sighed. "Well, hey. Could have gone a lot worse, right?"

Kody and Mariah couldn't help but laugh at the absurdity of his question.

Tegan listened as Aari and Marshall caught up with Jag, Mariah and Kody over the phone. Her head lolled tiredly against her shoulder where she was slouched rather unladylike in the backseat. They'd abandoned the truck Marshall had hijacked after letting Josh's contact know where to pick up the inactive pods, and were now back in their rented car. Exhausted as she was, Tegan forced herself to stay awake and be part of the conversation. They'd already reported on the success of their mission, and Jag and the others had just finished recounting what had happened with the Texas pod.

"It was *nothing* like the one in Ransom," Jag said. "But yeah, we got it anyway."

Marshall shook his head. "That's crazy. It's unfortunate that we weren't able to enlist a Sentry in time to help you in Texas."

"You guys can't be everywhere," Mariah's voice came consolingly over the speakerphone. "At least it's over. Are you and Aari gonna find a hospital and get your injuries looked at?"

"They're a stubborn pair," Tegan called, scowling. "When Marshall mentioned that he had more of his healing dust back in the farmhouse, Aari decided he'd bandage it and tough it out till we get back. Idiots."

When Mariah replied, Tegan was certain she could hear her friend shrugging over the phone. "Men! Gotta be macho."

Both Aari and Marshall snorted. Tegan smiled briefly.

"What's up with the other pod locations?" Kody asked. "Any news?"

"I'll reach out to Elder Nageau in a bit," Marshall answered, then tsked when he missed the turn they were supposed to take.

"He sounded jubilant when I told him we'd completed our mission, so hopefully everything's going smoothly."

"Okay."

"Hey, guys, I gotta put you on hold," Jag said. "My granddad's calling."

The line went silent for a couple of minutes before his voice returned. Tegan picked up an icy edge in it when he said, "Hi again."

"Everything alright?" Aari asked.

There was a long pause, then Jag said flatly, "Gran's passed. She's gone."

Tegan covered her mouth and met Aari's eyes as he whipped around in the front seat to stare at her in shock. They both struggled to find words for so long that Marshall had to step in. "I'm so sorry, Jag," he said softly.

"You're not the one who should be sorry. Tony and whoever the hell he works for—they're the ones. They're going to pay for this. I give you my word, they're going to pay."

Tegan realized that Tony and his men were locked up in the shipping container at the Sanchez farm and that Jag would reach them first. He'd successfully kept his temper at bay since returning from Dema-Ki—surprising all who knew him well—but there was nothing to keep him in check now.

"Don't say that," she mumbled nervously, biting her thumbnail. "Please. Don't do anything you'll regret later."

His voice was bitter and cold. "I hardly think I'll regret this."

"Jag—" Marshall began.

"I'll see you guys when you get back." Jag ended the call.

Tegan broke the silence. "Marshall . . ."

"I can't do much," the Sentry said grimly. "I'll get ahold of Nageau; maybe he can talk to Jag and calm him down."

Tegan curled up in the backseat, arms wrapped around her knees. Aari patted her foot as if to comfort her but in his blue eyes, she saw her own fear reflected. Jag's powers had grown and, in the state of mind he was in, would be devastatingly lethal. Even if she reached out to him telepathically, she knew he would only shut her out. There was nothing they could do but pray that he wouldn't act out of fury.

* * *

Nageau's eyes snapped open. "The last team has reported in," he announced. "Their mission was successful."

There were indulgent cheers as the Elders' tension melted away almost instantly. They shared elated smiles, the glow from the flames in the pit of their assembly *neyra* radiating warmly on their tired but triumphant faces. Tayoka sighed. "Wonderful."

"Except for the pod in Texas and one at another location, everything went smoothly and all the entities inside the pods were destroyed," Nageau said.

Elder Nageau? a voice entered his mind.

"Ah, do excuse me. I think one of our Sentries is trying to reach me."

The other Elders nodded as Nageau responded. *I am here, Marshall.*

I wanted to let you know that the inactivated pods are on their way to my contact's lab.

Splendid!

What's the update on the overall mission?

The incursion is a complete success! We have ended the scourge in North America. Well done, all of you.

The Sentry's thanks sounded distracted. He didn't speak for a moment, then hesitated before saying, *Jag received bad news, Elder Nageau. His grandmother has passed and I'm worried he'll do something reckless. There are four men confined at his grandparents' farm and he said that he would make them pay. With his abilities, there's no telling what he may unleash on them. Could you reach out to him? He's shut us out.*

Goodness . . . one moment, please, Marshall. Nageau returned his attention to the Elders and quickly informed them of the situation, then reconnected with the Sentry to get specific details about the men at the farm. *We will do our best to take care of it. Once we set things in motion, I will reach out to Jag personally.*

Marshall sounded relieved. *I appreciate that. Thank you.*

They severed their connection and Nageau nodded at the others, indicating he was with them once again. Tikina studiously patted down a wrinkle in her blouse with her thumb before heaving a quiet exhale. "My heart goes out to Jag."

"Mine as well," Tayoka said sorrowfully. Nageau felt a pang; Jag had, of course, been Tayoka's pupil during the five's training the previous summer and the flame-haired Elder loved the boy as if Jag was the son he'd never had.

"It will not be proper to pull him away from his family after such a loss," Ashack said slowly, "but that is something that we will not have control of with the five in the near future. This is far from over."

Saiyu looked miserable. "No. We are not pulling them away from their loved ones, especially not Jag. I will not accept it . . . I cannot accept it."

Nageau pursed his lips tightly, brow furrowed, and stared into the fire. "Perhaps it is time their families learned the truth about their children's true destiny. The Saplings of Aegis, our Bearers of Light, will soon become young trees with verdant branches. Their powers grow day by day, as will their responsibilities. We cannot keep this a secret any longer."

His suggestion was met with silence. None of the Elders were stunned by his proposal. Each knew this day would come. They didn't have answers regarding what was the right move, but if none of them were arguing against Nageau, it was a unanimous, though weary, agreement.

"If we are all in accord," Nageau murmured, "then I will volunteer to resolve this."

Saiyu tried to smile at him. "This will be unorthodox."

"Our traditions are in place to maintain accord and to safeguard our community and humanity at large, not to blindly cling to in the face of an impending cataclysm," Nageau said. "It is a means to an end and not an end in itself. However, we will continue to cherish them because to discard *all* time-tested customs is not only foolish, but dangerous."

"This is no small task to undertake," Ashack said. "The reactions of the five's parents are not likely to be positive."

"And they have the right to react as such," Nageau told him calmly. "Either way, it must be done. May the universe open the doors to their hearts and minds."

***

Concordia welcomed Jag, Mariah and Kody with a spectacular sunrise but the mood in the truck might have been better complemented by a moonless, arctic night. Rage seeped from Jag's pores throughout the ride back to his grandfather's house. He'd long since shut out Mariah's and Kody's pleas for restraint; the hurt and rage that had started within his heart had spread through every inch of his body, leaving him almost begging in a twistedly gleeful way for the chance to seek retribution for his grandmother's death.

Tony was the closest he could get to those who'd unleashed the nanomites upon the crops, pushing Julia Sanchez to the heart attack that ended her life. Her loss left Hugo without her sweet, loving presence and deprived the rest of the Sanchez family of a caring and uplifting soul. The pain of it all was unyielding. Jag kept hearing her voice singing softly somewhere in his mind.

He turned the wheel sharply and the truck skidded onto the gravel driveway to the farmhouse. He parked and, not bothering to remove the keys: stepped down from the vehicle. Feet hit the ground behind him, followed by two doors slamming shut. Kody and Mariah shouted at him to stop but he pointedly ignored them. A few jagged lengths of scrap metal rested beside the barn. He scooped one up and walked with long, steady strides to the back of the edifice. As the shipping container came into sight, heat shot up his body and his face darkened with hatred.

Before either Kody or Mariah could catch up to him, he was in front of the container. Waving the metal piece above his head, he brought it down on the latch with a roar, smashing it, then threw the doors open, wielding his improvised weapon like an axe.

The snarl he wore evaporated and he lowered the scrap metal. Kody and Mariah quietly stepped up on either side of him and gaped. Weak-kneed, Jag stepped into the empty container and looked around. "Where are they?"

His friends kept silent and watched as he paced in agitated circles. "What's going on? The door was still secured when we got here—there's no way they could have gotten out! *Where are they?*"

Using a two-handed grip, he dashed his weapon against the side of the container, gouging it. The piercing clang jarred his eardrums but he kept going. Mariah and Kody hurried out, wincing and covering their heads. Jag nailed the side of the container again and again. He didn't care if his ears bled.

"*How did they get out?*" he bellowed. He spun around, the container a dark blur from the motion and frenzy. Before he could register his thoughts, he bellowed again. "I'll find you, Tony! I'll find you and if you don't take me to your boss, I'll just kill you! I'll kill you, I swear it!"

In the midst of the storm in his head, a man's voice entered his mind. *Jag.*

Clang! Jag hit the side panel again, trying to drown out the voice.

Jag, the man repeated.

Clang!

Jag, please.

Clang!

Respond to me, youngling, I implore you.

CLANG!

Jag! Please!

"What!" he exploded. "What do you want?" Then, remembering that he hadn't been thinking the words, shot them out mentally to Nageau with just as much intensity.

The Elder sighed. *I heard the news, youngling. I am so—*

You're sorry. Yeah, everyone's sorry. Thanks. Jag swung at the container wall again but stopped when something warm trickled from his hands down to his elbows. He slowly walked over to the door and in the light, saw that the metal scrap he held was stained red.

Still gripping the improvised weapon, he rolled his hands slightly so they were wrist-up. Streaks of blood trailed down his forearms. He dropped the metal and stared at the crimson on his skin.

The Elder remained quiet for a time, then said, *We moved them.*

Jag's head shot up and he glared as if Nageau was standing in front of him. *What?*

The men you captured. We moved them. They are headed to a secure location for interrogation.

How—why? Why did you interfere?

Revenge is not what we are about, youngling.

Jag bristled. *You had no right to move them!*

What would you have done with them if they were still there?

He raged silently, refusing to respond.

Nageau's voice was gentle. *Tayoka speaks very highly of you, you know that? He watched you grow as he trained you last summer. There is so much goodness in you. He pleads for you to shine light in the darkness, not become the darkness. Stay true to yourself, Jag. Do not lose who you are.*

Jag kicked the metal scrap a good distance out of the container and stumbled outside. It hurt to hear the Elder echo his grandmother's last words to him. Shame followed quickly at the thought that his intentions for Tony would have let her down, shadowed by indignation and the need to justify what he'd wanted to do.

Do you believe your grandmother is gone, youngling?

She's passed on, Elder Nageau, Jag answered bitingly. *She's no longer here with us.*

But do you truly believe that she is gone?

If you're going to tell me that she's living on in my heart, I swear I'm gonna lose my—

No, that is not what I meant. Not entirely.

What did you mean, then?

Let me try to explain. This life here on Earth, this brief moment in time and space, is but a tiny piece of the entire fabric of our existence. Human language is bound by the limits of our physical experience. It is woefully inadequate to describe the next plane of existence that awaits us when we surrender this life. But there are signs here in the physical realm that gives us insights, a window if you will, to the next stage of our being, if we cared to look.

Meaning?

For example, an unborn child carried by its mother is comfortable and snug in its own world and does not have the capability to imagine, let alone understand, the world that awaits it. Though in reality, that world is right here and right now. All that separates the child from this beautiful place where it must eventually arrive is a layer of skin. Likewise, all that separates us from the next reality is our very bodies. When we lay ourselves down to rest one last time, we experience wonders of the next world just as a child experiences the wonders of this one when it is finally born. Your grandmother has stepped into an infinitely extraordinary plane of existence, not limited by the shackles of the physical world. Her love for you will never diminish and you will feel the evidence of this in a myriad of mysterious ways whenever the universe opens its portals. You must honor her by being the best you can be and continuing to walk the path you have been destined for.

And what path is that? It was a rhetorical question that really meant to say: *I've had enough of this destiny.*

The five of you have been chosen by the hand of fate to—

No, I know all that.

Ah, my dear boy, I know that you know, but there is a difference between knowledge and wisdom. Wisdom gives us lucidity so that we may use our best judgment, completely detached from impulse, and distinguish the right path to tread.

Jag slid down so he was sitting on the dirt. *You're not just talking about our destiny.*

It is all intertwined. I am not saying that this will be free from pain and challenges. Revenge can . . . can in some ways be an easier path to take than holding back. However, we cannot use the enemy's means to change the world. We can only change it with light.

And if the darkness swallows the light whole?

That is impossible, because darkness is but the absence of light.

May be so. But if it weren't for the people who created the nanomites, my grandmother would still be here. My grandfather wouldn't be alone and my dad wouldn't have lost his mom.

I am not saying darkness is incapable of inflicting pain, only that it grows when light dims. There is only so much consolation words can provide, youngling. Unfortunately, there is nothing we can do to bring our loved ones back to this realm once they have moved on. If you truly wish to honor her, the best way is to put a stop to the root of this evil that is spreading throughout the world. You have done a great deal and the Elders will never be able to sufficiently express how proud we are of the five of you. For now, though, Jag, you need to stay strong and take care of your family, especially your grandfather.

That's another thing. Elder Nageau, how long will we have to keep this part of our lives a secret from our families?

You will not have to hide it for much longer, I promise.

Uh . . .

Tend to your family for now. The five of you will be needed again soon as the dark clouds gather in strength and the world descends into turmoil. As Bearers of Light appointed by the prophecy, you, Tegan, Mariah, Kody and Aari have roles that will become more significant in the coming months. The Elder paused, then added ruefully, *Especially now that we know who is the catalyst behind the storm.*

Jag, startled, looked up from his bloodied hands. *Who is it?*

Nageau took a few moments before replying. *Someone I banished from Dema-Ki many years ago.*

Jag's mind reeled. Some things were falling into place while more fell out. *You—what . . . what are you . . . You have to tell me more!*

I will, Jag, I will. Soon.

The five sat with Marshall on the steps of the Sanchez farmhouse, facing the stalks that remained in the wheat field. The sun had nearly disappeared from the horizon but the sky was a canvas of color that the hand of no man could replicate.

It had been relatively quiet since Tegan, Aari and Marshall returned to Concordia that afternoon. As they waited for Jag's family to arrive at the farm, the friends stuck as close to Jag as they could. Though he showed little emotion, they knew he was grieving. Through persistence, Kody and Mariah had gone with him to fetch his grandfather earlier in the day; Hugo was now resting in his room.

The Jeep they'd used for the trip had made a sudden reappearance that afternoon as well. The friends had found the vehicle parked outside the farmhouse. Knowing that they could only credit this return to one source, they had all turned to Marshall probingly. He'd simply winked at them and said, "Connections. Don't want Jag's family coming here and wondering where their car is, do we?"

Tegan watched a crow soar over the field, its wings narrowly missing the headless stalks. She was tempted to jump into the feathered creature and fly into the sunset, to enjoy the feeling of freedom and briefly leave her memories of recent events behind. When she looked over at Jag, though, the sadness in his eyes persuaded her to remain where she was.

Marshall folded his arms on his knees. "You five surprised me beyond words. In a good way, of course. And you've also helped deepen my faith in the prophecy."

"You had doubts?" Mariah asked, somewhat in jest.

"Not doubts, per se. It's just that you're all so young. Having juggled the responsibilities of a Sentry and a Marine myself was a humbling burden, but then, I've had years to learn to cope with both tasks. When we first met, I was troubled because . . . because I've had a taste of what would be expected of you and I didn't want to see any of you losing your youth to this."

The five turned to him, and warmth blossomed in Tegan's chest. Marshall continued looking ahead at the field as he went on. "It worried me to the point that I felt almost . . . well, ill. But I've seen how you handle yourselves, how resourceful you are. You look out for one another and don't go down without a fight. You handled all these situations better than I could imagine. There's something special about you individually and as a group that seems especially rare in today's world, where selfish pursuits and the coarsening of culture is quickly becoming a norm."

"That's a lot of faith you're putting in us," Aari said. Tegan caught a hitch of meekness in his voice.

"As I said, I've seen what you can do. That gives me reason to have faith in you."

Jag extended his hand over the laps of Tegan and Kody toward the Sentry. "Thanks, Marshall."

The Sentry took his hand and shook it firmly, then after a few moments, stood up. "I think it's about time for me to get going."

The friends looked at him, confused, and got up as well. "You're leaving?" Tegan asked.

"Yeah. I have something that needs to be done." Marshall fished out his keys. "Egad, how many rental cars have we gone through the past couple weeks?"

Mariah covered her mouth, thunderstruck. "It's only been *two weeks?*"

"Mmhm." Marshall patted his styled hair into place as a gentle breeze stirred it. "Anyway, I should really get going. Take care, guys."

The five refused to let him leave before each of them took turns giving him a bear hug. The Sentry looked touched and colored a little when Kody said, "We're gonna miss you, Marshall."

"If you're ever around the Great Falls area in Montana, give us a shout," Jag said. "I know we'll be more than happy to have you crash at any one of our humble abodes."

As they walked the Sentry to his vehicle, Aari asked, "This isn't the last time we'll be seeing you, right?"

Marshall paused with one foot already in the car. He rested an arm on top of the open door and flashed the friends a devious smile. "Let's say that our paths are sure to cross again pretty soon."

The five converged upon him, demanding to know what he meant, but he dodged into the vehicle with a laugh. He waved at the teenagers as he backed out of the driveway. They waved back, questions still bubbling, and remained there even after the Sentry was out of sight.

"I miss him already," Kody sulked, kicking at the dust and sending a puff into the breeze.

Jag led them back to the steps of the porch and sat down, Tegan and Aari on either side of him and Kody and Mariah next to them. "We're lucky that we had him with us," he said. "We would have been handicapped if not for him."

The sun disappeared completely, leaving a full moon in its stead. It wasn't long before a car pulled onto the gravel driveway and Jag's family stepped out. Jag was the first to run to them; his siblings caught him in their arms and his parents joined them. Aari, Tegan, Kody and Mariah approached them afterward and greeted the newcomers with heartfelt condolences.

The door to the house opened and Jag's grandfather hobbled out. Lady walked by his side, her flank rubbing against his leg in support. The elderly man was enveloped in a long family embrace where nothing but love was shared.

"Come," he rasped, rubbing his eyes as he stepped back with his son's arm around him, "come inside."

Jag gave his siblings a light push, signaling them to follow the adults. He ignored their questioning expressions and waited until the door had closed behind them. Tegan nudged him. "Are we not going in?" she asked.

He tilted his head back to look at the stars that speckled the sky. "No. There's going to be a lot of hugging and crying and I'm done with that. If I dwell in that kind of environment for too long, I'll have an even harder time pulling myself out of it."

Kody took off his baseball cap and attached it to a belt loop on his jeans. "So we're just gonna sit out here, then?"

"Not quite. There was something I did when I was little . . . Follow me."

Minutes later, the five were lying on their backs on the roof of the house, gazing up at the heavens. The longer Tegan observed the constellations, the harder she found it to hold on to earthly problems. *This is so beautiful,* she thought. She raised her hand to pinch the stars between her fingertips. "I never knew you did this, Jag. Your parents really let you on the roof of your house?"

"Are you kidding?" he retorted amiably. "I had to sneak out. If they'd caught me, they would have grounded me for life."

"You always were a firebrand," Aari jibed. "Which is funny because I don't recall you stirring trouble in class."

"I just know when to pick my fights."

The others rolled into each other, laughing until their sides and chest hurt. "The only way that's true is that you stayed away from confrontation when adults were around," Kody giggled. "Now Aari, on the other hand, didn't even care that Mr. Goh was five feet away when he knocked the other smart kid in the class out of his chair."

"Oy!" Aari crawled over the others to smack Kody, who was on the other side of the group. "He was second-guessing all my answers on my history project *in front* of the class! I will *not* have my knowledge questioned!"

Tegan snickered as she pulled Aari away from Kody. The two boys sniped at each other good-humoredly before the friends settled down and went back to stargazing. For some reason, the worldly difficulties she'd been able to curb were crawling back into her mind. The last thing she wanted to do was voice her thoughts, but in the end she caved. "What now?"

"Mmh?" Mariah sounded preoccupied.

"North America is saved, somewhat, and that's great, but the rest of the world is going to be a different place real soon. The damage has been done, and my gut tells me that by the time Josh creates and ships out more of the anti-nanomite, it'll be too late."

"Yes, please bring up the topic I wanted to avoid," Kody groused.

"It's not something I want to visit either, you know. We can run from it for as long as we want but reality's gonna find us eventually. Might as well face it now."

Mariah pitched a deep sigh. "As we've been told by both the Elders and . . . Tony . . . this is just the beginning. No one knows what's in store next except for whoever Tony's working for. About the crop failure—"

"It's out of our hands," Aari chipped in. "This is global. It's in Josh's court now, and then the Sentries'."

Tegan pressed her hands to her temples. "What will happen next? War?"

"That's a worst-case scenario," Aari replied. "But that's entirely possible. Countries that lost their crops and have run out of food will go after countries that are still producing food."

"It's the twenty-first century. Aren't we a little more civilized than that?"

"One can hope. The things some will do to stay in power by making sure their people don't revolt is a powerful motive."

Tegan let his answer simmer in her mind instead of pursuing the discussion further. As the moon slowly traversed the sky, her eyelids grew heavy. She had just started nodding off when Jag said, "The plane crash last year."

Kody yawned. "What about it?"

"That crash was what led us to where we are. Our lives have changed because of it. There's no going back to the way things were before and I don't know if I want to shoulder all the responsibility that's about to come at us. We could just turn away. Say that this isn't for us and we don't want to do it. But then, that's kind of selfish."

"It's going to be a dilemma we'll be wrestling with for some time," Aari said. "There's no use pretending we'll be strong throughout all this. We're only human, I guess."

"But," Tegan cut in, "how about we acknowledge what we managed to achieve? Through everything that we've experienced, from the battle on the mountain last year to these crazy past two weeks, we came out alive and, in some way, victorious. That's something to think about."

"We had help," Kody argued.

"And there's nothing wrong with that! The Elders even told us back in Dema-Ki that we won't be alone. We have the means to make this possible but we're not comic book superheroes who have to carry this weight on our own. We . . . we have a family out there who will support us."

"The Sentries," Jag said, voice low. "Sentries like Marshall—and Gwen. We may not get to meet them, but they're there."

"Just knowing that lifts some of the burden, doesn't it?" Tegan insisted softly.

"It does."

"And as long as we're together," Mariah mused, "the five of us, I think we can help each other get through whatever else is going to be thrown our way."

"True," Kody agreed.

There was nothing more to be said. The friends stretched out to get comfortable and continued their stargazing in reflective but comfortable silence. They found strength in one another and Tegan knew it would remain that way for a long time to come. However much the world around them changed, they would still be able to plough onward.

Because the one thing that will always remain constant is our bond, our lifeline. We're strong on our own and we're stronger united. If we have each other, we'll take on whatever we have to

EPILOGUE

The sleek, white Gulfstream jet cruised at forty thousand feet above the Tyrrhenian Sea west of the Italian mainland. The luxuriously-fitted and technologically advanced aircraft showcased a cozy interior with windows that permitted ample sunlight to brighten the cabin. Though the plane could accommodate eighteen people, only one passenger was aboard the flight.

Sitting on one of the lush seats and speaking into a phone was the founder of Phoenix Corporation. "Hello, Dr. Nate."

"'Ello, Boss," the man on the other end of the line hailed. "I got your message that you'd just left the Middle East. Where are you 'eading to now?"

"I am en route to the Heart."

"Ah, the Heart . . . I wish I could be there! 'ow far out are you?"

"About thirty minutes."

"You know, Boss, the move to acquire the island from the Italian government a decade ago is nothing short of a tribute to your unrivaled brilliance."

"If you are done stroking my ego, Doctor, perhaps we can cut to the chase. I just finished reviewing the final report from Adrian about the damage sustained from the attacks on our pod sites, as well as the destruction of the Quest Defense lab, the Redding facility *and* the fact that we once again lost two of the five whom Tony had caught." The fingernails of the Boss's free hand dug into the side paneling of the cabin. "I need to know. *How* is this possible?"

Dr. Nate stammered. "I-it was a fully coordinated attack by a formidable f-foe."

The Boss stifled a response and looked out the window at the scattered clouds below, eyes aglow.

The pregnant pause had obviously made Dr. Nate nervous. "I understand you must be furious with us for letting our guard down," he said. "I will completely understand if you demand for 'eads to roll for this colossal mistake."

"Yes, I am tempted. But I will have to take some responsibility for not being better prepared. Heads need not roll . . . for now. However, we would have gotten an early warning if only that incompetent technician had reported the Ransom pod shutdown as an attack rather than a malfunction. Or even if she'd opted to include the possible tampered lock in her report."

"I agree, though in 'er defense, she said it was only a little loose and didn't think much of it. But I heard Luigi has dealt with that matter."

"He has. So I suppose there's nothing more to say." Reaching into a briefcase on the next seat to grab a tablet, the Boss tapped an icon to open up a calendar. "I assume you still haven't heard from Tony or his men?"

"N-no, I haven't. Doesn't sound as though you 'ave, either."

"It's like he and his team just vanished off the face of the Earth. We were unable to trace his phone or locate the vehicle they were using. As much as I don't want to say it, there are only two possibilities I can think of. One, he and his men are now being held hostage by our adversaries—or, he's dead. Killed in action at best."

"But Tony's an incredible fighter. There was a reason why you chose 'im to undertake your personal tasks."

"I *know* why I enlisted him under my wing, Doctor."

"My apologies. Still, 'ow could this 'ave 'appened?"

"Did I not tell you that the Elders of Dema-Ki are highly capable?"

Dr. Nate swore violently. "The mole. The boy, Aari—remember I mentioned to you that 'e said there was a mole the Elders 'ad planted among us?"

"And I highly doubted it because I know the people I picked to be in the Inner Circle. Rest assured, I did take another look at the list."

"And?"

"I stand by what I said. We're clean. All the same, it wouldn't hurt to have a chat with our people. I'd like you to see to that."

"Me? Ah . . . alright."

The Boss shifted beside the window to escape the sun's glare and gazed out at the dark blue sea below. The call was ongoing but neither end spoke for a time until Dr. Nate let out a quick breath over the speaker. "As bad as all this loss is, everything else is running as scheduled."

"I'm aware of that. I detest any part of our plan, no matter how inconsequential, being hindered. But you're right. What has happened is but a blip. It doesn't matter now because it will take time for North America to recover. Time they don't have. As long as the global pods are maintaining course, the world will soon slide into a very precarious state. We will, at the right moment, deal the next blow and they will never know what hit them. I spoke to Dr. Bertram earlier and he assured me that he has made good progress on the next phase of our strategy."

"'Ow long will we 'ave to wait?" Dr. Nate asked; the Boss heard fervor dripping from his tone like slobber.

"Three months at the latest. We are almost there, Doctor."

"I will await that day eagerly."

"As will the rest of us."

Dr. Nate nibbled on his lip. "One thing is bothering me, Boss. The Elders and these . . . children. They know about us. What's stopping them from going to the authorities with the knowledge they 'ave about our organization?"

"It's precisely because they have knowledge about us—about *me*—that they will do no such thing. The Elders know the consequence."

"Are you sure about this?"

"Do you have so little faith in me?"

"No! Of course not!"

"Then believe me when I say we will not have to worry about the authorities."

"Yes, Boss." There was a brief lull, then Dr. Nate said, "Uh, Boss, I really 'ate to cut this short but if there's nothing more to discuss, I 'ave some work to get back to. It's *orientation day* for our final batch of new recruits."

"By all means, take your leave. We wouldn't want to keep the future Stewards of New Earth waiting too long. I am expecting great results. Good luck, Doctor."

The call ended just as a seatbelt warning sign came and the captain's voice floated cheerily over the intercom. "Please fasten your seatbelt, Boss. We'll be landing at the Heart shortly."

Once buckled in safely, the tall figure relaxed back and pulled out the purple sphere, rolling the object between long, smooth fingers. The small orb slid down and the Boss caught it in a tightly-clenched fist, uniform lines of veins protruding from the back of a tanned hand.

In time, they will all be humbled to ashes.

* * *

It was a warm mid-July evening. At Jag's request, the five and their families had gathered together in the Sanchez household back in Great Falls, Montana. Though they would have preferred having dinner on the porch in the backyard, the friends insisted that the families eat inside.

The five had some idea of what was to come; Marshall had contacted Jag a day prior and asked for the group to gather their families together. He'd entreated them not to question him but to make sure that their parents and siblings were ready. Bewildered, the friends could do nothing but comply.

It was after dinner now and most of those gathered had drifted into the living room to chat over the drone of the television. Jag's and Mariah's mothers were in the kitchen, talking as they did the dishes together. Aari ambled in to clear his plate of chicken bones but Jennifer Sanchez scooped it away from him and gave him a one-armed hug. "Don't worry about this, hon. Go join the others. We'll be there shortly. Wish we had some notion of what this gathering's about, though. The five of you have been very tight-lipped about this get-together." She gave him a pointed look.

Aari responded with a hasty thanks and shuffled out of the kitchen. He didn't need Kody's hearing to pick up on Krystal Ashton's next words. "You know, Jen, I tried to pry it out of Mariah, but she wouldn't give me even a hint!"

Jennifer laughed. "Jag's the same. I think it has something to do with their road trip. But that's just a momma's Spidey-sense."

Curious, Aari sauntered about in the dining room, staying within earshot but out of sight.

"You're probably right," Krystal said. "They've been different since their return. I can't quite put my finger on it. Maybe they did re-discover themselves during this trip?"

"I noticed that in them too. That might just be it. In any case, I think we'll find out soon enough."

"Mmhm. Anyway, as I was saying, isn't it strange how the outbreak suddenly stopped in North America but not the rest of the world? And they *still* have no idea what caused it."

"To be honest," said Jennifer wearily, "I'm glad we don't have to worry about it here anymore. But don't get me wrong, it's horrible that the other countries are still suffering. There was a lot of speculation at the UN conference that Rob and I were in a couple of weeks ago. Nothing concrete came out of it, though. This whole thing is still a huge mystery."

"This is unbelievable," Krystal said. There was a clattering on the floor and she sighed; presumably, she'd dropped one of the forks or spoons.

"It's just . . . this is what happens when a nation lives hand-to-mouth on its food supply. I'm beyond furious that the government no longer stockpiles grain and other staple foods. And don't get me started on the amount of agricultural land lost to development and the monopoly of big agri-businesses. At the end of the day, you can't eat money. As a country we need to make sure that our farmlands are protected. They're priceless."

"Couldn't agree more. How *is* Hugo doing, by the way?"

Aari's ears perked further; ever since returning home, the topic of his grandparents was something Jag did not want to address.

Jennifer sounded deflated. "Hugo's staying at the farm. It's his home. We keep telling him that we have a room ready for him and Lady if he wants to come and be with us for a while, but I doubt he will. As difficult as it must be without Julia there, that's where his heart is. But we'll visit him often and he's promised to spend more time in Great Falls."

Leaving the conversation in the kitchen, Aari headed to the living room. He reached into his pocket and pulled out the small glass container that Marshall had tossed into their car a month ago, triggering their memories to return. He juggled it between his hands for a bit, then stuck it back in his pocket as he plopped between Kody and Mariah.

Jag entered the room, having stepped out to take a call. He looked anxious. "Is everyone—Mom! We need you in here!"

"Coming!" Jennifer called from the kitchen. She and Krystal hurried out a few seconds later and joined their families in the living room.

"I wish you kids would tell us what this is about, because this meeting's got us on pins and needles," Kody's father jested as Jag peeked through a curtain at the street outside.

None of the five friends answered him. Then Aari saw Jag stiffen, heightened tension in his eyes. He was about to ask what was wrong but Jag was already running toward the door. The bell rang before he reached it. As the others waited inquisitively, Jag could be heard greeting Marshall. Aari smiled briefly to himself—the five had missed the Sentry during their time apart.

Then another voice drifted into his ears, quiet but strong. A curious yet startlingly familiar scent wafted into the room; pine needles and mountain air.

The friends quirked their brows at one another as Jag walked back into the living room. Marshall followed him, looking fresh-faced in a black t-shirt and dark jeans. He greeted them with a tight grin and a small shake of his head, as if telling them not to say anything just yet. He stepped aside, then, and revealed a tall figure adorned in a black-and-silver cloak whose mere presence commanded attention.

With sharp eyes and a warm tone, Elder Nageau moved past Jag and the Sentry. "Good evening," he said. "It is my honor to finally meet the families of the five Bearers of Light."

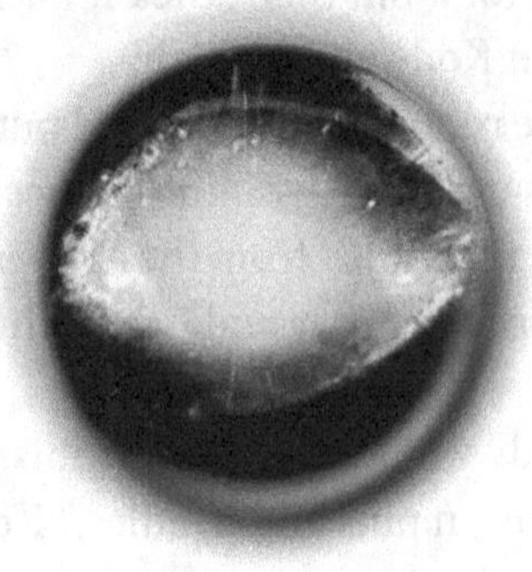

List of Characters

The Five:

Aari Barnes
Jag Sanchez
Kody Tyler
Mariah Ashton
Tegan Ryder

The Elders of Dema-Ki:

Ashack [Ay-SHAK]
Nageau [Nah-GO]
Saiyu [SAY-yoo]
Tayoka [Tah-YO-ka]
Tikina [Tee-KEE-na]

The Villagers:

Aesròn [Ay-zuh-RON]
Akol [AY-cole]
Hutar [HYOO-tar]
Huyani [HOO-ya-nee]
Magèo [Ma-JAY-oh]

Sentries:

Gwen Mboya
Marshall Sawyer
Related to the Five:
Hugo Sanchez — Jag's paternal grandfather
Julia Sanchez — Jag's paternal grandmother
Roberto Sanchez — Jag's father
Jennifer Sanchez — Jag's mother
Tristan Sanchez — Jag's older brother
Continued ...
Camilla Sanchez — Jag's older sister
George Tyler — Kody's second-youngest brother
Roshon Tyler — Kody's youngest brother
Samuel Tyler — Kody's father
Krystal Ashton — Mariah's mother

Supporting Characters:

Elwood McAllister
Roderick Davis
Kenzo Igarashi
Rosemary McDowell

Phoenix Corporation:

Adrian Black — CEO, Phoenix Corp.
Dr. Albert Bertram — Chief Scientific Officer, Phoenix Corp.
Elias Hajjar — Head of Security, Quest Mining and New Mexico Sanctuary
Jerry Li — Chief Financial Officer, Phoenix Corp.
Luigi Dattalo — Chief Executive, Quest Defense
Dr. Nate — Director of Human Resources, Global Sanctuary Projects
Tony Cross — Personal Assistant to the Boss
Vladimir Ajajdif — Chief Executive, Quest Mining and New Mexico Sanctuary
The Boss — Owner and Founder, Phoenix Corp. and all subsidiaries

Acknowledgments

There are so many people to thank for accompanying me in the creation of *Aegis Incursion*. This book was nothing short of a marathon and I will never be able to fully express my gratitude to those who encouraged me onward.

It goes without saying that had it not been for the support of my beloved parents, neither this novel nor Aegis Rising would have left the confined premises of my laptop. My mother's keen eye and insightfulness, as well as her unremitting love, and my father's help in research, editing and being the perfect partner for bouncing ideas are simply invaluable.

As well, I am deeply grateful for my wonderful friends, teachers and family who imparted both wisdom and encouragement. A particularly heartfelt thanks to my dear uncle Mark and aunt Renu for their amazing support, and who seem to be able to conjure a copy of the book from thin air whenever an opportunity to publicize my work presents itself. Sincere appreciation and an earnest salute to my editor, Gordon Williams, for his expertise and counsel, and whose steady support fortifies my effort to bring my readers a worthy read. To the wonderful souls at the Baha'i World Centre in Haifa; you have my deepest gratitude and love for your encouragement and friendship. You are an inspiration!

Special cheers to the Aegis Advance Reader team—Marco, Stefanie, Nancy, Renu and Shayda—for their astute observations and valuable feedback. You're the best! I would like to give a shout out to Larry Page and Sergey Brin, the founders of Google, for making the collective knowledge of humanity available at our fingertips; an outstanding achievement of historic significance often taken for granted. The number of places I've visited and information I've acquired whilst researching for my books without leaving the house is nothing short of a miracle, thanks to these visionaries.

The plot of this story would not have lifted off the ground if not for the remarkable advice from Dr. John Foster whose infectious enthusiasm and depth of knowledge makes a complex subject seem like a walk-in-the-park, even for me! I cannot thank him enough for helping me render the story as believable as possible. Any errors due to creative wanderings from the actual science of nanotechnology are solely mine. And yes, the delectable artichoke and baked swordfish lunch mentioned in the story is true and was expertly prepared by John and his lovely wife Kimberly, an accomplished scientist herself.

This list of amazing people would not be complete without acknowledging the one who is holding this novel; you, the reader. Whether you've been following the adventure from the beginning or just joined in, thank you for being a part of this journey. I'd suggest buckling up, because we're not done yet. Not by a long shot.

Shirin S. Segran

Haifa, Israel. March 21, 2015

About the Author

S.S. Segran's journey to becoming a bestselling novelist began in elementary school when she wrote extensions to books she loved. Her attempts to keep her favorite tales alive eventually led to the creation of her own characters and stories. Now, years later, her genre-defying novels are enjoyed by readers all over the world.

Even as she delves into her creative endeavors, Segran intends to help youth in less fortunate circumstances explore their potential through her non-profit, the Aegis League Youth Empowerment Program.

She's an ardent fan of horseback riding and parkour, and having enjoyed jumping out of a perfectly fine airplane at fifteen thousand feet — perhaps skydiving.

Segran lives in British Columbia and enjoys fall and winter in the Great White North. She loves to hear from her readers. You can reach her via her website at:

www.sssegran.com

www.ingramcontent.com/pod-product-compliance
Lightning Source LLC
Chambersburg PA
CBHW010451310726
48979CB00013B/2151/J

* 9 7 8 0 9 9 1 0 8 1 3 4 9 *